THE BLASPHEMER

✔ KU-466-320

www.**rbooks**.co.uk

By the same author

A Sympathetic Hanging

Last Action Hero of the British Empire:
Commander John Kerans 1915–1985

Flirtation, Seduction, Betrayal

Haw-Haw: The Tragedy of William and Margaret Joyce

THE
BLASPHEMER

NIGEL FARNDALE

Doubleday

LONDON · TORONTO · SYDNEY · AUCKLAND · JOHANNESBURG

TRANSWORLD PUBLISHERS
61–63 Uxbridge Road, London W5 5SA
A Random House Group Company
www.rbooks.co.uk

First published in Great Britain
in 2010 by Doubleday
an imprint of Transworld Publishers

Copyright © Nigel Farndale 2010

Nigel Farndale has asserted his right under the Copyright, Designs
and Patents Act 1988 to be identified as the author of this work.

This book is a work of fiction and, except in the case of historical fact, any resemblance
to actual persons, living or dead, is purely coincidental.

A CIP catalogue record for this book
is available from the British Library.

ISBNs 9780385617796 (cased)
9780385617802 (tpb)

This book is sold subject to the condition that it shall not,
by way of trade or otherwise, be lent, resold, hired out,
or otherwise circulated without the publisher's prior
consent in any form of binding or cover other than that
in which it is published and without a similar condition,
including this condition, being imposed on the
subsequent purchaser.

Lines from 'Memorial Tablet' on page 26, copyright © Siegfried Sassoon,
reproduced by kind permission of the Estate of George Sassoon.

Every effort has been made to obtain the necessary permissions with reference to
copyright material, both illustrative and quoted. We apologize for any omissions
in this respect and will be pleased to make the appropriate acknowledgements
in any future edition.

Addresses for Random House Group Ltd companies outside the UK
can be found at: www.randomhouse.co.uk
The Random House Group Ltd Reg. No. 954009

The Random House Group Limited supports The Forest Stewardship
Council (FSC), the leading international forest-certification organization. All our
titles that are printed on Greenpeace-approved FSC-certified paper carry the FSC logo.
Our paper procurement policy can be found at
www.rbooks.co.uk/environment

Typeset in 12/15pt Bembo by
Falcon Oast Graphic Art Ltd
Printed and bound in Great Britain by
CPI Mackays, Chatham, ME5 8TD

2 4 6 8 10 9 7 5 3 1

Mixed Sources
Product group from well-managed
forests and other controlled sources
www.fsc.org Cert no. TT-COC-2139
© 1996 Forest Stewardship Council
FSC

For my grandfather, Private Alfred Farndale,
who died in the mud of Passchendaele,
and again seventy years later in his bed

MORAY COUNCIL LIBRARIES & INFO.SERVICES	
20 28 42 19	
Askews	
F	

'Monkeys make men. Men make angels.'
Charles Darwin

PROLOGUE

Ypres Salient. Last Monday of July, 1917

WITH A FIVE-DAY BEARD AND A CRUST OF YELLOW MUD WOVEN INTO the fabric of his breeches, Peter Morris does not look like an officer. Instead of a peaked cap he wears a loose-knit trench hat. On his back is a sleeve-less leather jerkin. His skin is grey with fatigue and his hooded eyes, as he raises his head and stares at the entrance of the dugout, are shot with blood.

He has heard a scrape of metal. Now he sees the corrugated iron door open wide and a hairless hand push back the blanket on a string that serves as a gas curtain. A waxy-faced young private in a relatively clean tunic appears in the doorway, stamps in a tray filled with chloride of lime, and adjusts his eyes to the gloom. With his downy moustache and his narrow shoulders that slope down like a Russian doll's, he looks his age, twenty. 'Private Kennedy,' he says in a flat-vowelled voice. 'Shropshire Fusiliers. I've been told to find a Major Morris. You seen him? He's with the Rifle Brigade.'

The major lowers his gaze without answering. There are words vibrating in his head but they are random and meaningless. Someone has asked a question. A movement distracts him; it is his own hands coming together on the desk in front of him, the fingers steepling. Next to them, he notices, is a field telephone and a studded cosh with fibres of hair and cartilage attached to it, and alongside this an empty bottle of HP sauce with the label half picked off. They are acting as paperweights for a trench map. He places them carefully on a shelf, takes a sheet of folded paper from his wallet and

9

smoothes it out over the map. It is a musical score, annotated in German. He nods to himself as he studies it. There is meaning in these patterns. There is order and beauty.

'What's that?'

Kennedy's question does not reach Morris.

'Is it a sheet of music?'

All morning the sky has been buckling with noise. Now the barrage that has been creeping closer finds them. A Pissing Jenny — identifiable by its whistle — lands within forty yards of the trench. As the air compresses and a shower of soil falls from the gaps between the beams in the ceiling, the private cowers, but the major does not react. The score and the map are littered with dirt, making the cartographic trench system appear three-dimensional. A lantern hooked to a nail above the desk sways, pitching the map in and out of shadow. Morris brushes the soil away with the side of his hand, his movements mechanical and slow, as though underwater. A smell of cordite and damp, freshly turned earth crowds the space between the two men.

'I'm with the Shropshire Fusiliers,' Kennedy repeats, 'Eleventh Battalion.'

Morris remains silent.

'We've just got here.'

The older man levels his eyes at the younger. They are cold and bestial; the eyes of a man who has killed before and could, without hesitation or conscience, kill again. Kennedy steps backwards involuntarily. Makes as if to speak. Leaves.

As Morris stares down once more at the sheet of music in front of him, his right hand rises lightly and, with gradual undulations of the wrist, begins to conduct.

CHAPTER ONE

London. Present day

DANIEL KENNEDY STOOD NAKED IN FRONT OF HIS BATHROOM mirror and rehearsed in his head the lie he had told, the one he was about to tell again. His reflection was indistinct, more a shadow in the violet-edged dawn. As he stared at it, he felt behind his back for the light cord. Tug. *Click*. Release. *Clack*. When the darkness continued, he reached forward and gave the fluorescent tube above the mirror a double tap with his fingertip. It crackled for an instant before casting a sallow light over one half of the bathroom. Mounted to the left of the sink was a round, extendable mirror. He examined his magnified skin in it, captivated by the layers of epithelial tissue, by the orange peel, by the inherited, unchanging size of the pores. After half a minute he blinked, washed with a tea-tree-oil facial scrub and dabbed with a towel before applying moisturizer. This rubbed in, he rinsed his hands and teased his tufty hair with matt clay, spiking it in a way that looked dry and natural. He plugged in his shaver next, on a setting that left a suggestion of stubble. Its electric buzz was soon joined by the aggressive purr of Nancy Palmer's toothbrush. Nancy was his dentist, the mother of his child, the woman he loved.

As an associate professor of nematology – a branch of zoology involving Petri dishes, microscopes and steady hands – Daniel felt he had an excuse for occasionally studying Nancy as though through a powerful convex lens, observing her movements, analysing her behaviour. He watched her now as she lowered the lavatory seat, sat down and stared at the floor. She was running the oscillating head of the toothbrush over her tongue. The tendons on her neck were rigid. Her eyes were avoiding contact with his. After two minutes – her brush had a timer – she wiped, stood up and pushed the flush-lever. He admired the way she could multi-task like that.

'Don't wake the baby,' he said as he clicked off his razor and drew attention to the rushing water.

'Wasn't going to,' she countered too evenly, her voice tight.

'We should let her sleep for as long as possible.'

'*I know. I wasn't going to wake the baby.*'

(Although their daughter Martha was nine, they still sometimes referred to her as 'the baby'.)

Nancy was wearing the T-shirt she had slept in. It was too big for her – one of Daniel's – and her frame looked adolescent in it. When she tugged it off in order to stand as lightly as possible on the bathroom scales, her hair tumbled gently and the faded barbed-wire tattoo around her bicep became visible. This, along with her stretch marks and neatly trimmed pubic triangle was, to Daniel, incongruously adult-looking. As he sprayed under his arms with deodorant, he allowed himself a furtive smile, more a twitch of the lips. He couldn't afford to let Nancy gauge his mood yet. She hadn't: she was looking the other way, reaching for the main light switch.

'Don't turn that on,' Daniel said in a muted voice, crossing the bathroom and lifting the seat. 'You'll wake the baby.' His plan was to goad Nancy in such a concealed way she wouldn't understand why she was feeling annoyed. It would, he reasoned, make her appreciate the moment of unknotting all the more.

'But I can't see the scales.'

As Daniel relieved himself, he balanced on one foot and, behind Nancy's back, pressed his toes down on the scales.

'Unbe-fucking-lievable,' Nancy said flatly. 'I've put on four pounds.' She looked over her shoulder and noticed Daniel's toes.

'Hey!' She was laughing now. 'Bastard!' The tension that had been building between them was dissipated temporarily. Still smiling, Nancy flipped the seat back down, flushed again and reached the bathroom door at the same time as Daniel. When she opened it, Martha was standing on the other side, rubbing her eyes.

Three quarters of an hour later, Daniel was sitting in the driver's seat of what the advertisements had called a 'green but mean' hybrid utility vehicle. The engine was running, the heater was on, and he was worrying whether Martha was now too old to see him naked in the bathroom. It had, after all, been more than a year since he had stopped her getting into the bath with him. Making a mental note to consult Nancy – she always had a good steer on these matters – he unfolded his *Guardian* and turned to the sports section. England on tour in India. Batting collapse. What a surprise. When a council lorry hissed by in the slush, spraying salt on tarmac and parked cars alike, he noticed that his windscreen was icing up again where he had emptied the kettle over it. He turned the heater on as high as it would go and watched the glass steam up. The hot air was making him feel claustrophobic. He loosened his scarf, opened the window and looked out. Beyond the amber halo of the streetlights, blackness was shading into grey. It had been snowing steadily throughout the night and, in the absence of a breeze, flakes had settled on the tree next to the car. The phone lines that criss-crossed the square had also turned white, the extra weight causing them to belly. Daniel turned off his engine so he could appreciate the nakedness of the silence.

'Can I get out and make a snow angel?' Martha asked from her booster seat in the back.

'No. Mummy will be here any second.'

'Think she knows?'

'Hasn't got a clue.'

The sodium lights dimmed and went off, leaving the square eerily luminous. Daniel checked his watch again. 'Did Mummy give you your injection?'

'Not yet,' Martha replied with a yawn. 'Said she'd do it in the car.' The child gathered her hair into a ponytail. Pulled up her hood.

Shivered. Although it had been nine months since her tiredness, blurred vision and nightly thirsts had resulted in a diagnosis of type one diabetes, her father still couldn't bring himself to administer the required dose of insulin. He could inject rabbits and mice in a laboratory, but not his own daughter. Nancy had no such compunction. Being a dentist, she was used to the sight of other people's discomfort.

That was how they met, Daniel and Nancy. She had entered wearing a facemask that exaggerated her eyebrows: two fiercely plucked arcs. As he lay on her hydraulic chair thinking of the impacted wisdom tooth she was trying to wrest from his numbed gums, her eyes entranced him. They were bearish brown, flecked with gold. He fell in love with them right there as he lay on his back, with his mouth open, flinching intermittently. He also fell in love with the weight of Nancy's left breast, which, under several layers of material, was pressing against his arm. Pleasure and pain. Pain and pleasure. Their relationship had started as it was destined to continue.

What was she doing in there? They were going to miss their flight at this rate.

Daniel probed with the tip of his tongue the soft cavity that had been left by the wisdom tooth — something he often did without realizing, the equivalent of touching a comfort blanket. He tapped his watch again and shivered with excitement as the porch light came on and Nancy emerged from the house shrugging a grey duffle coat on over a fawn polo neck. The falling snow had softened a little, arriving in flurries, and downy flakes were settling on Nancy's hair as she turned the front door key in the lock, stood framed on the lip of the porch and closed her eyes — something she always did when making sure she had remembered everything. Watching her, Daniel felt a surge of tenderness. How beautiful you look, he thought. I don't think I've ever seen you looking more beautiful. 'We'll be late!' he barked through the lowered window. 'The traffic is bound to be bad with this weather.'

Snow that had settled on the path creaked as it was compressed under Nancy's sheepskin boots. *'Don't push it,'* she muttered, opening the back door and getting in beside Martha. 'And why did you turn the heating off?'

Think. Think. 'Global warming.'

Nancy narrowed her eyes. 'Now we'll use twice as much energy reheating the house when we get back. You should have just turned it down.'

Daniel drew breath as if about to reply, but stopped himself. He was becoming mesmerized by the speed at which Nancy was unzipping a medical pouch, removing a needle from a sterilized pack and slipping it on to a syringe. She did everything quickly: talk, eat, walk, reach orgasm, pick up new languages. Even sleeping was something she appeared to do in a hurry. Something to do with her REMs. Daniel could study her sleeping face for hours.

Nancy was now holding a small bottle of insulin to the car light and giving it an impatient shake. In the same movement, she pierced its rubber stopper, preferring this old-fashioned method to the 'pen' because it was easier to keep track of doses. A familiar clinical smell, sharp and metallic, pricked the air. Martha assumed a kneeling position, pulled down one side of her tracksuit trousers and pinched a fold of skin. Nancy positioned the syringe at an efficient right angle, inserted the needle up to its full depth, pressed down on the plunger and allowed a few seconds for the dose to be delivered before withdrawing the needle. 'There,' she said, massaging the skin. 'All done. You had enough to eat?'

Martha nodded, holding up a mottled banana skin.

Nancy stayed in the back and clipped up her belt: as she normally travelled in the front, this was intended as a statement of her annoyance. Daniel shrugged, turned the radio on and, recognizing the thumb positioning of Charlie Mingus, nodded approvingly. He then tuned it away from his preferred jazz station and found a raw, metallic Lenny Kravitz song instead. Better. Less relaxing. He started the engine. They had gone a hundred yards up the road before Daniel said: 'Dog!' The brakelights came on and the hybrid began reversing.

While Nancy ran back into the house, Daniel blew on his hands and patted the pocket of his cord jacket, checking he had the passports. He could feel two, but nevertheless pulled them out to make sure he had picked up Nancy's not Martha's. He flicked to the back page and stared at Nancy's photograph. It was recent and a good likeness: shoulder-length hair that had gone chestnut in the sun, swollen cheekbones, a puffy curve for a top lip. With a shake of his head he flipped open his own photograph page. It had been taken eight years earlier, when he was thirty, and he had not only looked younger – sandy hair thicker, not yet frosting at the temples – but also, somehow, more luminous: his long eyelashes paler, his blond eyebrows more feathery, the rims of his eyes pinker. He was, he felt, cursed with the fussy, delicate appearance of a Victorian clergyman. In recent years he had tried to compensate by growing sideburns and hair down to his collar, but this, he had come to suspect, made him look like a Pilgrim Father instead. He opened the glove compartment, pulled out a manila envelope and slipped the passports inside it next to the tickets, just as Nancy appeared with Kevin, a brindle-coloured mongrel of indeterminate age. She had rescued him from Battersea Dogs' Home and given him his name because it amused her to think of her socially ambitious parents having to shout 'Kevin!' in the park whenever they were looking after him. When she opened the hatch and Kevin jumped into the caged-off boot space, Daniel grimaced as he waited for her to notice the picnic blanket covering the two pieces of hand luggage next to the cage. She didn't and, having slammed the hatch-door shut, deigned to sit in the front passenger seat. As the car set off again, Martha caught her father's eye in the rear-view mirror, made a letter 'L' sign with her thumb and index finger – 'Loser' – and placed it on her forehead. They both grinned conspiratorially.

Nancy turned the volume on the radio down, flipped open the passenger-side shade-mirror and, in the partial glow of an interior light, began to apply mascara to her lashes. With her mouth open to stretch her skin, she dusted her cheeks with a brush and removed an eyelash. 'Explain to me again why we have to dump Martha at your parents',' she said, snapping the shade back up.

'Knew something was bothering you.'

16

'Of course it's bothering me. You didn't even ask me whether I minded.'

'We are not *dumping* her at my parents'. Martha *likes* staying with my parents . . . You like staying with Grampy and Grumpy, don't you?'

There was a pause before a fluty voice rose from the back: 'Grampy and Grumpy. Mum's parents. Whomsoever.'

(That was her new word, whomsoever.)

'If your mother wasn't so squeamish about doing the jabs . . .' Daniel said to Nancy, surreptitiously turning the radio volume back up.

'Don't start, Daniel,' Nancy said, turning the volume down again. '*Do not start*. I mean it.'

'I never feel it when Grampy gives me my injection,' Martha said. 'He told me he was awarded the Order of the Hypodermic when he was in the Medical Corps.'

'I still don't understand why the baby can't come with us to the airport,' Nancy pressed.

'Because there won't be room.'

'Because there won't be room,' Martha echoed unhelpfully.

'She can go in the back with your uncle Fritz and aunt Helga . . .' Nancy continued.

'Helmut and Frieda,' Daniel corrected, turning the volume on the radio back up as a Foo Fighters track came on. 'And they are not my aunt and uncle, they are my cousins. And, no, Martha can't go in the back because they're bringing Hans.'

'Hans?'

'Their son.'

'You didn't tell me they had a son.'

'Did.'

'He did,' said Martha.

'You did not . . . How old is he?'

'Fifteen.'

'*For fuck's sake.*'

'Mum, you promised you'd stop swearing in front of me.'

'Call me Mummy.' Nancy folded her arms. 'Where will he sleep? You thought of that?'

'We could put the camp bed up in my study. He's bringing a sleeping bag.'

The windscreen wipers thrashed against the thickening snow. The Foo Fighters began a growling chord progression. 'I still don't see why I couldn't have stayed at the house with the baby while you went to collect them.'

'Because you speak German.'

'They're bound to speak English.'

'Apparently not.'

'*Christ alive.*'

'Look, it's all organized now,' Daniel said in a neutral voice. 'Besides, they'll be expecting me to bring my wife. Germans are big on family.'

'No they're not. That's Italians. Germans are big on sausages and genocide. And anyway I'm not your wife, if you remember.'

Daniel sucked in air theatrically, as though Nancy had landed a low punch. As he regularly pointed out, he *thought* of her as his wife. They had been together for ten years, had a joint chequebook, a joint email address and a green but mean hybrid utility vehicle that they shared, and which they both usually needed at the same time. And they were named on the deeds of their house in Clapham Old Town, South West London, as Mr and Mrs Daniel Kennedy, a mistake that amused them and made them cringe in like measure. It had become a vinegary joke between them that he called her 'Mrs Kennedy' and she called him 'Mr Kennedy'.

Nancy spoke in an undertone. 'How could you forget to tell me that your aunt and uncle were bringing their teenage son? Are you a complete fuckwit?'

From the back: 'Mum!'

From the driver's seat: 'They are not my aunt and uncle. They are my cousins.'

Daniel did wonder whether he had gone too far with the German cousins theme. While he had been planning this trip to the Galápagos Islands for several months, as a tenth anniversary surprise for Nancy, he hadn't thought of a good excuse to get her to the airport until the day before. But this had proved a sound tactic, as it turned out. In her anger at having German cousins foisted upon her without warning, Nancy was too distracted to notice his suspicious behaviour, as well as the tracks he failed to cover: the almost illegible prescription for diazepam which he left on the kitchen counter, the one his doctor friend, Bruce, had written out to help him cope with the flight; the bag that Martha and he had packed full of Nancy's summer clothes and unthinkingly left in the hallway; the phone call he ended abruptly when she walked into the room – the one in which he had checked with the receptionist at the dental surgery that Nancy's appointments had been cancelled.

All other preparations for the trip had been worked out meticulously. After a day in Quito they would fly by seaplane to Santa Cruz Island where the four-berth yacht he had chartered would be waiting to meet them. Assuming they could get a signal, they would ring Martha, have a swim, unpack, and then, maybe, have sex – loud, sweaty, on-holiday-without-children sex. This would be followed by a siesta. They would wake in time to get a little drunk on whisky sours as they watched the sunset from their hammocks on deck. And after dinner they would take a motorized dinghy to the shore and Daniel would propose on a moonlit, barefoot walk along a beach patterned with worm casts, crab trails and dead jellyfish – his idea of a romantic setting. If Nancy could be persuaded, they would get married in a secular ceremony the next day; in the equivalent of a register office he thought he had located, or, failing that, in the Charles Darwin Research Station, which to Daniel was holy ground.

It was Daniel's turn to sigh. 'Said I was sorry.'

As the early morning traffic on the South Circular began to build, he drummed his fingers on the steering wheel, then felt in his jacket pocket for the box containing the emerald and diamond engagement ring he had bought. He was going to tell her about the trip when they reached the airport – he would ask her to check in the glove compartment for the arrival times, and she would find the passports and tickets there – but the engagement ring would have to be kept secret for a while longer. He gave her a sideways glance.

She was tugging at a strand of her hair, crossly examining it for split ends.

'And why have you never mentioned you had German cousins before?'

Daniel dipped his head to avoid an interrogative stare. 'To be honest, *I* didn't know I had German cousins. They're on Amanda's side.' Daniel smiled to himself. Amanda was his stepmother. Nancy didn't like her.

'Typical.'

It *was* typical, that was the beauty of it. Typical of him to forget to mention it. Typical of his stepmother to have German cousins. Typical of his German cousins to have a teenage son called Hans. What made the deception perfect, though, was the fact that Nancy often commented on how she could always tell when Daniel was lying; that he was a useless liar; that he couldn't lie convincingly if his life depended upon it. Ha.

Nancy clicked the radio off and stared at the road ahead. 'I'm not sure I feel up to seeing Grampy and Grumpy. They can be so . . . I mean, why does your stepmother always have to raise the subject of marriage?' She was holding up one hand, as though wishing to silence any objection.

Daniel ignored it. 'She doesn't.' He checked his watch again and lowered his window to flick snow off his side mirror. His father and stepmother lived in Kew, in a double-fronted, ivy-covered Georgian townhouse that was, to their regret, directly under the flight path to Heathrow. The first of the transatlantic red-eyes, Daniel noticed, was slanting down, beginning its descent.

'And why does your father always have to belittle your work.'

'He doesn't . . .' Daniel checked himself. 'He doesn't mean to.'

Nancy patted his knee with mock sympathy. 'You go on believing that.'

Daniel slowed down as his headlights illuminated an ethereal figure in white trousers and shirt standing on the verge twenty yards ahead. His arm was extended and his thumb raised. As the car drew closer, Daniel saw the hitchhiker was wearing the shalwar kameez, the traditional Muslim dress of long white shirt and baggy trousers. It was inadequate protection against the snow.

'Look at this guy,' Daniel said. 'He must be freezing his nuts off.'

Nancy was rummaging in her handbag.

As the car drew level, Daniel stared.

The man stared back and pointed, following the vehicle with his finger. A slow smile of recognition appeared on his face, the ghost of a smile, like a negative undergoing slow exposure.

Daniel was unnerved. 'See him?'

'See who?'

'That hitchhiker.'

Nancy swivelled the rear-view mirror. 'I can't see anyone.'

Daniel checked his side mirror and frowned. The hitchhiker was no longer in view. He had looked familiar.

CHAPTER TWO

AS THE TYRES OF HIS CAR CRUNCHED UP THE GRAVEL PATH OF HIS parents' house, Daniel felt the usual low-grade nausea – a reminder that he loved his father without liking him, and that the feeling was mutual. His father, Philip, was a retired – and decorated – army surgeon. He was also a remote and unreadable man, one capable of terrible, genial coldness. It wasn't anything he said; it was what he didn't say.

Once Daniel had parked and opened the boot, Kevin the Dog sprang out and bounded across to a stone-balustraded terrace massed with pots. 'Kevin!' Daniel shouted too late as one of the pots shattered. The front door opened and Amanda stepped out into a semicircular porch which had two Ionic pillars and a curved fascia that looked more grey than white against the snow. She was in her stocking feet and the cold of the stone made her retreat back inside. Kevin skittered past her, trailing powdery snow indoors behind him.

'Sorry, Mum,' Daniel said, kissing the figure silhouetted in the doorway. 'I'll get a dustpan and brush. Thanks for doing this. House feels nice and warm.'

'You've time for a coffee?' Amanda said with an upward tilt of her head as she returned to the kitchen. 'Keep talking. I've got some milk on the stove.'

Philip was carrying logs into his study. 'Hello, everyone,' he said in his unhurried, oaky voice. 'Have you brought Crush?'

Martha held up a squashy green turtle with a goofy grin and sleepy eyes, its velveteen skin worn smooth and greasy. Crush was the name it had been given by the merchandising division of Disney Pixar. Daniel had brought it back from America as a first birthday present and it still went everywhere with her.

'Phew. Wouldn't want to leave Crush behind. I think there might be some Coco Pops in the kitchen if you're hungry. Daniel, can I have a word?'

Because his father used words sparingly, storing them like a cactus stores water, Daniel felt hollow-stomached as he followed him into a panelled room cluttered with antique glassware, Penguin Classics stacked crookedly on shelves, and display cases containing row upon row of medals attached to colourful silk ribbons. Philip tipped the logs on to the fire he was laying, brushed off splinters of bark caught on his tweed jacket and straightened his back. Though he had shrunk slightly since reaching his seventies, he was still 6ft 1in, an inch taller than his round-shouldered son – and he still had a straight spine. He also still had a stern expression, which owed much to the feathery eyebrows that formed a 'V' above his beaky nose. Noticing the poppy in his father's buttonhole, Daniel folded his arms and half covered his own lapel with his hand.

'You like this?' Philip said, indicating a brown, smoky mirror above the inglenook fireplace. 'We bought it on eBay last week.'

'How much?' Daniel asked, wishing his father would come to the point.

'What?' Philip was partially deaf, having lost a section of his ear during a friendly fire incident in the First Gulf War. He rarely wore his hearing aid because, he said, it wouldn't stay in, there being little left of his ear to attach it to.

Daniel repeated his question, louder this time.

'Eight hundred,' Philip said.

'They saw you coming.' Daniel said this under his breath.

Philip knelt down, flipped his tie over his shoulder and, with his hand shaking slightly, put a match to the ball of newspaper he had rolled up in the grate. 'No, I saw them coming,' he said. 'It's Regency. Worth twice that.' His deafness could be selective.

Daniel was contemplating a sooty painting on the wall: a nineteenth-century naval battle in oil. Below this, in the light of an anglepoise lamp, was a side table and an open book. Philip's reading glasses, their arms joined by cord that could be tightened by a toggle to compensate for his missing ear, were resting on top of it. Daniel flipped the book over to see its cover: *The Conscience of a Soldier* by General Sir Richard Kelsey. 'Any good?' he asked.

'Bit pompous. Met him once.'

'Served with him?'

'No, Kelsey was long before my time.'

Conversations about great generals and historic battles were always, Daniel knew, an efficient way of cutting through the ice with his father, even if the water below was still cold. As a child he had sat at Philip's knee and listened in awe to tales about the world wars in which his grandfather and great-grandfather had fought. One of his favourite bedtime stories, indeed, had been from a war memoir, an account of how his grandfather had posthumously won his VC, shortly after D-Day.

Yet in recent years, whenever his father mentioned the army, Daniel had also felt a ripple of guilt. They had never discussed it properly, but it was obvious that Philip had hoped his only son would follow him into the Medical Corps. It was to do with his look of paternal pride when he was offered a place on a degree course in medicine, and his unspoken disappointment when he had dropped out of it and taken up biology instead. In the end, Daniel read zoology for his doctorate, specializing in nematodes, before getting stuck as a junior research fellow for eight years at Trinity College, London, and an associate professor awaiting tenure for a further four. At the age of thirty-seven came a glittering prize of sorts: he was asked to write and present a natural history programme on a cable television channel. And with a second series of *The Selfish Planet* in pre-production, he was, as he never tired of saying, close to being a certified media don. His father rarely asked him about his television work. His father didn't own a television.

'By the way, Dad,' Daniel said, as if remembering, 'looks like I got that promotion.'

'They've given you the zoology chair?'

'Yep.' It wasn't quite true. It had yet to be officially announced. But he had heard from his friend Wetherby, the professor of music who had also recently taken on the role of vice provost, that it was a formality. As good as his. Wetherby had been the only member of staff at Trinity he had told about the surprise holiday he had arranged for Nancy. And that was when Wetherby had said it could be a joint celebration, because his professorship was to be rubber-stamped at the next Senate meeting.

'About time,' Philip said. 'You must be relieved.'

'I've been practically running the department for the past six months anyway.'

'I know. Other men would have complained.'

Daniel could feel his blood pressure rise. He needed to score a point back. 'I suppose they thought I didn't need a pay rise after the success of *The Selfish Planet*.'

'*The Selfish Planet?*'

'My TV series.'

'Of course, yes.'

Father and son fell into a customary silence. Daniel, his mood dampened as it always was after an encounter with his father, half sat on the corner of a leather-topped desk, dangling one leg, helping himself to a Mint Imperial from an open packet. Around him in gilt frames were familiar family photographs that had lost some of their colour in the sunlight: Amanda on a beach looking annoyed at being photographed; Philip as a boy standing with his mother and sister next to his father's grave at the Bayeux War Cemetery; Daniel as a schoolboy in a Scout uniform; Philip again, standing outside Buckingham Palace on the day he collected his medal.

Set apart from them was a photograph he hadn't seen before. It was a sepia print of a group of grinning soldiers in a trench, the whiteness of their eyes contrasting dramatically with the muddiness of their faces. At the centre of the group, standing forward from the others, were two men with their helmets pushed back on their heads. One of them had his arm around the other's shoulder and was smiling widely, showing his teeth. The other wore a moustache and a more forced smile that was tight-lipped and inscrutable. Handwritten in block capitals across the bottom were the words: 'Private Andrew Kennedy, 11th Battalion, Shropshire Fusiliers. Ypres. 30 July 1917.'

'Which one is he?' Daniel asked, holding the frame up.

'Moustache.'

'Really?' Daniel examined it more closely. Though the young man in the picture had a wider face than either he or his father had, he could nevertheless see a family resemblance now: the heaviness of the eyelids; the dimpled chin. Daniel had seen a photograph of his great-grandfather before – a formal portrait of him in uniform, but he hadn't had a moustache in that one.

'Taken the day before he was killed,' Philip said.

Daniel looked at the date again. He knew his great-grandfather had died on the first day of a big battle, but he couldn't remember which one. He wanted to say the Somme but that didn't sound right. He read the caption again. 'So the Battle of Ypres . . .'

'The Third Battle of Ypres . . . They called it Passchendaele. That's a line from a poem by Siegfried Sassoon. "I died in hell – (They called it Passchendaele)."' Philip picked up his glasses, slipped the cord over his head and tightened it. Next he reached for a slim volume of poetry, looked in the index, flicked to the relevant page and handed the opened book to his son.

Daniel gave the poem a cursory glance and clapped the book shut. Something about his father's relentless seriousness always made him want to be flippant. 'Passchendaele was the one with all the mud, wasn't it?'

'Yes.'

'And it began . . .' He checked the date on the photograph again. 'On the thirty-first of July?'

'And lasted a hundred days.'

'And we won it, right?'

If Philip was irritated by this comment, he chose not to show it.

Instead he blinked slowly – an eagle's blink – before taking the photograph from Daniel and turning his back on him, so that he could study it against the light from the window. 'The British gained five miles of ground. Four months later they withdrew, leaving the ruins of Passchendaele to its ghosts. If it was a victory, it was a pyrrhic one.'

Daniel tried not to convey his annoyance at his father's pomposity, but he couldn't help himself, he was feeling annoyed. 'So Andrew was one of the lions led by donkeys? Have I got that the right way round? Yeah, lions led by donkeys.'

Philip stiffened but affected not to hear. He put the photograph in a drawer, face down, and got to his knees again in front of the fire. There was a wheezy sound as he lined a set of bellows up against the grate and began pumping.

Daniel walked over, opened the drawer and took the photograph out again. 'Where did it come from?'

'Your aunt Hillary. We found it in her garage after the funeral, in a biscuit tin . . .' Philip paused, momentarily lost in his thoughts, then shook his head. 'It was with some other personal effects. They must have been sent back from Passchendaele after Andrew was reported missing in action. We haven't had a chance to go through them properly yet. I'll show you.' There was a creaking of brogues as he stood up, walked to a cupboard and lifted a tin from another drawer. Though tarnished with rust, the word 'shortbread' was still discernible on its lid. 'Look, here's his hip flask, wallet, a lock of hair, some letters he wrote. And this . . .' He handed Daniel a copy of *Punch* magazine that was covered in doodles. Handwritten in faded ink above its masthead was 'Major P. Morris, 2/Rifle Brigade'.

'Is this musical notation?'

'There's more of it inside. There's also a music score tucked into the back.'

Daniel opened the back cover and a folded sheet of paper dropped out. When he smoothed it out on the desk he saw it had brown stains on it and was annotated in German. He read out loud: '*Das Lied . . . Der Abschied . . . mit höchster Gewalt . . .* This a passage from a symphony or something?'

'I don't know. There are two names at the bottom. Peter and Gustav.'

'I could get Wetherby to look at it. He loves shit like this.' Daniel cringed as the word came out. His father never swore.

'That's kind, but I'd rather hang on to these things for the moment. What's interesting is the magazine. Look at the date on it.'

'April the twentieth, nineteen eighteen.'

'Nine months after Andrew was killed.' Philip rested a hand on the fender as he got to his feet. 'Some of this Major Morris's personal effects must have been muddled up with Andrew's.'

Detecting a faint smell of uric acid, Daniel looked at the crotch of his father's moleskins. There was a small, dark patch. Feeling shocked that Philip hadn't noticed – how long had this been going on? – he looked away, slipped the music score into the magazine and handed it back. 'You wanted to talk to me about something, Dad.'

'I do.' He frowned for a moment. Nodded. 'It's about the tin. I wanted to ask your advice.'

'This is a first.' It sounded more sarcastic than Daniel intended.

'I've glanced at Andrew's letters but my French is not what it was.'

'They're in French?'

'I thought Nancy might be able to translate them properly, if she's not too busy . . .' He reached into the tin again and picked up a bundle of thin, yellowing letters bound with hairy string.

'Well, you could have asked her yourself, Dad. There was no need to call me in here like . . .'

His father looked at him.

'Sure,' Daniel said, backing down. 'I'll ask her to have a look at them.'

'But only if you think we should.'

It was Daniel's turn to frown. 'Meaning?'

'Sometimes it's best not to disturb the past.'

'Disturb? What are you getting at?'

Philip swallowed. His mouth groped for an answer. 'I . . . I don't know. My French is not . . . I think there was a reason your aunt Hillary never had them translated.'

'How do you know she didn't?'

'She told me . . . When she was dying. She said there was a tin in the garage she wanted me to have. Said she had never read the letters. I feel . . .' He searched for the right word. 'I don't know . . . Superstitious about them. Once opened. Once read . . .' He repacked the wallet, hip flask, lock of hair and copy of *Punch* in the tin.

'Dad, you worry too much.' Daniel's voice had softened. 'You should definitely get the letters translated.'

'So you don't mind?'

'Why should I mind?'

'I have your agreement?'

Daniel's brow puckered again. 'Don't get weird on me, Dad. Of course you . . . Do whatever you think best.' He took the letters, slipped them into his jacket and, for a moment, panicked as he felt for the passports. Remembering he had put them in the glove compartment of the car, he said: 'Anyway, we'd better shift. Thanks for looking after Martha and Kevin. I'll ring from the airport. Tell you . . .' He looked around and lowered his voice: 'Tell you how it went.'

Kevin trotted in, followed by Martha licking her fingers as she finished a doughnut. When Philip saw her, he clapped his papery hands together and opened them slowly to inspect. 'Missed,' he said with mock gloominess. 'Damn and blast.'

'Missed what?' Martha asked.

'A fairy. Been having trouble with them. They make holes in my clothes.'

Martha laughed indulgently. 'Fairies don't exist, Grampy. You're thinking of moths.'

'Of course fairies exist. What's this then?' He reached in his pocket. Martha's eyes widened and, despite herself, she walked over for a better look. Philip pulled out his pocket lining and showed Martha a hole in it. 'See?' he said.

Martha laughed again and punched her grandfather's leg.

Daniel shook his head. How could the old bugger be so at ease with his granddaughter, yet so awkward with his own son? He headed back out into the hall and called through to Nancy, who was talking to Amanda in the kitchen. With her rheumy eyes, soft cheeks and reserved manner, Daniel's stepmother gave the impression to strangers of being a passive and tolerant person. Nancy knew better. 'Amanda was telling me that your cousin Thomas is getting married,' she said pointedly as she emerged from the kitchen. A thin smile was playing on Amanda's granite lips.

'Mum,' Martha said. 'Grampy was pretending that he had a fairy in his pocket, but I know there aren't any fairies – Daniel told me.'

'Call me Daddy.'

Martha took her father's hand. 'He told me at the same time he told me there is no God and no Father Christmas.' Philip, Amanda and Nancy looked at Daniel accusingly.

'What?' Daniel said, pointing at himself. '*What?* . . . Well, there isn't.' He kissed Martha on the forehead. 'Bye, darling. Keep Grampy out of trouble.'

'*Auf Wiedersehen*,' the nine-year-old said with a grin. This was a game of theirs.

'*Au revoir*,' Daniel said.

'*Arrivederci.*'

'*Sayonara.*'

'*Do svidaniya.*'

'We'll be back in a couple of hours,' Nancy interrupted.

The snow had turned to sleet. '*¡Chao!*,' Daniel said in a stage whisper, pulling a guilty face as he turned his collar up, jogged to the car and opened the door. As he was reaching for his seat belt, arthritic knuckles rapped on the window. Daniel wound it down. Philip reached in and tucked a poppy into his son's buttonhole. It was the one from his own jacket.

'I have got one somewhere,' Daniel said, feeling a mixture of annoyance and humiliation.

'In case they don't have any at the airport,' Philip said.

'Thanks, Dad.'

'And guess what DVD I've rented,' Philip added in that slightly loud voice people use when talking to one person for the benefit of another.

'*Finding Nemo?*' Martha said from behind him.

'*Finding Nemo.*'

'Cool! Thanks, Grampy.' Martha warmed her hands on the bonnet of the car. 'Bye, Mum,' she shouted. 'Have a nice time.' She clapped a hand over her mouth as she realized what she had said.

Nancy hadn't noticed. She spent the short journey to Heathrow examining her nails. The windscreen wipers were on full speed. As the traffic slowed and thickened, Daniel wondered if he and Martha had left anything out of the packing they had done on Nancy's behalf. He was sure he had packed everything they would need, yet still he felt edgy. Was it something he'd forgotten? Phone numbers? No, he'd left them. He hadn't taken the pill he always took to counter his anxiety about flying. That must be it. He would take it once he had parked, once he had told Nancy what was really happening.

At Terminal 5, when he mounted the ramp marked DEPARTURES, Nancy waved her hands out in front of her, limp at the wrists, used her tongue to push out the flesh below her mouth and made a *Nnnugh!* sound.

'Bugger,' Daniel said, 'we need to go to arrivals, don't we?'

Nancy slapped her forehead in reply.

'Do you think I can park in this disabled bay while you check what time their plane lands?'

'Why not? I'm sure mental disability counts.'

Daniel pulled over to one side of the slipway and cut the engine. 'The airline details are in the glove compartment.'

When the two passports fell out of the envelope, Nancy stared at them blankly. She pulled out two plane tickets to Quito and looked at Daniel with confusion in her eyes. Next came a small guidebook to the Galápagos Islands. She blinked and looked up at Daniel again. He was holding his iPhone up, pointing its camera lens at her. He was about to say 'Happy anniversary,' when he became distracted by a blue van parking ahead of them. The hitchhiker he had seen earlier was getting out of it, his shape blurred by the slush on the windscreen. The man waved his thanks and strode off towards the revolving entrance door of the terminal. The only sound was the soft percussion of icy rain on the roof of the car.

CHAPTER THREE

Ypres Salient. Last Monday of July, 1917

PRIVATE ANDREW KENNEDY CANNOT UNDERSTAND WHY THE MEN
marching ahead of him have stopped singing mid-song. There is
something in the ditch – a carcass. Its lips are pulled back as if
baring its teeth and its bloated belly is moving, making one of its
hind legs shudder. It looks as if it is rising from the dead. As the
soldier draws alongside he can see it is not the horse moving but
the rats feeding inside it. One emerges from a leathery slit and stares
impassively back at the column.

Half a mile farther on, the 11th Battalion, Shropshire Fusiliers,
get their first sight of Dickebusch – 'Dickie Bush' – camp: smoke
rising from dozens of fires, hundreds of tethered horses and mules,
a long scaffold from which straw-filled sandbags dangle on ropes
like executed prisoners, crates of chickens, a confusion of chugging,
honking, backfiring trucks, motorbikes and staff cars, and soldiers –
thousands and thousands of soldiers assembling for roll calls, eating
from mess tins, arm-wrestling, digging latrines, dealing cards,
shining boots, lying on their backs, playing leapfrog, writing letters,
smoking pipes. As the column approaches, the noises and smells
intensify. A small steam train clatters into a makeshift junction,
followed by dozens of open cattle trucks packed with yet more
troops. They look precarious as they jostle each other and hang
over the sides. For the benefit of a newsreel cameraman whose

hand is turning a crank at an unvarying pace, they cheer and raise their helmets. In the fields beyond them are row upon row of white, well-guyed bell-tents, arranged as symmetrically as grave-stones in a military cemetery.

There are some tents waiting for the battalion, but not enough. Around a hundred men have to lie in the open, finding space wherever they can. Andrew and a few others from his platoon opt for a ruined barn. Despite their exhaustion from the march, sleep does not come easily. The pockmarked walls dance with faint colours: red and green flares being fired on the horizon. Also, they are sharing the barn with rats. Andrew feels, or imagines he feels, the straw moving beneath him.

Some members of the platoon regard the ubiquitous rats as companions in adversity, others as mere targets for bayonet practice. One private amused himself by baiting the end of his bayonet with a piece of bacon and shooting the first rat that came to eat it. But only one. He found himself on a charge for wasting ammunition. And bacon.

Andrew's attitude is different. He is not so complacent. In the three weeks he has been away from England, he has developed a morbid loathing of rats. It is to do with the bluntness of their muzzles and the glassy lifelessness of their eyes. It is also to do with the way they move, either trotting with purpose in a straight line, their hindquarters and long tails raised, or scurrying for cover – fat shadows in his peripheral vision.

But in moments of self-awareness, the soldier recognizes his hatred is varnished with cold, premonitory fear. He has heard how the rats at the Front are quite unlike the beach rats at the Étaples 'Bull Ring'. Here they grow to the size of footballs, bloated on the flesh of dead men. They usually go for the eyes first and then burrow their way right inside the corpse. When Andrew closes his eyes to sleep he can imagine the rank of rats heading with a steady, determined trot towards him, their coarse fur matted in the rain, their dark eyes fixing him, sizing him up.

He has encountered rats before. As a plumber in Market Drayton before the war he was sometimes obliged to inspect sewage pipes.

But the rats he had seen then never bothered him. They were more frightened than he was, apart from anything else. And now, as he lies awake gazing at the stars through the rafters of the barn, the Market Drayton rats are a world away. When was he last in his home town? Five months? Five years? A lifetime ago. He recalls the day he and another young man from his firm, William Macintyre, answered Kitchener's call for volunteers. As they cycled together to the recruiting office, a room in the town hall, they teased each other: about how one wouldn't be able to shoot straight; about how the other wouldn't know the difference between a stopcock and a Mills bomb. They were staggered to find a long queue of straw boaters and cloth caps snaking out of the hall and into the street. They parked their cycles and joined the end of it, playfully pushing each other out of the way.

Andrew allows himself a smile at this memory and turns his head to see Macintyre has managed to fall asleep. They have known each other since school. Took up their apprenticeships together, having both turned fourteen in the same week. The money wasn't bad but they knew that plumbing was a temporary calling, a means to an end. Their joint aspiration was to form a music-hall double act. In their tea breaks at work, they had experimented with vaudeville songs and comedy turns.

In the semi-darkness, Andrew tries to remember some of their routines but they remain out of reach, his mind too numb to summon them. Instead he reaches across to find his friend's hand. Macintyre grips it as a reflex without waking up. They had both found it funny when the medical officer had tapped their knees at the recruiting office. The memory prompts another smile. Although they had both recently turned twenty, the MO was suspicious they were under age. Andrew's tendency to blink excessively when talking didn't help, nor did his slight build and rounded shoulders. He nevertheless passed his examination and was issued with a uniform a size too big for him. Three months of basic training at Aldershot, followed by another two of hanging around the depot before his name appeared on a typed list outside the orderly room, had not given him an air of maturity, as it had certain other men. Even the

'Ole Bill' moustache he has since grown is too fine and pale to count as manly. As he lies in the dark, his head pillowed on his balled-up cape, he strokes his whiskers and tenses the sinews in his back whenever he feels, or imagines he feels, a movement beneath him.

It is still dark when reveille is sounded. Andrew has again not slept. He washes, shaves and eats his porridge in a trance before Colour Sergeant Major Davies, a thick-necked man with a dozen years of regular service to his name, orders the platoon to fall in. Though his nickname is the Creeping Barrage, on account of the way his voice starts quietly and builds to a roar, his voice this morning remains subdued and is all the more terrifying for this. He tells them what they have guessed, what they have feared and longed for at the same time, that they are going up the line in preparation for the Big Push – the breakout from the Ypres Salient that has been many months in the planning.

As he marches in step with his comrades across the reclaimed marshland of West Flanders, he feels as if he is daydreaming. Something about the percussion of studded boots and the hollow clink of bayonets against mess tins hypnotizes him. His legs and arms alone are doing the marching, without any conscious effort on his part. He also feels as if he is being carried along on a human river, his own marrow subsumed into that of the body of men moving inexorably forward together with momentum, strength and purpose.

The raucous singing starts again – 'Three German officers crossed the line. Parlez-vous' – and Andrew sings as lustily as any of the men he is with. He welcomes the distraction and enjoys the novelty of using vulgar, barrack-room vocabulary. 'Three German officers crossed the line. Parlez-vous.' Though sweat is running down his face and stinging his eyes, it is the sweat of exertion and heat, not fear. Andrew feels no fear as he marches. 'Three German officers crossed the line, fucked the women and drank the wine. With an inky-pinky parlez-vous.' Though the skies are overcast, the weather is humid and this means that the column needs regular breaks. When they stop alongside a destroyed railway track,

Andrew's thoughts return immediately to the CSM's icy words: 'Right, lads, we're going up the line.' For Andrew the fear is nebulous, no more than a vague tightening of the gut, but it is fear all the same. He is, and knows he is, a frightened man.

He takes off his helmet and dabs his brow with his sleeve. The men around him remove their haversacks and sit down with their backs to a dry stone wall, enjoying its warmth as they pass around canteens of water, light up Woodbines and swish with their hands at the ever-present horse flies. Inappropriately, they are looking out over a wildflower meadow of dandelion, white clover and cow parsley. Only the distant bark of guns and the sight of two observation balloons swinging on their mooring ropes ruin the illusion that this is an ordinary agricultural landscape in high summer.

As they resume the approach march, they pass between two growling minotaurs, a battery of rail-mounted howitzers manned by gunners stripped to the waist. Each thud is preceded by a hiss and followed by a tongue-flick of fire. Andrew has never heard a noise as loud in his life. It fills the world to its very edges, and he can feel each vibration resonate through his chest, so much so that he fears his heart might stop. Fear again. His ears are still ringing half a mile farther on when they encounter a team of pack mules. They are up to their hocks in mud. Soon afterwards they come to a dump of empty eighteen-pounder shell cases. Chalked on the side of one of them, as each row of men points out to the row behind them, are the words: 'To Willie with compliments!' This sight lifts their spirits and, when two Sopwiths skim overhead towards the enemy line, they break out into spontaneous cheering and raise their helmets. By the time they reach the mouth of a shallow trench a yard deep, Andrew is almost breathless with excitement.

CHAPTER FOUR

Quito. Present day

FLIGHTS TO QUITO ARRIVE AT NIGHT, BETWEEN A DARKLY FORESTED volcano to the west and a precipitous canyon to the east. As their 747 began its descent, Nancy and Daniel strained their eyes for a first glimpse of the city. They could make out the Guayllabamba River briefly, reflected in the moonlight, then the blackness became absolute as they entered a steep-sided valley. A minute later the city lights appeared below them as abruptly as a meteor shower.

Their hotel, a colonial building with a flaking stucco façade, was in the Centro Histórico, near the church of El Sagrario, and because Nancy's Spanish was fluent and Daniel had been to the city before, their ride there, in a taxi that reeked of stale cigarettes and warm leather, was direct.

They were intrigued to see the front desk lit by candles. The receptionist, a woman with hollow eyes and a despondent manner, explained that the power lines to the building had been damaged during El Niño the previous day, but that they were now being repaired. Another storm was forecast, she added, blowing her nose into a tissue.

'Will that delay our flight tomorrow morning?' Daniel asked. 'We're booked to take the seaplane from the Guayllabamba River to the Galápagos.'

'I shall find out for you, señor,' the receptionist said, staring at the poppy in the lapel of Daniel's jacket. 'Now, if you will follow me.' She picked up a candlestick and led the way to the stairs. 'The lifts are not working,' she explained.

Nancy and Daniel looked at each other, shrugged and picked up their bags. 'We have cable TV,' the receptionist continued as she opened the door to a double room. 'You can get the CNN, when the power it come back.' The receptionist used her candle to light the wick of an oil lamp on their side table. It guttered momentarily, filling the lamp's glass balloon with soot and the room with the smell of paraffin. With a whooshing sound, it caught brightly. 'There is a fridge in the cupboard,' the receptionist continued. 'It will work again when the power it come back. I put in there the champagne your friend he order.'

'What champagne?' Daniel asked. 'What friend?'

Nancy opened the fridge. It was empty apart from a dusty bottle of Moët et Chandon with a card hanging from a string about its neck. She reached in for it. ' "Happy anniversary. Yours ever, Wetherby." ' Wetherby? The music prof? *That* Wetherby?'

'I don't believe it!' Daniel said, reading the card for himself. 'That is so sweet of him. I told him I was bringing you here as an anniversary surprise.'

'How lovely! You must ring and thank him.' Nancy turned to the receptionist. 'How do you make an international call?'

'You dial nine, then your country number. But the phone line, that is also down.'

As she checked her mobile for a signal, Nancy tried to catch Daniel's eye. He was trying to avoid hers, his shoulders heaving. When the receptionist left they both started laughing. Nancy checked her watch. 'We're five hours behind, right?'

Daniel tapped his watch face. 'Yeah, so it's the middle of the night in London. Text Dad to let them know we arrived safely and he can read it in the morning.'

A minute later the mobile beeped again. Nancy read the text out. 'Night Mum.' Nancy replied by texting: 'Get back to sleep! Love you. And call me Mummy.' The message that came back said: 'Luv u 2. Will ring in AM.'

While Nancy unpacked, Daniel showered. When he emerged, towelling his hair, he poured two miniatures of Scotch. 'We'll save the champagne for when the fridge it come back on. That reminds me . . .' He dialled a number and listened. 'His answering machine at work . . . Wetherby! It's Daniel. Just ringing to thank you for the bottle of champagne. That was so thoughtful of you. Such a lovely surprise. And thank you once again for all your help with the zoology chair. I owe you big time. You're a prince among professors. Anyway, big love, will tell you all about it when we get back.' He touched the 'end call' button. 'Some of the dons don't get him, you know, but I've always found him to be . . .'

'Eccentric?'

'Old-fashioned. An acquired taste . . . Water's not very hot.'

Nancy was stepping out of her clothes and tiptoeing across the cold tiles into the shower cubicle. A hiss of water was heard, followed by a yelp. 'Think I'll wait for it to heat up,' she said, appearing in the bathroom doorway, half in shadow, wrapped in a towel. 'Look at this.' She held up a strand of dark hair. 'It's gone frizzy and we've only been here a couple of hours.' She lay down on the bed beside Daniel and wrapped his arm around her, placing the palm of his hand on the swell of her hip. The side of her face was resting on his chest and she could hear the thud of his heart. 'What you thinking?' she said, looking up.

He traced with his thumb the line of her jaw and the arc of her mouth before kissing her eyelids, chin, neck. She touched her lips to his and shifted position so that she was sitting astride his waist. She wanted to see his face as she lowered herself on to him.

Afterwards, as they were walking arm in arm across a cobbled square, Daniel asked: 'Do you fancy tapas? Or . . .' He couldn't think of another Spanish dish.

'Tapas is fine.'

A church bell chimed eleven o'clock. Having slept – or rather having been sedated – for most of the flight, Daniel wasn't feeling tired. On the contrary, the high altitude of the city was making him feel light-headed and energized. He took Nancy's hand and broke into a jog. 'Come over here,' he said, half dragging her. 'I want to show you something.' A flashing neon sign announced the Equatorial Monument. 'Here,' he said, planting his feet wide apart. 'Stand like I'm standing.' Nancy hitched up her skirt so that she could straddle the line. 'You are now standing with one foot on each hemisphere.'

In the glow of the streetlamps, Daniel took Nancy's hand again and led her down an alley and across another square. Here they found a café lit by strip lights swinging from bare electric wires and sat outside where they could listen to the cicadas. The evening air was heavy with the smell of lime and, as they studied the menu, this made them feel hungry. Nancy ordered for both of them: tortilla, sardines and lamb meatballs in chorizo sauce for her, a vegetarian omelette and salad for him, and a carafe of red wine for them to share. They ate and drank in a friendly silence.

'Look at the moon,' Nancy said, dabbing her plate clean with a chunk of bread.

Daniel turned in his chair. The moon was full and had an aura the colour of marmalade. 'Must be something to do with El Niño,' he said.

'Will we fly out over the rainforest tomorrow?'

'Can't miss it. The place is one big rainforest.'

'Did Bruce give you enough sedatives for that flight too?'

'I'm going to try it without. It's just over an hour. Should be fine.'

'He hates me, you know.'

'Bruce? No, Bruce loves you.'

'He hates me.'

Daniel thought for a moment 'He doesn't hate you. He's scared of you.'

'Me?'

'Everyone is scared of you. You're scary.'

'Funny to think we were being snowed on this morning and now . . .' Nancy yawned with her mouth closed and gazed at a small church across the square from them. 'Dan?'

'Yeah?' He was stifling a yawn now, one triggered by Nancy's. It was making the hinges of his jaws ache.

'You know "the argument"?'

41

Daniel crossed his eyes. They had not discussed marriage properly since 'the argument' a year earlier. They had been dicing vegetables together when it started, listening to the rhythmic sound of the knives tapping against the counter top. Nancy had said, apropos of nothing, that she assumed they would end up married one day, 'because that's what people who love each other do'. Daniel had joked absently that, as far as he was concerned, 'love' and 'marriage' went together like 'hate' and 'guts'. She had called him immature. He had sighed. She had slammed the door behind her. That had been on her thirty-third birthday.

'Yes, I know the argument,' Daniel said.

'Well, if we did get married, what difference would it make if it was in a church?'

Daniel's religious intolerance, as Nancy wrongly – deliberately – called his intolerance of religion, was the main reason they had never married, or rather the reason they had never had the church wedding she, an occasional Catholic, wanted. 'Exactly my point,' Daniel said.

'You know what I mean, Dan. What difference would it make? It's just another building to you.'

'Not now, Nance. Don't spoil it.'

A firework illuminated the night sky. The couple looked up. A second one followed it, a starburst of orange and green. There was a fizzing sound before three fireworks popped and crackled simultaneously, showering the sky with lights. They lingered on the retina, long after the sky had returned to darkness.

'Must be some kids messing about,' Nancy said. 'I don't think there's a fiesta.'

'Pretty.'

'Yeah.'

'Look at them.' A young Caucasian couple at a nearby table were kissing – leaning forward, returning to their seats, leaning forward again. The man had bleached dreadlocks and a sunburnt nose. He was wearing a T-shirt with the words WHAT WOULD JESUS BOMB? His girlfriend had sooty eyes and glitter-dusted cheeks. As she stood up, Daniel could see that the wicker chair she was sitting on had left imprints on the skin at the back of her legs. She looked fourteen.

Nancy gave them a sideways glance, grinned and crossed her eyes.

Daniel whispered, 'What's the Spanish for "Get a room"?' He opened his wallet. 'Do you remember our first date?' He knew the answer. They had reminisced about it before. He nevertheless held up the business card Nancy had given him, along with a prescription for antibiotics, on his first visit to her dental practice ten years earlier. ' "Dr Nancy Palmer BDS (Lond.), LDS RCS (Eng.)" ,' he read out. 'As you handed me it, I noticed your ring finger was bare.'

'Still is.'

'You told me to phone you if I had any problems, an obvious come-on.'

'Not at all, there can be complications with root canal work.'

'It was my wisdom teeth. You gave me stitches. They left me feeling like I had a mouthful of spiders. I remember I asked what I should do if I had any problems in the evening, after the surgery was closed.'

'You were dribbling as you said it. Attractive.'

'Yeah, but it didn't stop you taking back the card and writing your home number on it.' He turned the card round and tapped it.

'Let me see that.' She leaned over and took the card, looking at both sides. 'God, I remember that number. I can't believe you kept this. You're so sad.'

'You were being romantic.'

'I was being a slut.'

Daniel slipped the card back in the wallet, behind a grainy black and white scan of Martha in the womb. 'And three months later you were pregnant.'

They clinked glasses and looked across at the couple. The girl was laughing and throwing a strip of orange peel at her boyfriend.

Nancy said, 'I still can't believe you managed to keep this trip a secret.'

Daniel held up his hands in surrender.

'It's so unlike you . . .' Tears were beading her lashes. 'Had you really been planning it for months?'

'Months and months. Can't believe you didn't rumble me.'

Nancy was shaking her head. 'You know, I was *sure* you'd never mentioned your German cousins to me before, but I figured that that would be typical of you.' She was laughing. 'You sounded so . . . I can't believe I fell for it . . . You're normally such a useless liar . . . You know, I was really pissed off about you landing me with the Ninth Panzer Division.'

'I know.'

'I'm not sure which gives me more pleasure, the thought of going on holiday or the relief that your bloody relatives don't exist . . . And I can't believe the baby was in on it. Should I text her again? She can read it in the morning.'

'If you want.'

She began to tap out a message. 'No signal.' Without looking up she added quietly: 'I miss her. What if something happens to her while we're away?'

Daniel had been avoiding this thought. Now a shadow passed over the square. It was irrational, he knew. He did not believe that what he willed was itself part of a larger will, something already written. 'Nothing is going to happen to her,' he said, trying to remove all traces of expression from his voice. 'The baby will be fine.' He made a signature sign at the waiter. 'Fancy a brandy?'

'Why not.'

'I'll ask them to bring one with the bill.'

Nancy studied Daniel's face for a moment. 'I know you love me,' she said.

'Couldn't love you more.'

'And you know I love you, don't you?'

'Yes.' Daniel reached across the table. 'Give me your hand.'

Nancy's hand met Daniel's halfway, their fingers interlocking. 'You mean it?'

★

Back at the hotel, the receptionist told them their flight had been delayed for one day because another storm was expected. Daniel slept fitfully and, the following morning, was awoken by the sound of shutters banging and rain slamming down on a nearby tin roof. Feeling nauseous – partly from jetlag and a hangover, partly from mild altitude sickness – he lay in bed until noon, contemplating the ceiling. The chatter of rain on palm fronds summoned distant machine guns to his ears. Nancy woke up only when the noise had stopped. 'Did you hear the storm?' Daniel asked.

'What storm?' Nancy said with a yawn as she removed earplugs she had been given on the plane. She swung her legs out of bed, removed her T-shirt and walked naked over to the balcony. There she opened first the heavy curtains, then shutters. The brightness of the sun made her shield her eyes. When they had adjusted, she took in the scenery below: a busy street that was starting to steam in the heat. 'What storm?' she repeated over her shoulder above the sound of car horns, bicycle bells and equatorial frogs expressing their appreciation of the fresh rainwater.

Across the street an overflow pipe was running on to a rusty balcony and leaving a stain on the white wall. A cat was stretched flat on the red-tiled rooftop, enjoying the heat. Nancy looked down from the balcony to the walls of their hotel. The plaster was blistered by the sun and battered by the rain. A scooter was rasping and weaving over the cobbles below. In the silence that followed it, Nancy heard bells summoning the faithful. She shaded her eyes with her hand and looked across the town to the dome of the cathedral. 'Nothing beats a church service in Spanish,' she announced lightly. 'Think I'll wander over.'

'Have fun.'

'Will you come?'

'I can't.'

'No one will recognize you.'

'I would ruin it for you with my tutting and sighing and eye-rolling.'

'That's true.'

Nancy got dressed, gathered her shoulder bag and used her

sunglasses as a hairband. 'Afterwards,' she said, making a bottle of suntan oil wheeze as she squeezed the last remaining drop from it, 'I shall walk through the square in my floaty linen dress, trail my fingers in the fountain and enjoy the admiring glances of the local men.'

Daniel smiled. 'Give my love to Jesus.'

'I will.'

Hearing the landing door close, Daniel scratched and yawned. Without Nancy around to tease him, he suddenly felt flat and lonely. He sat up and saw the book she was reading lying open, face down on the bedside table. He tilted his head to see the cover. It was in Spanish, a novel. He picked up his own book and flopped back on the bed, his brow mantled with sweat. The heat was making him feel lethargic. He scratched at a mosquito bite on his ankle, a night-time attack, and turned the ceiling fan on. As he was listening to it pulsing, he plumped up the pillow and, underneath it, felt the T-shirt Nancy had slept in. He held it to his nose, closed his eyes and felt the spin of sleep. When he woke, Nancy was stand-ing over him at the side of the bed. He felt for the book he had been reading – a guilty reaction.

'How was it?' he said, wiping his mouth. 'I wasn't asleep.'

'It had the biggest altarpiece you've ever seen, all gilt-covered columns, saints with crowns, cherubs with halos. It went right up to the ceiling, thirty feet tall and twenty feet wide.'

'Tasteful.'

'I never said it was tasteful, I said it was big.'

She lay on the bed beside him. 'You would have liked it. All that Catholic kitsch. It would have given you much to scoff at.'

'Did *you* like it?'

'I liked the incense and the candles and the prayers in Spanish. The bit where you are supposed to shake hands with your neigh-bour, they kiss. The saints' faces were black. I'm going to try Martha again. Can I use your mobile? Mine doesn't seem to . . .'

'It's in my jacket.' Daniel gestured limply towards the back of the door.

Nancy patted the jacket pockets and raised an eyebrow. 'What are these?' She was holding up the letters that Philip had given him. 'Are they from your mistress?'

'Yeah. They're from my mistress.'

Nancy untied the string and opened the top one. It was brittle to the touch. 'She must be quite old.'

'Dad was wondering if you could translate them. They were written by my great-grandfather, just before he was killed in the trenches.'

'Did your great-grandfather have a name?'

'Andrew.'

'Kennedy?'

'Yeah, Dad's side.'

Nancy was frowning. 'They're almost illegible,' she said, reaching in her shoulder bag for her reading glasses. Once found, she held the glasses unfolded to the bridge of her nose and tilted her head back. 'The pencil has . . .' She rubbed her index finger and thumb together. 'These must be precious for Phil. Should you have brought them with you?'

'I meant to leave them in the car at Heathrow.'

Nancy read quietly for a couple of minutes, her lips moving occasionally, then she lowered her glasses and said: 'Well, Andrew's French is bloody awful. His syntax is all over the place. Sort of awkward and childish. Was your great-grandmother French?'

'No, she was from Shropshire, I think. They married after he joined up. When he heard he was going to be sent to the Front. Lot of them did that.'

'So when was your grandfather born?'

'My grandfather? You mean my great-grandfather?'

'No, I mean your grandfather. Phil's father.'

'I'd have to check. I don't think my great-grandfather ever saw him. Why?'

'Well, whoever these letters were to . . .' Nancy turned back to the first page to read the name again. 'Whoever "*Ma petite Adilah*" was . . . seems to have been expecting Andrew's baby.'

'I'm pretty sure my great-grandmother's name was Dorothy.'

'Well, naughty Andrew Kennedy then,' Nancy said, raising her glasses again. She continued reading. 'That's odd . . .'

'What?'

'He seems to have known he was going to die. Listen: "*Je mort avec votre visage sur mon esprit.*" I death, I think he means I will die, I will die with your face on my mind. He goes on, I won't be afraid if I can do that.'

Nancy fell silent as she read on.

'What else?' Daniel prompted.

' "*Pendant . . . dernière année . . .*" For the past year my wish when I saw the sun rising was to see it set, setting, again, that was the, the measure, yardstick of my life . . . You are my one *pensé*, thought, my darling, and I would not have swapped one moment, minute, I spent with you, not even if it would have meant escaping what is to come.'

She looked up. 'Quite the poet.' Her eyes returned to the letter. ' "*Ne pluie pas pour moi.*" Don't rain – no, don't weep for me. Be happy, be happy *pour moi* . . . I know God is with me . . . You know what I saw. "*Vous seul . . .*" You alone understand . . . Look after our child." Then he ends: "Tell him, I know it will be a boy, tell him that his father faced his death like a soldier, gallantly like a soldier." '

Nancy lowered her glasses once more and looked across at Daniel. Her eyes were glistening. 'That's . . .' She swallowed. 'That's so . . .'

'Can I see?' Daniel felt the texture of the letter, rubbing it thoughtfully. He held it up to the light and nodded. Like a primate, he sniffed its mustiness. It weighed heavily in his hand, with a gravitational pull of its own. 'Does this room have a safe?'

'Haven't found one.'

'Reception will have a safe. These letters should be . . . Come on, let's go and explore the town.'

Daniel handed the letters over at reception and, as an afterthought, slipped the poppy out of his buttonhole and tucked it behind the string. 'Can you keep these in your safe?'

'Of course, señor.'

'Are there any markets nearby?'

'Not far away, in a cobbled square called the Puerta del Angel. It is the highest point of the city.'

The walk cleared Daniel's head a little, but the sight of stalls laden with glassy-eyed rabbits, and geese with their heads still attached, made him feel nauseous again. The air smelled of spices, tobacco and incense mixed with burning hair and open sewers. The sticky afternoon heat did not help. 'It smells like my lab,' he complained, covering his nose.

Green and red bunting criss-crossed the square, evidence of a recent fiesta. In one corner three teenage girls were standing around an open-doored jeep, grinding their hips in time to a samba thumping from its speakers. Nancy copied them briefly, swaying her hips as she did a triple step backwards and forwards, her arms turning rhythmically outwards for balance.

Daniel grinned and shook his head in awe. 'Didn't know you could samba.'

'I'm an enigma. That's why you love me.' With this, Nancy turned and gave a little wave over her shoulder as she strolled across to a fruit stand. Daniel looked for a shady doorway to sit down in, away from the press of bodies. Unable to find one, he leaned against the crumbling plaster of a wall and watched Nancy testing the firmness of a mango, rolling it between her hands. When a dog appeared and began barking at him excitedly he moved a few yards on, to an area of wall sprayed with graffiti. He was feeling breathless. His eyelids were heavy. Distracted by a small, rust-coloured dust devil whirling across the street, he did not at first notice the young man in the white cotton *thoub* staring at him. With his fine features, long hair and bulging, wide-set eyes, the youth looked out of context to Daniel, more like a Moroccan beach boy than an Ecuadorian street trader. Though half in silhouette, he looked familiar, too. Daniel narrowed his eyes. When the young man invited him over to his stall with a wave of his hand and a broad, golden smile, Daniel stayed where he was. Feeling unnerved, he walked over to Nancy to ask if she recognized him.

'Recognize who?' she said, distractedly plucking a leaf from a bush, rubbing it and smelling her fingers. 'Is this a bay leaf? Smell it.'

Daniel walked the length of the stalls looking for the young man, all the while being jostled and accosted by traders with outstretched hands, but he was gone.

'You OK?' Nancy asked when he returned.

'I feel peculiar.' He rubbed the back of his neck. 'I feel . . .' His voice trailed away, his eyes closed and his knees buckled. When he slumped to the ground in a detonation of red dust, Nancy ran to him. She lifted up his head and, using water from a bottle she was carrying, splashed his face. He had cut his lip and the water made the injury look worse than it was, swelling the trickle of blood down his chin. Daniel came round to the sound of a stallholder hailing a taxi for them. Nancy supported his arm as he climbed unsteadily into it.

At the hotel, the receptionist eyed them suspiciously as they stumbled up the stairs. 'Good news, señor,' she called after Daniel. 'The electricity is back.' A pause. 'And your flight is cleared to leave in the morning.' When they reached their room they found the door ajar. A maid was vacuuming the floor with a machine that was so loud they couldn't hear, at first, that their phone was ringing.

CHAPTER FIVE

TOWARDS THE END OF THE FLIGHT, WITH HIS FOREHEAD PRESSED against the Plexiglas window, Daniel counted to three and opened his eyes. They were flying over a cluster of miniature islands – little more than sandbanks with gently scalloped bays – and between them he could see the white sail of a yacht and the dark outline of what he guessed was a shoal of dolphins. The Galápagos archipelago was not yet in sight but Daniel could sense its naked proximity. He closed his eyes again. After another count of three he opened them and saw the seaplane's undulating shadow, their shadow, below them. '"The spirit of God moved upon the face of the waters",' he said under his breath. As a practising atheist he was not normally given to quoting from the Old Testament, ironically or otherwise. He had surprised himself; an unfamiliar feeling.

He lowered the blind and checked his watch with a double tap of its face. It was 8.46am. Next he gave his armrest two taps with his knuckles, a ritual that helped him cope with his fear of flying – like touching wood, except that he was not superstitious or, rather, he had not allowed himself to be infected by what he called 'that virus of the mind'.

Nancy was sitting next to him, flicking with a licked finger through his copy of *National Geographic*. 'How long before we land?' she said.

'Mm?'

'How long before we land? . . . Hello?' She tapped his head. Her mood was frivolous. It had been that way since before take-off when the flight attendant, a thin-lipped Latino, had read safety instructions from a laminated card. He had included the line: 'In the unlikely event of a landing on water . . .' This had given Nancy the giggles; they were, after all, sitting in a sixteen-seater, twin-engine amphibian. Daniel managed a grim, nervous smile.

'How you feeling?' Nancy asked.

'Fine, fine,' Daniel said. 'I think it was altitude sickness. When I fainted, I mean . . .' He touched his swollen lip and frowned, losing his train of thought. 'Was I out for long?'

'A minute, maybe two. You remember getting back to the hotel?'

'Not really . . . I remember the phone was ringing.'

Nancy was polishing her sunglasses with a paper napkin. 'Didn't get to it in time.' She held the glasses up to the window and turned them to catch the light.

Daniel frowned. 'This bloody music.'

Incongruously, throughout the 600-mile flight, the pilot had been playing a Hall and Oates greatest hits CD over the speaker system – fairly quietly, but loud enough to annoy Daniel. He signalled the flight attendant over and asked if it could be turned down. Nancy began to sing along to it tonelessly, getting the lyrics slightly wrong: 'Because my kiss, my kiss is on your lips . . .' She was on her second half-can of Venezuelan beer.

Sitting in front of them was the youth with the bleached dread-locks they had seen in the restaurant. As he joined in with odd lyrics from the chorus he rose from his seat and began stretching. He was wearing boot-cut jeans so low half his Calvin Klein briefs were visible. His T-shirt carried the message I AM NOT A TERRORIST (I'M JUST BEARDED). He did not have a beard, nor did he look as if he needed to shave. Daniel felt a pang of envy. The young man was languid, carefree, clean-limbed.

'Cramp?' Nancy asked, flicking back a strand of hair. She had a very un-English habit of starting conversations with strangers; but this, to Daniel, looked more like flirtation.

'Yeah, right here in my calves,' the young man said with a

grimace and what Daniel recognized instantly as the springy accent of the Massachusetts north shore.

Nancy ground the palm of one hand against the other – a demonstration. 'Try massaging the balls of your feet.'

'Thanks,' the young man said, removing a flip-flop and hopping on one foot while rubbing the other. When he had finished, he gave a wide smile that exposed expensive American teeth. 'Greg,' he said with a pat of his chest. 'Greg Coulter.'

'Hello, Greg Greg Coulter. I'm Nancy. We saw you at the restaurant in Quito.'

'Yeah? You guys on holiday?'

Nancy nodded. 'You?'

'Honeymoon.' He pointed at the seat behind them. 'We got married three days ago.'

Nancy patted Daniel's knee, bare below Bermuda shorts. 'Did you hear that, Mr Kennedy? They've just got married.'

'Congratulations,' Daniel said, turning to smile at Greg's young-looking wife who was sitting behind them, her pale, goosepimpled legs tucked under her.

'Not afraid of commitment, you see,' Nancy added, not looking at Daniel.

'I didn't realize you two were together,' Daniel said to the child bride. 'You've been so quiet back there. Why don't we swap seats so you guys can sit with each other?'

'That's OK,' Greg said. 'We're nearly there.'

There was a lull in which the droning of the engines could be heard.

'Actually,' Nancy said, '*I'm* on holiday but my "biological pair-bond" here . . .' she patted Daniel's knee again, 'is working. He looks at things through microscopes. Spores, moulds, bacteria.'

'I only look at those things for fun. I specialize in worms.'

'He's an international authority on nonsegmented roundworms,' Nancy continued, enjoying herself. 'They're microscopic.'

'The first living organism to have its entire genetic blueprint decoded,' the child bride said, joining in with an uncertain smile, leaning over the back of Nancy's seat. A silver cross was swinging forward on a chain around her neck. She was wearing a microskirt and a clinging T-shirt with a peace sign drawn in diamante sequins. It was cut to show her midriff. It also showed she wasn't wearing a bra.

Daniel clasped his hands like an indulgent vicar. 'Very good!'

'They have a nervous system, can digest food and have sex, like humans,' the child bride continued with a chewy American accent. 'That's why they're so significant.'

'Now you're scaring me,' Daniel said.

'I thought I recognized you,' the child bride said. She turned to her husband. 'Told you I recognized him.' She faced Daniel again. 'You did that programme on the Natural World Channel, didn't you?'

Daniel helped her out: '*The Selfish Planet*.'

The child bride lowered her eyes and gave a shy smile. 'That's it,' she said. 'I thought it was real interesting. You always been into biology and stuff?'

'Yeah, I suppose I have,' Daniel said. 'My name's Dan, by the way.' He raised his eyebrows and paused for her to offer her name.

She nodded and smiled a second time.

He tried again. 'And you are?'

'Susie.' She leaned forward. 'Must be great being on television, giving people pleasure.'

'Thought you said you'd seen his programme,' Nancy said.

A look of confusion played across Susie's face.

'Take no notice,' Daniel said. 'You're from Boston, aren't you?'

Susie's lashless eyes expanded. She was blushing. 'How d'you know that?'

'Recognized the intonation. Lovely place, Bean Town. Lived there myself until quite recently.'

Nancy punched his leg playfully. 'As a student.' She turned to Susie. 'Before you were born, I imagine.'

'I was a postgrad, darling,' Daniel said. 'So it wasn't *that* long ago.'

'Harvard?' Susie asked.

The seaplane shuddered. Greg steadied himself by grabbing a curtain that was screening off the galley. Daniel began breathing slowly and deeply. He felt his belly contracting. Tap-tap of finger-tip on watch face: 8.54am.

'Fear of flying,' Nancy mouthed to Susie, directing a thumb at Daniel.

'No, not Harvard,' Daniel said as he recovered his composure. 'I was at MIT. And it's not fear of flying. Flying I'm fine with, . . .'

Nancy finished the sentence with him: '. . . it's crashing I don't like.'

Daniel gave her a patient look. The annoying truth, as far as he was concerned, was that it wasn't only the crashing he was afraid of. Planes made him feel claustrophobic. They gave him vertigo. More to the point, he hated ceding control of his life to someone else. Flying was an act of faith in the people who build, inspect and fly planes: as a scientist, Daniel knew he of all people should appreciate that. But he was not a great believer in faith.

'I keep telling him it's irrational,' Nancy said. 'He hates that. Thinks he's the most rational man on the planet.'

'The urge not to defy gravity is far from irrational,' Daniel said. Realizing this sounded pompous, he added: 'Besides, I haven't met everyone on the planet so how would I know whether I'm the most rational man on it.' He smiled to show he was joking.

Nancy smiled back. 'Statistically you are more likely to be kicked to death by a cow than you are to die in a plane crash, isn't that right, Mr Kennedy?'

Daniel sighed. '*Donkey*. And plenty of people are kicked to death by donkeys. Several hundred a year.'

Donkey. The word had an unexpected resonance for Daniel. Donkeys led by lions. No, that wasn't right. Lions led by donkeys. His great-grandfather Andrew had been one of the lions. A fearless lion roaring as he charged across no-man's-land . . . The letters . . . 'Shit. I've left those letters in the safe at the hotel.'

'Well, they'll be safe there,' Nancy said. 'Safe there! Christ, I'm funny. We can pick them up when we get back to Quito.'

Daniel rubbed his finger and thumb together as he considered the letters, what they meant, why they had spooked his father.

'He doesn't like it when anyone else uses probability,' Nancy continued, addressing the others again and breaking into Daniel's thoughts. 'Probability is his big thing. His catch-all explanation . . . He normally takes diazepam.'

This was true. His doctor friend, Bruce, usually obliged with the prescription, though Nancy had come to the prescriptive rescue on more than one occasion. Diazepam was a better cure for nerves than alcohol. Daniel had read up on it: if you drink alcohol when you are feeling anxious it makes you over-emotional and your blood less able to absorb oxygen, which it is being starved of anyway, because you are panicking. As this was a fairly short flight, Daniel thought he would risk it without diazepam.

'You OK, Dan?' Nancy whispered, sounding protective. Her breath smelled of chewing gum. At that moment Daniel's unease about the flight was coupled with an enveloping feeling of affection for his wife-to-be. Seeing that Greg was looking out of the window, he slipped his hand under the sarong tied low around her hips. Unbuckled his seat belt. Stood up. There were thirteen passengers on board – he counted them as he negotiated Nancy's legs on his way to the aisle. He opened the overhead locker, unzipped his bag, pulled out a map and struggled to rezip it. The padded box containing his specimen jars and test tubes had risen to the top. He pulled them out, removed his swimming trunks, fins and snorkel, stuffed the box down the side of the bag and jammed the trunks, fins and snorkel back on top of them. With a struggle, he was able to rezip. He surveyed the other passengers. A couple in row six had fallen asleep. In row eight, a septuagenarian with horn-rimmed glasses and skin hanging down in pleats was nodding to himself as he read the *International Herald Tribune*. The old-fashioned glasses made him look as if he was in disguise. A retired CIA agent, Daniel thought. Or an international paedophile. Either way, he had swapped seats at the beginning of the flight with the tall, solidly built black man with his legs stretched out in seat 1a.

'How many?' Nancy asked without looking up from the *National Geographic* she was again flicking through.

'How many what?'

'Passengers.'

'Dunno.'

'There are thirteen. I counted them, too. Don't worry, it's just a number.'

'I'm not worried.'

'Lots of people are superstitious about numbers. They're called triskaidekaphobes.'

'I know they are. And I am not one of them. I'm not superstitious. How many more times?'

'Do you know why the number thirteen is considered unlucky?'

'Yep.'

'It's because there were thirteen apostles originally, before Judas Iscariot betrayed Jesus.'

'I know.'

It amused Nancy to imitate his teacherly custom of offering unwanted explanations. She knew that, though Daniel pretended to find it annoying, he enjoyed it really. Daniel sighed again, because he knew Nancy liked to pretend that it annoyed her.

There was another shudder, lighter this time. It made the gut of the tall black man jiggle. Susie unzipped a bumbag and produced a bright yellow underwater camera. 'Can I take a photograph, Dan?'

Daniel pointed a finger at himself. 'Of me?'

'Here,' Greg said, taking the camera. 'I'll take one of you together. Stand next to him, Sus.'

Daniel felt embarrassed as Susie put her arm around his waist and the other passengers turned to stare, trying to work out why the young woman would want a photograph of herself with him. The picture taken, Daniel returned to his seat and strapped himself in. Susie took the camera back and framed another shot – of Nancy and Daniel sitting together. She took one of Greg half crouching beside Nancy. As the flash went off, Greg was staring at Nancy's cleavage, the weight and depth of the press between her breasts rendered more impressive than usual by a black 'deep plunge' bra purchased at Heathrow.

'Hang on,' Susie said. 'You weren't looking at the camera, babe. Let me take another.'

The seaplane trembled for a few seconds. Daniel gripped the

armrests and concentrated hard on keeping it in the air. Standard prop blades create a hum, which, along with the airstreams passing over the wings, becomes white noise after a while. Daniel focused on that for a few seconds and felt calmer. As he was sitting near the propellers, his body was vibrating in rhythm with the plane. That calmed him a little, too.

Nancy put an arm round his shoulder and pulled him gently towards her, so that the side of his face was resting on her neck. He closed his eyes and smelled the Ambre Solaire on her skin. She sometimes wore this in winter, to remind herself – and her patients – of holidays. They couldn't quite identify what it was, she reckoned, but it nevertheless lifted their spirits.

A jolt made Daniel sit back squarely in his seat. He checked his belt. Nancy removed her arm and signalled the flight attendant for another beer. Daniel stared blankly ahead, amorphous anxiety mounting. How, he thought, had he got himself into this situation? *Light aircraft are not safe. Light aircraft are not safe. Light aircraft are not safe.* He should have followed his instincts and taken the boat from Ecuador, as he had on his last pilgrimage to the Galápagos Islands.

Greg stood up again and used a Handycam to film the other passengers. When Daniel saw he was being filmed he gave a weak smile and distracted himself by reaching into the seat pocket for the safety instructions card. It was in Spanish. He put it back unread, remembered the map, unfolded half of it and laid it out on his knees to see if the sandbanks they had flown over were marked. He followed the line of their flight with his finger, but he could not see them.

The flight attendant brought Nancy another can of beer and said: 'The captain asked me to remind you to collect your CD when we land.'

Nancy chewed her lower lip, turned to Daniel and blinked her long, black eyelashes twice. Daniel's left eyebrow was forming a quizzical arch. 'That was *your* Hall and Oates album?'

'Bought it at the airport.'

Daniel was laughing. 'That's funny. Now *that* is funny. I like that. How the hell did you remember I hated Hall and Oates?'

Nancy shrugged. 'Just did.'

There was a second jolt. Daniel stopped laughing and folded the map away, breathing slowly and unobtrusively through his mouth. He began clenching and unclenching his fists, concentrating on breathing, on not hyperventilating, on keeping the plane in the air. The trouble was, as well he knew, once your heart rate goes up and you start sweating and struggling for breath, you begin to panic more. You start feeding your own anxiety. *Why did no one else notice the bumps?*

'How long before we land?' Nancy said. Thinking Daniel was pretending to ignore her, she repeated her question. 'Dan? How long before we land?'

More shuddering, lasting longer this time. Greg returned to his seat and buckled up. Daniel yawned. His fingers were tingling and a release of adrenalin was giving him butterflies. Blood flowing away from the stomach, he thought edgily – the fight or flight mechanism. He now felt his ears pop. We must be beginning our descent, he thought. He swallowed hard and tapped his watch: 9.00am. There was a gentle bump followed by a harder one, more of a lurch. Another yawn. Daniel couldn't stop yawning – his nervousness had gone up a gear and his brain was trying to get more oxygen. There was a film of sweat on his forehead. The FASTEN SAFETY BELTS sign came on, accompanied by a *ping*. Greg checked his seat belt. Daniel checked Nancy's belt and gently raked the backs of his fingers across a small, exposed part of her abdomen, over the stretch marks she had once compared to sidewinder trails in the desert. He swallowed again and checked the buckle on his own belt. He raised his blind and, without looking down, wiped the window with his sleeve, making a squeaking noise. Condensation was building up. The air outside was a clear, corn-flower blue. 'Do you know why the sky is blue?' he asked Nancy, trying to take his mind off the turbulence, trying to control the tone of his voice, trying not to give himself away.

'Yes.'

'Go on then.'

'Because if it was green you wouldn't know where the sky ended and the land began.'

Daniel cracked his knuckles. The back of his neck was feeling prickly. He rubbed it, trying to stifle another yawn. 'It's because light arriving from the sun hits the molecules in the air and is scattered in all directions.' He knew he was talking too crisply, too quickly; trying to disguise his tension.

Nancy continued her own train of thought. 'Of course, where the blue of the sky meets the blue of the sea, there you have a problem . . .'

'The amount of scattering depends on the frequency,' Daniel added. 'Blue light has a high frequency and is scattered ten times more than red light which has . . .' He swallowed. 'Which has a lower frequency.' He yawned again and stretched involuntarily. 'So the background scattered light you see in the sky is blue.' His mouth was dry; heart stuttering. He wiped the window again. Closed the blind.

'Do you know why the army term for a friendly fire incident is "a blue-on-blue"?' Nancy asked.

Daniel frowned. He knew this one. 'Is it because . . .' He shook his head. 'No, I don't.'

Nancy grinned triumphantly. 'It refers to the colour used to mark friendly troops on maps.'

A hissing sound came from the back of the plane. The passengers turned as one in their seats to see what it was. Then it happened: a dull explosion; a violent jolt; a gut-wrenching plummet. It was so sudden no one screamed. The dive lasted for several hundred feet before the plane levelled off. Nancy grasped for a handhold. '*Jesus.*' It sounded like she was in a wind tunnel. 'Dan? What's happening? Was that an air pocket? *What's happening?*'

An angry metallic sound came from the right side of the plane; the sound of metal ripping. This was followed by a popping noise in the fuselage below, like bubble wrap being burst. The plane banked left. People were screaming now. The flight attendant, who had been thrown the length of the plane, tried to stand up, grabbing a trolley to steady himself. He had a small gash on his head. For the next thirty seconds the plane pitched and rolled and there was a sickening series of thuds, like hammer blows against an anvil. The air tightened. The temperature in the cabin dropped – a chill of terror passing through the plane.

Daniel flicked his blind up. Five feet out on the wing the engine spluttered and stopped. It was missing a blade. Another blade was bent at a ninety-degree angle. The cowling was mangled, its aluminium peeled back and twisted, its wires and cables whipping in the airstream. Fuel was spewing from steel-braided hoses. With fumbling hands, Daniel reached for a sick bag from the seat pocket, but didn't manage to open it in time. The vomit splashed over his knees and shins and on to what Nancy always called his 'scientist's sandals'.

The left engine sounded louder on its own – so loud Daniel thought he had gone deaf in his right ear. Partial deafness. An image of his father's face flashed into his head for a second before his attention focused on the door to the cockpit. It was swinging open and closed and he could hear shouted snatches of the pilot's broken English: 'G362ES. G362ES.' Next came some co-ordinates followed by the word 'north', and some more followed by 'east'. The pilot shouted: 'We out at two zero zero at this time. Angels twenty. We losing power. We attempt emergency landing. Ecuador Centre. G362ES declaring an emergency. We have engine failure. Repeat. *We have engine failure.*'

The plane was gliding in a wide, downward spiral. The engine was no longer loud. A whistle of rushing air could be heard. The screams had turned to whimpers. Behind them, Susie was muttering: '*Ohmygod, ohmygod, ohmygod.*' Towards the back of the plane someone was praying in Spanish. Daniel turned round. An elderly woman was fingering a string of rosary beads. She didn't notice that she had a nosebleed. Incongruously, Greg was holding his Handycam up to his eye again, filming the scenes of panic. There was a powerful smell of aviation fuel and vomit. Oxygen masks flopped down from the overhead lockers. Daniel stared dumbly at his. We must be below 10,000 feet by now, he calculated with shock-induced detachment, because I am still conscious. With a rapid decompression you have only twenty seconds to get your oxygen mask on; after that you lose the ability to think clearly or co-ordinate properly. And after that a feeling of euphoria comes over you, a symptom of the brain not getting enough oxygen. *We are definitely below 10,000 feet. Because I am definitely not feeling euphoric.*

The flight attendant held a paper napkin to his head and made a surprisingly calm announcement over the Tannoy. 'You may notice, lady and gentlemen, we are experience some difficulty. But do not try to panic. We get through this together. This a twin turboprop. It can fly on one engine.' He began reading from his card. ' "In the unlikely event of a landing on water, you find you life vest under seat. Please remove pen and other sharp object . . ." ' Daniel could not concentrate. His mind had latched on to the words: *We get through this together.*

Nancy felt under her seat for her life vest. Daniel did the same. When they had put them on, they looked at each other for the first time since the explosion. Nancy's velvet-brown eyes were wide with confusion and fear, her pupils dilated. They kissed clumsily, their lips dry. 'I love you,' she said. Her eyes were beginning to water.

'I love you,' Daniel echoed, taking her hand, his voice sounding distant to him, disembodied. He looked at Nancy's tear-rimmed eyes. When wet they looked like melting chocolate. He wanted to reassure her, tell her any lie that would stop her looking so frightened. 'It's going to be OK, Nance. It's going to be OK. This is a seaplane. We're supposed to land on water. We'll be fine. We'll be . . .' He stopped. They both knew they weren't going to be fine.

Nancy gripped his hand. Her knuckles were white. 'Be brave, Dan,' she said. 'I love you.' Heavy tears were hanging on her lashes. She closed her eyes and repeated. 'I love you. I love you . . . *Martha!* I've got to ring her.' She felt for her mobile in her shoulder bag, turned it on and looked at its screen. 'No signal. *Come on. Come on.* There.' She pressed a speed-dial button and held the phone to her ear. 'Come on. Come on. Please pick up. *Please. Please.* Hello? . . . It's gone to voicemail . . . It's me, darling. I love you.' She sobbed and passed the phone to Daniel.

'I love you, baby. I love you. Be a good girl. Be a brave girl. Mummy and Daddy love you.'

They were the only words he could think to say, the only ones that could be said.

He thought about their life insurance, the wills they had made, how they had named his parents as Martha's guardians. Martha would be looked after. The baby would be looked after. Grampy and Grumpy would look after her. Daniel thought, too, of the second drawer of his desk, the one that was locked, the one that contained Nancy's Rampant Rabbit, the ecstasy pills he brought home from Glastonbury but never got round to taking, their stash of grass wrapped in clingfilm. Martha would find them all one day.

'We gonna be OK? We gonna be OK?' The tall, black man was shouting this to the flight attendant. The question brought Daniel back to the horror of the present tense. The plane was listing and it made him feel disorientated, as though delivered from gravity. He looked out at the wing but there were no visual references, no horizon, just lonely, cloudless sky.

They were floating rather than falling now. Daniel retched again. The fear had penetrated deep into his gut and was making his hands tremble uncontrollably. He stared at them as if they were not his own. From behind came the sound of Susie being sick, too. There was a jarring sensation as the plane banked right.

This can't be happening. Not to me. Not to someone who worries about this happening as an insurance against it happening.

They seemed to be taking too long to hit the water, given their rate of descent. Daniel rapped at his watch – 9.08am.

Let's get this over with. I can't stand this fear any more, this waiting, this living in fear of dying.

At this moment he realized that Hall and Oates were still playing on the sound system: 'I Can't Go For That (No Can Do)'.

The plane levelled out again, the wings dipping one way before correcting to the other. Daniel sat upright and saw they were within a few hundred feet of the water. The ocean was a deep, vivid blue, almost violet. A coral reef and dark shadows could be seen. It felt as though they were suspended. Time slowed down, distorted, warped, expanded. The intensity of the moment was almost physical, almost too physically painful to bear. Daniel sensed he was living more in the tissue of each of these last seconds, these final heartbeats, than he had in all the frozen years of his life so far.

The plane trembled, dropped, pulled hard left.

We get through this together.

Continuous juddering now. Sporadic screaming. An overhead locker flopped open. Bags of peanuts flew around the cabin. Nancy was clenching her teeth. Her eyes were bulging. She made the sign of the cross. Snatches of the pilot and co-pilot going through a checklist could be heard: 'Right condition. Lever right. Condition. Lever.' They were talking in English, the international language of air traffic control. It sounded like an abstract poem. 'We out at one zero. Angel. Repeat. We out at angel.' Beeps and synthesized warning voices could be heard as well. A metallic voice confirmed: 'Altitude one zero. Altitude angel.' There was another clatter, a howl of wind, and abruptly it felt as if the air had been sucked out of the cabin. The emergency door across the aisle had opened and the flight attendant had disappeared.

The pilot's voice came over the intercom: '*Brace! Brace!*'

Noticing a tingling sensation in his urethra, Daniel looked down and became mesmerized by a creeping dark patch around the crotch of his shorts. The image of his father's face flashed in his head again. The smell of Mint Imperials. The plane slewed left and right. It was soundless. Powerless. They were no longer at an angle to the horizon.

Silver shards of glass silently filled the air. The left wing clipped the surface of the water and the plane started its violent cartwheel. This, Daniel thought, is it.

CHAPTER SIX

THE ICE RINK IN FRONT OF THE TEMPERATE HOUSE AT KEW WAS, TO
Martha, a sanctuary. When she skated here she could forget about
insulin, about her condition, about what made her different from
the other girls. With each graceful sweep of her blades she was able
to slough it all off. From the moment her parents had driven away
to Heathrow two days earlier, she had been lobbying her grandparents to bring her here. Though they always found the botanical
gardens too crowded on a Saturday, and resented having to pay for
the skating on top of their senior citizen's admission fee, they could
hardly refuse. It was a short distance from their house. But they did
qualify their capitulation: they couldn't stay long. They were worried that Martha's blood sugar levels would drop if she exerted
herself too much in the biting cold. The weather forecast that
morning had predicted that this would be one of the coldest
November days on record, with temperatures dipping as low as -15
in parts of the north. Even London was expected to be -10 by late
afternoon, colder than Moscow. It was afternoon now.

As Amanda strode off to the cafeteria for two glasses of mulled
wine and a mug of hot chocolate, Philip watched his granddaughter describe lazy figures of eight in the ice. Though she was
easy to spot in her pink, fur-lined coat, a freezing fog was descending and every time she disappeared behind other skaters at the far
side of the rink, Philip's eyes watered as he strained to see her. His
breath was mushrooming visibly in front of him and, though he was

wearing a Russian Ushanka with the flaps down, and an Aran sweater under a padded wax jacket, the wind chill was reaching his bones. To try to warm up, he stamped his feet and clapped his hands. Beside him was a *Finding Nemo* rucksack he was looking after for Martha. Because it was on his deaf side, he could not hear the mobile ringing inside it.

When Martha scraped to a halt in front of him, sending up a spray of ice, he tried not to show he was shivering. Amanda returned and handed Martha the hot chocolate. The child cupped it in her hands for a few seconds before taking a sip. As it was too hot to drink, she handed it back and, after asking her grandparents to watch, began to spin, bringing in her arms to turn faster, obeying the laws of physics as explained to her by her father. After thirty seconds she slowed down and, with a wobble and a backward glance, set off on another lap, her skates hissing as they bit. When she had not reappeared after a minute, Philip became anxious. He checked his watch. Her next injection was due in half an hour. He began walking stiffly to the other end of the rink. Another skater, he could see, was trying to help Martha to her feet, but she was limp in his arms. Two rink marshals in jesters' hats appeared and carried her towards the pavilion. By the time Philip was able to shoulder his way in, a small crowd had formed. Martha was having convulsions. 'She's with me,' he said. 'She's diabetic.' He tipped the contents of the rucksack on to the floor, saw some glucose tablets underneath Martha's velvety toy turtle and put one on her tongue. Her undulations slowed and stopped. Philip held her mouth closed as the tablet dissolved. Flecks of saliva, he could see, had caught on her chapped lips. He pressed two fingers against her wrist and found the thread of her pulse. After a minute her eyes opened. They were dilated but she was soon able to focus them. 'Did I have another hypo, Grampy?' she asked blearily. Bubbles of saliva were appearing in the corner of her mouth.

Philip nodded and gave her a reassuring smile. He found her medical pouch among the scattered items on the floor and deftly administered a dose of insulin. Amanda joined them and gathered up the rest of the contents of the rucksack. The mobile was ringing again. One of the marshals, a man with windburnt cheeks and a pierced tongue, lifted Martha up and led the way to a small first aid room, backing against its swing door to open it. The bells on his hat jingled as he laid her down on a narrow stretcher bed. This made her grin. Amanda looked at the message on the screen of Martha's iPhone, touched it and held it to her ear. A look of confusion crossed her face. She tapped the message again, held the mobile to Philip's good ear and said: 'Listen to this. The message says it's from Nancy, but I can't make out what she's saying.'

CHAPTER SEVEN

COLD WATER WAS PRESSING AGAINST DANIEL'S CHEST AS HE CAME round. He could not work out where he was. When he tried to focus his eyes, he felt a searing pain between them, behind his sockets. Pain. It meant he had passed through death; that he was still alive. He focused on the empty space where the seat in front had been, the seat his head must have slammed against. To get his bearings he turned to Nancy. She was no longer there either. In panic he turned his head to his right and saw her slumped inertly forward in her seat, her profile hidden behind her hair, the water up to her neck. Daniel looked up and immediately his sense of disorientation deepened. The other passengers were upside down, hanging from the ceiling, suspended by their seat belts. The plane must have flipped over. Their double seat must have been wrenched from its bolted moorings and flung through the air to the opposite side of the cabin. Some of the passengers appeared to be screaming – their mouths were open and their faces contorted, but he could not hear their screams. One of them unclipped his belt and fell, landing with a splash in the water. Daniel did not hear the splash either. His ears were deaf with ringing.

The water.

It was over his mouth now. In his nostrils. Lungs. As he gasped, he swallowed; as he swallowed he lost his self-control. His balled fist was punching at his seat-belt buckle. He lifted its latch and it unlocked. By pulling his knees up, he was able to free his feet. With his eyes open underwater he could make out a blur of red light above an emergency exit.

It was now that he climbed over Nancy.

With a scrum-half's hand-off that flattened her nose and dragged her lips sideways, he pushed her cheek and jaw into the headrest. It was a reflex, visceral action slowed down by the water; an adrenal moment they would both replay time and again, always with the same damning frame frozen in time.

In a confusion of elbows, knees and grabbing hands, he half swam, half dragged himself towards the red light and once there, counter-intuitively yanked the lever down rather than up, following a direction arrow. As water was on both sides of the door, it opened easily. His lungs were burning. The urge to breathe was excruciating. Only a sphincter muscle at the top of his windpipe was keeping the water out, the drowning reflex that buys the body a few more seconds. It was enough time to get him to the surface and to suck hard for air. Painful, jagged gasps. A fit of coughing began. Salt water and mucus were stinging his synapses, grating his throat, choking him.

He looked around. The seaplane was on its back underwater, its floats on the surface, its tail pitched up slightly, its one good engine emitting steam. It had come to rest on a reef of coral.

Only then did Daniel think of Nancy. Remembered pushing past her as she struggled with her belt. Felt her warm face under the heel of his hand.

He dived back down. The cabin was almost underwater, the only air pocket in the tail. He refilled his lungs here. Got his bearings. Saw other passengers thrashing around and, as if performing in some grotesque ballet, pushing past each other in slow motion to get to the exit. Susie was trying frantically to open her lap belt like a car seat belt, pressing rather than pulling its latch. Daniel flicked it open for her as he half swam, half walked past. The water was clear enough to make out Nancy's shape. She was still strapped into their double seat, still struggling to unclip her belt.

An icy thought came to Daniel as he swam and pulled himself towards her: how was she managing to hold her breath? Now he saw: she had pulled the hose of an oxygen mask up between her legs from the ceiling – now the floor – and was holding the mask tight against her face. The trickle of air must have been enough. *Clever Nancy. Good thinking, Nancy.* He felt for her belt and tugged at it, but the clasp had buckled in the impact. And the seat was too heavy to drag across the ceiling. Feeling something sharp against his leg, he reached down. His fingers had closed around a shard of broken glass. It snapped off and, in the same motion, Daniel hooked it under Nancy's belt and began sawing. A wisp of blood snaked lazily up from his fingers, but the webbing would not give.

Nancy grabbed Daniel's right shoulder. He looked up. With the mask on, she looked as she had when he first saw her from the dentist's chair. She was making a stabbing motion with her fist. Understanding the meaning of this, Daniel lifted the belt as far off her as he could and tried to force the point of the glass through the canvas material. It would not give. He looked around and, though his vision was blurred, he saw a red light winking above a glass case that would have been above the entrance to the cockpit, but was now below it. The light was coming from a long, orange torch mounted on the wall. The glass case, he could see, contained a first aid pouch. He kicked the glass in, unzipped the pouch and rifled through the plasters, rolls of white bandage, safety pins, cotton buds and antiseptic creams, until he found what he was looking for, a pair of scissors. His lungs were crushing him and he had to return to the air pocket. After taking a gulp of air, he swam back across to Nancy. His second attempt to cut through the lap belt left a small rip and, after this, it cut easily. It was Nancy's turn to push past him, her actions slower in the drag of water. She was, he noticed, hold-ing one arm across her ribcage. They had to climb over a body on the way out and, as he looked down, Daniel realized abstractly that he had lost one of his sandals.

On the surface, neither could speak. Nancy was coughing. Daniel's throat was raw from the salt water. Both were drawing splintery breaths. Their life jackets were uninflated. The sea boiled briefly then went still as the remaining engine cut out and the water stopped churning. Two other passengers, the tall black man and the old woman with the rosary and the nosebleed, had also made it out and were bobbing on the surface. Susie appeared, surfacing like a mini-submarine that had blown its buoyancy tanks. She breached the oil-marbled water as far as her narrow hips before flopping back down, her hand still on the ripcord of her life jacket. There were small lacerations on her face, presumably caused by flying glass.

'You all right, Nancy?' Daniel said between gasps for breath.

She did not respond.

'Nancy! Listen to me! Look at me! Can you hear me?' She raised her head and looked at him but her eyes were distant, unfocused. She must be concussed, Daniel thought.

'Nancy?' he repeated. 'Nancy? Nancy? *Are you all right?*'

This time Nancy looked directly at him, and there was an unfamiliar coldness in her eyes. The print of his hand, the feel of it, still lingered on her face, as it would in her memory.

A pulse of guilt passed through Daniel. He had to look away. In that moment, he knew nothing could ever be the same between them. 'I'm going back down to see if I can help the others,' he said.

Once inside the plane, he swam towards the tail again where a couple of passengers were standing with their heads in the air pocket. As he stood up, too, he felt hands groping around at his feet. He pulled the passenger up by his dreadlocks, the only thing he could grab hold of. It was Greg, gagging and trying to catch his breath. Their faces were so close they were almost touching.

'Wait here,' Daniel said, feeling his way along the overhead – underhead – lockers until he found the one with his bag in it. He dragged it back to the air pocket, swimming with one arm, and unzipped it. The fins and snorkel were still on the top, but he had to pull out some clothes to locate his diving mask. 'Listen. The exit is over there,' he said, pointing as he put the mask on. 'You're going to have to go underwater to get to it. Follow me. You first, Greg.' At the exit, Daniel pushed Greg towards the surface. He guided the other two passengers to the surface, cupping his hand under the chin of one of them. It was a middle-aged man he hadn't noticed on the plane. The man was semi-conscious and had a deep gash on his arm.

Back on the surface, Daniel saw Nancy had inflated her life vest and was helping the old woman with hers, topping it up by blowing into a valve. 'This one needs mouth-to-mouth, Nancy,' he said, pushing the middle-aged man towards one of the plane's upturned floats. Nancy pulled the man towards her, turned him over, pinched his nose and began resuscitating him.

Daniel dived down again and headed for the cockpit. The pilot and co-pilot were dead. Both had their mouths open as if they had died mid-conversation. The windscreen was smashed: that was where the glass had come from. There was a locker that contained a bright orange flare launcher and an open box of what looked like twelve-bore cartridges. Daniel stuffed the flare launcher under his belt, filled his pockets with cartridges and gathered up the antiseptic cream and two sodden rolls of bandage that had sunk to the floor. Back in the cabin he saw a woman was still strapped in her chair, her hair fanning out gracefully around her in the water. Though this passenger was clearly dead, Daniel unclipped her belt and she drifted for a few yards before coming to rest against a man's body that was trailing blood from a big-mouthed stomach wound. There were plastic bottles, pillows, newspapers and items of clothing floating silently around him. A magazine, too: the *National Geographic*.

A creaking sound made him look up. The plane was shifting position. Daniel retrieved his fins from where he had dropped them and swam through the exit door, seconds before the nose of the plane broke away and began sinking down the steep side of the coral. He realized that the plane's landing floats had buckled in the crash and had been almost completely ripped away from the fuselage. The metal skin of the wing he was nearest to was badly pockmarked. What remained of the plane looked like a missile had hit it.

Daniel inflated his life vest. He was shaking convulsively and struggling to catch his breath. It took him several attempts to do a head count. There had been thirteen passengers when he had done this during the flight. Now he counted eight. Eight survivors. That meant there were five dead, seven including the pilots. More were alive than not; that was something. Aviation fuel, he now realized, was making the seawater so heavy and sticky it was almost impossible to swim in it. When those passengers not clinging to the upturned floats began swimming towards them, they panicked because of their sudden heaviness; some, their faces having aged years in a few minutes, were clearly in shock, others were sobbing and groaning. Susie, her face tattooed with trickles of blood from her cuts, was blowing the whistle on her life jacket. She looked around, stopped blowing and said to no one in particular: 'Why didn't the others get out?'

Daniel knew the answer. He had read about it. Given the slightest opportunity, certain people will always find a way to safety. They are known as 'life survivors' and they make up 8 per cent of the population. Twelve per cent won't escape under almost any circumstance. They lose the will to live, resign themselves to death, succumb to 'behavioural inaction'.

So now I know. I am a life survivor. And life survivors save themselves and leave their loved ones to die.

'You'd better come and hang on to these,' he said to Susie. Although the upturned floats were big enough for all the passengers to lie on, they were slippery and, because their undersides were a few feet above the surface of the water, they were hard to climb up on. Two passengers managed it, and they helped a couple more get a purchase. The others remained bobbing in the water, their hands on the floats.

'Oughta be a rescue plane on its way,' the tall black man said, revealing himself to be from the Deep South. 'I heard the pilots giv'n outa mayday call.'

Everyone looked up and searched the empty air.

'What happened to the pilots?' Greg asked.

'Didn't make it.' Daniel hardly recognized his own voice – he normally hated euphemism. 'Anyone injured?'

Several voices answered at once:

'Ma ribs feel bust.'

73

'Don't know. Think so. There's a pain in my knees.'

'Can't breathe properly.'

'My wrist . . .'

Daniel looked at his own hand. The bleeding had more or less stopped, but it was shaking. He also had a headache. Apart from these minor complaints, he appeared to be the only passenger without an injury. He circumnavigated the float so that he was facing Nancy, who was still in the water. Bruises were showing on her face. 'You OK?' he asked gently.

'Think I've broken my collarbone,' she whispered.

Daniel felt helpless, unmanned. Remembering the flares he had recovered, he tried to work out how to fire one off.

'Don't waste them,' Nancy said quietly as she checked her watch, a square-faced Longines Daniel had given her for Christmas. 'It's going to take a while for a helicopter to get here from the islands.' She shook her wrist and held the watch to her ear. 'Must have stopped when we hit the water.' She took the watch off, leaving an imprint of the strap on her skin, shook it again and strapped it back on.

Over the next hour and a half, a shadow of silence stole over the survivors, broken by occasional questions.

'What about sharks?'

'Should we fire off a flare now?'

'I'm so cold. Is anyone else cold?'

'There's a lot of blood in the water. Won't it attract sharks?'

'I'm a lay preacher,' the middle-aged man said carefully. 'If anyone wants to make peace with God, I'll say a prayer with them.'

'Hey!' Greg shouted, before anyone could answer. He was pointing at the old woman who had had the rosary beads. She was a hundred feet away, having drifted in the strong current, the light on her vest flashing.

'Should I . . .' The tone of Greg's voice indicated that he knew the answer.

'She's dead,' Nancy said. 'She's been dead for . . .' Her voice trailed off. 'Shouldn't there be a rescue plane by now? What time is it? My watch is broken.'

Daniel did a double tap of his watch face: 11.10am. Two hours had passed since the crash. Some of the passengers were shivering violently; the blood had drained from their faces. There were now seven survivors, eight dead; the balance was shifting.

The lowered morale was reflected in the questions:

'What should we do?'

'We should wait.'

'Yeah, let's wait.'

'What's the point in waiting?'

'What's the point in not waiting?'

Daniel found a catch that opened the barrel of the flare launcher, slotted a cartridge into the breech and snapped it shut. The others stared at him as he held the gun in the air and pulled the trigger. Nothing happened. He worked out how to cock it and tried again.

CHAPTER EIGHT

THE VICE PROVOST STEERED HIS BIKE LEFT INTO GOODGE STREET and grimaced. A pneumatic drill was biting into the road ahead of him and this meant he had to cycle through a cloud of cement powder. With his nose creased up in disgust, he weaved in and out of the cones that were corralling two lanes of traffic into one before coming to a skidding halt in the slush, his brakes squealing in protest. A workman was holding a red STOP sign up in front of him, blocking his path. His nostrils flared wider. They had detected the smell of beefburger and processed cheese – the workman was eating a Big Mac still half wrapped in greaseproof paper. There was another smell, more cloying and pungent. The vice provost turned his head and saw he was alongside a vat of boiling tar, its fumes becoming visible as they met the cold afternoon. He stared at the workman over the top of half-glasses, and, without changing his sight line, slipped his hand under his overcoat, as if going for a revolver.

A tall and bony man with a permanent air of desiccation and gloom, the vice provost contrived to look older than his forty-nine years. It was partly to do with the Crombie overcoat and weathered fedora he was wearing; partly with his tarnished sit-up-and-beg bike. Mostly it was to do with his old-fashioned glasses. He had begun wiping the cement dust from them with the silk handkerchief he had retrieved from his pocket when the sign swivelled round to show the word GO written in green. The driver in the car behind him sounded his horn. The vice provost's shoulders rose as his neck sank. He put his glasses back on, one arm at a time, and turned his coat collar up before peddling off again. As he passed through the wrought-iron pedestrian gate at the side of the Porter's Lodge and tasted the clean air of the college quadrangle, his expression did not adjust. He resented having to come into college on a Saturday afternoon for an Extraordinary General Meeting of the Senate Committee.

Despite the euphony of his name – Laurence Wetherby – the vice provost preferred to be known by his title. Wetherby was his second preference. The fashion for colleagues and strangers to address one another by their first names was, to him, an abomination. The only people who had called him Laurence were his parents, now dead, and the woman to whom he had once been briefly engaged – but she had not dared call him Larry. He had not been known as Larry at school either. Nor had he had a nickname. If his students had a nickname for him now, it had never reached his ears.

A CCTV camera on a metal pole followed him as he mounted a disabled ramp – to avoid a pool of slush – and peddled along for twenty yards, past leafless trees set in concentric circles of cobbled stone, before parking in the frosted metal of a vacant bike rack. He glanced up at the white clock above the Porter's Lodge before dismounting and slipping off his bicycle clips.

The riding of this bike, the wearing of these clips, the way he handled his fedora – a finger and thumb on the worn and shiny felt either side of the groove – all, for him, were deliberate acts of resistance against modernity. He knew they were futile, but he reasoned that everyone had to draw up their own battle lines and these happened to be his. In Wetherby's world, Victoria was still on the throne, a mass was still said in Latin and the horrors of contemporary syntax – contractions, split infinitives, hanging participles – held no dominion.

Wetherby's suspicion of the modern informed almost every aspect of his life, especially his work. As a professor of music he was obliged to teach modules on composers such as Birtwistle and

Schoenberg, but he found their experiments in atonality unbearable, almost as bad as free jazz, and he made this prejudice
obvious to his undergraduates. For him, classical music ended with
Mahler, Elgar and, if he was feeling generous, Vaughan Williams. On
this, as in so many areas of his life, there was no room for debate or
compromise.

As he was threading a bike chain through the spokes of his back
wheel, a security guard came panting up behind him. 'Excuse me,
sir,' the guard said in a bouncing but well-educated voice. 'You
didn't show your pass.'

Wetherby did not look at the man as he padlocked his chain.
Instead he spoke to his own shoulder, his gentle, croaky voice
barely carrying the required distance: 'You must be new here.'

'I've been here almost two years, sir.'

Wetherby turned as he considered this. The guard had a florid
complexion and a balding head. As compensation for this he had
grown bright white shaving-brush sideburns. 'Of course. That coat.
You look different in it.' He reduced his eyes in their deep bony
sockets as he searched the guard's donkey jacket for a name badge,
but could not see one. What he saw instead was a poppy.

'I'm under instructions from the provost not to allow anyone in
without showing their pass.'

Wetherby tried to disguise his irritation. 'I am about to have a
meeting with the provost. I shall compliment him on the diligence
of his security staff.'

'Thank you, sir.'

Thinking the matter dealt with, Wetherby picked up the scuffed
leather music bag that was sitting in the basket attached to his
handlebars and began to walk away.

The guard called after him: 'Your pass, sir?'

Wetherby looked at his watch and turned again. 'You are going
to make me late.'

'Sorry, sir. It's a new rule. No exceptions.'

With a heavy sigh, Wetherby set his bag down on a small drift of
cement-coloured snow and pulled out some examination papers, a
copy of *The Times* folded open on a page with a completed

crossword, and a bundle of sheet music. His college ID card was not there. He patted his pockets and checked his wallet before turning to face the guard once more with a spavined smile that exposed the gaps in his teeth.

'I can vouch for him.' It was one of Wetherby's students, her Chinese accent muffled by the purple and brown college scarf covering her mouth. She was descending the steps of the Portico two at a time. In her hand was her ID card.

'Thank you, miss,' the guard said. 'You'll have to sign him in. If you'll come back to the Lodge with me, I'll issue a temporary pass.'

The guard was enjoying this, Wetherby thought: something about the way the man was looking at him; about his voice not fitting his station. When they reached the Lodge, the guard asked him his name.

'Wetherby . . . Professor Laurence Wetherby, Vice Provost, Trinity College, London.' He paused for effect. 'I have been teaching here since I was twenty-four.' Pause. 'I am forty-nine now.' Pause. 'That is a quarter of a century.'

The guard was undaunted. 'And could I have your pass for a second, miss.'

The student handed it over. The guard tried to read out the name.

'Don't worry, no one can pronounce it,' the student said. 'It's Hai-iki buizi Yzu.'

'Thank you, miss. It is a bit of a mouthful.'

The student grinned. 'Think of the sound of a wasp trapped in a jar.'

The guard grinned back. 'Thanks, I'll remember that.' He wrote the name down carefully and handed Wetherby his temporary pass. 'There we go. Sorry to have kept you, professor. I do recognize you now. Must have been the trilby.'

'Fedora.'

'If you could remember your pass in future it would be a big help.'

Wetherby cast an unenthusiastic eye around the Porter's Lodge. As he took in the clipboard, the rack of keys, the boiling kettle and

79

the pictures of the guard's family – three teenage children – he nodded to himself. There was also a collection of books about the First World War, a model of a Vickers machine gun and a mug with a poppy on it. When he turned his gaze back upon the guard he fancied he caught the edge of a smile.

'Got one yet?' The guard was rattling a red, plastic poppy-appeal collection box in one hand and holding out a bunch of poppies in the other.

'Yes,' Wetherby said.

'I give tours of the Flanders battlefields during the summer holidays,' the guard said.

'Do you.'

'Ever fancied doing one?'

'No.'

The guard put the collection box back on the shelf. He looked deflated. 'Soon you won't be able to get in without an electronic pass,' he said. 'They're installing automated barriers.'

'I look forward to it with vigorous anticipation.'

Hai-iki was back outside, walking towards the Octagon Building under the central dome. She was rubbing her arms. When Wetherby caught up with her he said: 'Must be annoying, people making fun of your name like that.'

'You get used to it.'

'You should not have to.'

The student cocked her head as she reflected on this. 'It can be a bit frustrating.' She rubbed her hands together. 'I tell you what I haven't got used to . . . this weather.'

'I would prefer a heatwave to this, and I despise heatwaves.'

The student laughed. 'I heard you talking on Radio 3 last night.'

Wetherby gave her a sidelong glance. He knew she had a music scholarship – she was a highly promising pianist – but hadn't paid her much attention until now. She had clear skin and a black fringe, as well as a soft, expressive mouth. She wasn't obviously attractive and she barely came up to his chest – which made him feel self-conscious about his own height – but she had the confident, hip-rolling walk of a long-legged model. 'You will be the only person in this place who did hear me,' he said gently. 'These philistines,' he nodded towards the staff room, 'would not know where to find the Third Programme on the dial.'

'The Third Programme?'

'Radio 3. I am still in denial about the name change.'

'When was that?'

'Nineteen sixty-seven.'

As they reached the East Cloister he held the door open for her while he stamped the snow off his shoes and said: 'Do you have a moment?'

She gave a friendly, open shrug.

'I want to show you something in my office.' He led the way along a corridor lined with portraits of philosophers and statues of scientists and engineers, the leather soles of his shoes echoing dully on the marble floor. She padded after him noiselessly, as if velvet-footed. When they reached his office door he checked his watch again – still had a few minutes before his meeting was due to start – and tapped in four digits on a security keypad on the wall. The heavy door clicked open. 'Come in, come in.'

Wetherby took off his fedora to reveal a domed head barely covered by a tonsure of side-parted hair. He removed his coat and shook it before hanging it up behind his door. Next came his leather gloves, peeled off one finger at a time. Steady, Wetherby. Not too Gothic. Might frighten her. He smoothed down the hairs at the side of his head and checked his reflection in his glass-fronted bookcase. Not handsome in an obvious way, but distinguished. A donnish look which bluestockings found attractive. Grrr. 'How is your mid-term paper coming along?' he said.

'Getting there.' She shrugged again, yawned and shivered.

As Wetherby looked through his drawer for an old poppy he kept in there, Hai-iki wound up the metronome on his baby grand piano and set it ticking. She ran a finger over a spindly crucifix on the wall, felt the weight of a rosary hanging from it and trailed her finger along an open shelf of books, playing the leather spines as if they were piano keys.

Wetherby slipped the poppy into his lapel and looked up, a

question on his face. 'There is a project I am working on. I need a research assistant. Are you interested?'

Hai-iki cocked her head again. 'Why me?'

Wetherby hesitated for a beat before answering. 'Because you listen to the Third Programme.'

'I do think they play too much jazz though.'

'Any jazz is too much jazz.'

'And I'm not keen on the world music.'

Wetherby mimed sticking a finger down his throat.

The student smiled at this. 'I have to listen to Radio 3.' She patted her pockets. 'Can't afford the Royal Opera House.'

'You have never been?'

'Never.'

'Then you must go, you must.' Wetherby was sorting through papers on his desk again. 'I have a spare ticket for Covent Garden on Tuesday night.' He said this nonchalantly, without looking up.

'What is it?'

'*La Bohème.*'

She had heard a rumour about how the professor always seduced his students with Puccini. 'I find Puccini too saccharine,' she said.

'As do I,' he said. 'As does everyone, that is why I have a spare ticket. I will make it up to you afterwards with dinner at my club.'

'Your club?'

'The Athenaeum. We can leave the opera at the first interval and be there by nine.' He checked his reflection again. He was wearing a three-piece suit made from prickly, thorn-proof tweed and it had four buttons on its cuff, two of which had come open. He fastened them and ran a finger under his collar before adjusting the stud under his tie.

Hai-iki said, 'Can I think about it?'

'Of course, of course.'

The student scratched an itch on her wrist. 'What was it you wanted to show me?'

'I must swear you to secrecy first.'

The student blinked. 'Sure. Whatever.'

'Swear. Not a word to anyone.'

'I swear.'

Wetherby handed her a pair of latex gloves. 'Put these on.'

She looked at him suspiciously. Did as he asked.

He handed her a pair of tweezers and a yellowing letter in a plastic folder. She held it at an angle so that the light from the window wasn't reflecting on it.

'You can take it out.'

'I can see it clearly enough. German?'

'You speak it, do you not?'

'Enough to get by.'

'That was the other reason for asking you. There are some archives in Berlin . . .'

Hai-iki turned the letter over and saw the signature at the end. 'Gustav?'

'Mahler.'

She turned it over again. 'And who is Anton?'

'His cousin in Geneva . . . A collector sent it to me for authentication.'

As Hai-iki read the letter the whites of her eyes enlarged. When she reached the end, her mouth was slightly open, exposing an arc of pearly teeth and pink, wet gums. 'Is it genuine?'

'Oh yes.' Wetherby said this with a thin smile. 'I have known of the rumour for years, but this is the first time I have found any written evidence for it.' He stepped forward and took the letter back. 'Now remember . . .' He raised his index finger vertically, facing outwards, and pressed it gently to the student's spongy lips.

CHAPTER NINE

ALMOST THREE HOURS HAD PASSED SINCE THE SEAPLANE HIT THE water. Greg was the first to realize this. 'The flight from Ecuador takes under two hours,' he said. The clear blue sky was now feathered with clouds and the water that had been warm at first was cooling rapidly. Daniel knew why. Although the Galápagos archipelago lies on the equator, the water around it is cold because of the Antarctic Humboldt Current. It gets colder still at night. Anyone in the water who hadn't become shark food by morning would be close to death anyway from hypothermia. He thought it best not to share this information with his fellow survivors. Instead he announced: 'I think I can make it to the islands.'

Everyone looked at him.

Had he not been feeling ashamed about deserting Nancy, he might not have volunteered so readily. He knew his chances of reaching the islands were remote. 'I swim every morning for half an hour – twenty-two lengths,' he continued carelessly. 'That's a quarter of a mile. Besides, I've got fins.' He held them up. No one else spoke. 'I checked our position on the map before we went down. They're in that direction.' He pointed. 'West. I need to follow the sun . . .' He looked up; the sun was almost directly overhead. '. . . as it sets.'

'Shouldn't one of us go with him?' Susie said.

Odd trickles of salt water were still coming out of Daniel's nose; he snorted and pressed a finger against each nostril. 'No, I'll be fine.

Anyway, there's only one pair of fins. The islands can't be more than five or six miles away. As I get nearer to them, the currents should carry me in.'

'I think we should stick together,' the lay preacher said.

The African-American was the next to speak: 'If the guy want to risk it, it up to him. I got me a young family at home.'

Daniel and Nancy exchanged a look.

Greg swam up close to Daniel and said in a low voice: 'If I don't make it, can you tell my parents I love them? And that I'm, you know, that I'm at peace, or something.'

This was the point at which Daniel was supposed to tell Greg he *was* going to make it, that he should tell his parents himself. But he could not. He didn't believe it. 'Likewise,' Daniel said, slipping his fins on and spitting to clean the mask. 'Likewise.'

His T-shirt and life vest would protect his back from the sun, he figured, and the tall black man had handed him an Atlanta Braves baseball cap. This he put on back-to-front to protect his neck. He felt tired already and tried not to let the others see the way his arms were shaking. Greg noticed, grabbed a half-full plastic bottle of Lucozade that had floated to the surface and stuffed it into his life jacket. 'How far really?' he said in a muted voice the others could not hear.

'Eight to ten miles, I should think.' His teeth were chattering now. 'But I'll be fine. It'll be OK.'

Greg thought about this for a moment. 'That's a long swim, dude,' he said.

Not wishing to depart with this ominous observation hanging in the air, Daniel tried to make light of the situation, for Nancy's benefit. 'Do you think we'll get any money knocked off the holiday for this?'

Nancy didn't seem to hear. 'Good luck,' she said.

'Don't give up,' Daniel said, holding her hand. He felt in his pocket for the ring box. It was gone. 'I promise I'll be back with help. Trust me. Try and keep the others . . .' He couldn't think how to finish the sentence. 'Try and keep the others from drinking their own urine until I get back.'

Nancy gave a taut smile at this. 'I'll try.'

Daniel's eyes slid away as Nancy sought them. He wanted to tell her he loved her, but he knew he would choke on the words. They seemed hollow now. Instead he gently cupped the back of her neck and bowed his head so that his brow was touching hers. 'I can make it,' he whispered. 'Just stay alive.' He then turned and swam away. For fifty yards he kept his arms by his sides, using his fins to propel himself and his snorkel to breathe, then he raised his head to check he was still swimming in the direction of the sun. After half an hour he turned to look behind him. The floats of the plane were no longer in sight. He shivered, as much from loneliness as cold.

CHAPTER TEN

AT ONE MINUTE TO FIVE, WETHERBY APPROACHED THE DOUBLE doors of the Senate Room, his gown billowing behind him. As the minute ticked down, he composed himself. He had perfected, over many years, a look of unsmiling disapproval – at the frivolous, at the vulgar, at the pointlessly aesthetic. People expected it of him, and he did not like to disappoint. Today, he knew, he would have good reason to glower. The other male faculty heads would be gownless and wearing open-neck shirts under their jackets. Wetherby saw it as his moral duty to shame them. He was damned if he would allow his own standards to be compromised by the provost's new in-formal dress code. For more than a century and a half, dons had worn gowns for the monthly Senate meetings and he was going to ensure the tradition was upheld, even if no one else was, even if everyone else thought him affected. He paused for a moment. Checked his watch. Counted down the final five seconds to the hour before opening the doors.

He was surprised to see all the other heads of faculty seated.

'Afternoon, Larry,' the provost said, holding up his arms and pulling a mock-guilty face that made his rubicund cheeks wobble slightly. 'Didn't you see the email I sent round?'

'To which email do you refer?'

'My fault. We had to start half an hour early because the commissioner here has to go on to another briefing at Whitehall. He has been talking us through the new emergency procedures for campus.' Moving his head rather than his eyes, Wetherby turned his gaze slowly towards a uniformed policeman holding a braided cap. The commissioner was standing next to a flip chart that had a floor plan of the north cloister of the college on it. The officer acknowledged Wetherby with a nod and a compact smile. Wetherby flicked out his gown. Sat. Stared at the provost's open collar.

'Now, where were we?' the provost said airily.

'I think I'd more or less finished,' the commissioner said. He checked his watch and looked out of the window. 'Better be going. My driver's here.' He shook hands with the provost and gave a couple of nods to cover the rest of the room.

'We've been discussing how best to combat radicalization on campus,' the provost said for Wetherby's benefit. 'How to infiltrate political groups, how to detect warning signs of Islamist extremism. I'll fill you in later. Now. While I have you all here, I have some exciting news. We've been bequeathed some money by an alumni.'

'Alumnus,' Wetherby corrected under his breath.

The provost did not hear. 'A considerable amount of money, in fact. On legal advice I can't tell you at this stage who left it or how much they left because the family of the deceased are contesting the will. But the sum would be enough to pay for, say, a new library or theatre, a new sports hall, a gallery or museum, a new conference hall or a new lab perhaps. The only condition is that it must be open to the public. We would also be eligible for a building grant from the Heritage Lottery Fund which would match the bequest pound for pound. So.' He clapped. 'I'd like you all to go away and have a think about this and then put in your bids. Any other business?'

A secretary with a pageboy haircut checked the minutes. 'There's the zoology chair.'

'That's a formality, I think,' the provost said, reaching for his pen. 'No objections to Dan Kennedy getting it, are there?'

There was a brief silence before Wetherby cleared his throat softly. 'I think it should be advertised.'

A dozen pairs of eyes turned to him. The provost spoke first. 'Why?'

'I believe European employment law requires it.' He paused as he studied the faces of his colleagues. 'Also, I am not sure Dr Kennedy even wants the job.'

The provost laughed. 'Course he wants it.'

'That is not my impression.'

'Has he told you that?'

'Not in so many words, but I know he has a lot of other commitments.'

'Commitments?'

'His extracurricular activities. Television. That natural history series he does.'

The provost drummed his fingers on the table. 'What series? Why didn't I know about this?'

Pamela Henton, the professor of biology, slapped her pen down on her notepad. 'Look, Dan's been effectively running the zoology department for the past six months. You can't say he's not committed.'

'Oh, I do not doubt his commitment,' Wetherby said through closed teeth. 'And as you know I personally hold him in the highest regard as a colleague, and a friend.' He studied the faces of the other dons again as if challenging them to disagree. 'But I would feel it a betrayal of our friendship if I did not raise this matter with the Senate.'

'Well, I would have thought he was the poster boy for our new approach,' said Roger Eastman, a silver-haired history professor. 'Have you seen that photograph of him on the college website, the one of him wearing a leather jacket and sunglasses?'

'And designer stubble,' Henton added with a grin.

'I could not agree more,' Wetherby said, raking a hand through the remaining strands of his hair; his tonsure was not visible from the front and this recurring, nervy gesture was designed to keep it that way. 'He is most telegenic.'

'I saw him walking around campus the other day, with his iPod and manbag and thought he was a student,' Henton continued with a grin. 'Besides, his brand of militant atheism is terribly fashionable at the moment.'

'Like Marxism was fashionable, you mean?' Wetherby said. 'Yes, I can see that. It used to be terribly fashionable for middle-ranking academics to defend Mao and Stalin. Now that those heroes of atheism are out of fashion, Darwin has become the lad to follow. Darwin and Dawkins.'

Eastman was enjoying the light relief, too. 'Did anyone see that graffiti outside the Student Union? "Dawkins is God". Rather witty, I thought.'

'Hilarious,' Wetherby said in a voice heavy with sarcasm.

'Come on, Wetherby. It was a reference to "Clapton is God" . . . You must remember that. When were you a student?'

'Oh, I got the reference, and I do appreciate the wit involved in substituting the name "Dawkins" for "Clapton", but it took the caretaker a whole—'

'Dan's activism on the environment is very current as well,' Henton interrupted. 'The students really respect him for it.'

Wetherby seized his moment. 'As well they should. The man practises what he preaches. He told me the other day that he was planning to offset his global footprint for a trip to the Galápagos Islands by arranging for mahogany and cedar trees to be planted in, I think he said, the Bushenyi District of Uganda, as recompense for his flight to Ecuador.'

'What trip to the Galápagos Islands?' the provost said, his brow furrowing.

'I presumed he was filming part of his next series there.' Wetherby checked the date on his watch. 'I believe he is there now.'

Professor Nick Collins, head of psychology, was looking at some notes. 'I don't know why we're even discussing this. Dan's academic record is exemplary.'

There was a pout in the provost's voice. 'I wouldn't wish to make an appointment without the full backing of the Senate.' He looked at Wetherby. 'We shall advertise the post, but I don't imagine there will be any better candidates.' He scanned the room. 'And would all heads of department kindly remind their staff that I'm not keen on moonlighting. Also, I need to know when staff are absent, for whatever reason. Now,' he tapped his papers on the table.

'I, too, have to leave.' A dozen chairs scraped back in unison.

By the time the provost reached the door, Wetherby was at his shoulder, speaking in a low voice. 'On the subject of security,' he said, 'what do you know about the guard on duty at the Porter's Lodge today?'

'Donaldson? Been with us for two or three years. Good man by all accounts.'

'Not the accounts I have heard.'

'What do you mean?'

'One of the Chinese students has complained about him making racist comments.'

The provost came to a halt and turned to face Wetherby. 'Christ, that's all I need.'

'He was making mock of her name.'

'This is going to look bad. We'll have to have an investigation. For form's sake. Will you take care of it?'

'Of course.'

'But try and keep it quiet. We don't want the press involved.'

'Probably best to suspend him while the investigation is pending.'

'Do whatever you think best, Larry.' The provost caught a flicker of disapproval on Wetherby's face. 'You don't mind me calling you Larry, do you?'

'Not at all.'

'I think the less stuffy we can make this place the better.'

'Absolutely.'

'I'm glad you told me about Dan's television work.'

'Perhaps I should not have.'

'Don't feel guilty because he's your friend. It's best I know these things.'

'That is why I thought you should be made aware of his reservations about the job. He would never voice them himself.' The thin smile. 'You know Danny.'

CHAPTER ELEVEN

THROUGH HIS MASK, DANIEL COULD SEE STINGRAYS AND GROUPERS. He could also see pink marks on his skin: welts, grazes and weals where coral had scratched him. These, he knew, would attract sharks. He tried not to think about it and was relieved when a dolphin appeared and swam underneath him. Sharks don't like to hunt when dolphins are around. He could concentrate on worrying about the jellyfish. They were everywhere and he was being stung constantly on his bare legs, each sting a cigarette burn.

A second dolphin appeared and the two circled below, their swimming synchronized as they turned on their backs to get a better view of the strange fish they had found. Daniel knew he was approaching another shallow 'reef flat' because the water was alive with blue tangs and angelfish. As he swam over a coral garden, grazing it with his fins, he recoiled at the sight of volcanic funnels and what looked like human brains. Beautiful in any other context, they were sinister now. A school of yellowtail floated past within inches of his facemask, making him flinch. A blue-spotted ray scuttled off in a cloud of sand. Once it felt safe, it slowed down and, with graceful beats of its wings, disappeared from view. Daniel could hear parrotfish pecking noisily at the hard coral now. He could also hear the sound of his breathing amplified by the water. The ocean was too tranquil; too neon-blue. Clownfish were hovering among the waving tentacles of sea anemones. He wondered how they could be so oblivious to the plane that had crashed in their environment. How could everything be back to normal so quickly? A small reef shark appeared, the black tip on its dorsal fin sweeping back and forth as it patrolled the shallows. Daniel no longer felt afraid.

You can't hurt me. Not today.

He swam over a coral wall and looked down over a sheer drop. It gave him vertigo, making him feel as if he were floating in the sky, contemplating the ground. This thought triggered a sense memory of the crash; a feeling of panic; of falling out of the sky; out of time. He could make out a craggy labyrinth of rock below, and it looked like a twisted fuselage.

The crash, he figured, must have left him with mild concussion because memories were flowing back to him with frightening clarity, placing him back in his seat in the plane. He could hear the screaming of the engine. He could feel the noise, too, vibrating through his seat, through his groin, through his bones. He remembered thinking to himself: It's over. It's over. He shut his eyes as though to shut out the memory, and his mask began to steam up as hot tears wet his cheeks.

After three quarters of an hour, he brushed against an object floating on the surface. He shouted and recoiled with revulsion, thinking it was the decapitated body of the flight attendant. Now he saw it was something half eaten, a sea lion perhaps, and pushed it away, trying not to be sick. He realized that he hadn't counted the flight attendant. There were nine dead, not eight.

Not wanting to run into another dead creature, he opened his eyes and began swimming breaststroke, keeping his head above water to see where he was going. When his neck began to ache he alternated with front crawl. Every fifteen minutes or so he stopped for a sip from the Lucozade bottle. Soon after he had emptied it, he began to feel dehydrated and cold. His sense of direction, of time and space, was slipping. He was adrift now and, with the randomness of delirium, thoughts of his great-grandfather's letters began melting through his mind. He tried to recall what they had said, to picture Nancy's face as she was reading them, and his father's face as he handed them over, almost reluctant to let them go.

CHAPTER TWELVE

THE TEMPERATURE IN LONDON HAD RISEN BY TWELVE DEGREES overnight and the softly falling snow had sharpened to sleet and drizzle. This, Philip thought, is more appropriate. November weather. Remembrance Sunday weather. He usually travelled to Bayeux for the ceremony, officially because he was a director of the Commonwealth War Graves Commission, unofficially because that was where his father was buried. But this year he had been asked to lay a wreath at the Cenotaph on behalf of the Handbags, as members of the Royal Army Medical Corps were known.

The wreath he was holding, a red cross of poppies on a white cardboard background, was chafing his knees as he rocked back and forth on his heels, waiting. Umbrellas had gone up in the crowd around him but he had no need of one today: his dark-blue beret was keeping his head dry. He had angled it so that it covered his missing ear. Earlier that morning, he had checked and rechecked in the mirror that his cap badge – the rod of Asclepius – was one inch above his left eye. He checked, for the third time in ten minutes, the row of polished metal across the breast of his overcoat. Along with his campaign medals – Northern Ireland, the Falklands, the First Gulf War – there was a silver cross standing out against the charcoal grey of his coat material, an MC. With leather-gloved fingers, he flicked an imaginary speck of dirt off his shoulder, as if that, and not the medals, was what he had been staring at. He straightened his back, raised his chin and looked around.

From his position in Whitehall, a few rows behind the Chiefs of Staff, he could make out, through the gathering mist, Nelson's column. He closed his eyes for a moment and, when he opened them again, the column had disappeared from view. He studied instead the monolithic slab of Portland stone in front of him. It looked severe and beautiful. As he read and reread its simple inscription – 'The Glorious Dead' – the massed band of the Guards Division began playing Elgar's 'Nimrod'. Coming as it was from his deaf side, the adagio sounded more muffled and colourless than usual, but no less autumnal. Despite the cold there were still some leaves clinging on to the trees. In the overcast light, the branches had become almost invisible so that the golden and copper tints looked as if they were floating on the still surface of a lake. As Philip studied one particular branch, its leaves began to shimmer, stirred by a gust, and, almost as one, relinquished their hold and began spiralling slowly to the ground, only to be caught up again in a flurry. Dead leaves defining the shape of the breeze. He checked his pocket watch, a silver half-hunter inscribed with his grandfather's initials. The eleventh hour of the eleventh day of the eleventh month was approaching. He bowed his head and felt the silence deepening, like a shelf of sand sinking away beneath his shoes.

A numbing inner stillness descended upon him. There is no such thing as silence, the composer John Cage once said, and Philip knew the truth of this. When he went from being Lt Col Philip Kennedy RAMC to Lt Col Philip Kennedy RAMC (Rtd), he was presented with a silver sword and a rare collection of BBC recordings of the silences held at the Cenotaph since 1929. Whenever he listened to them he noticed the chimes of Big Ben were followed not by silence but by ambient noise: distant planes, birdsong, the shuffle of feet. Broadcasters knew that such near-silence had more resonance than shutting down the airwaves for two minutes. But for Philip the two-minute silence was crowded in other ways. In what amounted to a family tradition, he had not known his father, who in turn had not known his father. Neither man had grown old, as he, the son and grandson, had grown old.

They had instead been frozen in youth, their likenesses recorded in a few granular photographs, their names carved on stones in foreign fields. They were strangers to one another, grandfather, father and son, yet once a year, on the same November morning, they met for two minutes in the silence.

Though he was breathing in through his nose, the cold air was aggravating the back of Philip's throat, making him cough. It was making his eyes water, too, but that was as close as he ever came to tears. He almost envied the damp-eyed young widow holding a wreath next to him. Iraq possibly. Or Afghanistan. She was sniffing and dabbing at her cheeks with a tissue. It wasn't that he lacked compassion; merely that he had never cried in his life and was too old to learn how it was done. The closest he had come was when his first wife had died of ovarian cancer, or rather when, at her funeral, the five-year-old Daniel had felt for his hand by the grave-side. He thought of this now and of how, more recently, when his older sister had died, he had delivered a eulogy in a voice so steady Daniel had come up to him afterwards and said in an affectionately teasing undertone: 'Marble, Dad. You're made of bloody marble.' Actually, he thought – but did not say at the time – it is you who is made of marble, Daniel. When your mother died you decided there was no God, that it was all a lie, that you would have to put your faith in science. You have never once wavered. Never once reconsidered your rejection. If anyone is made of marble . . .

His thoughts on his son, Philip felt in his overcoat pocket for his mobile, turned it on to check for messages, and, seeing there were none, turned it off again. He did a mental calculation: Daniel and Nancy had left Heathrow on Thursday morning, they were due to fly on to the Galápagos Islands the following morning but their flight had been delayed by a day. So they should have got there on Saturday morning. Yesterday.

Philip had been trying Daniel's mobile every few hours, but had not wanted to leave a message about Martha's hypo. That would only cause unnecessary worry. Besides, he had wanted to talk directly to Daniel about another matter. He wanted to say that, upon reflection, he thought it would be best if Nancy did not translate Andrew Kennedy's letters from the trenches. He would explain why when they returned.

A frown knotted his brow. Why wasn't Daniel answering his mobile? He had said he would call when he reached the islands. Presumably he hadn't been able to get a signal. That must be it. It made sense actually, because when they were at the ice rink there had been a voice message left on Martha's iPhone that sounded like Nancy, but it had been too broken and crackly to make out what was being said. A bad signal. Unable to get through on Nancy's mobile either, Philip had rung the travel company. They had said that the seaplane had landed safely near the Galápagos Islands. But Philip was still uneasy. As a precaution, he had called in a favour from Geoff Turner, a friend who worked for the Security Services. Could he double-check about the flight? See if the British Embassy in Quito had heard anything? The friend would see what he could do.

Philip always felt a small stab of melancholy when he thought of Daniel. It wasn't that he thought his son a failure – far from it – it was more that, despite their best efforts, they had never managed to be close. As a child, Daniel had never caught his attention. Philip had pretended that he was interested in his games, and drawings, and songs, but his look of distraction had never been well concealed. The truth was, Philip had never even caught his own attention. He knew this. He was aware of his hollow centre, of his cauterized emotions, of the father-shaped hole in his own life.

He checked his medals again. They didn't just glitter, they cast a shadow. Philip had lived in the shadow of his father's posthumously awarded VC all his life. In the summer of 1944, Captain William Kennedy, 'Silky' Kennedy as he was known – the nickname came from his insistence on wearing silk underwear bought from Jermyn Street – had led his unit in a suicidal charge on a farmhouse, a German machine-gun position that was pinning down British and Canadian troops on the road to Tilly-sur-Seulles. Silky had managed to put it out of action with grenades but was shot several times in the chest as he did so. A glorious death. Philip often wondered what manner of man his father had been: brave, obviously, but also phlegmatic and good-humoured, he imagined. According to regiment folklore, Silky Kennedy had looked down at the bullet holes in his tunic as he lay dying and said: 'You have to admire the grouping!' His last words.

Philip studied the rows of Chelsea pensioners in their wheel-chairs. They were from the Second World War, Silky's generation. There were no First World War veterans left to take part in the march past, although he had noticed, with a disapproving eye, a Wren in her forties, thirties possibly, holding a wreath of poppies on behalf of the SAD campaign. Shot At Dawn. The red poppies had white centres. These symbolized the white patches of cloth placed as targets over the hearts of the soldiers shot for cowardice and desertion. Philip had been asked to support the campaign but had declined. He had also argued at a meeting of the War Graves Commission that the SAD campaigners shouldn't be part of the parade. They made a mockery of the men – men like his father and grandfather – who had given their lives gallantly in battle.

His thoughts were on his grandfather now. Private Andrew Kennedy's name was listed on the Menin Gate Memorial as one of the missing, and according to regimental records he had been killed in action on the first day of Passchendaele, but that was all that was recorded about him. There was no other mention of him in the day-to-day war diaries kept by the officers of the 11th Battalion, Shropshire Fusiliers. No latrine duty. No sentry duty. Nothing about his training at Étaples, the infamous 'Bull Ring'. He was the Unknown Grandfather. The letters he had written in French represented the first contact Philip had had with him, the first indication, after a lifetime of speculation, of what kind of a man he was. What would they reveal? That Andrew was cruel? Gentle? Lazy? What? The letters seemed to represent a threat to Philip's own legitimacy, somehow. They raised long-buried suspicions. Half-suspicions. Why were they written in French? This was why they made him feel uneasy. Sometimes it is best not to know these things. Would Nancy have begun translating them yet? Damn, he wished he could get through to Daniel on the phone.

He passed his cross of poppies from one gloved hand to the other and wriggled the fingers of the now empty hand to get the circulation back into them. This prompted a distant memory. When he had arrived at Sandhurst, his fellow officer cadets had wanted to shake his hand. Word had spread that not only had his grandfather been killed at Passchendaele, but his father had won a posthumous VC for his part in the Normandy Landings. It was quite a double: two generations of fighting men buried in foreign soil. It *was* remarkable. It *did* merit a shake of the hand. Philip accepted that. But he had nevertheless been a reluctant celebrity at the academy. Even the commandant at Sandhurst had joined in. 'If there is such a thing as heroic blood,' he had said, 'you must surely have it.' Philip had muttered something about how everyone was capable of self-lessness, given the right circumstances. But he had often wondered since whether that was the case, whether there might not be a bravery gene.

He checked his medals once more. Had Daniel lived in the shadow of his MC? He hoped not. He had tried not to talk of it, dismissing it almost. He hadn't even shown his son the short version of his citation, the one not covered by the Official Secrets Act. It described how, at the height of Operation Desert Storm, Philip had gone on treating his comrades after a ricochet had ripped off the top half of his ear and pierced his eardrum. The longer version of the citation explained that it had been a friendly fire incident – a 'blue on blue' in which a US helicopter gunship had attacked an eight-man SAS team travelling in two armoured jeeps. Two were killed and another five wounded, most of them seriously, with missing limbs and third-degree burns. By the time Philip and his medical team were helicoptered in, the Iraqis were also arriving. The one uninjured SAS soldier held them off while the medics evacuated the injured. His friend Geoff Turner was one of the survivors. That, indeed, was how they had become friends. Turner had since left 'the Regiment' and joined 'the Service'. Philip checked his mobile. Still no message from him.

The Bishop of London's procession was arriving. The royal family should be next but there was as yet no sign of them. Big Ben started chiming the hour. People in the crowd began looking at one another in puzzlement. Seconds passed and the silence filled with coughing and shuffling and distant traffic. Philip was too distracted to compose his thoughts. Something odd was going on. He could see the Prime Minister and the Leader of the Opposition being led by a policeman back inside the Foreign and Commonwealth Office. Another policeman emerged, whispering into a microphone on his lapel. The two-minute silence ended with the traditional firing of an artillery gun by the King's Troop and Last Post sounded by buglers of the Royal Marines. But before they could finish, a policeman ran out of the Foreign Office carrying a loudhailer. He stood in front of the Cenotaph facing the 10,000 former servicemen and women who were packing Whitehall all the way back to Trafalgar Square and barked: 'Will everyone please make their way to Horse Guards Parade. Everyone back! Now! This area is being evacuated!'

Six other policemen in luminous green jackets formed a cordon and began directing people back with their arms. The crowd erupted in noise: talking, shouting, the scrape of shoes. Some began shoving when it became apparent there was no give in the crowd. A bottleneck was forming at the archway leading on to Horse Guards Parade.

The policeman with the loudhailer turned towards the side area where Philip was standing. 'Will you people please make your way into Parliament Square. Quickly now! Move!'

Philip was almost carried along, so close were those around him huddled. He saw one old man stumble to the ground in the crush but couldn't turn round to help him. When other hands raised the man up, he concentrated on staying upright himself. The human tide of shuffling feet and pressing bodies roiled past the entrance to Westminster Tube before losing momentum. People were slowing down and breaking into a normal walk now. Mobile phones were being switched on. He carried on walking over Westminster Bridge, feeling confounded and anxious. What was going on? There had been no explosion. Was it a false alarm? Police must have had reports of a terrorist threat and evacuated the area as a precaution. He didn't stop until he was in Kennington, within sight of the

Imperial War Museum's copper dome. This was familiar ground to him. He felt safe here. Still carrying his wreath, he walked stiffly past the giant naval guns in the museum grounds, past a spray-painted fragment of the Berlin Wall, up the steps and through the lichen-covered columns.

Once inside, he stared ahead blankly as a broad-chested security guard frisked him. He paced back and forth, under a Sopwith Camel suspended from the ceiling, past a First World War tank, around 'Ole Bill', an omnibus that had seen action at Ypres, and returned to the entrance where he stood catching his breath, his heart palpitating.

He was in front of a plaque explaining that this building was the former Bethlem Royal Hospital – better known as Bedlam. Unable to take the words in, he stood for a few minutes reading and re-reading them. The museum was almost empty and so the same security guard who had searched him came over and asked if he was all right. He nodded in answer, turned and walked to the back of the hall, past a glass case containing the 1000cc motorbike on which Lawrence of Arabia had been killed, and down the stairs to the basement. Once there he followed signs to THE FIRST WORLD WAR and came to a framed poster of Kitchener pointing his finger at YOU. Beyond this was a cabinet containing wire cutters, chain-mail body armour and medieval-looking weapons used for hand-to-hand combat in the trenches: knuckle-dusters with blades, a mace, a nail-studded cosh, a gauntlet punch dagger. Philip stared at them. The next gallery was dominated by a wall of wooden signs: SUICIDE CORNER, PETTICOAT LANE, THAT TIN HAT YOU PASSED JUST NOW IS WORTH MONEY – PICK IT UP AND TAKE IT TO THE SALVAGE DUMP. Above him a large screen was showing flickering images of the Western Front on a continual loop: jerky footage of horses wearing gas masks and soldiers bustling over the top in fast motion, one of them not making it over the parapet before sliding back down the bank of soil.

He continued on to THE TRENCH EXPERIENCE, a walk-through recreation of a front-line trench. It was too dimly lit for his tired eyes, and the sound and chemical-smell effects did not register on his senses. He removed his gloves and ran a stiff hand over a sandbag that had been daubed with brown paint to make it look muddy. Beyond this was a cross-section of a recent trench excavation showing rusty shells, bayonets and bullets found below the topsoil. Philip thought again of his grandfather's newly discovered letters and felt restless. It was as if a shelf of soil had collapsed, disturbing the long-buried dead. Realizing he was still carrying the cross of poppies, he laid it against the perspex-covered soil and retraced his steps. Once outside in the crisp London air he checked his pocket watch – noon – and turned on his mobile. He listened to a message to call Geoff Turner. He pressed the 'return call' option and waited.

'It's Philip. You left a message.'

'Thanks for calling back. I can't talk now. There's been an incident at the Cenotaph.'

'I know, I was there. Hello? . . . I can't hear you very well.'

'We're being told it's a false alarm. But listen, I wasn't ringing about that. It's Daniel. I've just found out his seaplane never landed. I'm afraid it is being reported as missing . . . Hello? Philip? Are you there?'

'The seaplane never landed?'

'Afraid not.'

Philip was sitting down on a bench, next to the section of the Berlin Wall. The mobile was on the seat beside him. His hands were cupped neatly on his lap.

CHAPTER THIRTEEN

THE WATER HAD TURNED CHOPPY. DANIEL WONDERED ABSTRACTLY if he had found the current that would pull him to the islands, but he was too exhausted to swim any farther and find out. Lactic acid had built up in his legs. They felt like concrete, and cramp was knotting them. Part of him knew his swim would now not end other than in his own extinction. The long swim. He felt he had been swimming this distance all his life and all he wanted was sleep. To compound his agony, his eyes were stinging and blurred from the seawater and tears, and he felt as if he had swallowed splintered glass. His lips were cracked and swollen. Only the imperative of rescuing Nancy and seeing Martha again was now keeping him clinging to life.

Over the next two and a quarter hours he drifted as much as swam. The pain from the jellyfish stings had become so intense he found himself retching every few minutes. He was also shivering convulsively and feeling delirious: symptoms of sunstroke, or shock, or swallowing salt water – he was no longer sure which. Nevertheless, he managed to calculate that if he had been swimming on the right course, the islands would have been in sight by now. He stopped swimming as he realized this; and pictured himself alone in a vast, cold ocean, waiting for death to bear him away. As he had done on the crashing plane, he resigned himself to the inevitable – only this time his death, he knew, would be a slow and agonizing one, from dehydration and hypothermia. His only alternative was to remove his life jacket and allow himself to sink. Drowning is supposed to be painless. After the initial panic you feel nothing but tranquillity. Anyway, his life jacket had given him blisters under his arms. It was slowing him down. He would be better off without it.

The cramp moved to his feet and interrupted his thoughts. To relieve the pain, he pulled his fins off and watched them sink away into the velvety depths. With water-wrinkled hands, he removed his mask and let it float away, too, the snorkel still attached. An indifferent wind picked up and, as he bobbed in the swelling water, he thought about how he had abandoned Nancy, how he had pushed his hand against her face, how he deserved this punishment. As he fumbled to untie the cord across his chest, his head lolled backwards. So far, he had been avoiding staring at the sun but now, as he narrowed his eyes in its glare, he could no longer remember why. A stab of migraine jolted his head forward again.

Then he saw him. A young man with a lapidary smile and protuberant wide-set eyes was treading water no more than ten yards away, gently beckoning with his hand. Delicate-boned, olive-skinned and with contour, quiddity and mass, the man was completely present, yet could not be. Only his head and shoulders were visible – he wasn't wearing a life vest – and in the trough that followed a cresting wave he disappeared.

Daniel reached limply to his other arm and, in order to recover a connection with reality, tapped his watch twice. It was 5.40pm. No longer knowing what the numbers meant, he looked up at the man again, but he was gone. A hallucination. His face had been familiar though. Daniel longed to see it again. Left with a feeling of post-coital languor, he closed his eyes and a yellow glow lingered on his retinas. Already he was uncertain whether he had actually seen what he thought he had seen. He opened his eyes again and began swimming towards where the young man had been, the point at which the blue of the sky met the blue of the ocean. Twenty minutes later he lost consciousness and drifted, held afloat by the life vest he had, in a moment of distraction, failed to take off.

The water was as black and glossy as lacquer when Daniel regained consciousness. He blinked, trying to focus his eyes on what looked like phosphorescence. He looked up at the sky. A full moon. A canopy of stars.

He was moving.

His life jacket had snagged on the rim of something and it – slimy, leathery, barrel-shaped – was pulling him slowly along in its wake. It was a giant shell, at least seven feet long. Large, spadelike hind flippers were acting as a rudder. He could see a beak opening and closing silently. A leatherback turtle. The cord of his life vest, Daniel realized, had wrapped around one of its elongated forelimbs, keeping it on the surface. He unwrapped it and the creature swam away, shuddering with each sinuous stroke, leaving a trail of silver bubbles.

Faltering, milky light was bleeding into the darkness. Seabirds, shearwaters and a lone albatross, were wheeling and screeching overhead. Daniel's feet touched something soft. A sandbank. He slid out of his life vest, and lay half submerged in the water. Feeling warm – a symptom of hypothermia, he knew, of blood leaving the brain – he prepared to swim the final few hundred yards. A congregation of storm petrels appeared, soaring and swooping above high cliffs.

Cliffs.

He had reached the Galápagos Islands.

In the distance, he could make out a semicircle of jagged, black rocks. He recognized them: the Devil's Crown, a half-submerged volcanic crater. The island beyond them must be Floreana. Post Office Bay would be there, too, the site where visitors, from Darwin onwards, left their letters and postcards to be collected. Daniel saw another turtle walking away, its movements blocky and hesitant. He followed it, walking his hands along the sand, the shallow water bearing his weight. When he reached a brackish lagoon, he stood up and, feeling buoyant and dizzy, waded unsteadily. It led on to an estuary and, soon after, he passed eroded cinder cones, then a mangrove swamp framed by cactus clumps. He was navigating a gap between black lava rocks and could hear surf churning on a beach. The sun had risen and the water had turned emerald green, the colour of the engagement ring he had bought and lost. As he crawled heavily on to the pebbled shore, a sea iguana studied him unblinkingly and Sally Lightfoot crabs ran over his fingers, searching for food. He propped himself up on one locked arm and felt the full weight of his limbs, several tons of solid beached flesh. A wavering noise rose from his diaphragm, more an exhalation than a word, a cry to continue living.

CHAPTER FOURTEEN

Ypres Salient. Last Monday of July, 1917

ANDREW KENNEDY HAS LEARNED THE NAMES FOR THE DIFFERENT types of trench – 'support', 'reserve', 'communication' and 'front' – but has never seen a real one before. Nor has he smelled one. This trench reeks of newly ploughed earth, petrol and mildewed wood. A wooden sign stencilled in capital letters above it reads: KEEP TO THE TRENCH IN DAYLIGHT. BY ORDER. As they begin a three-mile, zigzagging walk to their position, Andrew's excitement turns to apprehension again. He is beginning to understand that fear and excitement, excitement and fear, are the twin emotions that define the PBI. The Poor Bloody Infantry. The fear this time is partly caused by the order to break ranks and walk in Indian file, a lonely feeling after the solidarity of the four-abreast marching.

Some of the reserve trenches are dry, but others dug below the water table are knee-deep – muddy water with which the drainage sumps cannot cope. Walking through the mud distracts Andrew from his morbid thoughts and when he sees his second trench sign – PETTICOAT LANE – and inhales the unfamiliar smell of chloride of lime, he feels excited once more. They have entered a properly built support trench system this time, with wooden fire steps, slatted duckboards and sides stoutly revetted with wood and piled with sandbags one and a half times the height of a man. There is a sump hole at one end and a solid-looking gate wrapped in barbed wire at the other.

Andrew and William, 'Andy & Will' as they styled their would-be music-hall act in Market Drayton, stare in wonder at the unfamiliar objects around them: a box periscope attached to the wall, a bayonet thrust next to it, acting as a peg for water bottles, an empty shell case hung from a bracket serving as an improvised gas alarm. They have all heard about the chlorine gas, about how it turns the skin greenish black and makes the tongue protrude. They have also heard the rumours about a new type of gas which smells of mustard and blisters the skin. The Devil's Breath they call it. You know you have inhaled it when your armpits begin to sting.

The weather is changing. It has turned colder and a fine drizzle is fattening the air. By the time they reach a trench marked CLAPHAM COMMON their uniforms are damp. They press their backs to the trench wall as the shapes of men loom up. It is the remnants of the battalion they are relieving, the 2/Rifle Brigade. As they ghost past like sleepwalkers, Andrew studies their cork-blackened faces. They are gaunt and chapped. There is matter in their eyes. Following behind them is a man with his arm in a sling leading a party of walking wounded – men with raw, blistered skin and bandaged eyes, each with his hand on the shoulder of the man in front.

Colour Sergeant Major Davies can sense that his platoon is spooked by this encounter. He holds up his arms and says calmly: 'All right, lads, we're going to wait here while we check this is our assembly trench. Don't make yourselves too comfortable. Cookie, let's get a brew going. The rest of you, check your equipment. Stand to at . . .' he glances at his watch, 'five o'clock. Kennedy!'

'Yes, Colour Sarn't Major?'

'You've just volunteered to check the officers' dugout in the next trench along. We're looking for . . .' He consults a piece of paper. 'A Major Morris of the Second Rifle Brigade. Tell him we're here.'

'Because we're 'ere!' Macintyre says from the back.

'All right, lads,' the CSM growls. 'Keep it down.'

While Andrew opens the gate to the next trench, the other men try to take in their strange new environment, looking around the trench like nervous teenagers entering a dance hall for the first time. They talk in whispers, thinking the Germans over the sandbags will be able to hear them and guess a new battalion has arrived. But when a lance corporal points out that no attempt has been made to keep the attack secret, they talk at normal volume. It's true. The clues that an attack is imminent have not been subtle. Metallic thunder has been building over the past three weeks, destroying the land drainage system and leaving the low-lying clay a succession of muddy pools.

When Andrew returns five minutes later, his face is freckled with dry mud. 'Couldn't find him, Colour Sarn't Major,' he says. 'Checked the next trench along as well. There was a bloke with a beard, but he wasn't an officer. I think he was suffering from shell shock or something. Waving his arms about, he was.'

'All right, Kennedy. Well, we've got through to BHQ on the field telephone now, so they know we're here.'

Andrew tamps tobacco into his pipe and, having been told what trench veterans do to avoid the unwanted attention of snipers, turns the bowl upside down before lighting it. He begins coughing and looks around to see if anyone has noticed. No one has. Keeping the pipe stem between his teeth, he removes from his wallet a photograph of Dorothy, his wife of only one month. It is a formal portrait in which she is wearing an ankle-length dress and is holding a parasol. Her long hair is coiled up in a bun. Her smile is false. She looks florid and plain, but not to Andrew's eyes. He has known Dorothy since school but only summoned the courage to ask her to marry him when he finished his training. Macintyre was his best man.

'How you managed to persuade a nice girl like that to marry you, I'll never know,' Macintyre says over his shoulder.

'She likes a soldier with a moustache,' Andrew replies, stroking his whiskers.

'*That's* a moustache? I wondered what it was.'

'Least I can grow one, Will.'

'You know she were always sweet on me, don't you, Andy?'

'Whatever you say, Will.'

'When you get shot, Andy, I'm going to go back and marry her.'

'You're a true pal, Will.'

Andrew is enjoying the musicality their Midlands accents bring to the exchange – to their 'Andy & Will' routine – but Macintyre ends it. While others in the trench sharpen bayonets and polish boots, Andrew finds an empty funk hole and rereads his most recent letter from Dorothy, the one in which she tells him she's volunteered to work as a 'canary' in a munitions factory, and her hands have turned yellow from handling TNT. As he takes out a small sheet of lined paper and a stump of pencil sharpened at both ends, he notices his own hands are shaking. He holds his pencil firmly between finger and thumb and presses it against the paper until the shaking stops.

30th July 1917
11/Shropshire Fusiliers
B.E.F. Ypres, Belgium

My Dear Dorothy,

   I am writing to you this short note to say we have arrived safely at the Front and are all verry cheery & bright so dont fret youre little self. The trenches are a wonder, they go on for miles. The engineers have done a marvellus job. Even the plumbing works! As I write, the shells are fair hairing over. You know, you get bemused after a few thousand of them. Still, itll be a great experience to tell our children about.

   We are going over the parrapet tomorrow & let me tell you the Bosch is going to get a right hiding in our quarter. I hope to spend a few merry hours in chasing him all over the place. I am sure that I shall get through all right, but in case the unexppected does happen I shall rest content with the knowledge that I have done my duty. So long, my dear, dont worry if you dont hear for a bit. Im as happy as ever. You will receive this only if anything has happened to me during the next few days.

   Will sends his best.

   Bye-bye ownest & best of love

   From yr hub

   Andy

Macintyre takes off his webbing and tunic, slips his braces and tugs out the tails of his collarless greyback shirt. The harsh texturing chafes his skin. He begins scratching feverishly.

'You'll only make it worse, Will,' Andrew says as he slides the letter under the canvas of his haversack.

'Look,' Macintyre says as he opens a medical certificate and brandishes it under Andrew's nose. 'Says here I'm free of vermin and scabies. I wish someone would tell the bloody vermin and scabies that.'

'No self-respecting chat would want to go near you, Will.'

'Chat?' Macintyre says quietly, unable to disguise the uncertainty in his voice.

'Chat,' Andrew repeats confidently, pleased with his superior knowledge of military slang. Lice, he has recently discovered, are known as 'chats' and soldiers are 'chatting' when they run a candle flame along the seams of their trousers. The term is to do with the crackling noise the burning lice make, or so he's been told. 'Don't tell me you don't know what a chat is.'

'Course I do.'

Tea is poured and men cup both hands around their tin mugs, taking comfort in the familiarity of the act. As it has been brewed in an old petrol tin it is almost undrinkable.

'Anyway,' Macintyre continues. '*I . . .*' He slips his braces back on and tucks his thumbs behind them. '*I* have got a tapeworm up me arse.'

Andrew spits out a mouthful of tea.

'The MO says it's the size of a cobra,' Macintyre goes on.

'Only thing of yours that is.'

Other men stop what they are doing and listen in to the routine.

'Look, Andy, me old chum, it may not be long but at least it's thin.'

Andrew is trying not to laugh. 'Anyway, Will, I being a gentleman have a gentleman's illness.'

'What's that then, Andy?'

'Trench foot, Will.'

'Trench foot. That's nothing. I've got trench leg.' Macintyre pulls his leg up behind his back and starts hopping around.

It begins to rain steadily. Men unwrap their ground sheets and use them as capes, swinging them over their shoulders and clipping the two sides together at the neck.

An officer appears at the entrance to the trench wearing a helmet and the uniform of a major in the Rifle Brigade. This is an unusual sight because trench officers usually avoid wearing any insignia that might make them high-value targets for snipers. Andrew does not recognize him at first – now that he has shaved off his beard and taken off his sleeveless leather jerkin. Then their eyes meet and he shivers. It is as if the heat has been drained from the major's face, as though the blood that pumps through him is cold. As he walks silently past, Andrew can see that his beard had been covering up a livid scar that runs the length of his jaw to his chin. As he opens the trench gate on the far side, the major passes Colour Sergeant Major Davies coming in, closely followed by Second Lieutenant Willets.

Macintyre notices the CSM approaching and whispers to Andrew: 'Look out, here comes the Creeping Barrage.'

'That was 'im,' Andrew says. 'That was the bearded bloke I saw. Major Morris.'

'Smarten up, lads,' the CSM says, 'the officer is coming to have a word.'

The men set down their mugs, button up their tunics and stand to attention. 'Bet you half a shilling he says that lessons have been learned since the last Big Push,' Macintyre says out of the corner of his mouth.

'You're on.'

Like every soldier in the PBI, Andrew and Macintyre know all about the last Big Push, one year and one month ago. They know that men were ordered to walk; not that they could have run if they had tried, weighed down as they were by 66lb of kit. They know that where the wire hadn't been properly cut, bodies had piled up seven deep, a scaffolding of bones. They had still been civilians when the cinemas played *The Battle of the Somme*, stunning audiences into silence. They had read the casualty lists in the papers

– 20,000 British dead on the first day, 40,000 wounded – but seeing the news footage had given the abstract figures an unwelcome reality. At least those who went over at the Somme had been afforded the luxury of ignorance. Along with the other quarter of a million soldiers now preparing for the Big Push at Ypres, Andrew and Macintyre know exactly what to expect.

Second Lieutenant Willets is the same age as them – a 'one-pip wonder' – but he bears himself like an older man. His tunic is well cut and made of whipcord, his brown field boots have been freshly polished by his orderly and, as he prepares to talk, he fingers the flounce of worsted braid on his cuff as if to remind himself of his own superiority. 'Stand easy, men,' he says in a clear, steady, high register, his public school having taught him well how to project. 'Now. Can everyone hear me?' There are affirmative murmurs. 'Tomorrow we will do battle in this place. For generations to come this battle will be spoken of in the same breath as Agincourt and Waterloo. Men who did not fight with us will think badly of themselves.' He folds his arms and adjusts his voice, lowering it a semitone. 'The first wave will be going over the bags at three fifty tomorrow morning. Zero hour. The second wave an hour after that. We will be going over in the third wave. Fire and movement. No walking.' He presses his fingertips together over his chest, as if he is a vicar about to give a sermon. 'Lessons have been learned since the Somme offensive.'

Macintyre elbows Andrew.

'We shall be following the Seaforth Highlanders who will have already taken the first Hun trench, which is on a ridge two hundred yards across. Our first objective is the village of . . .' He looks at an order paper in his hand. 'Gheluvelt. If you get lost just ask the Hun for directions.' Grim laughter at this. 'The overall objective for tomorrow is the village of Passchendaele, which is five miles due east of here. I don't need to tell you the importance of the channel ports.' He pauses. A coldness enters his eyes. 'Be bold in battle, men. Be brave. Be savage. Do your duty. Charge with hatred in your hearts, that way victory will be ours. Do honour to your uniform and your king. Ours is a noble cause and our enemy does not deserve mercy. Kill him before he kills you. We take no prisoners.' He pauses again and, while this order sinks in, he taps the wooden revetting that supports the wall of the trench. 'Any wounded men should wait in a crump hole and our stretcher-bearers will come and collect you after dark.' He pauses again and swallows. 'Some of you may not return. There will be no time for mourning to-morrow, but a time will come. You will have dignity in death and your bodies will be buried. Your graves will be marked.' He pauses and meets in turn several of the eyes staring widely back at him. 'You may have heard a little artillery bombardment going on these past three weeks . . .' There are more appreciative snorts at this. 'I promise you, nothing could have survived it. All their wire has been destroyed. Now,' he slaps his hands together, 'the padre will be coming round shortly. Try and get some rest. Stand-to will be at two fifty.' He pauses again. 'Remember what you are fighting for, men. This battle will bring the end of the war closer, and this war will mean the end of all wars.'

There is a thoughtful silence as the lieutenant returns to his dugout. As if to dispel the mood, the CSM says: 'Piece of advice, lads. Leave your mucky pictures here. You don't want them sent back to your nearest and dearest.'

As Macintyre empties his wallet of postcards, he says in an undertone: 'At least you know what a cunny feels like.'

Andrew looks embarrassed.

'You do know, don't you? . . . Don't tell me you don't know.'

'Don't want to talk about that. It ain't right.'

'I'm going to find some French tart. Pay for it first chance I get. Speaking of which . . .' He rubs his finger and thumb together.

Andrew hands over the sixpence. 'Seaforth Highlanders, eh, Will?' He wants to change the subject, to diffuse the tension, to retreat to the familiarity of their routine. 'They'll put the wind up old Fritz.'

'Saw the jocks marching past in their kilts yesterday.'

'We all saw 'em, Will.'

'I heard they've got a piper going over with them.'

'Imagine lining up to collect your rifle and being handed a set of bloody bagpipes instead.'

Macintyre adopts a Scottish accent. 'Hang on, Sarn't, can't I have a rifle like everyone else?'

Andrew slips into Scottish as well: 'Nae, laddie, it's the pipes for yous.'

'But why, Sarn't?'

'Because Fritz hates the sound of them. Drives him mad with rage. But this is good, see, because he uses up all his ammo trying to shoot the piper.'

'Oh . . . I see.'

There is laughter, but it soon dries. The men return to their mugs of tea and their private thoughts. The cook arrives with a pot of cold Maconochie's stew and disappears again in search of a dixie stove to heat it on. Macintyre sharpens his bayonet. 'You scared, Andy?'

Andrew starts guiltily. 'No.'

'Well, I am.'

'I heard they shot some poor toerag this morning. He'd been trying to get over to the German line, getting himself took prisoner. Court-martialled him yesterday.'

'Where you hear that then?'

'Cookie. He heard it from the CSM. They always do it before a big attack. Encourages the rest of us.'

'I heard that one of the rifles in them firing squads has a blank in it. You don't know which one it is.'

'That's not true.'

'It bleedin' is.'

The day has darkened. The clouds overhead are bulging and inky black. A moustachioed captain appears at the mouth of the trench, his young face framing old eyes. 'This Oxford Street?' Without waiting for an answer he makes his way forward, followed by a muddy-faced unit wearing the insignia of the Sheffield Pals. He turns to address them. 'You're going to have to wait here for a minute, men, while I find out from BHQ where they want us to go.' He turns to Andrew's platoon. 'Where's your officer?'

Five extended arms silently direct him to the dugout.

Macintyre offers a cigarette to one of the new arrivals and they light them off a single shielded match. An official photographer, as identified by his armband, begins setting up a wooden box on a tripod, an Imperial quarter-plate camera. 'Come on then, you two,' he says, pointing at Andrew and a man from the new unit. 'Big smiles for the folks back home.'

Andrew feels a comradely arm move around his shoulder. He smiles tensely at the camera, the whiteness of his eyes exaggerated by the dried mud splashes on his face. A fissure in the cloud affords a moment of watery sunlight and this coincides with the clatter of the camera shutter. As the two men pull apart, their eyes meet briefly. They grin shyly at one another and return to their own platoons.

The photographer asks Andrew his name.

'Private Andrew Kennedy, Eleventh Shropshire Fusiliers.'

'And his name?'

'Don't know.'

As the photographer heads over to the other platoon, the captain emerges from the dugout. 'Right, men,' he says. 'On we go. Next stop Piccadilly.'

'Piccadilly is back that way,' Colour Sergeant Major Davies says, cocking a thumb over his shoulder.

'Is it? Right, men, about face, back the way we came.'

Andrew lays his head on a sandbag and tries to get some rest, but once again sleep proves impossible. There is a constant rattle of discarded tin cans moving against each other. The rats are turning them over. The parachute flares they saw in the distance the night before are overhead now. One rocket hisses waveringly into the air directly above them. It leaves a trail of smoke as it begins its spinning descent. Andrew can hear Germans singing '*Wacht am Rhein*' and calling out in nasal voices: 'Hey, Tommee!' and 'Wake up, Tommee.' He gives up trying to sleep and rewraps his sodden puttees, working up from ankle to calf. Star shells are also illuminating the waiting night, silhouetting the corkscrew spikes across no-man's-land.

An hour before the attack, the weather sours. Black rain. And as the squall intensifies, so does the British bombardment. The

German guns answer back, though none of their shells is landing near the waiting infantry. What does land, with a clatter, feet away from where Andrew stands, is a mortar bomb, a 'plumb pudding' fired in error from a British reserve trench thirty yards behind them. Andrew stares at it, transfixed. Heat waves are rising off its metal casing. It is the size and shape of a football, with its solid tail still smouldering. A powerful smell of cordite reaches his nostrils, but the bomb does not explode. Other men who have also been staring at it dive for nearby funk holes, and Andrew joins them. Colour Sergeant Major Davies pounds around the corner and orders an evacuation of the trench. They wait in a communication trench for an engineer to arrive and take out the fuse. In shock at their near escape, the men begin laughing. Even the CSM manages a smile. 'Well, there you go, lads,' he says. 'Charmed bleeding lives.'

At zero hour, the ground undulates as a mine explodes half a mile away. Where Andrew is standing, he can feel its shock waves in his bones. The barrage that has been raging for three weeks stops abruptly. The dense silence that follows pounds in Andrew's head, pressing against his eardrums. He thinks there is ringing in his ears, but it is the first wave going over the top – dogs trained to respond to a whistle – and the sound is followed by the *zup-zup-zup* of distant machine-gun fire. The British bombardment begins again, with shrapnel shells arcing through the sky overhead, and Andrew and Macintyre take it in turns to look through a periscope at the long, jagged line of flames bursting from the ground fifty yards in front of the advancing troops. What was it they had been told? Advancing troops must follow the flames 'like a horse follows a nosebag'. Running. No longer weighed down by 66lb of kit. Lessons have been learned. The creeping barrage has begun. The German machine gunners will not survive it.

Ten minutes pass as the men of the 11th Battalion listen with colour-drained faces to the continuing patter of enemy machine guns. A commotion is heard in the trench ahead of them. Muffled shouting. Boots being sucked by mud. Stretcher-bearers wearing Red Cross armbands appear with a wounded soldier. Andrew steps to one side to let them past. There is no blood on the man.

'What's his trouble?' someone shouts.

'That mine,' the second stretcher-bearer says over his shoulder. 'He was bracing himself and the shock wave snapped his legs. Daft bastard.'

'Lucky bastard,' Macintyre corrects.

First light has still not punctured the nimbus clouds when the CSM gives the order to move up to the next trench. With the rain ricocheting off their helmets, the men scuttle like crabs, crouched over and moving from one side of the trench to the other as they follow its dogtoothed line. In the darkness up ahead there is scuffling and shoving. They make way for a steady stream of stretchers bearing wounded men from the first and second waves. Their eyes are cloudy, their skin pale. Andrew can smell the vapour of warm human blood following in their wake and, like a bullock spooked in an abattoir, he begins to shake. When a corporal with a blood-spattered face pushes blindly past him, he gags.

When they reach the front trench, the quartermaster comes round with an earthenware flagon marked SRD – 'Service Ration Depot' officially, 'Soon Runs Dry' unofficially – and pours rum into shaking tin cups. As soon as he has drained his, Andrew yawns uncontrollably. Feeling as if his bowels have turned to water, he wishes he had been able to go this morning. He opens and closes his hands to relieve the tingling sensation in them. He feels numb. More than anything he feels he needs more time – another year, another month, another day, even another hour. To take his mind off the attack he rechecks his kitbag. He unpacks his three days' rations, his folded waterproof sheet, his water bottle and entrenching tool, his four grenades, his ammunition pouches and his bandolier, before packing them all back in again. His box respirator is missing. He realizes he has it around his neck. Without taking it off, he tries to wipe clean the goggles set into the Phenate-Hexamine helmet, making the glass squeak – they are clouded over from the inside and will not come clear. The cloudiness reminds him of the wounded men he has seen. Their eyes.

When the order comes to stand by the scaling ladders, Andrew's pulse quickens and he feels his testicles contract. He is breathing heavily. Macintyre hears him and tries to smile reassuringly, but the smile comes out as a grimace. Andrew can see the fear entering his friend's heart too. 'Lice, Will,' he shouts. 'Chats is the name for lice.'

'Right,' Macintyre shouts back. 'Thanks.'

Andrew sees the CSM pacing up and down, shouting orders, but he can no longer hear him. Blood is roaring in his ears. He needs to urinate. A feeling of inertia is creeping over him. He's no longer sure he will be able to climb the ladder. All his fears, he knows, lie over these sandbags – fears not of pain but of annihilation, of ceasing to exist, of unimaginable emptiness. Yet for weeks he has been willingly drawn to this moment, pulled towards this line – on the overnight crossing from Southampton to Le Havre, on the cattle train from Étaples, on the road to Ypres, along the trenches to no-man's-land . . .

The name terrifies him. No-man's-land. A land where men do not belong.

'Fix bayonets!' the CSM orders in a rising growl.

There is a scrape of steel along the trench. Andrew's hands are shaking again and it takes him several attempts to align the hilt of his bayonet to the rifle's lug. He leans forward on to his rifle to set the weapon firmly and give it a quarter turn. His eyes close. When he opens them again he sees a rat squatting behind an ammunition crate. He stares at it. It stares back, its eyes two black beads. It runs a paw over its snout, as if scratching an itch. Andrew closes his eyes again. He can taste vomit in his mouth. He spits it out and opens his eyes. The rat has gone.

'Put one up!'

Bolts are drawn back and .303 bullets loaded into Lee-Enfield chambers. Andrew presses his back teeth together to stop them chattering and, quite unexpectedly, gravity falls upon him.

I'm not going to let the CSM down. I'm not going to let Dorothy down. I'm not going to let Will down.

He holds out his hand towards Macintyre. It is no longer trembling.

Macintyre takes it in his and presses it hard. Comrades shaking hands. 'When we go over, Andy . . .'

'What?'

'Try not to trip me up with your big clumsy feet.'

Andrew manages a smile. If this is to be the hour of his death, he thinks, he will meet it with a steady eye. Like a man. Like a soldier. He feels the heat of the rum and, with it, a surge of adrenalin. A new bombardment begins. It is more nerve-jarring than previous ones and so heavy the air liquefies – a heavy liquid, dense and metallic. Andrew tries to imagine he is back at home in Shropshire, caught in a lightning storm. He also tries to count the gaps between the flashes and the rolls of thunder like he did as a child, but the explosions are so loud he is unable to get beyond three – so loud that for one moment he cannot even recall his own name. Private something. Kennedy. Private Andrew Kennedy, 11th Battalion, Shropshire Fusiliers. There are no gaps in the thunder now anyway. It is rolling in unbroken waves. And the displacement of air caused by the shells overhead catches the whole of the line in a hurricane. At every report Andrew feels as if his scalp is being removed. Under his boots the earth is shuddering, ecstatic tremors that carry up his legs. In his confusion he imagines he sees the top of the parapet moving. It is only the terrified rats fleeing. They have become hysterical. Andrew looks at Macintyre and realizes what he feels for his old friend, at this minute, on this day, is something approaching love. Something beyond love. Macintyre shouts at him but his words are drowned out. Andrew can see his friend's lips move and tries to shout back but he cannot hear himself. He wants to tell Macintyre that they will keep together. Instead, he grabs his hand again. They will go over the top hand in hand, as they had gone to Sunday school. Andrew watches the subaltern stand on a firestep, a Webley revolver in one hand and a whistle in the other. He watches the whistle reach the officer's lips and his cheeks puff out as he blows. But he does not hear the sound. Others do and begin scrambling up the ladders. As Andrew follows them, still holding Macintyre's hand, the weight of his kitbag almost pulls him backwards. Then it comes to him: anger. He hears a voice saying: '*Shit, shit, shit.*' The word is repeated again and again. He realizes it is rising from his own throat, increasing in volume until it turns into a shouted noise, a battle cry. They are all doing it, hundreds of them along the line as they scale the ladders. They are swearing to give themselves courage, as they have been trained. Dogs responding to a whistle.

CHAPTER FIFTEEN

London. Present day. Three weeks after the crash

THOUGH SHE WAS LEFT-HANDED, THE SLING AROUND HER LEFT ARM meant Nancy had to hold her toothbrush with her right. In the days that had passed since the seaplane fell out of the sky, she had learned to do this with dexterity. She had also learned not to turn her head more than was necessary. As she brushed, she studied her reflection in the bathroom mirror. Her eyes were still puffy from sleep, or lack of it, and her neck and shoulders were still creased – the imprint of tangled sheets. They still had a ghost of a tan.

Daniel was also studying her reflection, from the doorway. 'It stimulates the brain,' he said.

Still facing the mirror, Nancy waited until her toothbrush clicked off automatically before answering. 'What does?'

Daniel took a bite out of his toast and chewed on it slowly, holding the plate near to his chin to catch crumbs. 'Brushing your teeth with your wrong hand. It's like showering with your eyes closed.' He took another bite and spoke with his mouth full: 'Why don't you let me brush your teeth for you, until your shoulder is better?'

'I've told you, I can manage.'

There was accusation in the tone of her voice. Daniel hesitated before speaking again. 'How did you sleep?' he asked.

Nancy ran a finger over the bump that marked the break in her collarbone, dabbed her finger into a contact lens carton, used a finger from her other hand to pull down the skin below her eye, tilted her head back and inserted the lens. After she had fitted the other one, she washed her hand, turned the tap off and jiggled her fingers dry. She was still staring at her reflection, running out of silence. 'I didn't.'

'Painkillers not working?'

'No, the painkillers are working. It's the sedatives that aren't working.' One-handed, she twisted the top off a plastic bottle of mouthwash, took a swig, sluiced and spat. 'I'm going back to the doctor's today to see if I can get something stronger.'

'That wise?'

Still facing the mirror, Nancy spoke to her reflection: 'I haven't had a proper night's sleep for three weeks. When I do manage to sleep I have nightmares. When I'm awake I have panic attacks. Yes, it's wise.'

They both turned as Martha's voice carried from her bedroom: 'Daniel, come quick! You're on the telly.'

'Call me Daddy,' Daniel said as he arrived in the bedroom with Nancy. A map of the Galápagos Islands was being shown on the breakfast news. A dotted line indicated the flight path of their plane. A reporter was mid-sentence: '. . . Islands, birthplace of Darwinism, of the theory that only the fittest survive. It was here that . . .'

'Turn it up,' Nancy said. 'What's he saying?'

'. . . has revealed that the mayday transmissions from the seaplane were never received, and a combination of factors meant its dis-appearance went unreported. According to the inquiry, the pilots had anticipated a further delay, having already been forced to wait twenty-four hours for bad weather, and so had left the details of their flight plan open, reclassifying themselves as "unscheduled". And because the seaplane came down close to the Galápagos Islands, air traffic controllers tracking its progress on a radar in Ecuador assumed it had arrived at its destination and landed safely on water. The four surviving passengers owe their lives to the bravery of one man.' A photograph of Daniel in his academic gown came up on the screen.

'It's you, Daniel!' Martha said.

The reporter continued: 'Daniel Kennedy, a thirty-eight-year-old scientist, swam fourteen miles in twenty-one hours. He was not available for comment but one of the other survivors had this to say . . .' A tall African-American man appeared on the screen. He was grinning. 'Don't know how he done it. Seems no one in Ecuador knew the plane had gone down. I'd have died out there if he hadn't come back for us. Man, I was gettin' very cold. I saw one old guy get eaten by sharks right in front of us. He'd fallen off the floats. One minute he was there, the next the water was red with blood. I'm telling ya, it was horrible.'

'Another of the survivors spoke to us from Boston this morning.' Susie came on the screen, her face marbled with pink lines where her scabs had recently been. 'I owe my life to Professor Kennedy,' she said, not looking directly at the camera. 'My husband Greg was one of the ones who didn't make it. He's with the Lord now. It was the cold that . . . that . . . We'd only been married for . . .' A sob interrupted her words.

The reporter came back on the screen. 'That was the moving testimony from—'

Daniel had pointed a remote control at the television and switched it off.

'Hey,' Martha said. 'I wanted to see the end of that.'

Nancy turned to Daniel. 'Did you know they had finished the inquiry?'

Daniel raised the slice of toast but instead of taking another bite he stared thoughtfully at where it had sweated on to the plate. 'Someone from breakfast television rang yesterday for a comment about it,' he said. 'I couldn't think of anything to say.'

'Were you going to tell me?'

'I was . . . I, of course, but . . .' Daniel stroked Martha's hair. 'You have enough to think about.'

'Poor Susie.'

'Poor Greg. He asked me to tell his parents that he was at peace. I'd forgotten about that. You weren't given any numbers for the other survivors, were you?'

'You could ring the people at the airline. They should have them.' She turned to Martha. 'You should be getting your uniform on. We're going to be late. Do you want peanut butter or Marmite sandwiches for lunch?'

It had been Daniel's decision to buy a bigger house than was needed, or than could be afforded on his salary alone should Nancy choose to give up work after having another baby. He had assumed that they would. A boy preferably. Instead, over the years, the couple had colonized a spare room each as a study. Even Martha had her own study, which doubled as a playroom. Each year the couple spent money on a house project: a roof terrace; a loft conversion; the solar panels. The most recent building project had been the most ambitious. They had extended into their side-return next to the kitchen and knocked through the wall separating it from their dining room. This had left them with a single open-plan room where the family spent most of their time together. One wall was windows and exposed brickwork, the other was hung with three large frames containing original film posters for *Jules et Jim*, *Le Notti di Cabiria* and *La Notte*. Despite its size and its chrome and glass minimalism, it was cosy, thanks in part to concealed spotlighting and the small, potted bay trees decorated with fairy lights which stood in each corner of the room.

Ten minutes after his mention on television, Daniel came downstairs and found Nancy wearing a rope-knitted jersey and appliquéd jeans. She was sitting on a high stool pinching the bridge of her nose. He studied her from the doorway. She looked older, he thought. The crash had aged her. She was reduced, as if limp and boneless. Her eyes were swollen and red from crying and he could see odd strands of grey hair. Had she had them before? When did she stop dyeing them? Her hair was greasy and unwashed. There were nail scores on her neck where she had been scratching. The varnish on her toenails was chipped. She was confused and forgetful. The doctor had said it would take time.

When the toaster launched two slices of golden bread with a loud clunk, Nancy looked up, saw Daniel and looked down again.

He walked past her and shook some Nurofen from a pot.

'Headache no better?' Nancy said, spreading peanut butter and jam on two slices of bread.

'The same.' Daniel washed the pills down with a pint of water, refilled his glass from a water filter on the table and drank that as well. Since the crash he had had an unquenchable thirst. 'You seeing that counsellor again today?' he said, draining the glass and refilling it.

'Tom.'

'First names is it?'

The coffee maker gave a raspy gurgle.

'You should come with me.'

'Sit around holding hands and singing kumbaya? No thanks.'

Nancy cut the crusts off the bread and placed the sandwiches in Martha's *Finding Nemo* lunch box. 'It's not like that.'

'I could sign up for the crying workshop. Maybe bring Dad along.'

'He's a professional therapist.'

'He's a charlatan.' Daniel picked up a corner of a child's painting and pushed it across to Nancy. 'Seen what the baby has drawn?'

Nancy turned the painting right way round and held it at arm's length. Coloured crayon marks showed an island with palm trees and a plane crashing towards the sea. Black smoke trailed behind the plane and flames leaped from its wings. Matchstick passengers with arms raised were hanging out of the windows. Some were falling out of the sky into a blue sea dotted with black shark fins. Nancy stared at it for a moment and blinked. A tear beaded her cheek.

'Sorry, darling, I didn't mean to . . .' Daniel gently extracted the painting from her hand and laid it on the kitchen counter top. 'Martha was trying to . . .'

Nancy waved the thought away and swallowed. 'You haven't met him.'

'Haven't met who?'

'Tom. How can you say he's a charlatan?'

'All counsellors are charlatans.'

Martha walked in and asked: 'What's a charlatan?'

'Someone who preys on the vulnerable and panders to the egotism of the unhappy.'

'For God's sake, Daniel. She's nine.'

'Martha knows what egotism means, don't you, darling?'

The child took hold of her father's hand. Reached for her mother's. 'I know what unhappy means,' she said.

If Tom Cochrane was a charlatan he was a sympathetic one: a Scotsman with kind eyes, handsome, angular features and a mouth that turned up at the corners, even in repose. When Nancy went to see him later that morning, he was wearing a linen jacket over a pale blue shirt, but no tie. Professional, yet casual.

'My husband thinks you're a charlatan,' she said as she lowered herself on to his sofa and, as though for protection, held a cushion over her lap. 'Are you?'

'Your husband?' Tom said in his soft, Morningside accent. He had the counsellor's habit of answering questions with questions.

'I thought of him as my husband.'

'Thought?'

'Think.'

'I read about him at the time of the crash. There was a lot in the papers about him.'

'My mother saved some cuttings. Haven't read them yet.'

'You must feel proud.'

Nancy shrugged and began twisting her hair. The fluorescent light above her was humming gently.

'I think I saw something about him on BBC online today.' Tom swivelled in his chair so that he was facing a PC covered in yellow Post-it notes. He double-clicked his mouse with a slender finger, paused and clicked again. 'No, I can't find it. There was something, though.'

'You haven't answered my question,' Nancy said. 'Is there any point to these sessions?'

'Do *you* feel there's a point?'

'Daniel says talking constantly about traumatic incidents only makes them worse.'

'He might be right,' Tom said.

'He also said that veterans of the First World War didn't need counsellors. They coped by repressing their memories.'

'It doesn't work for everyone. How have you been feeling?'

Nancy stared at a polystyrene coffee cup on the pine table in front of her. 'Daniel insists I take my own mug to Starbucks. To save the planet.'

There was a silence that Tom did not attempt to fill.

'Tearful,' Nancy continued. 'I've been feeling tearful and . . . I don't know . . . claustrophobic.'

'That's normal. The fight or flight mechanism floods the body with adrenalin, heightening the senses. So when you were trapped on the plane it would have been like having one foot on the accelerator and the other on the brake.'

'Will it go away?'

'The claustrophobia? It takes several weeks for adrenalin levels to return to normal.'

Another silence.

'I feel angry all the time,' Nancy said.

'That's normal, too. Angry with yourself?'

'A bit. I felt angry as the plane was going down. I kept thinking, why me? I also felt angry with those passengers who were scream-ing, because they were disturbing my last moments. Afterwards, when some of them were killed, I felt guilty about having felt angry with them.' She picked an elastic band up off the floor and began stretching it. 'I think I felt angry with God. I prayed to him, you know, on the plane.'

'Thought you were an agnostic.'

'A Catholic agnostic.'

'Ah.'

'What's that supposed to mean?'

'Just means ah.'

'Anyway, there was no one there. I had no sense of Him. I cried out for help and God was silent, just as he was silent when the

Zyklon B was being tipped into the gas chambers, and silent as the babies were having their heads bashed against the trees in Cambodia, and silent when the Tutsis were being hacked to death by the Hutus.'

'Have you talked about this with Daniel?'

'He's the one I feel angry with the most, though that anger is more like a background whisper. Everything he does annoys me at the moment.' With her teeth, she worried the fatness of her lower lip, biting on one corner. 'He keeps smiling all the time. Since the crash. Makes me want to punch him.'

'Trauma affects people in different ways. If Daniel has been feeling positive it might be survivor's syndrome . . . It makes some people feel invincible and godlike. Have you talked about it with him? The crash?'

Nancy shook her head and began breathing more quickly. She could feel loose contours of anger inside her narrowing to a peak. In her hand she repeatedly stretched and released the rubber band, gripping it as tightly as her anger gripped her. 'After the crash I kept repeating in my head, "Why hast thou forsaken me? Why hast thou forsaken me?" You know, from the Bible.'

'You felt God had forsaken you?'

'Daniel.'

'Daniel felt God had—'

'No. No . . . It doesn't matter.'

'How has Daniel been feeling?'

'He gets headaches.'

'Is he sleeping?'

'Dunno. I've been sleeping in the spare room.' She held up her slinged arm by way of explanation. 'Trying to sleep. When I do manage to fall asleep I wake up feeling anxious. Wide awake, with blood pumping in my ears. Can't sleep beyond four am.' She looked around the room. There was a sterility to it which the few books, the DAB radio and the hatstand with the mac hanging from it did nothing to dispel. On a wall opposite the window was a framed medical certificate. 'You're a doctor?'

'Not as such,' Tom said with a shake of his head. 'I don't do this full time. It's voluntary work. The local authority pay my expenses and provide me with this office. I'm a surveyor in my day job.'

Nancy inspected Tom's bookcase. There were biographies of Freud and Jung and textbooks on cognitive therapy and behavioural psychology but also, on a lower shelf, some titles that would make Daniel hyperventilate: *Alternative Medicine – the Truth*; *Psychic Energy, Crystal Healing and the Power of Chant*; *Inner Expansion – Guardian Angels and How to Contact Them*. 'What kind of a therapist are you exactly?' she asked.

'The psycho kind.'

The joke reassured her. She smiled.

'I am a qualified trauma counsellor,' Tom added. 'That is my certificate.' He pointed to the frame on the wall. 'Those books you were looking at were given to me by patients. A lot of people find that New Age stuff useful, even if it is a placebo.'

Nancy knew that Daniel would argue that 'New Age stuff' relied on gullibility and superstition, but he didn't understand why an increasing number of people were turning to it. He didn't understand that they were unhappy, that they wanted answers, that they wanted placebos – that she, Nancy, the woman he had lived under the same roof with for ten years, wanted a placebo.

She untwisted the top of a bottle of fizzy water, making it hiss angrily. Tom was staring at her. She took a sip from the neck and swirled the bottle round and round absent-mindedly. Bored now.

'Do you want to see what they do with healing crystals? For fun?'

Nancy shrugged.

'Lie down then.'

As Tom stood over her, Nancy studied the crystal he was dangling over her chest, intrigued by the way it caught the light. She knew it wouldn't make any difference physically, but she thought it might make her feel . . . something, anything, anything other than lost.

★

Enveloped in the dark, wooden panelling of the confessional, his knees cushioned by the prie-dieu in front of him, Wetherby shivered and stared up at the crucifix hanging over the grille. He remained in this position for a full minute, lost in his reflections, in his contemplation of sin.

The priest on the other side of the lattice screen tapped.

'Forgive me, Father, for I have sinned,' the penitent began in a brittle but well-modulated tone, one that, for the priest, evoked the BBC Home Service. 'It is one week since my last confession.'

'What is it you wish to confess?' The voice was gentle, disembodied.

'I have committed both venial and mortal sins.' Wetherby placed the gloved palms of his hands together. 'I also missed mass on Sunday.'

'On purpose?'

'No, Father.'

'Go on.'

'I suspended an employee, a security guard, even though I knew he was only doing his duty.'

'Why?'

'Spite, I suppose . . . I also blocked the promotion of a colleague, even though he deserved the job.'

'Now why did you do that?'

'Because I am a small and envious man, Father.' As he spoke Wetherby lowered his head and closed his eyes. 'Because I envy his looks, his hair, his wife, his popularity, his social ease, his decency, his certainty . . .'

'Jealousy is a terrible thing,' the priest interrupted. 'We must resist it. Is there anything else you wish to confess?'

Wetherby thought.

He thought of the vulnerable students he had seduced over the years. He thought about the envy he felt for the celibacy of Locke, a thinker whose mind had been free from sordid distraction. He thought, too, about how much he resented the appetite for sex he shared with Bertrand Russell, the vile atheist who considered it an immoral duty to sleep with the wives of other men. He hated himself for being more Russell than Locke. He hated himself for being weak. He hated himself. 'I took advantage of someone who trusts me,' he said. 'Someone in my pastoral care.'

'In what way now?'

Wetherby became overwhelmed, partly with self-pity, partly with a feeling of deep love for his own piety and candour. If anyone deserved to regain the grace of God, he thought, it was he. He longed for it and that longing was enough for him, enough evidence of His existence. 'Though I was having lustful thoughts about her, I engineered events so that she and I could be alone together.'

'God understands the weakness of the human spirit.'

'I then had sex with her.'

There was a silence as the priest weighed this. 'Is she above the age of consent?'

'Yes.'

'Did you use contraception?'

'No.'

'Well, that's something. Is there more you wish to confess?'

A single tear ran down Wetherby's sharp cheekbone. It felt cold and ticklish. He sniffed loudly. 'In my guilt, Father, in my wickedness, I . . .' He wrung his gloved hands as if washing them. 'I struck this girl.' He always enjoyed the formal language he used in confession; he felt cleansed by it. 'I did not mean to. In the heat of the moment I called her a temptress and struck her across the face with the back of my hand.'

'These are serious sins,' the priest said. 'Have you examined your conscience?'

Wetherby's words were blurred by the sob he was stifling. 'Yes, Father. I have. I have. I ask your forgiveness. God's forgiveness.'

'Yes, well, the intent of this sacrament is to provide healing for the soul. Are you truly contrite?'

'Truly, Father.'

'Then I suggest you see a counsellor. You need to talk about these matters properly and at length. Now you must say the Act of Contrition.'

'*Deus meus, ex toto corde poenitet me omnium meorum peccatorum, eaque detestor, quia peccando, non solum poenas a te iuste statutas promeritus sum . . .*'

There was a pause when, thirty seconds later, Wetherby finished and said, 'Amen.' The priest cleared his throat again. 'It's been a while since I heard that said in Latin. I'm afraid we must do the absolution in English.' He coughed. 'God the father of mercies, through the death and resurrection of his son, has reconciled the world to himself and sent . . .' When he reached the end he coughed again. 'Say ten Hail Marys, and may the Lord be with you.'

Outside the cathedral, the city was trembling with energy. The sidestepping pedestrians walking through the slush, the chasing sirens, the dull grind of techno music as a pub door opened and closed, the rolling chatter of overland trains arriving at Victoria station, the whistles of the guards, the clatter as the juggler in the beanie hat dropped one of his clubs: all were a comfort to Wetherby. They offered anonymity and sanctuary. He inhaled the cold air deeply, rewrapped his scarf and stood in the great doorway looking for Hai–iki. She was wearing his Crombie overcoat, hunched up with her back to him, feeding crisps to the pigeons. Wetherby walked over, wiped the step and sat down beside her. When she looked up at him he winced. The swelling around her eye had disappeared, but a dark blue circle had appeared instead. He extended a protective arm around her supple waist and said quietly, 'I have asked for God's forgiveness, now I ask for yours.'

'I forgive you.'

He pressed his cold lips to her forehead. 'Thank you . . . You know, Evelyn Waugh once said he would be much nastier if he were not a Catholic. I think I fall into that camp. I am sorry. I truly am. It will never happen again.' He stood up, led the way across the square and raised his arm in the direction of an approaching cab. If we catch this, he thought, I can have her back home and bent over the chaise longue within half an hour. It had been a long time since he had felt so exalted, so alive, so aroused.

★

After picking Martha up from school, Nancy returned home, listened to four answerphone messages and went up to Daniel's study to see if he had come back from work early. As she watched him hunched up over his desk – drawing something, she couldn't make out what – she realized he had not heard her. 'Is it true?'

He lurched forward guiltily, covering up his drawing.

'Is it true?' Nancy repeated.

Daniel turned his chair so that his body was blocking her view of the desk. 'Did you just say . . .' He stopped himself. 'I didn't hear you come in.'

'What? What do you think I said?'

'Shame on you.'

'I said, "Is it true?" Well, is it?'

'Is what true?'

'You're going to be given an award?'

'I don't know. There was a message on the answering machine. Someone from the *Mirror* wanting a comment.'

'I heard it. That's why I asked.'

'Haven't been told anything.' Daniel scraped back his chair, turned over the picture he was drawing and, without making eye contact, brushed past Nancy to get through the doorway.

Nancy did not move, the soft cogs of her mind unable to find a purchase. She was staring at the well-bruised cricket bat propped against his desk. Her sight line rose to take in familiar objects: the bust of Mao wearing a cricket cap, the chess clock, the microscope, the sunglasses, the novelty Father Christmas nailed to a cross that one of Daniel's students had sent him from Japan, the rugby ball signed by the England team. She took a step farther into the room. The desk had some ornaments she hadn't seen before, a collection of three turtles. There was a hard rubber one with a flattish shell, a small marble one and a suede one with a nodding head. An empty box distracted her. Chinese writing on the side. Dirty chopsticks sticking out. It had been left on a bookshelf in between a Nick Hornby novel and an untidy stack of science magazines. There was also an empty bottle of German beer and, in the ashtray, a stubbed-out joint. Nancy wondered how Daniel could work like this. The untidiness was unbearable. As she walked over to collect the Chinese food carton, she picked up the down-turned picture. It was Martha's crayon drawing of the crash. Daniel had added a turtle and a man in the sea. The picture had been covering a notebook. After a backward glance at the doorway, Nancy flicked through it. On almost every page there was a sketch of a man with wide-set eyes. In every picture, the man was smiling.

CHAPTER SIXTEEN

ALTHOUGH THEY HAD TALKED ON THE PHONE SEVERAL TIMES, Daniel had not had a chance to meet his friend Bruce Golding face to face since the crash. When he did, in the County Arms, a pub equidistant from their two houses, he did not recognize him. He had known Bruce – a rugby-playing hospital consultant – since university, but a four-week beard and a bulky leather jacket had rendered him invisible. It was as if light was flowing around him and carrying on, like water around a rock in a stream. Daniel scanned the pub a second time and when Bruce, standing at the bar a few yards away, gave a small wave, he slammed into focus.

'What the fuck has happened to your face?' Daniel said with a snort of laughter as he strode over and gave his friend a handshake that turned into a hug.

'Like it?' Bruce asked, scratching under his chin.

'You look like the Yorkshire Ripper.'

Bruce was a heavily built man with thick wrists and an untidy tangle of hair. To friends and colleagues he was known as the Bear. 'Well, my new tenant likes it. Did I mention that I have a new . . . ?'

'Once or twice.'

'I tell you he was an actor?'

'Yes.'

'And that he's twenty-two?'

Daniel nodded. 'How's that going?'

'He hasn't slapped my face yet.'

'Probably afraid to touch that beard. Doesn't it scare the patients?'

'Haven't had any, you know, complaints. Not that I . . .' Bruce stroked his beard again, more defensively this time. 'Anyway, it's just an experiment.'

When they were together it was usually assumed that Daniel, not Bruce, was the gay one. It wasn't that Daniel was effete necessarily, it was more that Bruce looked and sounded like the rugby player he was. The bridge of his nose was flat where it had been broken. His shoulders were broad, his thighs were stalwart. There was nothing gathered or defensive or apologetic about him. When he sat down it was solidly, knees apart. Women adored him.

'You look more like Captain Birdseye,' Daniel said, brushing the beard with the back of his fingers. 'You've gone grey.'

'It's called salt and pepper,' Bruce corrected. 'Anyway. Piss off. What you drinking?'

'Nah, I'll get them in. What's that?' Daniel nodded at Bruce's half-empty pint glass.

'Bitter.' Bruce tucked his hair behind his ear. 'Not sure what it's called. Old Tosser or something.'

The words 'Old Tosser' echoed in Daniel's head. Where had they come from? His friend could do better than that. They were being stilted with one another; trying too hard to feel relaxed in each other's company. Something had come between them. He caught the barman's eye, pointed at Bruce's pint and held up two fingers.

'So how, urm, how is, you know, everyone?' Bruce said. 'Morticia OK?'

'Nancy is fine.'

'She still carry a knuckleduster in her handbag?'

Daniel smiled and handed over a note as the barman placed two pints on the bar. He took a sip from his, leaving a moustache of white foam on his top lip. 'Well, when I say fine, I mean as fine as can be expected. She was badly shaken by it all. She's seeing some charlatan counsellor. I sometimes catch her crying.'

'Those aren't tears, they're leaks of battery acid from her brain.'

'How about you, my ursine friend? They haven't struck you off yet?'

'Nope. They can't prove a thing . . . And how's my little goddaughter?'

'Fine . . . Good.' Daniel paused. 'She asked me where babies come from the other day.'

'What did you tell her?'

'That the stork brings them.'

Bruce frowned. '*You* said that?'

'And then she said: "Yeah, but who fucks the stork?" '

'What!'

'It's a joke, Bear.'

'Oh, right.' Bruce had a sip of beer and noticed his friend's darkly circled eyes. 'Anyway, how are you? You look like shit, and I'm not just saying that.'

'Thanks.'

'Taking any exercise?'

'Haven't been able to swim since the crash. Sounds nuts, but I can't put my head underwater.'

'You mentioned headaches on the phone.' Bruce sounded too nonchalant.

Daniel nodded and rubbed a two-inch square of hair that had turned white since the crash, the spot where he had hit the seat in front. 'They come and go. Quite painful at times, like a migraine. This helps . . .' He took another sip.

'Are you, urm, taking anything?'

A shake of the head. 'Just fistfuls of Nurofen.'

Daniel pocketed his change, Bruce collected a half-eaten packet of cheese and onion crisps and the two walked across a sawdust-sprinkled wooden floor to a brass-topped table. Though it was still early December, the Christmas decorations looked tired: windows sprayed with fake snow, red and green tinsel dangling from framed pictures of hunting scenes, a menu on a blackboard advising patrons to book their Christmas parties early. It had been up since October.

'Actually,' Daniel said, pulling up his chair, 'I've been feeling pretty weird, to be honest.'

'Weird how?'

'Thirsty. Can't stop drinking.'

'What colour is your pee?'

Daniel found his friend's bedside vocabulary comforting: Bruce always said pee, never piss, tummy, never belly, and all actions were described as popping – 'pop up on to the bed', 'pop your under-pants down and cough', 'if you wouldn't mind popping your bra off. I need to do a UBE.' (It stood for Unnecessary Breast Examination, a medical student joke.) 'Purple,' he said.

'Good. Purple is normal for a man your age.'

'I'm not dehydrated or anything, it's more . . .' Daniel searched for the right word. 'I feel trippy.'

'Hearing colours and seeing noises trippy?'

'Not quite. It's more . . . There are smells. I keep smelling cake. And I have a tingling sensation.' He leaned over and held the tip of his finger to the space between Bruce's eyes, without touching the skin. 'You feel that?'

Bruce said, 'Mm, it tickles.'

'Yeah, well, I'm feeling that all the time, right across here.' He ran his fingers across his own brow.

'That prescription I gave you. The diazepam. You been taking it?'

'Only on the flight out to Ecuador. Not since. Why?'

'It can make you delusional.'

'Thanks for telling me.'

'Don't you ever read warnings?'

'Does anyone?'

'Well, anyway, it can.'

'No, it's more like dizziness. Room spins.'

'What about the crash? You bumped your head . . .'

Daniel rubbed his brow and nodded.

'Maybe you should come in for some, you know, tests. Would you like me to arrange some?'

'Tests?'

'Routine stuff. Safe side. Did they give you a CAT scan?'

Daniel touched the side of his head again, as if contemplating the prospect. 'Should they have?'

'Not necessarily. They wouldn't unless . . .' Bruce's tone had changed. 'How you fixed for the rest of this week? I can book you in for an MRI. I'll be in the hospital tomorrow afternoon if you can . . .'

'Bear!' Daniel was laughing. 'You're starting to freak me out!'

Bruce ripped the cellophane off a packet of Marlboro, tapped a cigarette out and stared at it. 'They can't stop you looking at cigarettes in pubs,' he said. 'I should stop anyway. I wake up in the morning aching from arse to elbow. Coughed up something black the other day. Not well. Much worse than you.'

'You're so competitive.'

'No, really, I'm falling apart.'

'I'll stand outside with you if you're desperate for a smoke.'

Bruce shook his head. The wounded martyr. 'Are you getting compensation?'

'Someone mentioned it but, to be honest, I don't want to go there.'

'May as well.'

'Nah, I'd rather forget it. You know, move on.'

'Look, come to the hospital for your own peace of mind. It'll take an hour and a half, tops.' He drained his glass and put it down next to the full one that Daniel had bought him. 'Apart from the headaches and the smells, how you been? It's normal to feel a bit down, you know, for a few weeks . . . afterwards.'

'Not really down. The opposite. I keep . . .' Daniel shook his head and grinned. 'I keep smiling unexpectedly. I only know I'm doing it by the look on people's faces. I went back into work the other day and some of my students stared at me like I was mental or something. I feel sort of . . .' He took another sip. 'Safe . . . I drove across three lanes on the motorway the other day without indicating. Didn't think about it. Wasn't looking.'

There was a metallic chatter as a slot machine paid out dozens of coins. Both men turned to look at it, momentarily lost in their own thoughts.

'I'm sure it's a temporary thing,' Bruce said.

'You reckon? I keep thinking about . . . I saw something . . .

Since the crash nothing has been quite real, as if I'm living in a shadow, waiting for the sunlight to return.'

'What was it you saw?'

A background murmur from the other tables – football, credit crunch, more football – filled a long silence between the two men. Daniel tried to get the word out. 'I saw . . .' He closed his eyes and grimaced. He couldn't say it. 'I . . . I don't *know* that it was . . . I thought I . . .' He imagined Bruce laughing if he told him. Why wouldn't he laugh? It was laughable. 'It doesn't matter. The point is . . .' Daniel's shoulders started heaving.

'I know, it's all right.' Bruce put a big paw on his friend's shoulder. 'You've had a tough time.'

A man playing darts stopped mid-aim and stared at them.

'You don't know, Bear. There's something I haven't told you.' He sniffed. 'Haven't told anyone.'

'Finally. You're coming out.'

'The papers were full of what a hero I was, rescuing the others and all that but . . . The truth is . . .' He rubbed the back of his neck. 'I panicked. The cabin was filling with water and I panicked.'

'What's wrong with that? I'd have shat myself.'

Daniel reached for one of Bruce's cigarettes and began tapping it against the table. 'There was one guy, one of the passengers, who left his wife. Climbed over her to save himself. Left her down there to drown. Deserted her. He was a deserter.'

Bruce fell silent as he reflected upon this. He took a sip of beer and wiped his mouth. 'But he came back for her, right?'

'Yes but . . .' A fat tear was rolling down Daniel's cheek.

'Mate, what he did was normal. The survival mechanism is . . .'

'You don't understand. He left her there.'

'But he didn't leave her there to drown, right? He went up for air then came back for her – is that so awful?'

'I suppose not.'

'People have to learn not to blame themselves. There have been cases documented of mothers escaping from planes and then realizing that they left their children on board. They'd seen a gap and gone for it.'

'This was different, he could have, I mean, others didn't get out. But . . . He put his hand on her face like this . . .' Daniel demonstrated.

Bruce gently removed his friend's hand. 'Look,' he said. 'The official advice given by airlines is that families shouldn't try and stick together. You should make your own way to the exits and meet up afterwards.' Daniel's halting speech was making Bruce uncharacteristically fluent. 'And think of the, you know, safety announcement on planes. "Always put your own mask on first before helping children to put theirs on." . . . Sounds like you've got survivor's guilt, Dan. Have you talked about it to Morticia? A little heart-to-heart while lying in the crypt at night?'

Daniel sniffed again and shook his head. 'I'm not sure she . . . I'm not certain she knows what happened . . . She hasn't mentioned . . . I want to talk to her about it but . . .'

'I'm sure she will understand.'

Daniel blew his nose. 'The truth is, Nancy and I . . . She has disappeared into herself. Something is missing. It's like she's in mourning for herself, like part of her died in that plane.'

Bruce drained his glass. 'I'm not nearly pissed enough for all this. Same again?'

Daniel looked up, a pale smile on his face. He wiped his cheek with the heel of his hand. 'James Robertson Justice.'

Bruce looked puzzled.

'That's who you look like with that ridiculous beard. James Robertson Justice in *Doctor in the House.*'

'Look, matey, when I get back with the drinks, you're going to stop blubbing like an old poof and tell me what it was you saw. OK?'

CHAPTER SEVENTEEN

Ypres Salient. Last Tuesday of July, 1917

ANDREW DOES NOT KNOW HE IS BURIED ALIVE. LIFE DEMANDS breath and he, with his mouth and nostrils blocked by Flanders soil, is not breathing. He has neither sight nor sensation; no sense of up and down, right and left. There is pressure on his chest, a dead weight pinning him down, but he cannot work out from which direction it is coming – the confusion of the avalanche victim.

The earth convulses abruptly and a fist of clay punches his face. He is tossed high above no-man's-land in a fountain of black soil. His compressed lungs inflate again. He splutters and gulps the metallic air, gasping his way back to consciousness.

The soldier is lying on top of the soil now, surrounded by cadavers that have been disinterred with him. Some are putrefying, others are freshly mutilated, empty containers that were inhabited by men only hours earlier. There is a severed hand lying across his chest. He brushes it off and spits the soil out of his mouth. A rising whistle overhead signals an incoming shell and, instinctively, he scrambles to his feet, runs for a few yards and dives into a waterlogged crater. He turns in time to see the bodies he has been buried with vomited back into the air and buried once more. Foaming black smoke leaves him disorientated for a moment, but when it lifts in great wreaths he sees the moon. It is blood red. There is a warm wetness on his legs, distinct from the cold wetness of the dead water. He touches it with his hand, expecting to find an injury. None is found. He has been shocked into incontinence.

As his concussion subsides he realizes he is crouching behind the lip of a shell hole that is at least twenty yards in circumference. He feels a burning thirst. This at least means he is still alive. It begins to rain heavily again, in vertical sheets that almost blind him. He tries to get his bearings. The smoke is blue and rising in coils. Through them he can make out concrete bunkers.

He knows where he is now. He remembers being told about this place in Sunday school. Abandon hope, all ye who enter here.

On the ridge ahead of him, the German pillboxes are chattering with sporadic machine-gun fire, a desultory conversation with the bodies lying scattered and torn on the wire in front of them. Andrew grasps that the Germans must have retaken the positions they lost after the British first and second wave attacked that morning. With every staccato bark of their guns they are riddling flesh that is lifeless, tearing at it like demented harpies.

As Andrew's awareness of his surroundings grows, he realizes he has neither helmet nor rifle – and this makes him question abstractly if he is still a soldier. Where is his unit? Has he been left behind? He tries to piece together what has happened. He remembers running towards the German trenches and then stopping, feeling paralysed with fear as bullets began to puncture the mud around him. He could not hear them, but he could see the ground bubbling as they blindly sought out their soft targets: the impact of bullets on mud and skin was not so different, each a lazy perforation. The faceless demons could not see their targets, firing from raised ground a mile and a half away, creating a moving wall of metal, a swarm that anything living could not escape.

He remembers seeing Second Lieutenant Willets stagger backwards with blood pulsing from his throat. He had dropped to his knees and pawed the air, his chest swagged with bright crimson. Andrew tried to help him stand, but he fell on to his back and drummed his heels on the ground. The young soldier had never seen a man die before. As he stared, he too was hit, by a bullet or a piece of shrapnel, a glancing blow that penetrated his helmet and sent him spinning to the ground. That was his last memory. A whole day must have passed since, because he has now returned to the relative safety of darkness.

He touches his scalp with his fingers. It is caked with dried blood, or mud, he cannot tell which. He dabs at it and licks his fingertip. The taste of iron confirms it is blood. There is a welt. A stinging sensation. Feeling is returning to him. He hears the groans of dying men around him, like a thousand wet fingers being dragged down a pane of glass. It has been a background noise that he was unable to focus on before, a constant white sound that could not be isolated and identified until there was a variation in its tone. A last breath is exhaled, not inhaled, it causes a rattle in the throat. It is the rattling he hears now.

There is a rushing scream and a white phosphorous artillery round bursts overhead. A ball of claret hangs in the air and explodes, showering blazing hot tendrils and illuminating a honeycomb of shell holes and the skeletons of trees. It also reveals thousands of bodies. Perhaps millions. The dying and the already dead. The landscape is black with them.

With gluey mud clinging to his boots, Andrew attempts a crouching scuttle, wading through the darkness, trying to keep to the small spits of land that join shell holes. But he cannot go three yards without slipping and the heaviness of his legs means he is soon out of breath. He trudges past a sunken tank and follows with his hand some white tape left by engineers to guide the damned across the pitted ground to the very edges of the earth. He comes to some slippery duckboards and follows them for a hundred yards, jumping at the shadows that flicker on the margins of his sight lines. There is a horse screaming somewhere and men calling out for help, but he cannot see them in the gloom or work out from which direction their calls are drifting. When he strains his eyes he can make out giant rotting teeth – ghost trees reduced to charred stumps.

The sudden flaring glow of a Verey light makes his silhouette visible to the guns and he dives for cover in a nearby hole. He finds himself feet away from the face of a man whose moustache is a parched yellow. There are bubbles of blood in the man's open mouth and confusion in his dying eyes. A blinding explosion fills the air with shrapnel. In the light of the blast, Andrew sees the dying man's face sliced off with surgical precision. It is hurled like a rubber mask against the side of his own face. The sweet effluvium of cordite and newly spilled blood crowds his senses. The mask feels hot and wet. He claws at it and dives into the water as another shell lands. When he surfaces, it is to a hellish rain of soil, blood and steaming intestines. The blood mixes with the water. The dying man has gone. Only his haversack remains. Andrew crawls out and drags it back into the hole. He tips out its contents and fumbles through it looking for iron rations. There is one tin of Fray Bentos bully beef and another of hardtack biscuits. He peels back both lids and crams the food into his mouth. The biscuits make him thirsty again. He scoops up a handful of muddy water but it is un-drinkable, poisoned by chlorine and corrupted flesh. He becomes aware of an ungodly stench: sweat, excrement, sulphur. Only now does he see the other occupants of his hole: one man scalped by shrapnel, his brains spewing over his forehead; another dissected, the whole of the front of his chest down to his stomach carved open and spread apart as if in an anatomy lesson. Carbon mon-oxide is lingering in the crater, left by the shell that made it. As he lies here, Andrew slips into a stupor.

After an hour the shelling subsides and the rain eases to a drizzle. The soldier shivers and checks his pocket watch. It has stopped. He gives it a tap with a cold and trembling fingertip and then winds it up. His head is aching. The night sky fills with flashes from flares and whiz-bangs. Seeing a shadow approach from the enemy line, he pretends to be dead. When he feels it is safe enough, he looks up and sees a man staring down at him, his face illuminated by light, poised like a German star shell. He is a British soldier, a ranker, his uniform intact. He is standing perfectly upright, apparently oblivious to the danger. When he smiles at Andrew, his teeth are luminous against his mud-darkened features. The soldier looks at once familiar and strange. More ghost than man. He belongs here in no-man's-land. When he holds out his arm and beckons with repeated rolls of his wrists, Andrew obeys, grateful for any contact with life in this place of death. He crawls through the mud, using bodies for cover. Then, as if tugged upwards by strings on his hands, he gets to his feet.

For more than an hour, the soldier leads Andrew through the dark landscape, between the trenches, always staying ten yards ahead. Eventually they see strands of barbed wire that look orange and golden as they loop up out of the mud. Sprawling against these are grey-green uniformed corpses, two or three deep, covered in clay and flies. The night is hot and windless. The horizon is shot with purple. It begins to rain again. As they approach the wire, Andrew can see it is draped with entrails. Men have been tortured by demons here; are being tortured still, their wounded cries unstanchable. The leg of one of the German bodies has been ripped off, leaving the ragged end of the femur sticking out. The other leg has been twisted back to front. What remained of the man's uniform has been ripped open to reveal a similarly ripped abdomen gaping with bowels. Steam is rising from them.

In the distance is a strip of land that, despite its bowl-shaped cavities, is recognizable as a track. The Menin Road. Andrew can make out a sign handwritten in English, HELLFIRE CORNER. The only other features in the landscape are grey, splintered trees and hedges of glistening wire. As his eyes focus, he realizes the landscape is also clotted with dark shapes. A distant party of stretcher-bearers runs between them looking for survivors. The ground is undulating and covered with coarse grass. After a few hundred yards, the gap between them never closing, the two men come to a river, snaking out, crossing the front line. With red moonlight reflecting on its rain-pummelled surface, it looks like a river of boiling blood. The soldier in front points to what looks like a giant turtle shell: half an empty wooden beer barrel part submerged in mud. Andrew recognizes the man now. They had been photographed together in the trench the previous night. He hesitates for a moment before wading out through the mud, pulling the barrel free and dragging it to the water's edge. With firm kicks he is able to push himself out into the current, his body resting on the convex centre. The river is deep. As he drifts away from the noise, he turns to wave his thanks, but the soldier is receding from view, a shadow returning to his line.

CHAPTER EIGHTEEN

London. Present day. Four weeks after the crash

'Good morning, Thomas.'

'Good morning, Mr Ibrahim.'

'Good morning, Vicky.'

'Good morning, Mr Ibrahim.'

'Good morning, Martha.'

'Good morning, Hamdi.'

An appreciative giggle erupted from the rest of the class.

'That's enough,' the teacher said in his gentle voice. 'Martha, see me at break.'

The child's plan had worked: she was to be given a chance to be alone with Mr Hamdi Said-Ibrahim.

As the ticking-off of names in the register resumed – 'Good morning, David . . .' – Martha closed her eyes and fantasized about being kissed by Hamdi. Although she was only nine, Martha knew about sex. Her father had told her about it, using the terms 'penis' and 'vagina', after she had appalled him with her ignorance by asking: 'Do you sex Mummy?'

Nancy had been furious. Both father and daughter learned from that episode. When Daniel had subsequently explained to Martha how Darwinian natural selection was proof that God did not exist, he had sworn her to secrecy, at least until she was twelve. Martha had agreed. She wasn't convinced by her father's arguments anyway, partly because he had been clearly wrong about sex. He had told Martha that sex and love do not become 'issues' for a girl until she reaches puberty at about the age of twelve. She knew this wasn't true because she regularly fantasized about being kissed by Hamdi. She was in love with him and, as soon as she was old enough, she was going to marry him. That was another reason why she thought her father might be wrong about God: Hamdi believed in God, only he didn't call his god 'God', he called him 'Allah'.

When the bell for break sounded, Martha remained at her desk. Hamdi didn't notice her at first as he was marking homework sheets. 'Martha,' he said when he looked up. 'Why are you still here?'

'You told me to see you in the break, sir.'

'Oh.' A faint smile. 'I did, didn't I. You were cheeky to me this morning, weren't you?'

'Yes, sir.'

'Why did you use my first name when I had told everyone to address me by my surname?'

'Because I like the sound of it, sir.'

Hamdi pursed his lips to suppress a smile. 'I want you to copy out the first five lines from this page.' He handed her an opened book of poetry. As Martha took it, Hamdi resumed his marking. Martha retrieved a pencil from his desk and surreptitiously snapped the point of it with her thumb. She took the pencil sharpener from the teacher's desk, sat down cross-legged on the floor at his feet and began sharpening the pencil into his bin.

'You don't have to do it here, Martha. You can do it at home.'

'I want to do it here,' she said.

Hamdi frowned and, after a minute, looked down. 'Are you all right there, Martha? That pencil is taking a lot of sharpening.'

Martha gave a shrug and jutted out her lower lip.

'Anything you want to talk about?'

Martha shrugged again. 'Is it true Muslim men have, like, lots of wives?'

★

At 3.30 that afternoon, Martha's class filed out into the playground and children began raising their arms when they spotted their mothers, or nannies, standing behind a yellow line. Hamdi shook hands with each child in turn as he checked them out. When it came to Martha's turn he gave Nancy a little wave and mouthed: 'Can I have a word?' He shook Martha's hand and said: 'I just want a quick word with your mummy.' Martha ran off to where a friend of hers was throwing a tennis ball against a wall.

'How is everything?' Hamdi asked, glancing at her sling.

Nancy tugged at her hair. 'Oh, you know. Surviving . . . Martha been OK?'

'Well, that is what I wanted to mention. She seemed a little upset today. Thought I should tell you.'

'Upset in what way? Crying?'

'No, she seemed like she needed a hug.'

'Oh.' Nancy looked across at Martha, who was dribbling the ball past her friend. 'Thanks.'

'Is she keeping up her cello practice?'

'Yeahyeahthanks,' Nancy said distractedly, eliding the words and bringing the conversation to an end.

'Her playing is coming along.'

'I know, yeah.'

Hamdi realized Martha's mother was not taking the hint. 'A cheque for the past two weeks would be fine.'

Back in the classroom, Hamdi untied his laces, removed his shoes and rubbed his stockinged feet. He enjoyed this moment in the day when the silence was heavy and enveloping. The unrolling of his prayer mat came next. The placement, facing east. The kneeling and the touching of his forehead to the mat in the same movement. The sitting back on his heels with his hands resting on his knees. In this way, five times a day, he absorbed the comfort of submission. When he had finished his prayers, he studied the article he had cut from the newspaper three weeks ago. SURVIVAL OF THE FITTEST, the headline read. Underneath this were the words: 'Professor swims miles to rescue fellow passengers when plane crashes into sea.' The photograph showed passengers being winched to safety by a helicopter. There was a map of the Galápagos Islands and an inset of 'Professor Daniel Kennedy'. Hamdi thought he had a kind face.

He got to his feet with a supple jump and looked in his drawer for his MP3 player and noticed a handmade card. Teachers were often given cards by the children – 'I love you' is one of the first things children learn to write and they like to leave cards, especially the girls. But this was different. His nine-year-olds had mostly grown out of it. And this one wasn't signed.

CHAPTER NINETEEN

DANIEL HAD INTENDED TO CYCLE TO THE HOSPITAL, BUT ON THE short walk from his front door to the shed where he kept his bike he had felt his brow dampen with sweat. He heard barking overhead, looked up and, through half-closed eyes, saw a skein of Canada geese flying north. They exaggerated both the silence they disturbed and that which they left behind. Migrating in December, he thought. That can't be right. He checked his watch with a double tap. It was 10am and already the day was stifling and oppressive. There was a smell of heating rubber and melting tar. Two days earlier there had been a silver rime on the grass. 'This weather is insane,' he said out loud. Feeling dizzy at the notion of cycling through traffic, he looked across the street to where his car was parked. It had air conditioning and cool leather seats. He would drive. The bonnet seemed hot to the touch as he trailed the back of his hand over it before clicking off the central lock with a double beep. Inside, he popped open the glove compartment and felt for his sunglasses and, as he slipped them on with one hand, began texting Nancy with the other. 'Have got car x.' When he started the engine, he was blasted by one of Nancy's hip-hop CDs. He ejected it, looked at the label – 50 Cent – and replaced it with Chet Baker.

As he approached Vauxhall, police cones reduced two lanes to one: a diversion. London had been raised from the severe to the critical security level for the past month, since the evacuation on Remembrance Sunday, but Daniel couldn't help moaning inwardly.

His destination, St Thomas's, was in view. The diversion would mean him having to cross over Vauxhall Bridge, only to double back across the river at Westminster. He drummed his fingers on the steering wheel and thought about how Bruce had tried not to alarm him about his headaches. He thought too about the way his friend had been questioning him about what had happened in the Pacific, what he had seen.

Daniel had not mentioned the turtle: partly because he did not think his friend would believe him; partly because he did not quite believe himself. He had also resisted telling Bruce about the young man he had seen, or thought he had seen, treading water. What could he say? That as someone newly in love cannot stop thinking about the object of their love, so he could not stop thinking about the young man in the water? That he was always on the edge of his mind? That he thought about him when he came down the stairs in the morning, and when he turned on his radio, and filled his kettle? Thought about him when he sat at his computer screen? Thought about him while delivering lectures, and having showers, and reading newspapers?

No. On balance, it was probably best not to mention this.

Daniel decided to analyse what had happened as if it were one of his scientific investigations: he would systematically rule out possibilities. What he 'saw' might have been something illusory, a sheet of water caused by atmospheric refraction by hot air, perhaps. More likely, the 'young man' had been a dugong or a manatee, the creatures which mariners used to call sea spirits. Perhaps it had been the turtle. Perhaps it had been a fisherman standing on a sandbank. He had seen sandbanks from the seaplane. And from his perspective in the water the waves would have made it look as if the man was appearing and disappearing. Except that his face had been familiar. The most plausible explanation was medical. Daniel had been dehydrated, traumatized and suffering from sunstroke. He must have been hallucinating. What was that thing called where healthy people reported seeing faces in the clouds, or on the moon? Pareidolia? Something like that. He would ask Bruce.

After driving across the bridge, he followed the police diversion down Victoria Street and into Parliament Square. In front of Westminster Abbey, he saw a ring of policemen jostling what looked like a row of shapeless, walking tents, women wearing burqas. He had heard on the news there was to be a demonstration outside parliament about a Muslim teacher who had been sacked from a Church of England school for teaching his class that Jesus was not the son of God, but a prophet of Islam.

As Daniel drew closer he wound down his window and could hear chants of *'Allahu Akbar!'* He could see Union flags and Stars and Stripes being burned for the benefit of a TV crew. An effigy was also in flames – judging by its makeshift mitre it was supposed to be the Archbishop of Canterbury – and the smell of burning hair made Daniel wrinkle his nose. It reminded him of the market in Quito. He had to squint to read some of the slogans on the placards: WHAT ABOUT FREE SPEECH FOR MUSLIMS? and LEAVE MUS-LIM TEACHERS ALONE. One bearded imam in white robes was waving his banner, pumping it up and down. It read: BEHEAD THE BLASPHEMERS! A younger bearded man was being escorted away by police. He was wearing a bandanna and an obviously fake vest of explosives: wires and tubes strapped on with duct tape. The faces of the men in the crowd were contorted in anger. Hands were punch-ing the air. Daniel scanned them without emotion and noticed that a policeman was doing the same, only with a video camera held to his eye.

It was at this moment that he saw a young man in a jacket and tie who was not shouting, whose features were composed, whose protuberant eyes were set wide apart. Recognizing him, Daniel swerved to the side of the road, causing the driver behind him to blast his horn, the pitch starting high then receding as the car passed. Daniel parked on an angle and lunged out of his own car, leaving his door open. As he jumped a concrete security block, a policeman with a machine gun on a sling turned and started running towards him, shouting: 'You! Back in the car! Now!'

Daniel stood still, held up his hands and called back: 'I have to see someone. He's over there.' He pointed. The young man was staring at him, smiling.

The policeman aimed his gun at Daniel. 'You cannot leave that car there, sir. Get back in. Now!'

Daniel returned to the car and climbed back in, all the while searching the crowd. He noticed the TV camera was trained on him now. He followed the diversion signs up Birdcage Walk and felt frustrated about being taken farther away from the hospital. Then he saw a ball of white light about a hundred and fifty yards ahead of him. At its centre a van lifted off the ground. A vibration that compressed the air against the small bones in his ear followed this sight almost immediately – a shock wave passing through the car, sucking out the oxygen. This was followed by a sullen thud.

CHAPTER TWENTY

Northern France. Last Wednesday of April, 1918

AS AN ACT OF WILL, THE MARKET TOWN OF NIEPPE HAS CHOSEN TO ignore the Great War, meeting its psychopathic rages with a shrug. Though German, French and British soldiers have, in their turn, marched through its square, they have carried on marching, visitors passing through. The town's only acknowledgement of the conflict comes in what it does not have. There is no water in the fountain and a tall building on the corner of the Rue de Bailleul has been stripped of its roof tiles by a stray shell, leaving a ribcage of charred beams. The window in the charcuterie has straw and empty crates on display – but the only meat hanging upside down from a hook is a solitary hare still in its fur. There are teenage boys running errands and old men sitting outside cafés playing dominos, but no young men. The streets are empty of them.

One of the few is a relative newcomer to the town, a bearded Englishman. Every morning he shoulders the haversack that holds the tools of his trade – a wrench, a set of spanners, a pair of canvas work gloves – and cycles from his lodgings on the Rue des Chardonnerets to wherever his work is taking him that day. He always rides his bike back home for lunch, however inconvenient the journey.

This is what he is doing as the church bells peel noon. In his basket is the baguette he has promised his landlady, Madame

Camier. She is a widow, her husband having been atomized by a German shell at Verdun. Andrew feels protective towards her. After her husband's death she had volunteered as a nurse at an advanced dressing station, but had been sent home on permanent medical leave after only four months: shrapnel having severed her left arm at the elbow. She was awarded the Légion d'honneur in compensation.

Andrew speaks little French and Madame Camier little English, but over the months they have been living under the same roof they have developed a non-verbal language, one of exchanged glances and suppressed emotions. There is a formality to their relationship that they both find reassuring. He addresses her as 'madame', she calls him 'monsieur'. Sometimes they listen to songs on the gramophone, or play cards, or read books, but more usually they sit together in companionable silence watching the fire burn down in the grate, listening to the echoey throb of a longcase clock. When nothing is left but embers, Andrew will bid her '*Bonne nuit*', and she will say 'Goodnight' – their private joke. They go to their separate rooms, she to her double bed with its brass frame, he to his single – and she will sometimes hear him screaming and wonder whether she should go in and comfort him. She did once and found him drenched in sweat, his eyes wide open in terror, still asleep.

Some of her neighbours were scandalized when she took in the young plumber from England. But she ignored their stares and whispers. Her neighbours had never been particularly friendly towards her anyway, coming as she did from another part of France, the Pyrenees. That was where she had met her husband, a cloth merchant on a business trip. He brought her back with him to Nieppe, away from her family and friends. They had two children and both were stillborn. Hers had been a lonely life, until Andrew Kennedy knocked on her door. Her late husband's clothes were a perfect fit.

Andrew is wearing them now as he cycles home through the sunlit morning: a leather jacket over a collarless shirt and waistcoat, a handkerchief knotted around his neck, a beret. His route takes him past the Château de Nieppe, a Flemish structure with gothic gables and a slender turret. He slows down to stare at it, as he always does, then freewheels along a cobbled path that leads him under a row of overhanging timber-built shops, their bellies bulging out into the street, casting it in permanent shadow. By the time he reaches the market square, the vibrations of the handlebars have left the palms of his hands pleasantly tenderized. As he crosses, the only sound, apart from the squeak of his brakes, is the clatter of a rope against a flagpole, paying out slack, then taking it up. Attached to it is a Tricolour, flapping lazily, stirred by a gritty breeze. The red, white and blue bands look beautiful to Andrew against the cloudless sky. Ugliness, the flag says, has no place here. An old man studies the young plumber from a bench by the market cross, his grizzled chin resting on his hands which, in turn, are balanced on top of a cane. The pug by his side looks up and trots towards the cyclist, its hackles raised.

'*Bonjour*,' Andrew calls out.

The old man nods and calls his dog back. It returns immediately, satisfied its territory has not been compromised. Andrew continues up between the line of gas lamps and poplars on the Rue d'Armentières and on past the town's unofficial tip – a discarded perambulator, a bicycle wheel, some bedsprings and a pile of rotting apples. He turns on to the canal path, a short cut to his lodgings, parks his bike up against the back wall, removes his clips and tucks the baguette under his arm. Madame Camier's house is not large but with its cream walls and blue-painted shutters it has a certain dignity and presence. When he reaches its gate, Andrew takes off his beret and flattens down his hair. He can see Madame Camier in the kitchen wearing a high, lacy collar under a damp pinafore. She is lifting clothes off a washboard laid across the sink. Her hair is pinned up but stray strands are hanging down and, as she emerges into the melting sunshine carrying a clothes basket under her arm, she blows at them out of the corner of her mouth. Her lips are not full but there is a softness to her face, an aura of downy hair that catches the light. She feeds a sheet into a mangle set up in the yard and, as she straightens her back afterwards, rests her hand on her hip, splayed fingers pointing backwards. She holds the sheet, now cardboard stiff, by its edges, one corner in her hand, the other in her teeth, and then, with rapid movements, she parachutes it open before snapping it crisply and billowing it out again. Andrew envies the sheet its proximity to Madame Camier. He also relates to its billowing. That is how he feels as he watches her, his soul floating gently outward, riding the warm air. Next she drapes the sheet over the line and puts two clothes pegs in her mouth. As he contemplates her golden, blurred beauty, Andrew forgets to breathe.

Adilah Camier is older than him by fourteen years. She seems taller than she is, the impression of height exaggerated by her slender figure and the coarse hair coiled up on her head. Ghosting in a rhombus of sunlight it looks reddy brown. Normally it is darker. Her brow is beaded with sweat. Andrew sees the high-collared shirt she is wearing has three buttons at the neck. It is pastel green: she no longer wears mourning black. The cuff of her empty left sleeve is pinned up to her shoulder. She frowns. Andrew frowns, too. Of what is she thinking? Her face clears and she smiles to herself. Her thoughts, Andrew concludes, are of him.

He checks his breath against a cupped hand and announces himself with a cough. When she does not hear this, he walks up behind her and places his hand over hers. She does not reel. Perhaps the sight of her late husband's cuffs reassures her. 'Allow me,' Andrew says, taking the peg.

Madame Camier closes her eyes and rests her head momentarily against the young man's shoulder. He can smell the soap on her skin. Half hoping she won't notice, he gently touches his lips to the crown of her head. She is breathing through her nose: rapid, shallow breaths. She turns to face him and something passes between them, a pulse, a look of almost sexual intimacy.

He follows her inside past a rocking horse in the hallway, its paintwork bright and unchipped. She carefully clears a space on the kitchen table, lays out two plates and holds the baguette with her knee so that she can cut it. They eat in silence, as though nothing has changed between them.

CHAPTER TWENTY-ONE

London. Present day. Four weeks after the crash

THE ONLY PERSONAL TOUCHES IN BRUCE GOLDING'S OFFICE WERE the signed photograph of Kylie Minogue and the Christmas decorations hung on the large yucca plant on his windowsill. The dust on them revealed that they had been up for more than a year. His desk was untidy: specimen bottles, a stethoscope and several trays stacked with files, magazines and medical books. Bruce himself was partially hidden by a flat screen. In his hands was a PlayStation console. He was wincing and pulling faces when he heard the explosion in the distance. He pushed his chair back on its rollers and swivelled around so that he could look out of the window across the Thames towards Buckingham Palace. There was a pall of black smoke rising over the buildings there. Without taking his eyes off it, he felt for his phone and pressed the conference call button followed by a speed-dial button. When a scratchy voice answered, he tilted his head towards the machine and spoke out of the corner of his mouth: 'You know those code words we were supposed to learn?'

'The emergency procedure codes?'

'Yeah. What's the one for a bomb?'

★

The van was in flames. Above it was a column of black, bubbling smoke. Daniel removed his sunglasses and watched in confusion as the cars behind it swerved. There was a sudden incongruous smell of fireworks in the air. Nitro-glycerine? Cordite? The flames were fifteen feet high. A water main began spraying. The traffic light across to his right was stuck on green. His iPhone interrupted his thoughts. He put it on speaker.

'Is that Professor Kennedy?' It was a woman's voice, brisk and confident.

'Associate Professor, actually.'

'My name is Kate Johnson, I'm a producer at the BBC. I work on *Forum*. I think we met once at a book launch. You were . . .'

'Who? I can't . . . There's been an explosion. A car bomb, I think.'

'Where? Where are you?'

'Birdcage Walk.'

'*Shit.*'

Already a cordon of police tape was going up in front of him and a policeman was standing in front of Daniel's car ordering him with urgent arm signals to drive down Queen Anne's Gate.

'Hang on, I have to move,' Daniel said. The road was now emptying of traffic. His senses sharpening with panic, Daniel saw broken glass ahead of him and looked up to see that some of the windows of the buildings around him had been broken. He found himself heading back down Victoria Street, where he pulled over to allow a convoy of three ambulances with lights flashing and sirens sounding to pass as they headed towards the explosion. There was now a helicopter overhead.

'I'm seeing pictures of it on *News 24*,' Kate Johnson said.

Daniel had forgotten she was still on the phone.

'You OK?' she added.

Though he had not exerted himself physically, Daniel was short of breath. 'I'm fine.'

'Did you see it happen?'

'Yes. Yeah.'

'A car bomb?'

'An explosion. It was a car, yeah.'

'You better get away from there. They often plant two near each other to maximize . . .'

'Can't move at the moment. Roads are blocked. I'll wait here.'

'Tell me what you saw.'

'It was about a hundred and fifty yards ahead of me. A van. Think it was black.'

'So it wasn't parked?'

'No, moving.'

'Must have been detonated by mistake.'

'I saw a flash, then saw the van lift off the ground, then I heard this dull thud. Couldn't see whether there was anyone hurt. There were cars swerving and broken glass everywhere.'

'Will you talk to one of our correspondents if I give them your number?'

'Sure.'

'Stay on the line a sec . . .'

The significance of the explosion was beginning to sink in. Daniel would have been driving directly behind the van had he not . . . He pictured the face of the young man at the demonstration. There had been recognition in his wide-set eyes. He had smiled. It was possible that the man had recognized him from his natural history series – that did happen occasionally, a fleeting shadow of uncertainty as they tried to place him. Where was the young man now?

'Daniel, are you there?'

'Yeah.'

'I'm looking at the pictures from the helicopter now. There seem to be three other cars that were caught up in the explosion.'

Daniel saw his reflection in the rear-view mirror. 'What were you ringing about, Kate? It is Kate, isn't it?'

'Yes. Right. Sorry. We were wondering if you could come on *Forum* tonight. Obviously this bomb might have changed everything but I think it is even more relevant now. We're discussing religious intolerance and thought you would have a good take on it.'

Daniel tried to sound nonchalant, but he had been hoping for this call for years. 'So you want a token atheist?'

Kate Johnson did not laugh. 'We've got a good line-up. A

bishop, a Muslim leader and the chief of police. Will you do it?'

'Sure. Count me in.'

'Great. It'll be live so we'd need you at the studios by ten. We'll send a car. Someone will ring for your address. I'll give you a proper brief later . . . Take care.'

As soon as he hung up, Daniel turned on the radio. A news bulletin was being broadcast. Police believed it was a car bomb. Three killed, four including the driver of the van, several injured. Daniel rang his father. Amanda answered.

'Have you heard?'

'Daniel?'

'Yeah.'

'Heard what?'

'About the bomb. Birdcage Walk. Turn on the TV . . . I forgot, you don't have a TV. Put the radio on.'

'Is anyone hurt?'

'Four killed . . . I saw it go off. There was this ball of light then I saw the van lifting off the ground. Can I speak to Dad?'

'He's having a nap,' Amanda said. 'I'll go and get him.'

'No, don't. Tell him when he wakes up that . . . I'm all right. Also . . .' Daniel hesitated. 'Tell him I'm going to be on *Forum* tonight. BBC2, ten thirty. I know you don't have a TV, but if you could tell him.'

'We do have a TV. It's in our bedroom.'

Pause.

'Didn't know that.'

Pause.

'He's always proud of what you do, you know, Daniel.'

'He is?'

'Course . . . By the way, has he said anything to you about his grandfather's letters? He's worried about them.'

'I know, I've left another message with the hotel manager in Quito. He's promised to FedEx them to us. I'll check my credit card bill to see if he has charged us yet.'

'OK. I just thought I'd mention it. You know what a state he gets in.'

165

The only indication that Bruce was a doctor was the photo ID badge dangling from a chain around his neck. In his black jeans and tight black polo shirt he looked more like a bouncer.

'There's something different about you,' Daniel said.

Without taking his eyes off the screen, Bruce held up a hand.

'Don't you ever do any work?' Daniel continued.

Bruce continued playing for a few seconds, weaving the console from side to side, before saying, 'Bollocks!' and tossing it down on his desk. He looked up. 'Don't you ever knock?'

'I did.'

'Hear the bomb?'

'Saw it,' Daniel said. 'I was driving towards it at the time.'

'Fuck.'

'Fuck indeed.'

'You OK?'

'Fine. A little freaked, but fine.'

'They took them to the Chelsea and Westminster. This place is on terrorism alert in case there are more. Had to clear a few beds.'

'Police think it was an isolated incident.'

'Yeah.' Bruce rubbed his hands together. 'Well, let's get on with it then. Pop your trousers and pants down. Have you brought a credit card?'

Daniel acknowledged the joke by putting his hand to his mouth, as if to cover a yawn.

'For some bizarre reason they won't let me charge for these scans. They should. When I'm running this place I'll make sure we do.' As he talked, Bruce flashed a light in his friend's eyes and ears. 'Actually, I do need you to take off your shirt.' He sounded his chest with latex-gloved fingers, pressed his fingers at various points on his back and neck and took his blood pressure. 'Normal,' he said, wrapping up the pump and applying an elastic tourniquet on the other arm. 'Better take some bloods. You OK with needles?'

'Fine, unless I'm having to stick them into Martha.'

'How is she? Any more hypos?'

'Not since the ice rink. Seems fine physically. We're a bit worried about her, about how the crash might have affected her, made her feel insecure.'

'You up to a pee sample?'

'Sure.'

'Through there then. There's a small plastic bottle with a label on by the sink. Leave it in there when you're done.'

Two minutes later, when Daniel reappeared, Bruce said, 'Follow me.' He held the door open and led the way to the lift. 'How you feeling generally?'

'OK. Still getting the headaches. What happened to the beard?'

'Peter decided he didn't like it.'

'Peter?'

Bruce turned and raised his eyebrows significantly. 'My new tenant.'

'How's that going?'

The lift door opened and they stood to one side as a bed was wheeled out.

'I'm in love.' Bruce's monotone did not change as he said this.

'Oh shit.'

'Don't worry. It's early days yet. He might be straight for all I know. He had some little slapper with him the other night, but it was obvious their relationship was platonic.'

'You were spying on him?'

Bruce drew himself up. 'I happened to be at my window when he came home with her. Wasn't what you would call, you know, a looker. Certainly not as beautiful as he is. Did I tell you he has big, sleepy brown eyes and cheekbones like wing mirrors?'

'Have you told Rob about him yet?'

Bruce raised a disdainful eyebrow. 'Robert and I are no longer speaking, other than through our lawyers.' The lift made a pinging noise and the doors opened. When they reached the scanning room, Bruce introduced Daniel to a radiographer, a round-faced woman with a bubble perm spilling over her green hospital gown. Bruce said goodbye, giving Daniel a reassuring pat on the back as he left.

The radiographer gathered her perm into a green paper hairnet and went through a medical checklist with the patient.

'Do you want me to change?' Daniel asked when she had finished.

'Not for a brain scan, but the MRI uses a very powerful magnet so it is best to empty your pockets. And it takes an hour, so if you need to go to the bathroom best go now.'

'Just been actually. Into a bottle.'

Daniel lay on his back and tilted his chin up so that he could see the mouth of the Magnetic Resonance Imaging scanner behind his head. It looked like a giant white doughnut at the opening of a tunnel. He felt he was about to be swallowed whole.

'Lie as still as you can,' the radiographer said, 'but breathe normally. Any movement can blur the scan. You'd better put these in.'

Daniel was handed some earplugs.

The radiographer went out to the control panel where she could see the scanning room through a window. 'OK, Daniel?' she said through an intercom.

Though Daniel felt lonely and anxious, he raised a thumb and a loud humming noise began. He felt himself being carried slowly backwards. Once his head was in the cylinder he heard a loud clanging. He closed his eyes and felt a sensation of tightness around the temples. As he lay there, claustrophobia stole over him: a flash-back to the air pocket on the plane.

In a blank-walled room in a glass and chrome office on the bank of the Thames, James Bloom, a thirty-eight-year-old, shaven-headed surveillance specialist on secondment from the CIA, clicked his mouse and froze the image on his screen. With a flick of his wrist and a second click, he zoomed in on a face in the crowd of Muslim demonstrators and simultaneously enlarged it so that it filled half his screen. He cocked his head and the blue glow of the screen reflected in his metal-framed glasses. 'Geoff?' he said without his eyes leaving the image. 'Come and look at this one.'

A lean, older man with a buzz cut appeared at his side and stared at the screen. His weathered face was cross-hatched with lines. He was wearing a suit and open-necked shirt. Geoff Turner was Bloom's liaison to the counter-terrorist section of the Metropolitan Police.

'Haven't seen him before. You?'

'Can't say I recognize him,' Turner said, chewing thoughtfully on the inside of his left cheek. 'Don't think he's a player. Would have noticed the shirt and tie. But send him over to me and I'll run a check.'

While Turner ran the image of the man in the shirt and tie against the hundreds of thousands in the database, Bloom tried to get audio on him.

Ten minutes later Turner said: 'He's a clean skin. The Passport Office have him. Second-generation British. Grandparents from Karbala. Not getting a criminal record. Doesn't even have a driving endorsement. He's a teacher. Should we do a nibble on him?'

'Can't hurt. One of the 7/7 virgin hunters was a teacher.'

Turner was studying the CCTV footage again. He tapped the screen. 'See this bloke here, the one getting out of the car? I know him. His name is Daniel Kennedy. He's the son of a friend of mine.'

That evening, feeling nervous and excited, Daniel laid three shirts out on the bed before settling on a blue one. He would wear it with an open neck, he decided, under a charcoal-grey suit. He checked his watch. Kate Johnson had still not rung to brief him. As the BBC car was not due to arrive for an hour, he flicked on to *News 24*. There was an item about the car bomb that the police thought had been detonated by accident. There was also footage of the demonstration. He scanned the faces of the protesters but could not see the young man he had recognized. The protest, according to the newsreader, was supposed to be a peaceful march by Muslim teachers but Islamist militants intent on provoking the police had hijacked it. It had also been co-ordinated with demonstrations in Damascus and Jakarta. And in Pakistan, the foreign ministry had called in ambassadors from Britain, France, Germany, Italy, Spain, Switzerland, Holland, Norway and the Czech Republic to explain that his government thought the sacking of the Muslim teacher an unjustifiable provocation against the Muslim world. In London meanwhile, the headmaster who had sacked the Muslim teacher had been receiving death threats and had been given twenty-four-hour police protection.

A reporter came on and spoke to camera: 'Muslim fury over the sacking erupted on to the streets of London today as politicians and religious leaders argued that there must be limits to free speech. The extremist faction that infiltrated today's protest is believed to be Hizb Ut-Tahrir, an Islamist splinter group. One of the protesters, originally from Pakistan but now living in London, said the sacking . . .' he looked down at his notes: '"degraded Islam".' The item cut to the protester, a young man. He was waving a placard bearing the slogan: BEHEAD THE ONES WHO INSULT THE PROPHET.

'The blasphemer who sacked this teacher should be punished!' he was shouting. 'If we had Sharia law in this country an insult like this would not happen.' The reporter turned to the chief rabbi, who said: 'The only way to have both freedom of speech and freedom from religious hatred is to exercise restraint. Without that, we can have one freedom or the other but not both.' He turned to a bearded spokesman for Lambeth Palace and asked if he thought the headmaster of the school could be prosecuted for unfair dismissal. 'We believe there is no case for doing that,' the spokesman said, nodding sympathetically. 'What the headmaster did was not gratuitously inflammatory. That said, we are truly sorry if we have caused any offence to the Muslim community. We believe the right to freedom of thought and expression cannot entail the right to offend the religious sentiment of believers, be they Muslim, Christian or Jewish.'

As he watched, Daniel muttered the word 'tosser' under his

breath. How typical of the Church of England to be so inclusive they employed a Muslim teacher in the first place – then so woolly they apologize for sacking him after he offended them. He reached for a notepad and began jotting down some ideas in preparation for his appearance on *Forum*, circling keywords and linking them with arrows. He would begin by arguing that it was up to Muslim leaders to caution their followers not to allow themselves to be provoked. Through their silence they were allowing extremists to hijack the controversy. He would argue that the government, as usual, was trying to deal with Muslim radicals by aiming its measures at the rest of us – religious hatred legislation, banning crosses because of concerns about veils, attacking all faith schools because they couldn't single out the madrassas. The present laws, he would argue, were aimed at a symptom of Muslim disaffection, not the malady itself. The problem was not that some excitable young men had set fire to the Union Jack – sorry, Union flag – but that they were defying the normal pattern of evolution by becoming less assimilated than their parents. This, he would conclude, was to do with changes within Islam. The 1979 Iranian Revolution was an epochal event that began to replicate itself across the world through a process of mimetic natural selection. This would bring the debate back to the biological ground where Daniel felt safest. He was feeling a rush of adrenalin at the prospect of his television appearance.

He checked his watch with a double tap of its face, got dressed and stared at his reflection in the bathroom mirror. His nose and forehead looked shiny. Would they use face powder in the studio? Where was Nancy's? He found her brush and dusted himself with it before taking several deep breaths to steady his nerves. He went downstairs, opened the fridge and took out some cooked sausages in a bowl covered with clingfilm and a bottle of HP sauce. He was running over some arguments in his head when his iPhone rang.

'Hi Daniel, it's Kate. Look, sorry I didn't get back to you earlier but you'll be relieved to hear you can stand down.'

'The debate is cancelled?'

'Um, actually we've got Richard Dawkins coming in now. We

double-booked because we didn't think he would be available.'

Daniel closed his eyes. 'No worries.'

'Sorry to mess you about. Let's get you on soon.'

Daniel sat at the kitchen table and began picking at the label of the HP bottle.

CHAPTER TWENTY-TWO

Northern France. Last Wednesday of April, 1918

THREE DAYS PASS BEFORE ANDREW AND MADAME CAMIER TOUCH again. It is evening. They are sitting with their chairs facing the fire, though he keeps shifting position so that he can cast a sideways glance at her, without her noticing. She is too present. The atmosphere around her too charged. It is as if her molecules extend towards him, spilling out, disturbing the air. The ticking of the longcase clock is excessively loud tonight. Each pulse fills the room, as if thickening the particles of dust. 'It is slow,' Madame Camier says, rising to her feet in one liquid movement. She adjusts the time by a fraction, and, as she closes the glass face, Andrew's hand covers hers. They are standing so close to one another he can smell her hair. His heart is hammering with such force it is rocking his whole body. She must be able to feel it. He wants to put his arm around her waist but its heaviness prevents him. She is breathing through her nose again – rapid, shallow breaths. Is she nervous? She yawns, frees her hand and stretches. If she turns and smiles, he thinks, it will be my permission to kiss her. She turns and smiles. He does not move. Cannot speak. The silence is raw. It is Madame Camier who breaks it. 'Goodnight,' she says.

'*Bonne nuit,*' he says.

★

173

A thick, steel gramophone needle is scratching against a 78-rpm disk. Major Peter Morris VC, MC & bar, DSO & bar, DFC, Mons Star, BWM, VM, does not notice it as he sharpens his razor on a strop of smooth leather hanging from the coat hook on the back of the door. After testing the blade with the side of his thumb he works his shaving brush up into lather and, eyeing his reflection in a small mirror, begins applying the white foam to his broken-veined cheeks. The act of tilting back his head to shave under his chin makes him wince and, once he has splashed his face with cold water and dabbed it with a thin khaki towel, he stares at the deep weal that follows his jaw line from chin to ear. This is his morning ritual. The scar has taken on a totemic significance for him, a savage reminder whenever he looks in the mirror of who he is now and what he stands for. The German who tried to cut his throat had not lived long. Morris had hacked his head off with an entrenching tool and tossed it, helmet still attached, over the parapet.

He is distracted from his staring by the specks of blood appearing on his cheek, watching as they grow in size, drip down over his chin into the sink, and mix sickeningly with the water. After splashing his face again, he looks around for a sheet of paper and tears off tiny strips that he uses as plasters. There is a further minute of staring before he becomes aware of the scratching being amplified through the gramophone horn. He raises the gooseneck, lifts the record off the box and snaps it across his knee. It breaks neatly in two. One half of the label reads, 'I'm Henery The'. The other half reads, 'Eighth, I Am'. Perhaps this is part of my punishment, Morris reflects. In my own circle of hell the only recordings available are from the music hall.

Standing in his vest and braces, with the towel draped around his neck, Morris takes from his wallet a tattered score of the first movement of Mahler's last completed symphony. He smoothes it out on the desk before him and contemplates it. It had been presented to him by the composer himself – the two had met for dinner in Leipzig in 1910 – and it is annotated in Mahler's own pencil marks: 'das Lied', '2×3, 3×2', 'der Abschied', 'mit höchster Gewalt'. It includes words in English, too. 'Like a shadow'. 'Love and hate'. 'Youth and death'. It is signed 'Gustav'.

In the restaurant that day, a young woman had come to their table asking for an autograph. After that, an excited chatter had run between the tables like an electric current, and the quartet playing waltzes in the background increased their volume and tempo. Mahler, awkward in wing collar and pince-nez, looked discomfited by the attention and when, at a murmured signal, three waiters simultaneously lifted the silver dish covers and an expectant hush fell on the restaurant, he looked as if he might be sick. Gradually, other diners lost interest and got on with their own meals. Morris was hungry and made short work of his braised duck with port wine, but Mahler barely touched his, instead pushing mushrooms around his plate with his fork. He was agitated. Morris, having heard the rumours about the composer's failing health, asked if he was unwell. Mahler shook his head and, in a subdued voice, confided his terror of writing a ninth numbered symphony – 'the curse of the Ninth', he called it. Beethoven and Bruckner had died soon after writing their ninth symphonies. So had Dvořák and Schubert. Mahler was afraid the same would happen to him. 'The ninth is a limit,' he said. 'The ninth circle of hell is the last. You can go no farther.' This, he explained, was why he had not given a number to the symphonic work – *Das Lied von der Erde* – which followed his Eighth, but instead described it merely as *Eine Symphonie für eine Tenor- und eine Alt- (oder Bariton-) Stimme und Orchester (nach Hans Bethges 'Die chinesische Flöte')*.

This confession brought him to the point of their meeting. He had written two versions of the opening and this, he said, handing over a score, was the more contemplative. No one knew about it and no one was to know, not while he was alive at least. The composer felt that for as long as it remained a secret, the symphony would remain uncompleted and he could go on living. Mahler wanted Morris to conduct it in London, but only after his death. A conductor himself, he had long admired Morris's integrity, as well as his light hand. He was convinced that only Morris could do it justice. Only Morris would understand the melancholy beneath the anger: the composer looking back over his life and saying goodbye.

Mahler's terror had been prescient. Shortly after completing the symphony he discovered he was dying. The doctors hadn't told him this in so many words, but he knew. He fell ill with a streptococcal blood infection and conducted *Das Lied* in a fever. He died soon after. And before Morris had a chance to conduct the alternative version, the war began.

Now, as his dove-grey eyes flit over the notes in front of him, Morris feels a tingling in his brow, as if some soothing balm has been applied there. His spirit is being raised to some higher meta-physical plane and an invisible hand is leading him to some inner world, the resting place of Mahler's soul. This version of the first movement seems to be more sublime, tender and full of hope than the original. Although he has memorized it, he cannot quite hear it in his head, yet. The prospect of conducting it in public one day is, he knows, his only bulwark against insanity, his only defence against the hounds baying at the door.

Andrew is whittling a stick in the garden, filling the hours until his next call-out in the afternoon. Four days have passed since he missed his moment to kiss Madame Camier, and he has been able to think of little else. She has been behaving as if it never happened. He begins to doubt himself. Perhaps nothing did happen. The sharp sky is empty and the warmth of the morning sun, after the cool interior of the house, is melting through to his bones. He rolls up his sleeves and plucks a blowzy white rose from the garden. It loses a couple of its petals as he removes its thorns.

'Is that for me?'

Andrew turns to see Madame Camier standing directly behind him.

'Have you no work today?'

'Not until this afternoon.'

Madame Camier considers this. 'Would you join me for a walk?'

'Where to?' He doesn't mean to say this. He should have said yes, of course he would.

'There is a river half a mile away. We could have . . . We say *déjeuner sur l'herbe*. What do you call it?'

'A picnic?'

'Yes, a picnic.' She gathers her skirt and walks inside the house. Ten minutes later she emerges carrying a small hamper under her arm. She puts it down as Andrew, having regained his composure, presents the rose to her with a half-bow. She holds it to her nose and tucks it behind the ribbon in her hair before reaching for the hamper again. There is fluency to her movements drawn from habit. Since her amputation, her simplest actions take on a three-stage complexity.

'Let me carry that,' Andrew says.

'I am fine,' Madame Camier says, putting the hamper down and lifting one side of it so that Andrew can lift the other. 'I am strong, you know.'

They walk slowly, following a path that skirts woodland, swinging the hamper between them, crackling beechmast underfoot. When they come to a stile, Madame Camier hands the hamper to Andrew, gathers her skirt up and climbs over. As she leaves the path to stroll in an arc, Andrew stays on it – and when Madame Camier catches up with him she begins treading on his heels deliberately. Smiling, he pretends he hasn't noticed. She overtakes, plucks a long feathery wild grass and, walking backwards, begins swishing at his face. It tickles. He tries not to laugh. They walk over a carpet of wood anemones, savouring the mushroomy, pine-woody smells, and reach a meander in the river where the water is sluggish and damselflies are skimming the surface with their gauzy wings. They lay the hamper down and break off chunks of bread. Madame Camier pats the ground beside her. Andrew shuffles over, avoiding a bed of nettles, enjoying the warmth of the soil under him.

Madame Camier throws a pebble and they watch the ripples slap and plunge against the reed-fringed bank.

Andrew uncorks a bottle of red wine, takes a swig from it and shudders at its warm and bitter taste before handing it over.

Madame Camier takes a sip, lights two cigarettes and inhales quick jabs of smoke before handing one over to him. They both lie on their backs, staring at a single fleecy cloud that has appeared. It is motionless. They blow languorous smoke rings to keep it company. When they finish they toss the butts in the river and listen to them hiss.

I can't stop thinking about you, Madame Camier.

Andrew wants to say this but the words will not come. Instead he lies on his front and studies her eyes. The colour changes according to the light, sometimes grey, sometimes blue. Now they appear green. When she closes them, he wants to kiss the lids. She raises her chin. His own eyes are closed. When he opens them again he can see her cheeks are flushed. She holds his hand.

Five minutes pass before Madame Camier sits up and reaches for some cheese, breaks off a piece and chews on it in silence. Andrew does the same. Knowing that the taste he is experiencing is the same as that which she is experiencing makes him feel an almost claustrophobic intimacy with her. They eat small rations of cold tongue and ham that Madame Camier has saved and both drink again from the neck of the bottle. Andrew thinks he has never felt happier and knows that he can never be as happy again – it would be impossible – a sweetly melancholic thought. He swallows and looks inside the hamper for a knife. When he finds one he uses it to try to cut off a small lock of Madame Camier's hair. It takes several attempts and only works when he makes the lock smaller.

'*Pourquoi?*' she asks.

'Proof.'

'Of what?'

'That you were here with me. The two of us alone.' He lies on his back with one hand pillowing his head and touches her lips with the tip of his finger. A moment later, when an old man appears on the opposite bank following the river path, Madame Camier smiles but Andrew turns pale. Strangers make him nervous. The old man looks across at them in puzzlement before becoming distracted by a smell that has reached his nose. He inspects the sole of each shoe in turn then continues on his way.

Madame Camier rests her head in the crook of Andrew's arm and slaps at a bluebottle on her calf. They both stare at the cloud, lost in their feelings, before sleep closes their eyes.

It is cooler when Andrew wakes, the sun having disappeared behind scudding clouds. Feeling dryness in his mouth, he opens and closes it several times, and his gummy noises wake Madame Camier. He scratches, props himself up on his elbows and realizes that it was the sudden coolness that woke him, as someone sleeping in front of a fire might be woken by a passing body. Madame Camier steps out of her dress to reveal that she is wearing a full-length swimming costume underneath, one that has sleeves long enough to cover her stump. She strides to the river's edge and hesitates a moment before jumping in. Andrew strolls over, stretching and yawning. The water is a greeny-brown, its undercurrents stirring up silt. When Madame Camier resurfaces, flicking her hair back and gulping for breath, Andrew asks: 'Cold?'

Madame Camier can't keep her teeth from chattering as she replies. 'N–no. I–t is l–lovely.'

The atmosphere is close and sultry. The river is smoking. 'Going to rain soon,' Andrew says in English. 'Midges are low.' As if in acknowledgement of this there is a distant roll of thunder.

'Come in.'

'Don't have my costume.'

'You don't need one.'

He looks around before slipping his braces and tugging off his shirt, trousers and boots, so that he is wearing only his long johns. As he removes the second boot, he hops on one foot. With his fingers pinching his nose he takes a running leap. The water is so cold that, when he comes up for air, he cannot, for a moment, breathe. Madame Camier splashes him. He splashes her back. After they have been treading water for a while, the cold begins to bite and they can feel the first pinpricks of rain. Soon large raindrops are puckering the surface of the water, and, as they fall more intensely, they bounce off it. On the bank, the dusty soil absorbs the water and begins to turn greasy.

'We must get our clothes undercover,' Madame Camier shouts

above the noise of the rain. As she scrambles out, she slips over. Andrew splashes after her, catches hold of her ankle and flops down beside her. Their cold, goosefleshed calves scrape together as Madame Camier struggles free and crawls on a few yards, laughing to herself. The soil is turning to mud and, as Andrew squelches it in his fist, he has a sense memory of the trenches. He smears the mud on his arms and over his long johns, which are sagging with the weight of water. As gently as he can, he rolls her over so that she is resting on one hip. This makes her sleeve slip back. Seeing him glancing at her stump, she reaches across to cover it with her hand. Andrew lifts the hand away and kisses the meld of skin where the amputation was performed. He kisses her neck, enjoying her involuntary shiver as his whiskers tickle, then he touches her mouth with his fingertip again. When she takes the finger in her mouth, the sudden sensation of warmth and wetness makes Andrew's heart dilate. He withdraws the finger in shock. They lie together, she with her back curled up to him, he with one arm looping under her neck, the other tucked under her knees, clinging to her, oblivious to the rain.

Andrew's next job is out of the town along a potholed lane corrupted by tussocky grass and lined with tall poplars. At the end of this he comes to a spinney. He recognizes it as the route he followed with Madame Camier three days earlier. The riverbank must be near. Why has she been so distant with him since that happened? Is she embarrassed that he saw her stump? Did she want him to kiss her? Why had he let the moment slip away once more?

There is blossom on some of the trees and lime-green buds on others. A smell of garlic and elderflower pricks the air. Andrew inhales deeply, not caring that he might be lost. Another lane hidden by thickening hedgerows leads on to a blue haze of open meadow. This looks more promising. On closer inspection he can see the ground is misty with bluebells nodding in the breeze. Beyond it is the farmhouse, his destination.

Two hours later he has sealed a leaking water tank and removed a dead pigeon that was blocking a drainpipe. On his way back to Nieppe, for the first time in months, he finds himself whistling. He stops at the Estaminet du Cerf for a glass of *vin de table*, a taste he has acquired. The waiter, a square-faced old man with coffee-coloured skin, is wearing a black waistcoat and carrying a white cloth over his forearm. He smiles when he sees his regular customer and pulls back a chair near the bar. As the café is empty, Andrew gestures that he would like to sit outside where he can watch people go by. The waiter returns with a gingham tablecloth, floats it open and spreads it over one of the outside tables. Without being asked, he brings a glass of red wine. Andrew likes this waiter. He is friendly and is the only brown-skinned man he has ever seen. Is he a negro? He has seen pictures of them. Perhaps he has come from one of the Empire countries, India or Australia. Except that he speaks only French. Andrew is certain that they speak English in Australia. He is halfway through his glass of wine when two British officers appear and, with the leather of their burnished boots creaking loudly, sit down at the next table but one. He studies their faces, their cap badges, the pips and crowns on their epaulettes. One is a lieutenant in the Royal Garrison Artillery, the other a major in the Rifle Brigade. They look the same age but the lieutenant is taller and, with his deep-set, soulful eyes, more handsome.

The major has bags under his eyes and wiry hair brushed forward. Below his right ear is a livid scar that follows the line of his jaw to his chin. Andrew has seen this officer before. He tries to recall his name. Morris. Major Morris. He had been sent to look for him in the trench at Ypres. Morris places his baton on the table and, in the same easy movement, tosses his cap beside it. A click of fingers and the waiter appears. '*Deux cognacs s'il vous plaît*,' he says, holding up two fingers.

With his boot, Andrew surreptitiously nudges his haversack under the table.

Once he has brought the cognacs, the waiter disappears behind the bar and reappears with an accordion strapped to his chest. As he starts to play, he winks at Andrew and mouths the words: '*Pour les touristes.*' Andrew has never heard him play before and soon realizes why: his talents as an accordionist are modest. He nevertheless keeps winking as he wanders back and forth, pleased with himself. Andrew waves him away. Apart from anything else, he wants to listen in to the tourists' conversation. He finds officers intimidating. They appear inhumanely composed and cold-blooded and, contrary to the myths, are more ferocious in battle than rankers. He pictures Second Lieutenant Willets screaming in rage as he led the charge at Passchendaele, moments before he was cut down. But the sound of English voices is nevertheless welcome.

These two are like old friends, addressing each other by their first names – Peter and what sounds like Rayf. They talk about acquaintances from their time at a place called the Royal College of Music, about concerts they heard in Paris and Vienna before the war, about composers they worked with: Ravel, Mahler, and – a name Andrew has heard before – Elgar. The one called Rayf makes jottings on a *Punch* magazine cover and, as he shows them to the other officer, he uses words that hold no meaning for Andrew: 'tonality', 'pianissimo', 'counterpoint'. The obvious conclusion, that they must have been musicians in Civvy Street, is confirmed when the waiter comes close and they stare at him until, sensing their disapproval, he stops playing the accordion.

Morris takes a sheet of paper from his wallet and smoothes it down on the table. Andrew hears the words 'Mahler's Ninth' but does not know what they mean. The one called Rayf studies the paper, nodding thoughtfully, then he gestures for the waiter to hand his accordion over. As he takes it he runs his fingers over the keys for a moment, getting used to the shape of the instrument, then he plays a passage of music so soft and lyrical it makes Andrew want to sink to his knees. He has never heard a more haunting sound in his life. The officer stops abruptly, breaking the spell. Running his finger along one of his jottings, he becomes immersed once more in conversation. The unfamiliar words again. Without looking up, he holds the accordion out to be collected. The waiter takes it away and returns with a piece of paper. He hovers over the lieutenant briefly before placing the paper on the table and saying in heavily accented English, 'Please, monsieur, your autograph. *Merci.*' As the officer signs with a flourish – he is clearly used to such requests – he looks down his shoulder directly at Andrew, but he pays no attention to him, as if looking through him. Andrew wipes his wet eyes with the heels of his hands. The waiter reads the paper and does a half-bow. 'Monsieur Vaughan Williams. This is an honour.'

Major Morris takes the copy of *Punch* now and begins scribbling something across the bottom of the cover. When he has filled the white space he moves to the inside front page and then on to the next page and the next, until half the magazine is filled with scribble. Vaughan Williams reads over his shoulder, nodding to himself and occasionally tapping the page with a finger.

The conversation between the officers tails off as a young woman wearing a lacy shawl around her shoulders walks past and smiles at them.

'Was she smiling at you or me?' Morris asks.

'Both of us.'

'I thought so. How much do you suppose?'

'Perhaps she will give a group discount.'

'A liberator's concession.'

Andrew takes a copy of *Le Temps* out of his bag and unfolds it. He has been reading the same edition for weeks, trying to improve his French. When the officers drain their glasses, toss some coins on the table and scrape back their chairs, Morris looks across at him, noticing him for the first time. His eyes are hard and wintry; filled with suspicion. The two men regard each other for a moment then Morris gives a terse nod, picks up his baton and cap, and breaks into a jog as he catches up with Vaughan Williams, who is following the woman down the street.

Andrew scratches his beard distractedly and orders another glass of wine. And another. When this comes he asks the waiter to leave the bottle. It is unlabelled. There is half a litre of wine left in it. As he drinks, he can feel a prickly heat across the nape of his neck. It reminds him of the tot of rum he had been given before going over the top. His confidence is evaporating. When he stands unsteadily, he reaches in his pocket for some coins, takes out a handful of holed five and ten centimes and, as the officers did, slaps them down next to the empty bottle. As he lurches past the table where the two officers had been sitting, he notices they have left behind the copy of *Punch*. There is cross-hatching in the white space in the letter P, but most of the doodling on its cover is, he sees, musical notation. When he picks it up he sees the sheet of paper concealed under it. More music. He slips the sheet of music inside the copy of *Punch*, then rolls that up and stuffs it in his haversack.

It is dusk by the time Andrew returns to his lodgings and tries to lift the latch-tongue on the front door. As it is stuck, he uses his shoulder to force it. It opens with a clatter. The shutters are closed. Madame Camier is standing by the fire. She has changed into her Sunday clothes. Her hair is down, covering the pinned-up sleeve. They look at each other for a moment before she takes a step backwards, causing her skirt to rustle. Andrew sways before striding over. He pinions her wrist with one hand, rests his hand on her hip with the other, and kisses her. She does not protest. Emboldened by this, he tugs open her starched collar and moves his hand under her blouse. She frees herself, steps to one side and holds up a finger. '*Un moment*,' she says. It takes her several attempts to blow out the two candles on the fireplace and several more to unbutton her blouse, one-handed, to reveal a whalebone corset. Turning her back to Andrew she says: 'Please.' He unlaces it with trembling fingers and wonders how she managed to lace it up in the first place. With the waxy smell of snuffed-out candle lingering in the air, she again turns to face him and shrugs her shoulders forward to help him remove the bodice. With her eyes fixed on his, she pushes her silk petticoat over her hips and lets it sigh to the floor. Stepping out of it, she clears a space at the end of the kitchen table, pushing back a pepper grinder, a colander, and a heap of garlic bulbs and courgettes that make rubbery squeaks as they rub together. She sits down. In the long, dancing shadows from the fire, she balances one of her lace-up boots on the back of a chair, unclips a stocking and rolls it down over her knee and calf, leaving it ruched on her ankles. She does the same with the other leg before holding out her hand. As Andrew steps towards her, he removes his jacket and lets his braces fall. She runs a fumbling hand under his shirt. When he tugs at her camisole she raises her arm and her stump above her head to help him, revealing an attenuated web of black hairs under her armpits. He cups her small breasts with his hands, kisses her shoulders and glances at the pursed scars on the end of the stump. When he tries to kiss them too, she recoils. Even in the amber glow of the fire her skin is as translucent as alabaster. Her nipples, when he directs his attention to them, are as hard as dried figs. She shivers as he flicks and circles them with his tongue. In a gesture of trust, she rotates so that he can kiss her raised stump. The skin feels coarse to his lips. Still sitting, Madame Camier hitches up her skirt and opens her legs. Andrew glimpses a dark triangle. He feels her legs moving around his waist. The mallowy softness of her thighs against his hips makes him shudder and close his eyes. As he works his hands underneath her, she arches her back so that he is half supporting her, feeling the heft of her body. She touches his beard tenderly with her hand and, as they kiss again, he feels a billowing sensation from his feet to his head. Her sudden enveloping warmth makes him cry out, as though a bullet has ruptured his heart.

Afterwards, a moment later, Andrew's body sags until he is sitting on the chair with his face buried in Madame Camier's lap. As he feels her fingers stroke his hair, he sobs drily, quietly at first then convulsively until his sobbing turns to laughter.

They sleep in the same bed for the first time that night and, in the morning, make love again. When it is over, Andrew feels the same post-coital tristesse he felt the night before, but it lasts only a brief time. What he feels most, as he brings the sheet up over their naked bodies, is relief, a sense of having been frozen and now melting, a glacier sliding into the sea. That morning, as she lays her head on his arm, Andrew calls his new lover Adilah for the first time. He notices that her bedroom smells of camphor and determines that, in whatever time remains to him, in whatever time he can borrow, he will make love to her here every morning and every evening, and, work permitting, every lunchtime, too. Love, he reasons, is all he has left, all he has to throw at death, his only protection against the firing squad. Only lovemaking can blot out his thoughts, cauterize his fears, quell the terrors of his sleep.

He dresses as he walks downstairs, humming to himself and trailing his fingers along the wall. A wash of sunlight is slanting through the windows. As he waits for the pan on the stove to boil, he checks in his haversack and finds the copy of *Punch* the officers in the café had left behind. He freezes when he reads the date under its masthead. It is a recent edition: 10 April 1918. The war has gone on without him, and is going on still.

CHAPTER TWENTY-THREE

London. Present day. Five weeks after the crash

AS HE FUMBLED IN HIS JACKET FOR HIS PADLOCK KEYS, DANIEL hunched up his shoulder to try to prevent the water trickling down the collar of his cagoule. The posture suited him. Whenever it was his turn to do the school run he would play, as subtly as he was able, the reluctant martyr. It wasn't that he objected to the 4×4s – though he did – it was that he would come away feeling unkempt and, in some hard-to-define way, fraudulent. Other fathers appeared richer and more secure. They seemed more mature, too, making both an effort to talk about house prices and to look presentable: they brushed their hair, polished their shoes and had creases in their trousers. Their Audis and BMWs looked new and clean. Daniel always felt as if he was being judged as he cycled into the playground in his tracksuit.

This pattern of reluctance ended on the afternoon he saw Hamdi Said-Ibrahim.

The rain eased, turning the trees on the common into a fuzzy wool that merged with the blur of the passing cars and joggers. By the time he cycled into the playground, the rain had stopped altogether and weak sunshine was causing steam to rise from the tarmac. He dismounted, removed his helmet and saw Martha wave at him. She kept her hand in the air as she tried to catch the attention of the teacher, who had his back to her. When she walked in front of him and pointed at Daniel, he noticed her, looked across at Daniel, smiled in acknowledgement, and shook the child's hand. Martha ran towards him trailing her school bag and, when she reached him, he picked her up and swung her in the air.

'Who's that?' Daniel asked, shielding his eyes against the sunlight. Martha blushed guiltily. 'That's Mr Hamdi Said-Ibrahim, my form master.'

Hamdi was the man Daniel had seen at the protest. His gentle, bulging eyes were unmistakable: a hyperthyroid condition, presumably. He must have smiled at Daniel because he recognized him: from school runs and PTA evenings. Daniel shook his head. 'I recognize him,' he said. 'How long has he been working here?'

'Since halfway through last term.'

'What did you say his name was?'

'Hamdi Said-Ibrahim. He's a Muslim.'

'What does he teach?'

'Everything. He's training to be a full-time music teacher. Takes me for cello in music club. Yesterday he taught me a passage from Mahler.'

Daniel's euphoria changed to relief. The man he had 'seen' treading water in the Pacific Ocean might have been a figment of his imagination, but at least the figment was based on a real person.

As Daniel cycled home across Clapham Common, with Martha following on her bike a few yards behind, his relief turned to an odd sense of gratitude. Whether he knew it or not, Hamdi, or at least a simulacrum of Hamdi, had saved him. He had, after all, been trying to take his life jacket off when 'Hamdi' distracted him. He had stayed afloat. In terms of timing at least, there was a connection between the hallucination and his being saved. Daniel decided to send the teacher a present by way of thanks. A bottle of champagne. No. Hamdi was a Muslim. A CD box set. That would be better. Mahler. He could order it online, when he got home. He tried to think of a message – something along the lines of 'thank you for saving me' – but realized whatever he wrote would sound insane, so he would send the gift anonymously, next day delivery.

The phone rang. Nancy answered. 'Is that Mrs Kennedy?' The voice was graceful and measured.

Nancy hesitated. People often assumed she was married. 'Speaking.'

'It's Mr Said–Ibrahim from the school. I was wondering if I could have a quick word with you and your husband one afternoon this week. Or first thing, if that would be easier.'

'Anything wrong?'

'No, no. Not at all. But I would like to see you both together if that's possible.'

'Of course. This afternoon? Martha is going back to a friend's house for tea.'

'Should we say three forty-five? I'll be in the classroom.'

Nancy was surprised when Daniel readily agreed to the meeting. He normally tried to get out of school events.

Hamdi was sitting at his desk marking homework when Nancy tapped on the door.

'Thank you for coming at short notice,' Hamdi said, standing up and crossing the classroom to shake hands. 'Can I get you a coffee?'

'No, we're fine,' Nancy said.

'Take a seat.' Hamdi gestured apologetically at two children-sized chairs in front of his desk. 'Sorry.'

When Nancy and Daniel sat down, their knees were almost level with their chests. They both sniffed and looked around. The classroom smelled of glue, gym socks and Cup-a-Soup. There were essays on the wall, a project about Ancient Egypt, a paperchain, an overhead projector and a blackboard which had the day's date written in chalk and the word 'equations' underlined twice. There were also piles of Oxford Reading Tree books, colourful trays stacked with textbooks and pots of pencils sharpened to fragility and leaking smells of carbon.

Hamdi came straight to the point: 'Is everything all right at home?'

The couple looked at one another in surprise.

'Martha has been behaving oddly,' Hamdi elaborated. 'She seems unable to concentrate in class. Hasn't been her usual, carefree self. And the thing is, I wouldn't normally mention this as it is bound to happen from time to time, but she seems to have developed . . .' He shifted uncomfortably. 'How can I put this? She has become a little fixated with me.'

Daniel noticed Martha's handwriting on one of the fact boxes on a volcano project. He saw, too, a chart of stars by pupils' names and Martha's had the most. His eye fell on the news cutting on the board behind the teacher's desk: SURVIVAL OF THE FITTEST. Hamdi followed his eye. 'Martha brought it in to show me,' he said. 'She's very proud of you.' He paused again. 'She's been bringing in quite a lot of things for me. Gifts, I suppose you would call them. She leaves them in my desk.'

'Gifts?' Nancy asked, folding her arms defensively.

'Cards that were unsigned but in her handwriting. Lines of poetry. Pictures she had drawn. Chocolates. When a half-used bottle of aftershave appeared, I did wonder then whether I should say something.' From his desk he produced a black bottle of Calvin Klein Eau de Toilette Spray.

'I wondered where that was,' Daniel said.

'But I didn't want to embarrass her,' Hamdi continued. 'And I assumed the phase would pass. I decided I would slip the aftershave into her satchel at the end of term. Then a CD box set arrived. There was no message attached so I rang the internet store and was told it was paid for by a credit card belonging to a Dr Daniel Kennedy.'

Daniel found it hard to take all this in. He watched Hamdi's lips move but could not concentrate on what he was saying, the words slipping through his mind like mercury through open fingers. It was partly to do with Hamdi's appearance − androgynous, almost sexless − partly with his voice. It was unnaturally neutral and elusive, like soft rain. Daniel could not detect an accent, something he was normally good at. And he found Hamdi's expressions impossible to read, too, as if he was slightly out of focus, as though he had no edges. Yet for all his impersonality, Hamdi appeared familiar to Daniel, as if he had known him all his life. It was to do with the way his eyes bulged, a pressure of acuity.

Nancy had no difficulty concentrating on his words. 'Thanks for being so tactful, Mr Said-Ibrahim.'

'Please, call me Hamdi.'

'We'll have a word with her.'

'And if there is anything you want to talk about regarding Martha, please feel free to call me at any time. My home number is on the school list. She is a gifted little girl.'

As had become her habit since the crash, Nancy did not wear her seat belt in the car on the way home. She was in the passenger seat and when she reached in the ashtray for a pound coin and slipped it under her bra Daniel asked, 'What are you doing?'

'It's so I don't forget to leave it under Martha's pillow tonight. When I get undressed it will fall out and remind me.'

'Why do you want to leave a pound under her pillow?'

'She lost a tooth this morning.'

'But she doesn't believe in the tooth fairy.'

'She believes in money.' Nancy studied Daniel's face. 'What did you make of Hamdi?'

'Seemed nice.'

'He's right, you know. She has been behaving oddly. I think we need to get some play dates and sleepovers sorted out for her. I don't think she's mixing. Not eating properly either. Small for her age. We should have family mealtimes.'

'What about getting her to a child psychologist?'

'Couldn't hurt.'

'Think I should be the one to have a word with her, father to daughter.' Daniel tapped the steering wheel. 'As it was my credit card she used.'

He looked at Nancy and fancied there was a cloud of suspicion in her eyes, but he dismissed this – she couldn't have known that he had no intention of having a word with Martha. When he got home he went to his study and phoned Hamdi.

'Hello . . .' Daniel couldn't remember the name; it slipped through his mind, unable to find traction.

'Hamdi.'

'It's Daniel, Martha's father.'

'Professor Kennedy. Hello. Thank you for coming to see me . . .' That unplaceable voice again, part warm beer, part Arabian incense. 'I hope you didn't think I was being melodramatic.'

'No.' Daniel hunched his shoulders and spoke in a low voice. 'I'm glad you asked me. Contrary to what Nancy and I said, we have been under strain since the plane crash. This may be why Martha has been behaving oddly.'

'I see. Thank you for letting me know . . .' Silence. 'Was there anything else?'

There was hesitation in Daniel's voice. 'I know this is going to sound odd, but I have a feeling I've seen you before.'

'I've been at the school since the middle of last term.'

'No, somewhere else.'

It was Hamdi's turn to hesitate. 'I believe you saw me at that demonstration outside Parliament.'

'Yes, I did see you there.'

'I wasn't taking part, you know.' Hamdi sounded anxious. 'I was passing. Went over to have a look. I was curious, that's all.'

'No, no. I wasn't suggesting . . . I was passing, too. But it wasn't there I was thinking of. Have you always lived around Clapham?'

'Only for six months. I was at Birmingham University before I came here.' He paused. 'I read music. A doctorate. My plan was to teach music at university, but nothing has come up.' Another pause. 'I think when they see my name on the application . . . I've considered changing it.'

'You should come along to Trinity. I'm there most days. Ask the porter to ring for me and I'll sign you in. The music professor is a friend of mine. I could introduce you. It can't hurt.'

'Thanks. That's generous. Remind me, what is it you teach there?'

Daniel hesitated. He had come to accept from years of awkward moments at dinner parties that nematology was a discipline so obscure it could not pass without explanation. And when he did explain it, people always sounded embarrassed on his behalf. He thought he had perfected a technique for sparing people the awkwardness – and he deployed it. 'I'm a nematologist. No, I hadn't heard of it either. It's an obscure branch of zoology.'

'I have heard of zoology. You study elephants and tigers.'

'Not exactly, I study worms.'

'Oh.'

'So where were you before university?'

There was silence.

'I'm sorry, Mr . . .'

'Hamdi.'

'I don't mean to sound nosy, I just . . .'

'It's OK, professor.'

'Associate professor. But call me Daniel.'

'My family live in Birmingham. My parents were born there. My grandparents came to this country in the fifties.'

'From?'

'Iraq. Karbala.'

'Ever been there?'

'Been asked . . .' Hamdi hesitated. 'But it is a dangerous place.'

'Sectarian tensions?'

'No, everyone in Karbala is Shia. It is a holy city, a place of angels. A thousand came down from heaven in the ancient days and never returned.'

Daniel fell silent. He was finding it hard to concentrate on Hamdi's words again. They were evaporating like breath on a mirror.

'Hello? Professor Kennedy? Are you still there?'

'Yes, I'm still here. Look, I'd better go. I'm serious about Trinity. And call me Daniel.'

Daniel sat at his computer screen and self-consciously googled the words 'guardian angel', barely able to look at his screen as he typed. His 'angel', after all, had inverted commas for feathers. There were thousands of results, flapping in the electronic ether like trapped birds. He found most of the sites too nauseating to open: New Age offers to 'identify who your guardian angel is, based on your birthday'; or sites promising to show photographs of 'angels' supposedly seen in the smoke clouds of the falling Twin Towers. One, under the heading 'how to recognize an angel by its smell', intrigued him enough to click on it: according to medieval angelology, he read, angels were accompanied by an aroma associated with angelica, an ingredient in cakes and puddings. He smiled and shook his head. A site dedicated to Shackleton's claim that he experienced a 'guiding presence' as he crossed the mountains of South Georgia looked promising, but turned out to be more nonsense.

It took a news site to make his eyes widen in appalled disbelief: a *Time* magazine poll revealed that 78 per cent of Americans believed in angels, while 63 per cent believed they had their own guardian angel. Unsure what it was he was looking for, he continued scrolling until he reached a pseudo-academic-looking site dedicated to something called the Royal Society of Angelology. There was indeed a royal crest, as well as a detail from Fra Angelico's 'The Annunciation' and a brief history of the society, but that was all. The society had been founded by the Duke of Norfolk in 1615 and given a royal warrant by King James I the following year. A chair had been founded at New College, Oxford, but no one had held it for more than a century, it having been amalgamated with the theology and philosophy chairs. 'Belief that God sends a spirit to watch every individual was common in Ancient Greek philosophy,' he read in an introduction, 'and Plato alludes to it in *Phaedo*, 108. But it is with the Judaeo-Christian tradition that angelology is more commonly associated. The Hebrew for angel is *mal'akh*, which originally meant the "shadow side of God" but came to be translated as "messenger" . . .' Among the patrons listed was one Professor Laurence Wetherby. Daniel reached for his copy of *Who's Who*. Wetherby's entry listed 'angelology' under his interests, along with 'humiliating modernists and liberals'. Daniel tapped his teeth with a pen, nodded to himself and sent Wetherby an email.

Martha returned from her friend's house and ran up the stairs, as she always did, to see her father. 'What you reading, Daniel?' she asked.

Daniel was smiling. 'Nothing important. And call me Daddy.'

Martha jumped on his lap. 'Can I see?'

'No.' He tickled her ribs. 'It's private.'

'Is it porn?'

His ringtone interrupted further discussion. Though there was a photograph of a grizzly bear flashing on the iPhone screen, Daniel hesitated before picking it up. The phone was also on vibrate and as it rang it turned slightly on its axis. 'Bear,' he said in a voice that sounded calmer than he felt.

'Hi, Dan. Where are you?'

'Home, just sitting with Martha. Say hello to Bruce, darling.' Daniel pressed the iPhone to his daughter's ear.

'Hi, Uncle Bear. He won't let me read his emails.'

'Emails from who?'

'Whom.'

'Whom.'

'Don't know. Says they are private.'

'Quite right too. You on the same insulin dosage as before?'

'Yeah.'

'Any more hypos?'

'Nah. My doctor says I'm allowed to self-administer soon.'

'Great. Can I have Daddy back please?'

'He wants to speak to you.'

Daniel took the phone. 'So what's up?'

'Just wanting to arrange a time for you to swing by my office.'

'My test results?'

'Yeah.'

Martha signalled for the phone back. Daniel put his finger in the air. 'So what do they say? Pass? Fail?'

'When can you come in?'

'Can't you tell me over the phone?'

'Probably best to come in, then I can go through them with you, urm, you know, properly. How are you fixed for this week?'

'Thursday morning would suit me best.'

'Great. See you then.'

'Should I be worried? Hello? Bear?' He looked at Martha. 'Gone.'

As he stared at the phone, Daniel's fingers rose slowly to his scalp and began to massage.

CHAPTER TWENTY-FOUR

WHEN AN ANNOUNCEMENT WAS MADE OVER THE PUBLIC ADDRESS system that the Deutsches Rundfunkarchiv was closing in half an hour, Hai-iki buizi Yzu shook her wrist and held her watch to her ear. It was working, but the hours had crept up on her. Since ten that morning she had been checking the collection of drafts for Mahler's symphonies – one to eight – in the hope of finding something relating to the Ninth. A doodle. An annotation. A sketch. It had been laborious work, not least because each symphony comprised a box of around 160 separate sheets of music. It didn't help that Mahler, out of superstition, had avoided referring to the Ninth as the Ninth. He had been a prodigious and messy scribbler with a spidery scrawl and a propensity for crossing out – and the hours of hard concentration were making Hai-iki's eyes sore and bringing on a headache. Also she felt sick, or at least she had in the morning session, which was why she had wanted to leave that afternoon in time to get to a chemist. The other reason was that her period was late.

She had been feeling frustrated anyway. The previous two days she had been working her way through the Mahler family letters and diaries for 1908–1910, the ones held at the Abteilung Potsdam, but her research had produced none of the material Wetherby had assured her it would, and she was dreading telling him this. There was something about him that made her want to please him all the time. It wasn't just that he was the master and she the pupil, it was more to do with his vulnerability. On the one occasion when he had struck her he had been so contrite afterwards she had found herself feeling sorry for him. Besides, she knew she had provoked him. She had wanted to play a sex game, had thought that was what he wanted. He would be the submissive and she the dominant – insulting him, slapping him, calling him a worm. She had not bargained on his self-esteem being so low. She pictured him now – his look of wounded dignity, his soulful eyes, his expressive hands – and felt a rush of longing. She loved his fierce intellect, his dry humour, his tenderness when they kissed. She loved him.

There was a loud click as she shut her laptop. She smoothed her hands over its lid, lost in thought, then coiled up its lead and gathered the two remaining archive boxes under her arms before returning them to the front desk and heading for the antiquated wooden lifts – 'continuation chambers' that Berliners hopped on and off as they trundled slowly up and down without stopping. The lifts had been the height of modernity when the archive was built in the 1930s. In fact the whole building, triangular in shape with interlinking courtyards and covered throughout with dark brown glazed tiles, had been considered a fine example of Third Reich architecture: futuristic, angular, Teutonic. That it had survived the carpet-bombing of the war was a mystery to the local residents. It was the only building for miles around that hadn't been reduced to rubble.

As Hai-iki stepped outside into the Berlin suburb of Charlottenburg, she inhaled the *Berliner Luft* and turned up her collar. Although sticky spring buds were appearing on the beeches and oaks, a wintry chill was in the air. The days were still short, too. The streetlights were warming up. A giant radio transmitter opposite the Rundfunkarchiv was a silhouette. In the gloom, farther down the street, Hai-iki could make out a stumpy cylindrical column carrying theatre schedules, and several yards beyond that a small, green neon cross above a shop window. The blue-coated pharmacist was about to bolt the door as she reached it. When she asked for a pregnancy testing kit in her rough German, the man looked confused. But when she asked again, this time also describing with her hand an exaggerated shape of her belly, he nodded. A tram took her to the door of her hotel on the Albertstrasse. She ripped open the packet and drank a glass of water as she read the instructions. Five minutes later she returned from the bathroom, lay on her bed and stared at the indicator tube to see what colour it would turn.

Wetherby, fastidious and elongated in a double-breasted chalk-stripe suit, considered the hateful object on his desk, one of the flatscreen computers that had recently become standard issue for members of staff at Trinity. He didn't mind the laptop he was obliged to use, because that could be folded away and hidden, but the desktop was a permanent affront to his aesthetic sensibilities, squatting on his desk in a space that should be occupied by books. He moved his mouse so that the cursor was hovering over the first of six unopened emails, all from the same sender. She was still in Berlin, still waiting for a 'discovery' to fall into her lap, still letting him down. He should have known better than to entrust such delicate research to an undergraduate. And now she was becoming high maintenance, making emotional demands, declaring her devotion to him, expecting some level of commitment or reassurance from him in return. He enjoyed her company, enjoyed listening to her play the piano, enjoyed talking to her about the great composers. But he had no need of an acolyte at this stage in his career, not even one who allowed him to sleep with her. He hesitated then logged off. He knew what the emails said anyway. She had been sending them for the past two days, as well as leaving messages for him on his home answering machine.

A rapid triple knock distracted him. A head framed by a thick bob of dyed blonde hair appeared around the door. 'Dr Kennedy to see you,' the secretary said.

Wetherby stared at her over the rim of his half-glasses.

'You had a meeting with him at eleven.'

Wetherby rolled his eyeballs upwards in the manner of St Peter. 'I remember now, I did. Show him in. Oh and . . .' The head reappeared. 'Could you check something for me regarding student visa applications?'

'Sure.'

'I believe foreign students need to obtain permission from the Home Office before they are allowed to travel abroad in term time on a student visa. Could you get chapter and verse on that for me? Find out what the implications are in terms of deportation. Thank you. And do send in Dr Kennedy.'

As the secretary disappeared, Daniel appeared, grinning broadly. Wetherby eyed him, his gaze moving down his body then up, taking in the hipster jeans and the V-neck jumper worn over a blue-and-white-striped matelot shirt. '*Danny*,' Wetherby said with undue emphasis as he rose from his chair and extended a hand. 'How are you? Recovered from your ordeal?'

'More or less. Good to be back at work.' Daniel was distracted by the fireplace, a tall and wide construction made from puce and grey marble banded by diagonal seams of turquoise enamel. It soon became apparent that it was not the fireplace that had arrested his attention, or the bust of Dante on its mantel, or the white embossed invitation to a dinner at the House of Lords, but the small object almost hidden at the end behind a decanter: a frosted glass angel five inches tall. He picked it up and examined its hands pressed together in prayer, its wings extending vertically upwards above its head, the length again of its body. 'I guess I was lucky,' he continued, replacing the angel. 'Not everyone walked away from that crash.'

Wetherby was gliding across the room towards him. Without comment he moved the angel back to where it had been, three inches farther along the fireplace. 'Anyway,' he said rubbing his long, thin fingers together and bringing the small talk to an abrupt end. 'What is this project you want to discuss?'

'It would be easiest if I showed you.'

As the two men walked side by side along the marble-floored corridor, the one looming over the other, neither spoke. 'Can I ask you something?' Daniel said into the silence. 'You ever had an aesthetic experience?'

'A strange question.'

'I know, but . . . have you?'

'Yes, I believe so.'

'Listening to music, I presume.'

Wetherby considered this for a moment. 'I was fourteen. Bruckner's Seventh at the Queen Elizabeth Hall. I felt overwhelmed, exalted, reduced to tears. *That* I interpreted as an aesthetic experience. My first.'

'And what is going on when someone has an aesthetic experience, in the brain, I mean?'

What is he up to, this flat-footed biologist? Why the sudden interest in philosophy?

'Kant defined it as the free play of the cognitive faculties of imagination and understanding. It is intersubjective, as opposed to objective or subjective. Everyone who attends to a piece of music or a work of art in a disinterested way ought to have the same aesthetic experience.'

'And what's the difference between an aesthetic experience and a religious experience?'

Ah.

Wetherby eyed Daniel suspiciously, inclining his head as they walked. 'Are they the same, you mean? I think not. A religious experience takes the form of a revelation, an epiphany, a vision and so on.'

'And have you ever had one? A vision, I mean. Is that where your belief comes from?'

Wetherby came to a halt alongside a marble statue of Locke. 'Sadly no, I do not believe I have. Like Kierkegaard I have had to make a leap of faith.' He started walking again. '*Credo quia absurdum*, as Tertullian put it. I believe it because it is absurd, also sometimes translated as *certum est quia impossibile est*, it is certain because it is impossible. I have come to the view that God does not reveal himself to those of us who are actively looking for him. He appears in the peripheral vision, when you are not expecting him, when you are not trying.'

'Like the way to remember a word is to stop trying to remember it? Think of another subject and the word will come to you?'

Of course not, little man. 'Something like that.' Wetherby began walking again. 'The Lord likes to keep us on our toes, reveal Himself at times of his choosing, in unexpected ways.'

'Won't do it on demand, you mean?'

'A God who could not help revealing himself would not be a terribly impressive God, would he? Anyway, what has prompted your sudden interest in visions? Planning one of your mocking lectures, are you? Or a paper that pokes fun at we simpletons who splash around in the shallow waters of faith?'

They had reached the heavy oak door leading out on to the quadrangle. Though Wetherby was a step in front, it was Daniel who opened it.

'No, not at all,' Daniel said. 'Far from it. Your religion must be a great consolation to you. I'm just . . .' His brow creased. A thought.

Wetherby wondered whether Daniel had realized at last that whenever the two men were together they played pre-assigned roles. Master and pupil. Wetherby always liked to give him the impression he was being tested. This habit of waiting for doors to be opened for him was part of that.

'It's just I've been giving the subject a lot of thought,' Daniel continued, 'from a biological perspective. There's a theory doing the rounds that the irrationality of religion is a by-product of our in-built urge to fall in love, the temporary fanaticism and mania of falling in love, I mean. The neurally active chemicals produced by someone in love are the same as those produced by someone obsessed with the idea of God.'

'Yes, I have heard that. It is possible, I suppose . . . You could say the same of music, of course. What is the part of the brain that releases dopamine?'

'The name of it? Um, the, um . . .' Daniel clicked his fingers. '*Nucleus accumbens*. It regulates our moods.'

'Exactly, but it also regulates the way we experience music.' They stood to one side as a student in a wheelchair trundled past, then they cut across the lawn, a privilege of dons. 'Although I said aesthetic and religious experiences are not the same, I do think there is one connection. You almost have to become childlike to have them.'

'As in naive?'

'As in innocent. Open. Curious. Part of what convinced me of the truth of Christianity was a tour I embarked upon as a seventeen-year-old – not exactly a Grand Tour but certainly a cultural one, through France, Austria and Italy. There seemed to be so much beauty associated with the church. The sonatas of Bach. The frescoes of Giotto. The statues of Michelangelo. All the great composers and artists seemed to claim God had guided their hands, that their genius was God-given. And I came to see why. Wittgenstein described Mozart and Beethoven as "the true sons of God". I am not sure about Beethoven, some of the late bagatelles perhaps, but when I listen to Mozart I do hear the divine. His music is angelic. Perfectly poised. To be lost in it is to be lost in oneself. Everything in his music is ecstatic. Change the position of a single chord and the whole thing falls to pieces. That is why it moves you. And if music does not move you, if it does not inwardly reduce you to your knees, what is the point of it? I am trying to say, I suppose, that when I listen to Mozart I have my proof of God. I have my certitude.'

They had reached the bronze statue of Charles Darwin that guarded the entrance of the Zoology Department. It depicted the naturalist as an old man, seated and distinguished with his wing collar, bald head and flowing beard. At his feet were a pile of bronze books and rolled-up maps. He was frowning. 'Been thinking for some time now that we don't make enough of our connection with Darwin,' Daniel said, pausing to stare up at the statue. 'Follow me.' He led the way through the building, down the stairs and along a dark corridor to a basement door marked DRY STORE. He turned lights on, felt in his pockets for keys and opened the door. Once inside, he flicked more lights. After a brief delay they came on, illuminating long tables laden with prehistoric bones and fossils. Along the length of the walls were glass cases filled with stuffed monkeys, specimens preserved in fluid and, in the centre of one display, a giant mammoth skull. 'I love this place,' Daniel said. 'No one ever comes here. Darwin himself collected most of it . . . Let me ask you another question. What was Darwin famous for?'

'I believe he was the great-uncle of Ralph Vaughan Williams.'

Daniel grinned. 'I was thinking more in terms of his trip to the Galápagos Islands in the *Beagle*.'

Wetherby ducked his head slightly to clear the doorframe. There was something about Daniel's manner which he found especially annoying today. He was being ingratiating. That was it. Hadn't stopped smiling. The smiling was making Wetherby want to punch him.

'Much of this collection is from that trip,' Daniel continued. 'And I think members of the public would pay good money to see it, if they knew about it. We could make it an interactive experience, with computer graphics and holograms. Get school parties coming in. We could call it "The Darwin Experience", or, and this is what I really wanted to try out on you . . .' He held his arms above his head and spread them wide, miming a sign, ' "On the Side of the Apes: a Journey through Darwinian Evolution by Natural Selection".'

'But what Disraeli said was: "The question is this: is man an ape or an angel? I, my Lord, I am on the side of the angels." '

'I know.'

'So why misquote him? I don't understand.'

'It's a play on . . .' Daniel caught Wetherby suppressing a grin. 'Look, it doesn't matter. The point is, it could be the first thing visitors see through the door. You could have it here . . .' He pointed to a space above the doorway. 'A painting of Disraeli standing up in the Sheldonian with the quote underneath it. Look, I've done some sketches.' Daniel laid out a sketchbook showing different sections and vistas. 'Obviously I'd get these all mocked up as a virtual reality tour, so you can see what it will look like as you walk from room to room. I know there's this bequest to the college and I just thought . . . Of course, I'd need to do a presentation to the Senate. The museum would draw in different departments. History. Theology. Biology. Political science. Philosophy. The

Courtauld could loan us some quattrocento paintings of angels. This was one of the reasons I wanted to run it past you first. I know about your interest in angelology . . . We could present it as a joint idea, you coming from the one direction, me the other. I see it as an antidote to all the misinformation that is being pumped into schools by the Creationists. Did you know, there is a Creation Museum in Ohio that has a model of Stone Age children playing with a pet dinosaur?'

'What is wrong with that?'

'What's wrong with that! Dinosaurs went extinct almost . . . Oh I see. You were joking.'

Wetherby's fingers were tapping his chin. 'A better quote to have above the door might be "Monkeys make men. Men make angels." '

'That's good. Who said it?'

'Darwin. Notebook B.'

Daniel looked embarrassed.

Wetherby took pleasure in this. 'You see this as an exercise in atheistic propaganda?'

'Not at all. I see it as a way of stimulating debate, getting students thinking about the subject. We could inaugurate it with a recon-struction of the Disraeli debate, only do it here at the Union. You could propose the motion, I could oppose it. Or the other way round, depending on what the motion was.'

'But I would win, and that would never do. Fashion dictates that the atheist must always win.'

Daniel gave a short, dry laugh. 'So how would you win then? What would be your clincher?'

'I would win because there is no poetry in your idea of man as a lumbering robot servicing the interests of his genes. People like poetry. Consider the profession of faith: "All that is, seen and unseen." Is that not poetic?' Wetherby was enjoying himself, savour-ing the polite tension and the academic one-upmanship. 'God cannot be found by looking through a microscope, or a telescope. That would be like unravelling a human brain in order to find thoughts and feelings.' He picked up a small, yellowing bone and held it at arm's length to see it better, feeling its weight as if con-templating using it as a club.

Daniel said, 'That's from a quagga. Very rare.'

Wetherby laid the bone down gently on a case containing beetles, cockroaches and locusts stuck down with pins. He let out a long sigh. 'You know, I almost envy you your Enlightenment certainties. Life is so much messier when you have to accommodate the numinous and the mystical. Messier, but more human. Our intellect craves certainty, our nature craves mystery. Are you familiar with Sir John Tavener?'

Daniel nodded.

Wetherby was sure he was bluffing. 'Sir John refers to "the angel of inspiration" and talks of having "auditory visions" in which music is dictated to him. Blake spoke of something similar . . . You look shocked.'

'You've reminded me of something.' Daniel sounded distant.

Wetherby raised his eyebrows but Daniel, looking as if he had seen a wraith, did not take the prompt. 'Well?' Wetherby said.

'There was a Canadian neurosurgeon in the fifties who per-formed surgery on the brains of epileptic patients. He found that when he stimulated certain areas of the temporal lobe with electronics, his patients began to hear voices and see ghost-like apparitions. This prompted Aldous Huxley to ask if there was a part of the brain from which the probing electrode could elicit "Blake's Cherubim". It was staring me in the face. I can't think why I didn't . . .'

Wetherby removed his glasses, breathed on them, rubbed them and put them back on. 'Even if you were blessed with a divine intervention you would not accept it,' he said. 'Such is the arrogance of the scientist. You would explain it away. Murder in order to dissect.'

'The dissection of an angel, now that I would like to see.'

'Milton believed their vital organs were evenly dispersed throughout their bodies, so that they were all heart, all head, all eye, all ear.'

'As a Catholic, you believe in them presumably?'

'Angels? You do not have to be a Roman Catholic. Angels profess no single confession.'

'You've lost me.'

'All three of the monotheistic religions, the Abrahamic ones at least, share the same angels. Belief in the same angels, I mean.'

Daniel made an apologetic face. 'Didn't know that.'

'Islam, Christianity and Judaism. The archangel Gabriel being the… your generation would call him "the Daddy".'

'Wetherby!' Daniel was laughing. 'We're the *same* generation!'

'We are?' It struck Wetherby that Daniel was wrestling with something, something that he wanted to get out in the open. It was to do with his falseness of tone, his pretence at nonchalance. He studied him narrowly, watching him chew on his lip. 'What, may I ask, has aroused your curiosity in angels?'

Daniel hesitated, backing up against a cabinet containing glass models of jellyfish, sea anemones and gastropods. 'What would you do if you heard that someone had seen one?'

'That would depend.'

'On whether there were witnesses?'

'Yes, and how reliable the witnesses were. I might inform the appropriate authority at Westminster Cathedral. It could be some-thing the Vatican would need to investigate. But there are thousands of claims made each year, and almost all prove to be false or fraudulent. The Vatican has a whole department dedicated to unmasking fake miracles and sightings of angels.'

'Seriously? That's hilarious! So only Vatican-approved fake miracles and angels are allowed? I suppose they don't want to flood the market. Devalue the currency.'

Daniel led the way to the far end of the display cabinets. 'Come and look at this.' He pointed to a taxidermic duck-billed platypus. 'The bill of a duck, the tail of a beaver, the paws of an otter. Preposterous in evolutionary terms. Like it's thrown together from leftovers. When this little fellow was first brought over from Tasmania at the end of the eighteenth century, European naturalists assumed it was an elaborate fraud . . .'

'When in fact it was proof that God has a sense of humour.'

'Or proof that evolution works through random mutation – the natural world trying on different things to see what fits.'

Wetherby exhaled noisily. 'Perhaps you are right. Perhaps that is why God makes angels, immaterial beings whose identity resides in the world of thought. The unseen world. The abstract world. They are creatures that can't be explained away by scientists.'

'Thought you said men make angels.'

'No. I said that Darwin said men make angels.'

'So you *do* believe in them?'

'They have been described as the most beautiful conceit in mortal wit, and I would go along with that.'

'And the museum?'

'The idea has merit. Let me try it out on the provost.'

Wetherby turned to go, turned back again and gently placed his hand across Daniel's forehead. 'You have an injury here, I think.'

Daniel shrank back slightly but did not remove the hand.

'It hurts because you think too much. You should try to think with this.' Wetherby pressed the hand over Daniel's chest. 'Ponder with your heart.'

CHAPTER TWENTY-FIVE

Northern France. First Monday of September, 1918

THE WEDDING CEREMONY IS TO BE A SIMPLE ONE, OF NECESSITY. Neither the bride's family, nor the groom's, will be attending. The priest has explained that Adilah will need to provide him with her late husband's death certificate. The only other documentation required will be their birth certificates. Having written to the Registry of Births at Somerset House in London asking for a copy of his, and having received a letter in reply asking for proof of identification and a fee of twopence, Andrew has sent his army pay book by return, along with the fee in loose change. As soon as the certificate arrives they will marry. Their child will not be born a bastard.

The light is dying as Andrew returns home from work. When he goes to lie on the bed, aching pleasantly from his labours, Adilah joins him, bunching up her skirt so that she can sit astride him. She leans over to cut a lock off his hair. As he stares up into her eyes, his face tickled by threads of her hair, he traces the length of her spine with his thumb. His hand moves under her skirt and feels the loose silk material gathered at her knees. Her skin is almost as silky: fine-textured and delectably soft to the touch, like flour – like dipping fingers into a bag of cool flour.

Adilah leans forward to kiss him and the wetness of her kiss carries down to his groin. A thin, clear trapeze of saliva stretches between them as she backs away so that she can remove her clothes. Supporting herself on her good arm, she crawls back across the bed towards him, her slightly swollen belly and compact hips looking hugely foreshortened, as if she is a giantess looming towards him. Her small breasts are two downward-pointing conicals, the pigmentation of the areolae pink. Cupping the back of his head in her hand she draws his mouth to her left nipple, shivers, and swivels her shoulder forward to press the other nipple to him. They make love and, afterwards, wrap themselves in towels.

Later, as Adilah heats three pans of water on the stove, Andrew drags the tin bath in from the pantry and places it in front of the fire. Next he pours two glasses of Armagnac and stares at the fire through its amber lens, shivering intermittently before helping Adilah plait her hair into a single fat rope. As she steps into the bath she flips the hair over her shoulder so that it covers her left breast. She no longer covers the pucker of her stump with her hair. Being naked in front of Andrew does not make her feel shy or awkward any more. The fatty deposits beneath her skin, the lines at the corners of her eyes, the freckles on her shoulders, Andrew, she knows, adores them all. She cups the slight swell of her belly and rakes her fingernails upwards, leaving tiny white trails on her skin. No kicks yet but she calculates it must be four months since she last bled. As she lowers herself into the bath, Andrew feels the reflex of desire. He lathers a bar of soap, pauses to pick a hair from it and rubs it over her back. When it is his turn to get in, Adilah puts on a dressing gown and tops up the bath with water from the pan. When he has washed, he asks her to pass him the towel. She holds it at arm's length while he stands up and, as he reaches for it, she drops it. Laughing, and leaving wet footprints on the stone floor, he chases after her. She runs behind the table and feints left as he tries to anticipate which way she will run next. They are laughing so loudly they do not at first hear the knocking at the door.

'Open up.'

An English voice.

Andrew feels a trickle of ice in his veins.

Adilah tosses the towel across to him. As he wraps it around himself he reaches for a comb and parts his fringe to one side.

'Open up.'

Andrew nods to Adilah to open the door. Instinctively he stands to attention; something about the tone of the man's voice. Four military policemen, identifiable by their red-topped caps and armbands, are crowding the doorway. They are holding pistols in their hands. The tallest of them, an assistant provost marshal, looks at Adilah in her dressing gown then at Andrew. 'Private Andrew Kennedy?' he asks with a Scottish brogue.

Andrew swallows. 'That's right.'

'You'd better get some clothes on, laddie. You don't want to face the firing squad with a bare arse, now do you?'

'Andrew?' Adilah looks frightened.

'It'll be all right,' Andrew says with rapid blinks. Turning to the APM he adds: 'My clothes are in the bedroom.'

'Well, you'd better go and fetch them, then. On the double. And get that horrible thing shaved off.'

A redcap follows Andrew into the bathroom where he slips on a singlet and a pair of shorts, before cutting off his beard with scissors. He has a shave after this and finds the sudden smoothness of his cheeks strangely disgusting, as if he were unpeeled, his skin exposed and raw. The redcap escorts him into his old room and watches uninterestedly as he pulls out from under the bed a blanket tied with string. It springs open as he tugs the string apart, revealing a uniform covered in dry mud and dark stains. It smells of mildew. As he puts it on, its scratchiness against his newly bathed skin makes him shudder. Though he has filled out slightly since he last wore it, it is still a size too big for him. He picks up the lock of Adilah's hair that is lying on the bedside table and slips it in his pocket. When he returns to the kitchen, Adilah is crying.

'Can I have a moment with her?'

'Fraid not, laddie.'

CHAPTER TWENTY-SIX

London. Present day. Six weeks after the crash

BRUCE CAME IN JIGGLING CHANGE IN HIS POCKET AND SMELLING OF disinfectant. He had a stethoscope wrapped up in his waist pocket. He could not meet his patient's eye.

'Shouldn't you be wearing a white coat with pens sticking out of your breast pocket?' Daniel asked.

'Urm, take a seat, Dan.'

Daniel clenched his fists, bracing himself. 'Bad as that?'

Bruce clipped a negative to a light box and said through a sigh, 'I don't think it's, you know, anything we need to worry about. But there is a small shadow on your brain.' He pointed a thick and hairy finger. 'More a bubble on the lobe that controls perception, memory and so on. The temporal lobe. This bit here.'

Daniel touched the back of his head. At first his mouth was too dry to speak. 'It's a tumour, right?'

'Not typical of a tumour. It could be a form of aneurism. Could be. But again it's, urm, not typical of one. I would need a second opinion.'

Daniel rubbed his head again. He could feel the skin capillaries on his face cool as the blood left them. 'Think I will sit down. Feel a bit faint.'

Daniel knew that Bruce had been trained how to break bad news. They had talked about it. As a medical student he had done role-play sessions with students from RADA, learning how to cope if they reacted badly, how to console, how to impart information efficiently and tactfully.

'What do *you* think it might be?' Bruce said slowly.

'Let's not play that game.'

'My guess is that it's a blood clot from when you bumped your head. A minor haemorrhage that stopped before becoming a major one. If that's what it is, it will probably disappear in a few weeks. You need to take things easy, that's all. You've been feeling OK, haven't you?'

'Apart from the headaches, yeah. And the thirst.'

'Then I don't think it's anything to get excited about.'

Daniel shook his head. 'Can you give me five minutes, Bear? I feel a bit . . . I need five minutes on my own if that's OK.'

'Sure. I'll get some coffee. Milk, no sugar, right?'

'No, put some sugar in mine, I'm feeling a bit shaky.'

Five minutes later, when Bruce returned carrying two steaming polystyrene cups, Daniel was standing again, by the window. 'What about the smells and the noises?' he said. 'They're associated with tumour development, aren't they?'

'Not necessarily.' Bruce handed a coffee over and took a sip from his own. 'We'll need to do some more tests.'

'Is there a test you can do for epilepsy?'

'You didn't tell me you'd had a seizure.'

'It's more . . . I did see a blinding flash. That's associated with epilepsy, isn't it?'

'It can be . . . The brain tissue behind the eyes is weak and when hit there the brain, you know, urm, bounces back and can cause an electromagnetic field . . .' He trailed off and when it sounded like he had finished he added, 'or seizure across the temporal lobes. A sensed presence, perhaps in the form of a blinding flash, can be stimulated in that way . . . There are some electromagnetic tests we can do. Look up at the ceiling for a moment.' Bruce shone a small torch in his friend's eye. 'Nothing unusual there . . . although . . .'

'What?'

'I wasn't going to tell you this but I ran what we call "a comparative" on your scan and . . .'

The two friends stared at one another.

'And what?'

'You're going to love this, Dan . . .'

'Go on.'

'The only recorded example of a shadow pattern like this dates back to nineteen ninety-three. A monk who had a scan after complaining of headaches.'

'A monk?'

'Think he was a Buddhist.'

It was Daniel's turn to sigh. He stood up and walked back towards the window. He was still rubbing his head. 'You know that thing you wanted me to tell you about?'

Bruce took another sip from his mug and wiped milky foam from his top lip with his sleeve. 'Go on.'

'I had a sort of . . .' Daniel searched for the right word. 'You're going to laugh at me.'

'I won't laugh at you.'

Daniel pouted. 'OK.' He sighed again. 'I had a vision.'

Bruce laughed.

Daniel picked up the photograph of Kylie Minogue. 'I was going to say "hallucination" but . . .'

'*You? A vision?*'

'Yes, me. But I was going to say . . .'

'What did you see?'

'A man. A young man. He was in front of me treading water when I was swimming for help. I was about to give up when I saw him. I was actually taking my life vest off. He smiled and signalled at me to swim towards him.'

'You recognized him?'

'Can't say for sure. He looked familiar. I think I've seen him since. He's a teacher at Martha's school.'

Bruce nodded again. 'So you *had* seen him before?'

'Guess I must have.' Daniel drew in his shoulders defensively. 'Well, there it is.'

214

'It's not really my, you know, area, but given your condition at the time, the bump on the head, I mean, and the heat exhaustion, I think it would have been a miracle if you hadn't been hallucinating. Hallucinations can seem very real. What we see is driven as much by what we expect to see, or want to see, as by the actual patterns of light and colour picked up by our eyes. Brain scans have shown this. You didn't want to die alone out there. You wanted to see another human face. This was a guy you had seen around the school, that confirms it for me. Hallucinations are nearly always of things that we have seen before. Memories. People.'

'It *was* a hallucination, wasn't it?'

'Course it was.'

'The reason I called it a vision was because of the way it made me feel. I felt . . .' He searched for the right word again. 'Exalted.'

Bruce grinned. 'That's why you asked about the epilepsy, wasn't it? Frontal lobe epilepsy is associated with religious visions.'

'You think that might be it?'

'Could easily be. Also you were probably still traumatized from the crash. Seeing those people killed. Feeling guilty about having survived. It's like with bereavement hallucinations. A lot of grieving people believe they have caught sight of the dead person. It makes them feel better. It's all to do with the, urm . . .'

'Frontal cortex.'

'Exactly. Decision-making. Hallucinations relate to the, the . . . higher cognitive functions of the brain. I was reading about someone at Columbia who asked volunteers to differentiate between houses and faces. Signals in the frontal cortex became active whenever subjects expected to see a face, irrespective of what the actual stimulus was. They would look at a house and "see" a face. It's called, you know . . .'

'Predictive coding?'

'Predictive coding. The brain has an expectation of what it will see, then compares this with information from the eyes. When this goes tits up, hallucinations occur. Our eyes don't present to our brains exact photographs of the things we see. They are more like sketches and impressions chattering along the optic nerve for the brain to interpret. That's what optical illusions are about. The brain's software is perfectly capable of simulating a vision in this way.' Bruce smiled again and raised his hands. 'What can I say? It was *definitely* a hallucination, Dan. Definitely, definitely. There is no doubt in my mind. The only thing we need to check is whether it was triggered by temporal lobe epilepsy. Has it happened since?'

'Nope.'

'Then stop worrying about it.'

'What happened to him? The monk?'

'His shadow went away eventually.'

'Makes sense in a way. Do you know what I mean by the "God spot"?'

'Read something about it in *Nature* once. They did an experiment in which quasi-religious epiphanies were induced under laboratory conditions. Didn't they use nuns?'

'Carmelite nuns. But they were also able to produce these visions in non-believers. Basically they showed that there's a circuit of nerves in the brain which explains belief in God.'

'There you are then. Angel, my arse.'

Daniel started guiltily. 'I never said anything about an angel.'

'Look, if it makes you feel exalted, enjoy it while it lasts. I normally have to prescribe pills to achieve that effect.'

'There's something else.' Daniel gave an embarrassed laugh. 'I'm, sort of, priapic.'

'Poor Morticia.'

'Poor me. Since the crash we haven't had sex once. Six weeks.'

'I'm no expert but that's not so unusual after ten years, is it? For heterosexuals, I mean.'

'It is for us. Before the crash normality was two or three times a week.'

Bruce shook his head. 'Poor, poor Morticia.'

'It's probably because of her shoulder. The other night we tried sleeping in the same bed and . . . I shouldn't be telling you this . . .'

'But you're going to.'

'We always used to have this thing where . . . when we lay back to back we would touch our toes together. We don't even do that any more.'

'You told anyone else about your . . . whatever it was?'

'I nearly told one of the professors at Trinity. Wetherby. Do you know him?'

'Why didn't you?'

'Dunno. Didn't seem fair. He believes in all that bollocks. Probably been waiting all his life for a vision . . . You know, he's a pious man. If anyone deserves to have a vision-like hallucination it's him. He'd think it was wasted on me.'

'I'm sure he's a bigger man than that.'

'Yeah, I'm sure he is. Perhaps I will tell him . . . Bear?'

'Yeah?'

'If something happens . . . If it is a tumour, I want you to look after Nancy and Martha.'

Bruce grinned. 'I'll look after Martha, but Morticia's on her own.'

'What is it between you two?'

'To be honest, Dan, she terrifies me.'

'She's only terrifying with people she knows.'

'And strangers.'

'And strangers, yeah, but she's like that because she's vulnerable.'

'Yeah, right. About as vulnerable as the north face of the Eiger.'

'OK, I ask you to look after her as a friend. You're the only man I trust with her.'

'You can look after her yourself, Dan. Nothing is going to happen to you. Now, I need to . . .' He nodded at the door. 'And so do you. Go home. Get some rest. Ring me in the morning. And Dan . . .'

'Yeah?'

'Have a wank. Doctor's orders.'

★

When he got home, Daniel sat in his car for a moment with the engine running. The sun glinting off the bonnet was making him squint. He slapped the steering wheel and smiled to himself.

He had his explanation.

Martha was reading a Harry Potter book in the kitchen. 'Can I watch a DVD, Daniel?'

'Call me Daddy. And why not carry on reading?'

'I've been reading for, like, half an hour. Mum said I could watch a DVD if I did half an hour's reading.'

'OK. If Mummy said.'

'She also said you had to give me my injection. Shall I go and fill it up ready?'

'I'd better do it.'

'I can do it. I've been practising doing the injecting, too. On an orange. Can I show you?'

'OK, but don't tell Mummy.'

Martha filled her syringe as expertly as Nancy would have done and held it up for Daniel to see it was the right amount. She pinched loose skin on her waist and slipped the needle in without hesitating. 'See?'

'Very good.' Daniel ruffled her hair. 'How are things at school?'

'Fine.'

'You're happy?'

'Sure.' Martha shrugged. 'I guess . . . Daniel?'

'Call me Daddy.'

'Daddy?'

'Yeah.'

'Why is Mum always crying?'

Daniel blinked. 'When does she cry?'

'All the time.'

Ten minutes later, as Daniel sat waiting on the sofa in the drawing room, Kevin the Dog nudged the door open with his nose, slunk across the room and exchanged a guilty glance with him before creeping up over the arm of the sofa and curling into a ball. Martha followed the dog into the room, shuffling as she tried to keep Nancy's stilettos on her feet. She was holding one of her mother's handbags too and wearing one of her hats. Her face was made up. She was trying not to grin.

Daniel played along, affecting not to notice.

Martha took a DVD of *Finding Nemo* out of its sleeve, slotted it into the player and pressed 'play' on the remote. When nothing happened, she opened up the back of the remote and rolled the batteries around with her thumb. It worked.

As Martha watched the television screen, Daniel stole glances at her, studying the detail of her face, the pores in her freckled skin, the delicate whorl of her ear, her thick lashes, the slight tilt of her nose, the bow of her lips. She was so pale – a pale imitation of her golden-skinned mother. Even the wash-off tattoo on her arm was a mockery of the real thing. Compared to Nancy, Martha was plain and mousy. She was more like Daniel. She had his colouring. Would adolescence favour her with good looks? He put a protective arm around her and smelled her hair. She tucked herself into him – father and daughter on a big blue sofa with chocolate stains on its arm. *Finding Nemo* was her favourite film. Daniel and she had watched it often. When it came to the part where the clown fish hitches a ride on the shell of a sea turtle, Daniel said: 'Ah.'

'Why did you say "Ah"?'

'Because Daddy's been seeing things.'

'What things?'

Daniel did not answer. Instead he pulled his daughter towards him, in the crook of his arm. After a while, feeling bored with the film, he extracted himself and opened the metallic lid of his MacBook Air. Unable to get online, he called up the stairs. 'Nancy? I'm not getting a signal. Have you got one on your laptop? Nancy? You there?' He took the stairs two at a time. The door to her study was open. As he crossed the threshold, an energy-saving, movement-sensitive lightbulb came on. He picked up the empty wine glass on her davenport desk. It had a print of her lips on its rim and, when he raised it to his nose, he closed his eyes. The scent of her lipstick made him ache, in his legs, his stomach, his chest. He thought of the 'five unobvious things' he loved about her, the things Nancy had once asked him to list. One of them had been the way she wore Ambre Solaire in winter. He tried to recall the others: the way she wore her watch on the wrong wrist when she had something cooking, to remind her to take the pot out when it was ready; the way she could work her whole fist into her mouth, as a party trick; the way she snored gently, almost imperceptibly, as if the sound was carrying across a foggy valley; the way she learned new languages, just for fun; and the way she tugged her sleeves down over her wrists when feeling self-conscious. What was it she had said when he listed them? Yes, he remembered now. 'That's six things, you moron. I asked for five.'

Her laptop was a PC – he had never paid attention before to the fact that he was a Mac and she was a PC – and it was open with a standard PC screensaver on: tropical fish making bubbling noises. Daniel was transfixed, transported in his reverie back to the Pacific Ocean. He closed his eyes, massaged them with his fingers, walked over and touched a key. The machine booted into life. He checked for a signal: there were four stepped vertical bars indicating green, which meant that the laptop had a broadband connection. He noticed a file on the screen titled 'Diary'. Perhaps Nancy had gone out, he thought, clicking on the file to check. It wasn't an appointment diary; it was a journal. He looked away guiltily and moved the cursor to close it down. Then he stopped. Nancy would know he had opened it; there would be a time record, if she wanted to check it. She was behaving so strangely she might just do that. Upon reflection, he thought that perhaps he should read it. It might help. Perhaps Nancy intended him to read it. The file wasn't locked, after all. They both knew each other's passwords. There was only one entry. It was dated a week ago. It had been written in a hurry; hadn't been spellchecked.

Tom, my counsellor – I can't believe I have a counsellor – says I have to keep a diary. So this is it. Actually he said I should keep a 'sleep diary', to record when I sleep, or rather when I don't sleep, which is every night, pretty much.

Daniel sat down, not taking his eyes off the screen. A stillness fell over the house as if the air was thickening; the only sound was the muffled knocking of the steam in the radiators.

i'm stalling. i've never kept a diary before. I'm not sure what to put it in. tom says diaries are useful – 'therapeutic' – because they help you come to terms with thingjgs that arebothering you. It it's written down it stops buzzing round nad round your head. You should just record whatever is on your mind. So what is bohtering me? Well, daniel mostly. It's not the things that used to bother me, like him not helpingwith the shopping and keeping the house tidy and never helping with martha's homework and never putting the loo seat down and always beingon his computer instead of spending time with us and always asking me what's wrong in front of Martha so I can't tell him and always having to be right about everything and always finishing my sentences and never listening to me and taking me for granted and ignoring me. He walked right past me while I was washing the pans the other day, didn't even notice. But that's not it.he's a good father. He's a good man at heart. But for years I have felt lonely and permanently as if his time is more important than mine. I have always ignored these feelings because I knew he loved me but since the crash . . . He never looks me in the eyes. And he keep smiling all the time . . . and I'm feeling better all ready.

Daniel frowned. The complaints were familiar but he couldn't recall the washing-up incident. He was the one who always did the washing-up. He wiped his mouth.

His work always has to come first, even though I'm the one who earns most money.

Daniel shook his head and raised his hands at the screen in exasperation.

He is so fucking selfish. I don't like him touching me at the moment. He keeps coming over my sideof th e bed, puttinghis arm round me but familiarity has made the touch of his hand feel like the touch of my hand . . . and he has a permanent hard on.

221

Daniel frowned again, annoyed at the thought that Martha might read this.

I can't stand the pain in my shoulder.i smoked a spliff on my own at 9am yesterday morning. It made the pain and nausea go away but when it came back it was worse. I'mgoing to have to get some stronger painkillers. I shouted at the baby this morning. She wouldn'tget dressed, I'd told her ten time, so I went into flamethrower mode with her. a complete over reaction. She started crying, then I started crying. Then she came up and put her arms round me and began stroking my hair. What kind of a BITCH mother from hell am I? I feel so fat and miserable and lonely and angry. Ihate myself more than anything. i thought going back to work might help but I just kep bursting into tears.mrs crawford looked at me like I was mad.. I think tom might be right. There is unresolved stuff between dan and me, since the crash. I want to talk it through with him but I can't. we haven't talked about what happened.

Daniel felt his heart pounding. He glanced over his shoulder before reading on.

I keep thinking about it. It keeps me awake at night. He left me. He left me.

Daniel held his hand out in front of him, fingers splayed. It was as if it belonged to a stranger. He examined the hairs on its back before turning it slowly to study the creases on its palm. It rose up to his face and with his finger and thumb he dragged his eyelids closed and pinched the bridge of his nose. He sank back into the chair and remained like this for a full minute before exhaling loudly, opening his eyes and reading on.

I still love him. Of course I do. But I don't know whether I'm ever going to be able to forget what happened. I see it in his face every time I look at him . . . there is fear in his eyes. He is afriad that we will never get over this . He climbed over me to save himself. I could have died. What happened to women and chilrden first?. He came back for me but his first

instinct was to save himself and leave me to die. How could he do that if
he loves me? I know he loved me but he didn't love me ENOUGH . . .
I think he was going to ask me to marry him while we were away..i
would have said yes. Of course I would. if me asked me today. Right now.
I don't know what I would say. I Know he loves martha. I know he
would save martha . . . don't know where this is going.i'm crying again
now. I'mnot sure it has helped writing this after all. I don't think I shall
write anymore.

Daniel closed the file, went downstairs and poured himself a
Scotch. Half an hour later, when Nancy came in flossing her teeth,
he stood up, moved across the room to her and, when she turned
her back to him to tidy up the magazines scattered on top of the
piano, he put a hand on her shoulder. She shrank away – her injury
– and his hand slipped on to her face. He removed it quickly.
Neither of them moved. He was desperate to hold her now, but he
could no longer get close enough. The distance between them was
too great. Nancy avoided his touch by bending down to pick up a
DVD case. She straightened and walked towards the door. In the
doorway she stopped, scratched her neck and said: 'By the way, a
couple of policemen called today asking for you.'

CHAPTER TWENTY-SEVEN

Northern France. First Monday of September, 1918

MARCHING SOON COMES BACK TO ANDREW, AS IF HIS UNIFORM HAS a memory of its own. He tries not to look left and right as they cross the cobblestones in the market square, but he can sense curtains lifting. His escort leads up to the town hall, which has, on three parallel flagpoles, a Union flag and a Stars and Stripes flying alongside the Tricolour. The British 4th Division and American 33rd have recently requisitioned the building as their temporary joint headquarters. As Andrew is led up its steps and through its corridors he can see it is a place of fevered administrative activity, piles of papers, phones ringing, maps being pored over by sun-tanned men in broad-brimmed cavalry hats. They're planning a final attack, Andrew thinks. They always bring out the firing squad before an attack. He continues through to a courtyard at the back leading on to a walled garden that he inspects for bullet holes. He cannot see any. What he can see, at the end of the garden, is a wooden hut freshly painted green. Andrew recognizes it as the potting shed that had once belonged to the baker. The Scottish APM opens the door, which is a little loose on its hinges, and stands to one side as Andrew walks in. The door closes behind him with a creak. A bolt is slipped.

'Guard!' Andrew calls out.

The bolt sounds again. The door opens.

'How did you know where I was?'

The APM reaches into his pocket, removes an opened envelope and hands it to the prisoner. It is addressed to Private A. Kennedy, 11/Shropshire Fusiliers, BEF, c/o Madame Camier, 11 Rue des Chardonnerets, Nieppe, France. He studies the words, intrigued by them. It is the first letter he has had in more than a year.

'The postman wasnae sure what to do with it so delivered it to Divisional HQ.'

Andrew looks inside the envelope and finds his paybook, a copy of his birth certificate and a receipt for twopence. 'Can I keep these?' he asks.

The guard shakes his head and gestures for the letter to be handed back. The bolt clatters again.

It is dark inside and, as his eyes adjust, Andrew sees there is nowhere to sit. The hut is empty apart from a broken chicken coop and some garden pots. He turns one of these over and sits on its base. It is now he notices the smell. The hut has clearly been used as a latrine, not an official one though, as there is neither a bucket nor a hole. Ten minutes later he hears footsteps approaching. The guard shouts 'Attention!' and the door opens. An officer looks in. He is holding a hurricane lamp in a hairy-backed hand. Andrew recognizes him as the major he had seen in the café four months earlier – the scar below his jawline is unmistakable. The three braid bands on his cuffs confirm his rank. He stares at Andrew but says nothing. He then turns and leaves the prisoner blinking in the gloom and listening to the boot steps receding. Several faces poke around the door after this: rankers who have been out drinking and have come by for a stare at the deserter. Word has spread of his capture.

Three hours after the arrest, a guard with a broad Dales accent and kind brown eyes asks Andrew if he has eaten. He shakes his head. The guard hands him four biscuits and a can of water. The bolt clatters home again.

'Am I going to be shot?' Andrew shouts through the door.

'Tha'll 'ave to wait for t'court martial to find that out. They's coming for yus in t' mornin'. Tekin yus t' brigade at Chapelle d'Armentières.'

'Can you let my landlady know?'

'One thing at a time, lad.'

Andrew welcomes the brief conversation, though he can barely penetrate the guard's accent. He hasn't spoken to an Englishman properly in more than a year. 'Where you from?' he asks.

'Keithley.'

'What did you do there?'

'I were a miner.'

'Do you know Market Drayton?'

'Aye, 'eard of it, like. That where yus from then?'

'I was a plumber there.' He thinks for a moment. 'How long you been a redcap?'

'Too bloody long.'

It ends the conversation and Andrew falls silent as he eats. For a few seconds he doesn't notice the movement in the shadows, then he sees it: a rat on its haunches testing the air with its whiskers. Andrew shrinks back but when he sees the rat standing its ground he breaks off a corner of his biscuit and tosses it over. The rat does not move. Andrew throws it another piece. This time the rat disappears into the corner of the shed. Andrew crawls over on his hands and knees and sees that where the floorboards meet the wooden slats of the wall there is a small hole with rough edges. Teeth have gnawed through. There is soil directly underneath. He looks back into the centre of the shed and sees that it takes two floorboards end to end to cover the length of the floor. Those that meet the back wall are loose.

As quietly as he can, he prises one of the boards out. It is damp and crumbling. When it breaks in two with a dull crack he looks up at the door. The guard does not appear. He removes the board next to it, working it out like a rotten tooth, and begins digging with his hands. The soil is compacted on the surface but soon gives way to looser loam. After twenty minutes' digging there is a pile two feet high on the floor and moonlight visible underneath the wall. He takes off his cap, tosses it through the hole and lies on his back, savouring the fresh air. Though he is able to work his head into the hole there isn't enough room for his shoulders, so he levers

226

himself back inside and digs deeper. Ten minutes later he can undulate his body through the space like a contortionist, breathing through his nose and stopping every few seconds for fear of making a noise. There is sweat on his brow and, when he wipes it with his sleeve, his face is left smeared with soil.

Once outside, he crawls on his belly and elbows to the garden wall and looks back at the courtyard. There are lights on inside the town hall and sentries walking up and down outside it, but they have not heard him. His friendly guard is standing several yards away from the hut, warming his hands on a brazier. He inches over the wall and, in a crouching posture, jogs along an alley until he comes back out into the square. Two officers are approaching. Andrew pulls his cap down and salutes as they pass. They pay him no attention. He can see the dismembered bones of a building, the burnt-out shell on the corner of the Rue de Bailleul, and he walks towards it briskly. There is rubble inside but also stairs leading up to a first floor. The glass has gone from the landing window. As he crouches under it, looking out over the square, he tries to work out what to do next. If he can, he figures, he should make his way back to the Rue des Chardonnerets to collect his bike and arrange a time and place to meet Adilah once the redcaps have stopped searching for him. He will not be their main priority, not for long anyway.

A commotion in the square interrupts his thoughts. There are whistles and shouts. Soldiers are running around with torches. Dogs are barking. Andrew tucks his knees up under his chin and wraps his arms around his legs. He will have to stay where he is for the moment.

Hours pass as his mind replays the day's events. Plans of action come to him and evaporate, round and round, slipping in and out of his conscious thoughts until his limbs grow heavy and sleep drags away his anxiety. It takes the sound of a horse whinnying to wake him. The blue-edged darkness means it is dawn. He rubs his arms against the cold and looks out of the window. The soldiers have gone. There is a horse and cart below, and an elderly man on a bike. It is the postman. Andrew curses him under his breath. The doddering old fool had given him away. How could he have been so stupid as to go to the army with that letter? He knows Andrew well enough. Does he have an eye for Adilah? Is that it? Yes, that must be it.

Andrew feels a stab of hunger. His eyes are stinging. A yawn. It will be no good his going to Adilah's house yet, the redcaps will be waiting for him. He will have to lie low for a few days. He checks his pocket watch with a tap of its face. Five thirty. From his elevated position he can see through the milky half-light that a camp has been erected in the field on the outskirts of the town. Some fifty bell tents are visible through an early morning mist. It is an American Expeditionary Force camp – a Stars and Stripes is flapping from a pole. There are dozens of horses in a corral, swishing their tails, breath pluming from their velvety noses. He can also make out dark shapes. Sleeping giants. Heavy artillery guns on their way up to the Front.

The cold is biting into his bones. He can smell woodsmoke and realizes that it isn't mist but smoke from still-smouldering fires. Ash is floating on the breeze. He watches an arrow of barking geese spiral down towards a pond beyond the camp and, in an echo of the noise, hears a bugler sound the reveille. Breakfast time. He feels in his tunic pocket to see if he has any iron rations left and finds his wallet instead. The picture of Dorothy is still in it, unseen for more than a year. He replaces it guiltily. Whatever they had done in bed together, it hadn't been sex. He knows that now. And whatever it was he felt for her, it had not been love. Love is what he has found with Adilah. She has caused some chemical change in his brain. She is his single thought during the day, and when he sleeps at night he dreams of her. He pats his breast pocket and feels his dog tags. Once he has put these on he feels his army identity return. It is dawn, a significant time for a soldier. He breathes deep and savours it as though it is his last.

The sound of a woman crying in pain rises from the square. When Andrew peeps over the sill, he freezes. The scar-faced major is dragging Adilah by her hair. She is trying to stand but keeps stumbling. The major will not let her get her footing. He is carrying

228

a pistol in his hand. When she trips and falls on her face, he presses the muzzle of the gun against her head and shouts: 'Up! Get up, you bitch! Get up, or I swear I'll put a bullet in your head!' He pulls on her hair again, making her whimper. She crawls on for a few yards but, unable to get her balance, staggers again. She is sobbing. Andrew screws up his eyes and sinks his teeth into his fist. He looks down at the square again. Adilah is kneeling. The major is standing over her, holding the pistol to her head. He has an arm stretched out. 'Up! Up!'

Andrew turns away, presses his back against the wall and draws his knees up to his chin to make himself as small as possible. He can still hear Adilah. To block her out, he presses the palms of his hands against his ears. He can still hear her. He looks over the sill again, down to the square. The major has his pistol pressed against Adilah's head. At this moment Andrew knows he is going to pull the trigger. He also knows that he would rather surrender his own life than watch Adilah die. The ache of fear that has defined him for so long lifts from his heart. He understands what he must do. There can be no cowardice. He stumbles towards the stairs, half falling down them because his legs have gone to sleep. Five seconds later he is standing outside the building with his hands above his head. 'Enough!' he shouts. 'Let her go.'

Keeping his arm straight, the major raises his pistol so that it is pointing at Andrew's head. Without looking at Adilah he presses his boot against her shoulder and pushes her to the ground. As he walks towards his prisoner, his gun still raised, he puts a whistle to his mouth and blows.

CHAPTER TWENTY-EIGHT

London. Present day. Five months after the crash

THE LIGHTS IN THE AUDITORIUM OF THE GREAT HALL DIMMED AND simultaneously rose on Daniel standing in one corner of the stage. He was at an intricately carved walnut lectern that was as old as the college itself. When the coughing and murmuring subsided, he waited a further thirty seconds so that the silence could deepen, a speaker's trick.

'Some of you . . .'

He stopped.

This was not part of the technique. His thoughts had liquefied; could not find a grip in his mind. He felt dazed, waiting for them to cool and harden. He was aware of the students in the front row looking at one another; noticed the red light of a camera. Was it pointing at him? Yes, he remembered, this lecture was being broadcast live as a webcast. He tapped his notes. Smiled.

'Some of you may have attended this lecture out of curiosity about its title,' he began again, his voice amplified through speaker panels at the back of the hall. 'Some of you, those who never check their pigeon holes, may not have been aware that this lecture had a title.' He paused, looked around at the blank faces and thought: hmm, tough crowd. 'Some of you may have attended this lecture because you were curious to know what a lecture is.' There were smiles at this. Can you smile louder please? he thought. At least he had their attention. 'The title, for the record, is "Apes or Angels: whose side are you on?" Those of you sitting your finals in a few weeks may be wondering what the hell this has to do with nematodes. Well . . . everything.'

Daniel clicked a button and an illustration of a nonsegmented roundworm was projected on to a large screen behind him. 'The nematode, though lacking in biological complexity, is perfectly adapted to its environment. And I mean *perfectly*.' He made a hard chopping motion, one hand against the other. 'It *cannot* be improved upon. In fact, over millions of years of evolution, it has reached a peak of efficiency and perfection. A zenith. An apotheosis. If it evolved legs or ears or eyebrows it would go from being a biological success story to a biological flop overnight – species survival to species extinction in one generation. Now, what is the explanation for this perfection? The religious mind doesn't even *try* to explain it. It gives all the credit to the Big Fella, to God, to Allah. In other words, it gives up, it surrenders, it regresses to childhood fantasy. This lack of explanation is then passed from religious mind to religious mind like a replicating virus. It then reinforces itself through repetition. People believe it because they want to believe it. Priests preach to the converted . . . And I suspect I am doing the same here.'

He paused again. 'Is there anyone present who is not an atheist?' No hands were raised. 'Good. Although if there had been a believer among you I suspect they would not have raised their hand. That is how peer pressure works. That is how religion works. Our job as scientists is to save religious people from their own ignorance, their own herd mentality. We want to encourage individualism and free thinking. You cannot call yourself a true scientist if you believe in God. As a scientist it is your duty to dismiss religion as the empty, shallow and infantile propaganda it is. As Einstein put it, "The word god is for me nothing more than the expression and product of human weakness, the Bible a collection of honourable, but still primitive legends which are nevertheless pretty childish." '

Daniel walked to the front row, feeling intoxicated by what he was about to say, about the perversity of it, the sheer, private recklessness of it. 'Imagine I had a vision. I think I've seen an angel, say. My first reaction might be to think it was religious. But there are always rational explanations if you look for them. Always. It would almost certainly – we're talking about a probability of 99.9 per cent here – have been a hallucination brought on by medical factors. You know, dehydration, exposure, sunstroke, hypothermia, medication, that sort of thing. After all, it's not hard to have a hallucination. Such have been the advances in neuroscience, it is now even possible to reproduce visions in laboratory conditions. Mystery solved.'

A student at the front raised a hand.

'Yes?'

'What the hell has this to do with nematodes?'

There was appreciative laughter. Daniel joined in with it. 'Very good. Nice timing.' He drew himself up and stared directly at the student who had asked the question. Theatre again. 'Though a nematode is perfectly adapted to its environment that does not mean it might not try something else, a random mutation, an experiment that will help it. Like the Madagascan frog born with an eyelid on the roof of its mouth.' Another slide clicked in the carousel. 'Evolution is capricious. Why else would human embryos develop gills at twenty-four days only for them to disappear almost immediately, then, later, after five months in the womb, grow a coat of hair, only to shed it straight away? Nature likes to try things on. See if they fit.'

He was talking without notes now, pacing back and forth. It felt like an out-of-body experience, as if he were high above the lecture theatre looking down. He was like a god. A zoology god with a room-filling ego. And he knew he had his students with him for the performance. 'We can be absolutely certain we evolved from apes and that any quirks we have are the result of random mutation. We can be absolutely certain there are no such things as angels because it is not biologically possible for angels to have evolved. They have no physical dimension, after all. No corporeal presence. They are immaterial. Figments of the imagination.'

He reached the lectern again, stopped pacing and leaned

forward, riding the silence. 'You may have been reading in the papers about a ring-tailed lemur that has been born in captivity at the Wildlife Foundation in Massachusetts. It appears to have two small dark feathers on its back. In a few days I'm flying to Boston to film it, so I'll report back on the accuracy or otherwise of this observation. The point is this – Creationists in the Midwest are hailing it as evidence of Intelligent Design, because they say it could not be explained in terms of evolution by natural selection. An "atheist's nightmare", they are calling it. Actually, it is a *perfect* example of natural selection. The feathers can easily be attributed to the Darwinian process of crafting fit organisms with no plan, no view for the future and no mechanisms more sophisticated than random genetic shuffling. This is the "crossing over" that occurs in reproductive cells during "random mutation". There is no intelligent designer, no supreme being, no watchmaker – and even if there was, he would be blind.'

'I have a question.'

Daniel shielded his eyes to see who had spoken. There was a man standing at the back. He was wearing a long white shirt and baggy trousers, the traditional Muslim shalwar kameez.

'Yes?'

'What if you are wrong?'

Daniel looked puzzled. Slowly a smile melted his features. It turned to laughter, a splutter that mounted in intensity. He propped himself against the lectern, doubled up and wiped his eyes with the backs of his hands. Eventually he caught his breath and managed to say, 'I don't know!' before collapsing into giggles again. The sounds of coughing, murmuring and zipping of bags could be heard in the auditorium now and, after a couple of minutes, some of the students began leaving, their seats clattering into the upright position, their embarrassment palpable. 'Sorry, folks,' Daniel said into the microphone as his laughter finally subsided. 'Let's leave it there for the day.'

A young woman with studs in her lip, nose and brow approached the stage. She was holding a camera. 'For the newspaper?' The raised intonation at the end of the sentence suggested she was Australian.

He had forgotten he had agreed to be profiled for the college newspaper. 'Oh right, yeah. Sure. Where do you want to take it?'

The rest of the students were now leaving. All except one, who was walking down the steps towards the lectern. '*Salaam alaikum*,' he said. 'I hope you don't mind me sitting in on your lecture.'

It was Hamdi, and Daniel could now see he was also wearing a chequered Shemagh scarf and was growing a beard. 'Not at all. How did you . . . ?'

'I just walked in. I was going to tell security that I was a friend of yours, but when I reported to the gatehouse there was no one there.' He shrugged. 'So here I am.'

Daniel extended his hand for Hamdi to shake. 'Glad you came.'

'You rushing off?'

A tap of the watch face. 'I do have to be somewhere. But . . . Fancy a quick drink?'

'An alcoholic drink?'

'No, I meant . . .'

Hamdi grinned. 'I know plenty of Muslims who drink whisky. The Koran only mentions wine by name. But as it happens I don't drink whisky either. I could go for a coffee though.'

When they had met at the school, and again later when they had talked on the phone, Daniel had found it hard to concentrate on Hamdi's voice. Now he noticed Martha's teacher had a hypnotic loud-quiet, long-short speech pattern, as if his batteries were running low, or he was experimenting with an unfamiliar language. There was little consistency in the way he placed emphasis: it was always on the first syllable of a word, but the word could be anywhere in the sentence.

They walked to the refectory where Hamdi found a seat while Daniel queued up for skinny lattes and cream cheese bagels. An inchoate thought was beginning to take hold: that if he could get a sample of Hamdi's DNA he could have it profiled in the university's lab. It might answer a question that was nagging him. The problem was how to extract it. A hair follicle? Some chewing gum he spat out? There might be enough of a saliva trace on the rim of the paper cup. 'I bought you a bagel as well,' he said when he returned to the table.

'Thank you,' Hamdi said.

'You don't have to eat it. I needed something. Always feel ravenous after a lecture. Now, I didn't answer your question.'

'My question was ridiculous.'

'No, it was a good question.'

'It made you laugh.'

'I'm sorry, I don't know what happened. I sort of lost it. Didn't mean to be rude. God knows what the students thought.'

'Scientists like yourself only understand the world in terms of questions that have an answer.' Hamdi paused but did not take a sip of coffee. His androgynous face was empty of expression and a dark sheen on his eyelids made him look as if he was wearing eye shadow.

'What if I am wrong, you asked. Well, I'm not wrong. I have certainty.'

'Just as the believer in God has certainty? I am a believer, by the way. I raised my hand in that lecture when you asked if anyone was a believer, but you could not see me at the back.'

'Sorry about that. I would probably have pretended not to notice you if I had. Would have ruined my pay-off. Anyway, my certainty is different to your certainty, if you will forgive the presumption. Mine is based on science and knowledge and empirical evidence. What is religious certainty based on?'

'Belief.'

'But not proof.'

'Can you prove to me that there is no God, professor?'

'I could prove there is no need for a god, which is the next best thing.'

Hamdi raised his eyebrows. 'You can?'

'The Big Bang is the explanation. The Big Bang followed by billions of years of evolution by natural selection.'

'But what was there before the Big Bang?'

'Nothing.'

'Surely that is based on belief, too. You believe there was nothing. You cannot prove it.'

Daniel gave a soft laugh, which he intended to sound indulgent but not too patronizing. He liked Hamdi. He had a friendly face. He found his presence comforting. 'Just as there are laws of physics, so there are laws of biology and the main one, the one which explains every living thing on the planet – and every planet in the universe, for that matter – is that all things must start simply and become complex. The complex dolphin began its evolutionary journey hundreds of millions of years ago as a simple, single-celled prokaryote. For a god to create the universe he would have to be hyper-intelligent. But intelligence only evolves over time. The argument for a god starts by assuming what it is attempting to explain – intelligence, complexity, it amounts to the same thing – and so it explains nothing. God is a non-explanation. The Big Bang followed by billions of years of evolution *is* an explanation.'

'You have told me how, professor, you have not told me why.' There was laughter below Hamdi's surface, which was something else Daniel hadn't noticed before. When the young man said something that amused him, he punctuated his sentence with an almost inaudible snuffle – mm – the suppression of a laugh, a hint of satisfaction at what he was saying.

Daniel exhaled slowly. 'Everyone throws that one at me . . . I know *why* people want to believe in God. Because they are in denial. Because with God comes the comforting fantasy of life after death. Because people cannot face the fact that every living thing must die. Yet it's natural, it's what we are born to do. Death is part of life. It is programmed into our DNA. I can even tell you, more or less, how long you will live, barring accidents. Here—' Daniel reached for a tub of cotton buds that he kept in his shoulder bag. 'Dab this on your gums.'

'Why?' Hamdi asked, taking a cotton bud.

'Trust me.'

Hamdi ran it around his mouth and dropped it in the plastic specimen pouch Daniel was holding open.

'The entire genetic history of your family is in this pouch,' Daniel said. 'From this we can calculate your chances of contracting

Alzheimer's, heart disease, cancer, everything. Would you like us to find out for you?'

Hamdi shook his head. 'No, not really.'

Daniel looked disappointed. 'Well. If you change your mind . . . Hello?' The female student with the studs and the camera was standing in front of them. 'Sorry, I got distracted. Do you want to take it here?'

'Here's fine,' the young woman said. When her camera flashed, students at nearby tables turned round. 'Can I have one of you two together?'

Daniel shrugged and edged his chair closer to Hamdi's.

'And can I have some of whatever it was you were smoking in there.'

Daniel grinned and shook his head. 'Sorry about that. Haven't had the giggles like that in ages. Don't know what got into me.'

The photograph taken, Hamdi stared at the specimen pouch in Daniel's hand. 'If evolution is the explanation,' he said, 'I mean, supposing it is, why is a belief in God hardwired into our brains? Every culture has a variation on the same belief, so what evolutionary purpose can that serve?'

'I suppose it keeps us sane. Stops us thinking and questioning. Stops us going mad contemplating the vastness and complexity of the universe. The nothingness. Mental health is an important part of the survival of the species . . . That's why the Marxists called religion the opiate of the masses.' Daniel put the specimen pouch in his shoulder bag, picked up the bagel and began jabbing with it. 'Personally, I think it's more a poison than an opiate. Poisons every-thing it touches. Fills hearts with hatred and prejudice. Causes wars. Divides families. Look at honour killings. A father would rather murder his own daughter than allow her to have sex with a man he thinks his god might disapprove of. That's insane.' He took a bite. 'Sorry. Don't mean to offend you or your religion.'

'I am not offended . . . You keep looking at me. It is my beard, I think.'

'Suits you.'

'I figured if they are going to treat all Muslims as terrorists, I might as well start looking like one.' He tugged at his clothes. 'And dressing like one.'

'Have they approached you?'

'The terrorists or the counter-terrorists?'

Daniel took a sip of coffee. 'It's not only Muslims who are intolerant, of course,' he said. 'Catholics are as bad. And born-again Christians. And Mormons. Complete intolerance. And for what? For a random flight of fancy. I reckon adults want to believe in God in the same way that children want to believe in Father Christmas. They cling to it, even after they suspect it cannot be true, because it makes them happy. They are capable of believing and not believing at the same time.'

'Does Martha believe in Father Christmas?'

Daniel shook his head emphatically and took another bite from his bagel. Its dense, doughy interior prevented him from answering for a moment. 'No.' He swallowed. 'Though she did briefly, before we talked about it. I asked her how probable it was that one man could get around the world in one night and visit all the world's children. We worked out that he would have to be travelling at the speed of light.'

'How old was she?'

'Five or six.'

'And in that brief time she believed in Father Christmas, did it make her happy?'

'Possibly, but that's not the point.'

'And did her belief in him make him true, in her mind at least? He existed in her mind for a while, didn't he? He was real to her?'

'Yes, but that is mere subjective truth. The only useful and relevant truth is objective.'

Hamdi thought about this for a moment, folding his hands neatly in his lap. 'Have you ever been to Greenland?'

Daniel shook his head again.

'But you believe it is there?'

'Won't be for much longer, not covered in ice and snow . . . but yes.'

'Why do you believe it is there?'

'I know people who've been there.'

'So you take it on trust.'

'And I've flown over it dozens of times on my way to America.'

A line wrinkled the skin of Hamdi's brow. 'Perhaps Greenland wasn't a good example. The point is, just because a truth happens to be subjective, it doesn't mean that it isn't objective also.'

Daniel checked his watch again and dabbed with a licked fingertip at the sesame seeds that had fallen from his bagel. 'There is no god. There's nothing subjective about it.'

'That is blasphemy, professor! You will have to be punished!' Hamdi grinned to show he was joking and added unnecessarily, 'I am joking, mm.'

Daniel smiled. 'Didn't know you were allowed to joke about such things.'

'*Allahu akbar!*' Hamdi said, raising his arms in the air and waving his hands. Two hair-chewing female students at the next table stared at them.

Daniel tapped his watch again. 'I have to go.'

'You have a stressful job, I think.'

'There's a lot more red tape these days.'

'You should convert to Islam. We have no red tape.'

'Maybe I should. "There is no God but Allah." If I say that twice in the presence of two witnesses I'm a Muslim, that right?'

'Depending on the state of your heart.'

'Then you have to surrender your life to Islam? And it governs everything from dress to forms of greeting and even the way in which a glass of water is to be drunk?'

Somewhere in the refectory a pile of plates was dropped and this was met with an ironic cheer. Hamdi looked across in the direction of the noise before directing his dark, bulging eyes at Daniel. 'Yes, my life belongs to Islam, to Muhammad, to Allah . . . but it is not blind submission. We pray and fast to show that we are with Him in our daily life. When you drink you take it with your right hand to remember Him. It's a question of remembrance.'

Daniel noticed Hamdi hadn't touched his bagel, nor was he drinking his coffee, with either hand. 'That OK? Did you want it black?' He pushed the plate with the uneaten bagel towards him. 'Try it.'

Hamdi placed his hand on top of Daniel's. It was cold. 'No.'

'You're fasting?'

Hamdi smiled ambiguously. 'You know, a lot of Westerners think they understand Islam but . . . Did you know that death by stoning is not mentioned anywhere in the Koran?'

'Can't say I did.'

'Its scriptural sanction comes from the Old Testament, from your tradition, mm.'

'Not mine, I'm afraid. My only testament is *On the Origin of Species.*' Daniel held up his hands and, at that moment, saw Wetherby gliding towards him, staying, as always, one pace ahead of a coarse, uncaring world.

'Wetherby,' Daniel called out. 'Meet my friend . . .' He blinked. 'I'm sorry, my mind has . . .'

'Hamdi.' The young Muslim stood up and held out his hand.

'I am the head of music here,' Wetherby said. 'Are you an undergraduate?'

Daniel rubbed the back of his neck. The name had gone again, as if it were written in water. 'My friend has a doctorate in music.'

Wetherby raised a laconic eyebrow. 'From?'

'Birmingham.'

'They have a good department there.'

'He's a teacher at Martha's school, but I think he's looking for a university post. That right?'

Hamdi looked embarrassed.

'Do come and see me,' Wetherby said. 'Arrange a time with my secretary.'

'He seemed nice,' Hamdi said as he watched Wetherby glide away.

'He is nice.' Daniel took a sip of coffee and checked his watch again. 'Once you tune in to his sense of humour. He's deeply religious, you know. He was telling me the other day that the three Abrahamic religions believe in the same angels.'

'The belief in angels is central to Islam. The Koran was dictated to Muhammad by the chief of all angels, Gabriel.'

'And you, I mean Muslims, believe they take human form?'

'Angels are created out of light. They can assume human form, but only in appearance. Angels do not eat, procreate or commit sin as humans do.'

'And what do they do, these angels? What are they for?'

Hamdi knitted his fingers together. 'They are the agents of revelation. According to the Koran, they do not possess free will. They record every human being's actions. They place a soul in a newborn child. They maintain the climate, nurturing vegetation and distributing the rain. They take the soul at the time of death.'

'You believe they watch over us . . . protect us, I mean?'

'Oh yes. Protection is what they do best.'

'But if they are out there protecting everyone, why is there so much suffering in the world? Is that Allah's will? I don't want to sound facetious, but does he sometimes call off his angels, when he thinks people deserve to suffer?'

'Allah is all-merciful, professor.'

'Please, call me Daniel. And strictly speaking, I'm not a professor yet.'

'The attitude to suffering is, I think, the main difference between the Jewish, the Christian and the Muslim traditions. We are all born innocent but we lose our innocence when we become adults. That is when we have to take responsibility for our own lives.'

'So it's OK by Allah if a child suffers . . . If Martha were to suffer, say.'

'You know, all the kids, all the children in the world, they are going to paradise, according to the Islamic tradition, because they are innocent.'

'So it's all right if they suffer on earth because afterwards they will go to paradise?'

'This is life. To live is to suffer. Life is suffering. Even Martha must suffer one day, but you can take comfort in the thought that she will be in paradise. If she dies in childhood, I mean.'

The conversation was making Daniel feel uncomfortable, for all its being hypothetical. He became aware of the two hair-chewing students at the nearby table nudging each other. They were talking about him, he could sense it. In recent days he had sensed other students talking about him, too, making jokes about the way he went around smiling all the time. 'I'm afraid that's not much of a comfort for me. I don't believe in paradise.'

'Does Martha?'

'Well, I guess it doesn't matter whether she believes it or not because, as a child, she's got a guaranteed, gold-embossed, one-way ticket there? Right?'

'Right.'

'And what about me? Can I as an adult non-believer go to your paradise?'

'Allah knows best. I don't know.'

'And what about suicide bombers and Muslims who fly planes into buildings, will they go to paradise?'

'Allah knows best. I don't know.'

Daniel set down his half-eaten bagel.

Hamdi still had not touched his. He looked at Daniel with concern in his glaucous, bulging eyes and asked, 'You OK?'

Daniel was staring at Hamdi with what looked like an expression of puzzlement. He gave a weak cough and, after a laboured breath, emitted a high-pitched noise. His face was turning blue and both his hands had risen up to his throat.

CHAPTER TWENTY-NINE

WHEN NANCY HAD SUGGESTED TO TOM THAT SHE SHOULD START having sessions with him more than once a week, she had the strange feeling that he had steered her into making the suggestion. She did not mind, if that was the case. She appreciated the chance to think out loud about Daniel, about how her peace overtures to him always ended in an argument. Tom was an attentive listener, a natural empath. When she told him how her relationship was struggling, he nodded sympathetically. Their meetings always ran over the allotted time and, one evening, at the end of a long session, he asked almost as an aside: 'When was the last time you and Daniel laughed together?'

'I can't remember,' Nancy said. 'It's like living with a stalker. He follows me from room to room. Sometimes he sits there staring at me. Do you know what I mean? There's that fine line that separates eye contact and the piercing stare of a psychopath. He often crosses it.'

'Are you sleeping together?'

At first the question floated between them as lightly as a dandelion seed. It was innocent and appropriate. Now its implications began to weigh on Nancy. 'You can't ask me that,' she said with a shake of her head that set her dark locks tumbling around her strong-boned face. 'Not you.'

'Forgive me.'

'I can't at the moment.'

The ambiguity hung between them.

'Can't what?'

'He wants to.'

'But you don't.'

'Don't know what I want. Sex between us was always great.'

'Freud once said the sexual life of adult women is a "dark continent" for psychology.'

'And what do you say?'

'I reckon men and women aren't so different sexually.'

'We haven't had sex since the crash. Dan wants to but . . . The trouble with being together for so long is that you become wholly known. Nothing I could ever do could surprise him in the bedroom, or he me. We've become too familiar. Too used to each other. Too tender. Too predictable. I suppose that's the reason a kiss from a stranger feels a thousand times dirtier and sexier and more exciting than the dirtiest sex imaginable with someone you know.'

Tom shifted in his seat. 'Go on.'

'It's funny, we used to try and make each other jealous by talking about the lovers we had before we met. It would always end in an argument and it made the reconciliation sex afterwards so much better. So much rougher. So much sluttier. It made me feel as if I was the mistress and he was being unfaithful with me.' Without losing her train of thought, Nancy leaped up to whack a wasp with a rolled-up magazine. 'That's the trouble with Englishmen. Never jealous enough. I've been out with Spaniards and Italians and they are too jealous. But Englishmen aren't jealous enough.'

'Don't look at me, I'm Scottish.'

Though Nancy smiled at this, tears appeared in her eyes. Tom comforted her with a pat on the back and, when she leaned into him, with a hug long enough to constitute an embrace. He cancelled his next appointment and offered to walk her back to her car. As he linked her arm with his, he asked her gently whether she thought she might benefit from some time away from Daniel. She did not answer, but when they parted she gave him a kiss on the cheek and he returned it with one on her mouth. It happened so fleetingly she felt uncertain about whether it had happened at all. If she felt shocked, it was mostly with herself because the kiss did not make her feel guilty.

The two men at the door were not in uniform. The younger one had a shaven head and was wearing a T-shirt and stone-washed jeans. The older was wearing a suit but no tie. He had close-cropped hair, military style. 'Geoff Turner,' he said, holding up an ID card. 'I'm with the Security Services.'

'Haven't we met?' Daniel asked, with a tilt of his head.

'I know your father.'

'Oh, OK . . . So what's up?' Daniel still had a knife in his hand from chopping garlic and mushrooms for a soup he was making. The sound of Charlie Parker's alto saxophone carried through from the kitchen.

'Is that Bird I can hear?' the younger man said with an American accent.

'Yep.'

'With his quintet?'

'Sextet. Dizzy Gillespie. Teddy Wilson. Specs Powell . . . I'm sorry, did you say the Security Services?'

'We wanted to ask you a few questions.'

'Come in . . . Coffee?'

The two men sat at the kitchen table while Daniel put the kettle on.

'How is Philip?' Turner said.

'Fine, fine. Remind me, how do you know him?'

'He saved my life. Kuwait.'

'Really? That's where he won his MC.'

'I know.' Turner rolled up his shirt sleeve to reveal an area of dark scar tissue that looked like a map of Australia. 'I would have burned to death.'

Daniel turned the music down using a remote. 'You were one of the ones he saved?'

'One of them, yes.'

'He's never talked about it to me. What happened?'

'He risked his life to save ours.'

'Yes but how? What actually happened?'

'He's never told you?'

'Not really, no. Said something about the Official Secrets Act.' Daniel poured steaming water into two mugs. 'Instant OK?'

'Fine,' Turner said. 'Milk, no sugar.'

'Same,' the American said.

'If Philip has never told you then I probably shouldn't,' Turner said.

'Oh,' Daniel said. 'No worries . . . What was it you wanted?'

The American fanned out photographs of Hamdi on the table. 'You know this man?'

'Yes. He's my daughter's teacher.'

'You sent him some CDs.'

'Is that a crime?'

'He was asked to go to Karbala. Has he said anything to you about that?'

'How do you know?'

'We know.'

'Well then, you'll know why I sent him the CDs as well, and why he came to see me. It had nothing to do with . . .'

'With what?'

'When you say Security Services do you mean . . . ?'

'Counter-terrorism,' Turner said.

'You suspect my daughter's teacher is a terrorist?'

'We didn't say that. But he was seen at . . .'

'He was at the protest. I know. I was there too. Does that make me a suspect? He was passing by, like me. Curious. He told me. I've never met a less likely terrorist in my life.'

The shaven-headed American gave Daniel a patient look. 'He's what is known as a "person of interest". It's routine.'

Daniel shook his head. 'No, what's that term you guys use? Clean skin? He's a clean skin, isn't he? You've tried but you can't get any dirt on him.'

Turner gave a flicker of a smile. 'Clean skin means there is no trace of him on police records. But yes, he's a clean skin. And my advice to you is keep away from him. I tell you this as a friend.'

'This really is routine,' the American said. 'Can you let us know if you see or hear anything suspicious? That is my direct line.' He handed over a card.

'You know I'm going to tell him, right?'

Turner looked at the American and gave his tight smile again.

Daniel rang Hamdi as soon as he closed the front door behind the two men. 'I need to tell you something – and if anyone is listening in on this conversation, my name is Daniel Kennedy and I don't care if you know – you are on a watch list. I've been questioned about you. You're what's known as a clean skin.'

'Cleanliness is something to which Muslim men aspire.'

'Did you know you were under surveillance?'

'Every young Muslim I know is under surveillance,' Hamdi said carefully. 'But thank you for telling me. I reported a fault on my phone the other day and an engineer came round to fix it almost immediately. Normally it takes weeks. I've heard they can create the fault . . . Thank you for warning me.'

'The least I could do. And thank you again for saving me in the refectory. I was really choking there. I must have exhaled just before swallowing because I didn't seem to have any air left in my lungs. Then I had black spots appearing before my eyes. Never a good sign.'

'Anyone would have done the same.'

'But not everyone knows the Heimlich manoeuvre.'

'All teachers have to learn it. It is part of our first aid training.'

'You were very calm in the way you did it, even if you did nearly break one of my ribs! No fuss. No panic.'

'It was Allah's will that you be saved.'

Daniel laughed. 'Well, Allah be praised.'

★

His bike safely parked and padlocked, Wetherby checked his watch. Twenty minutes early. He looked across the car park to the polished chrome and pale wooden entrance of DR NANCY PALMER'S DENTAL STUDIO. With its mood lighting and its discreet neon bulbs advertising 'cosmetic consultancy', 'facial aesthetics' and 'teeth whitening, veneers and implants', it looked more like a wine bar than a dental surgery. It also looked expensive. Scowling to himself, Wetherby walked around the corner and entered the east gate of Battersea Park. He was wondering whether Nancy would recognize his name in her appointments book. They had met a couple of times and on both occasions he had thought her intelligent, beautiful and a little frightening. When he had told her about how he hated the gaps between his teeth, she had suggested he come and visit her. But that had been three years earlier.

As he headed towards a bench overlooking the boating lake, he saw her fifty yards away, unmistakable in a white coat, walking towards him arm in arm with a man he did not recognize. As she hadn't seen him he considered changing course but, realizing she was too deep in conversation to notice passers-by, continued walking towards her. She was not only talking animatedly but also smoking – taking urgent, agitated jabs and barely pausing to hold the smoke down before exhaling, presumably so that she could finish her thought. She dropped her cigarette on the pavement half smoked and ground it out with her foot, causing a jogger behind her to swerve. There were big gestures from her now; arms spread wide, fingers open. Her hair looked vivacious in the sun, painted by a Pre-Raphaelite. She undid a hairclip and, holding it between her teeth, shook her head, regathered, coiled and reclipped. The man held out a hand to stroke her hair. With his other hand he rubbed her arm. Hello, Wetherby thought. What's this? When the man removed a lash from her cheek she wrapped her arms around his neck and held him.

Wetherby was only a few yards away from them and, as he walked past, he saw that Nancy was crying. He glided on for twenty yards before turning to see her checking the man's watch and saying something he could not hear. He presumed she had realized she was going to be late for her next appointment: him. She kissed the man on the cheek and he took hold of her hand briefly before letting it slip from him as she pulled away, trailing her fingers like a lingering fragrance. As she walked briskly towards the exit gate, putting in extra steps, the man stood staring at her. Once she had disappeared from view he checked his watch but did not move. Wetherby began walking back towards him. 'Hello,' he said with a double-take when they were level.

The man looked confused. 'Hello?'

'Sorry,' Wetherby said. 'Have we not met?'

The man studied his face. 'Not sure.'

Wetherby frowned. 'London University perhaps? I am the vice provost at Trinity College.'

'I know a professor there, well, know of him.'

'His name?'

'Kennedy, Professor Daniel Kennedy.'

'Perhaps that is it. Though I believe he is not a full professor yet. Are you an academic?'

'No, I'm a trauma counsellor.'

'So you're Daniel's therapist?'

'I'm sorry . . . client confidentiality. Actually, it's his wife Nancy I know.' He held out his hand. 'Tom.'

'Ah yes, the crash.'

'You know about that?'

'Through Daniel. I am a friend of his. How is Nancy? Do you see her regularly?'

Tom hesitated. Wetherby sensed a shadow of guilt play across his face. 'Next time I see her I'll mention . . . sorry, I don't know your name.'

'Wetherby. Actually, I am about to see her now. She is my dentist. You should be careful.'

'What do you mean?'

'Patients often fall in love with their therapists.'

The shadow of guilt again. 'I'm not a therapist, I'm a counsellor. And I didn't say she was my patient. Besides, that's a myth.'

'Really? She seems very fond of you.'

Tom looked confused again. Made as if to speak. Checked his watch again and gave a half-salute. As he walked towards the band-stand in the centre of the park, Wetherby checked his own watch and walked off in the direction taken by Nancy. He was smiling to himself, his thin version of a smile.

'That Muslim friend of yours seemed pleasant.'

Daniel jumped. Though the refectory was almost empty, he hadn't heard Wetherby approach.

'He *was* a Muslim, I take it.'

'Yeah, he's a Muslim, unfortunately for him.'

Wetherby silently placed his empty tray alongside Daniel's. 'Why do you say that?'

'MI5 have been hassling him. They even came round to my house asking questions.'

'Did they say why?'

'Because he's a Muslim, I guess. Because they are all fascist bastards.'

'What did you tell them?'

'Nothing. There was nothing to tell.' Daniel shunted his tray along. 'Might try the soup.'

'Did the MI5 officer give a name?'

'Think his name was Turner. Geoff Turner. Why?'

'The provost has asked me to be police liaison for his new emergency policy. Thought I might know him.'

'I'm just glad Nancy wasn't in.'

'How is she?'

'Fine.' Daniel nodded distractedly as a woman wearing a green apron and hair net gestured with a ladle at two soup tureens. 'Well, as fine as can be expected. Tomato, please. Still seeing her counsellor.'

'Yes, I had heard. I gather she is seeing a lot of him.'

Daniel looked at Wetherby, trying to read his face. In his

confusion he gave a short laugh. 'How do you know that?'

'We only have onion left.'

Daniel looked at the woman holding up the ladle. 'Fine,' he said.

'I tell you as a friend.' Wetherby didn't so much speak these words as breathe them.

'What do you mean, you tell me as a friend? Tell me what exactly?'

'Careful, it's hot.' The woman in the apron was holding up a steaming bowl of onion soup.

'I am sorry,' Wetherby said, 'it is none of my business.'

'What *is* it you are telling me as a friend?'

Before Wetherby could answer, a short man in a black silk shirt, black denim jacket and black jeans set his tray down between theirs. Though the thick hair that came down to his shoulders was silver, the skin on his hands and face was smooth, like a teenager's. A smile tugged gently at the corners of his mouth and, as he examined what hot food was on offer, he hummed to himself.

'Ah, Professor Sang-mi,' Wetherby said. 'You two met?' He looked across at Daniel, talking over the top of the professor's head. 'Professor Sang-mi has recently joined us on secondment from MIT. He is going to teach theoretical physics here for two terms. We are very lucky to have him . . . You were a research student at MIT, were you not, Daniel?'

'What? . . . Yes . . . Sorry.' He held out his hand. 'Daniel Kennedy. Zoology.'

'Hello.' Sang-mi spoke with a gentle American accent infused with Korean. 'I know all about you. I've seen your programmes. Most interesting.'

Daniel grimaced. 'They have to be fairly simplistic. For a television audience, I mean.'

Wetherby indicated a table. 'Do join us.'

The three men sat down together but the conversation was mostly between the professors of music and physics.

'So have we read the mind of God yet?' Wetherby said, gathering his eyebrows in mock seriousness, the extravagance of his vowels giving an ironic connotation to his words. 'Have we cracked that elusive theory of everything?'

Sang-mi had a lazy, sprawling voice – soft and mallowy, as if his mouth wanted to swallow all his words. It was a shy voice and an attention-seeking one at the same time. 'We prefer the term "quantum gravity",' he said.

'Well, we are all looking for the mind of God, in our own way,' Wetherby continued. 'And if we find it we hope that mind will be even rather than steep. *Aequam memento rebus in arduis servare mentem.*' Wetherby gave a sideways glance at Daniel who, his own mind elsewhere, did not notice.

Sang-mi spoke through a smile. 'I think the physics department will get there sooner than the music department. With respect.'

'The day you are able to play some Bach on one of your particle accelerators will be the day you come closest to knowing the mind of God.'

'You joke, but I have a doctoral student working on the beauty of equations at the moment. He has a whole chapter on Bach. Such a mathematical composer.'

'Indeed. What do you think, Daniel?'

'Huh? Oh definitely. Bach will do it. Or Miles Davis. It's all good.'

The shape of Sang-mi's smiling mouth did not change. 'No, I think it would have to be Bach. There is even some discussion about whether Bach could help with string theory. You are familiar with string theory?'

Daniel nodded. 'The stuff about the universe having eleven dimensions?'

'Exactly. The vibrations on our tiny, one-dimensional strings can be interpreted as particles. String theory – you'll like this, Wetherby – is just music, different harmonies you can play on the strings. This is the only candidate for a theory of everything that would be consistent with the beautiful symmetry of the universe.'

Wetherby leaned forward. 'Perhaps I have this wrong, but I have heard that string theory is going to help simple, unimaginative

Christians like Dante, Milton and me prove the existence of God. That must be an annoying prospect for you.'

There was a bubble of laughter from Sang-mi. 'Not at all! The mind of a scientist is open to all possibilities. Take the uncertainty of the subatomic world. It is supposedly full of fluctuations that apply to space-time as well. So up and down, left and right, even past, present and future are no longer predictable at the subatomic level. The past could walk in on the present. Your great-grandparents, Daniel, or yours, Wetherby, could walk into this room right now.'

Daniel was raising a spoonful of soup to his mouth but stopped in mid-air.

Sang-mi nodded at him. 'I know! Sounds crazy, right? But as Einstein showed us, time is relative to space. There is no absolute *now*, and no absolute *then*. Not that any of this means that God created the world in seven days.'

'Six,' Wetherby corrected. 'He rested on the seventh.'

'Six then.' Sang-mi's knee was jiggling up and down. 'Or six billion years. It doesn't matter because there is no mathematics for your God. None. Certainly not for the personal God of inter-vention in people's lives. I mean, how do you write the mathematics for it? You can't. But if you define God as harmony, you might be on to something. Then you could say all your equations must be harmonious and unifying. That becomes a testable theory. Is there harmony and symmetry in the universe? If that is your idea of God then that is testable.'

Wetherby stared at the physics professor with the hollow eyes of an El Greco saint. 'I personally would not presume to define God, other than to say He is indefinable.'

Professor Sang-mi laid down his knife and fork. His smile had gone, along with his slightly patronizing tone. 'The point is, the fundamental particles of the known universe are not made of different material, but the same material. The reason they display different characteristics is because their internal strings are vibrating differently. If string theory is correct, and it is, the sum total of the unimaginably small vibrating strings equates to the harmonic symphony of the universe we see around us. That is why if an equation is correct it will be beautiful. It will have harmony and symmetry and simplicity. If you look at a score by Bach it looks like chicken scratches, unless you can read music. But to a musician it resonates and has beauty. In a similar way equations resonate to a physicist. They speak to you. They jump out at you. Look at $E = mc^2$. Beautiful.'

Daniel was staring in front of him, lost in his own thoughts. 'Beautiful,' he repeated distantly.

'Oh, but biology is a much sexier subject than theoretical physics,' Sang-mi said, trying to draw Daniel in.

Wetherby was studying Daniel's face. 'You have been doing some interesting things with worms, have you not? Did I not read that you have been playing God and reversing the ageing process?'

'Huh? Oh. Yeah. Yes. Sorry.' Daniel was aimlessly stirring his soup now. 'We can double the life expectancy of the nematode to forty days, which is, you know . . .' The sentence went unfinished. He was staring at the spoon in his hand. Eventually he looked at the physics professor and said, 'Did you say the past could walk in on the present?'

Wetherby and Sang-mi exchanged a look.

'Yes,' Sang-mi said. 'Are you OK? You seem . . .'

'I'm sorry. I don't mean to be rude. I've . . .' Daniel closed his eyes in concentration. 'Scientists are not as anti religion as you think, Wetherby. We just want evidence. One shred. It's not so much to ask. Something testable. Something we can hold in our hands . . . I mean, you can say anything without evidence. Anything! *A Brief History of Time* tells of the lady who insisted that the Earth sat on a giant turtle. When challenged as to what held that creature up, she replied that the cosmos was "turtles all the way down".' Daniel blinked. The word turtle had produced some cognitive friction. He tried to repeat it but it clotted his tongue.

Wetherby touched his arm. 'Daniel, are you unwell? You have not touched your soup.'

'Soup?' Daniel said. 'Turtle soup . . . Mock turtle soup . . .' He rose from his seat, muttered, 'Excuse me,' and left the refectory.

Sang-mi looked shocked. 'Did I say something to upset him?'

'Do not mind Daniel,' Wetherby said, playing with the cornelian intaglio ring on his finger. 'He can be a bit territorial, that is all. He probably feels you are stepping on his turf. Also . . . I probably should not mention this . . .'

Sang-mi looked left and right. Leaned in closer.

'His nerves have been a little strained lately. It has been a great worry to his colleagues.'

CHAPTER THIRTY

NANCY THREW HER FRONT DOOR KEYS ON THE SIDE, JOGGED UP the stairs, opened her laptop and clicked on the file marked 'diary'. It was empty. Good. She had remembered to delete its contents before leaving for work. It had been nagging her all day. She descended the stairs as quickly as she had gone up them, the heels of her boots clattering on the wood. She found Daniel waiting for her in the kitchen. 'Why didn't you ring and say you were going to be late?' he said. 'I was supposed to be going to a faculty meeting tonight. I've had to cancel it.'

'My watch is still broken.'

'Well, why don't you get it repaired?'

'I keep it like this to remind me of the crash.' There was hardness in her voice. She was surprised by it.

'Why would you want to be reminded of the crash?'

No answer.

'Oh, *obviously* you would want to be reminded of the crash.' Daniel's tone had a sarcastic edge that he must have known would provoke her. 'Why would you *not* want to be reminded of the crash?'

She shifted her weight from one foot to another, her hands on her hips. It annoyed her that he was fixating on the watch. Bloody hell, he had nothing to get upset about. He had no right. She was the one who should be feeling irritated. 'Just do, that's all.'

'Time frozen. I get it. Like you. Frozen.'

'Let it go, Daniel.'

He moved a step closer to her, squaring up. 'You've calcified and you can't see it.'

'Stop it.'

'Anyway, you need to keep thinking about the crash so you can go on seeing your counsellor. How often do you see him?'

Nancy gathered her hair over one shoulder and teased two strands of a fringe down so that they hung dangerously over her eyes. 'Most days. Why?'

'What do you talk about?'

'None of your business.'

'Is that all you do? Talk?'

'What are you saying?'

'You tell me.'

'Don't be pathetic.' Nancy's nostrils were flaring, her eyes flashing in anger.

'Well?'

'I'm fucking him? You think I'm fucking him?' Nancy shook her head in disbelief. Her expression hardened and she nodded. 'Yes, I'm fucking him.'

'You can't be.'

'Of course I'm not, you arsehole.' She threw a can of deodorant at him, the closest thing to hand. It bounced off his arm. She threw a mug next; it broke against the wall behind him.

Daniel stared at the pieces in silence for a moment, then said, 'It's getting crowded in here,' and left her standing on her own.

Neither spoke to the other while they made their own breakfasts the next morning, though each clatter of plates and cutlery felt like a reproach. When Nancy went upstairs to floss and gargle, Martha said to Daniel, 'I heard shouting last night. What was happening?'

'Mummy and Daddy were having an argument.'

Martha thought about this for a moment before saying, 'Who won?'

'Well, both sides did, in a way.'

'So Mum did.'

The silence continued into the school run. Daniel was driving and, as usual, he dropped Martha off first, then Nancy at her dental surgery. Neither said goodbye. Trying to change the subject of his thoughts proved enervating and futile. Nancy kept seeping back, filling the mental space like a liquid: her face, her voice, her smell. Stop it. Think of something else. What had Wetherby and the new physics professor been talking about? It had sounded interesting. Something about the past walking in on the present. His mind furred around the conversation, unable to give it shape or substance.

In the evening, when Daniel came home from work, he got straight into the bath vacated by Nancy – as he always did, to save water, to save the planet – and began itching. He held up his arms. The skin was turning red and blotchy. His eyes were streaming and, when he wiped them, he felt a stinging sensation. It was now he noticed the smell coming from the bathwater: sodium hypo-chlorite. He lurched from the bath and reached for a towel. 'Nancy!' he shouted downstairs. 'Have you put something in this bath?'

There was a pause. 'Sorry. I'm cleaning it. I put some bleach in it.'

Ten minutes later Daniel stood in the doorway of the kitchen watching Nancy wiping the counter top with a damp cloth. He spoke first. 'You did that on purpose.'

'Did what?'

'Put bleach in the bath.'

'I know I did. I was cleaning it.'

'You knew I'd get in it after you.'

'Said I was sorry. I forgot.'

'Of course you didn't forget. I've been doing that for years.' He was breathing loudly through his nose. 'That was really *fucking* dangerous, Nancy. I'm still itching.'

'Sorry. OK? I didn't do it on purpose. You didn't put your head under, did you?'

'I might have done.'

'You said you couldn't put your head underwater since the crash.'

Daniel glared at her. 'Unbelievable.'

Nancy stood her ground. 'Are you going like that?'

They had been invited to a dinner party in Hampstead but Daniel was wearing jeans with a rip in the knee, plimsolls without laces, and a tight, navy blue crewneck jumper over a white T-shirt. He looked down at himself then up at Nancy, who was dressed smartly – knee-length suede boots and russet skirt, and a polo neck which served as a plain backdrop to a string of rough-cut amethyst stones. 'Yep,' he said. 'You going like that?'

The couple managed to look cheerful as they kissed their host, Camilla, on both cheeks. She had been widowed six months earlier, her husband Mark, a don at Trinity, having died of a heart attack at the age of forty-seven. This was her first attempt at a formal dinner party since the funeral. Nancy and Daniel were introduced to another couple, an architect and his barrister wife, and made small talk with them for a few minutes before seeing, above the heads of the other guests, Wetherby's lank frame in a three-piece suit and tie. He was talking to a dishevelled-looking Bruce and a young, Oriental-looking woman with a black fringe. Daniel led the way through the press of bodies and noticed that both men looked guilty and stopped talking when they turned and saw him. 'Talking about me?' he asked with a laugh, clinking his champagne glass with those held by Bruce and Wetherby.

'There are other subjects,' Bruce said.

'Didn't know you two knew each other.'

'We both knew Mark,' Wetherby said, revealing a thin track of metal across his front teeth, 'and we have realized we both know you.'

'So you *were* talking about me.'

'Allow me to introduce my friend Hai-iki,' Wetherby said, standing to one side. 'A most gifted pianist.'

'Hello,' Daniel said, taking her small hand in his. 'What sort of stuff do you play?'

Hai–iki's full lips parted into a wide smile. 'I've been working on some Ravel recitals lately. Debussy. Delius. The impressionists mostly. Do you play?'

'Not really, but I do listen to a lot of jazz.'

Hai–iki and Wetherby exchanged a look.

Daniel didn't notice. 'Wetherby, you remember Nancy?'

'Of course, of course.' Wetherby kissed Nancy on the hand she had held out to shake, an extravagantly antiquated gesture, even for him. 'She is my dentist.'

'Yeah? Better watch out then. That was how she got me into bed.'

'I remember you saying.'

Nancy snatched her hand away in mock indignation. 'So that's why you wanted to become one of my patients!'

Wetherby smiled, exposing his brace again. 'Of course.'

While Wetherby introduced Nancy to Hai–iki, Bruce led Daniel to one side and, speaking softly, said: 'Actually we, urm, were talking about . . . Wetherby was asking about you and Morticia, saying that they're worried about you over at Trinity.'

'They?'

'You know, the provost. Members of staff.'

'Really? What did you say?'

'Nothing compromising. You all right? You look like you've got fleas.'

'Got a rash,' Daniel said, scratching his hips. 'Nancy put acid in my bath.'

'Ooh, that's dark. Even by her standards.'

'She didn't intend to. I mean, she didn't know I was getting in it.' He was scratching his ribs. 'What did you make of Wetherby?'

'Very tall.'

'Apart from that.'

'Quite liked her. Is she single?'

Daniel was scratching his chest. 'I didn't mean like that. Anyway, she's – he's – straight. I mean, did you like him? I've always thought you two might get on. He looks a bit mad but he's a decent bloke.'

Bruce dropped his voice. 'Thought you'd told Wetherby about your, you know, whatever it was, hallucination, vision thing . . .'

'No, did you tell him?'

'You didn't want me to?'

'You're a credit to your profession, Bear. Did you show him all my medical records while you were at it?'

'Sorry. It sort of slipped out.'

'What did he say?'

'Think he was surprised.'

'Surprised?'

'He was holding a breadstick and it snapped in his hand when I told him.'

'Bruce and I were talking about this angel you saw,' Wetherby said, appearing at Daniel's shoulder and making him jump.

'Wasn't an angel,' Daniel said distractedly, his eyes searching the room for Nancy. 'It was an . . .'

She was talking to a man who looked to be in his mid-thirties and was wearing an expensively tailored, cream-coloured suit that showed off his tan. He had the sculpted face and curling hair of a Michelangelo statue and something about the way Nancy was standing, like a ballet dancer with her arms behind her back and the heel of one foot tucked into the arch of the other, made it look as if she was trying to impress him.

'Of course,' Wetherby continued, '99.9 per cent of all sightings are hoaxes. People make these claims to get attention, or to compensate for some inadequacy.'

Bruce shot Daniel a look, but his friend had not heard this slight. He addressed Wetherby instead. 'Wasn't there a famous sighting in the First World War?'

'The Angel of Mons?'

'Yeah.'

'A textbook hoax. Do you know much about it?'

'Don't know anything about it, apart from the name.'

'Well, the name refers to the first major battle of the war and, for the heavily outnumbered British, the first major defeat. They called it an orderly withdrawal but it was a full-scale retreat.' Wetherby dipped his shoulder slightly in order to follow Daniel's sight line. When he saw he was staring at Nancy talking to the handsome man he said: 'Do you know about Mons, Danny?'

'Huh?' Daniel looked at him with confusion in his eyes. 'The *mons*? Sure. The soft mound of fatty tissue just above the vagina. Protects the pubic bone. Why?'

Wetherby raised his eyebrows and turned back to Bruce. 'Anyway, the point is, something odd happened while the British were retreating. The Germans failed to press home their advantage. Just stopped in their tracks. A rumour spread that an angel had intervened. The Angel of Mons.'

'Well, obviously,' Bruce deadpanned. 'What other possible explanation could there be?'

Daniel was looking around Wetherby's shoulder again, only half listening. He could see Nancy was enthralled by the statue's conversation, touching his arm as she laughed at his jokes. Unbelievable.

'What is?'

Daniel must have given voice to his thoughts because Wetherby was looking at him and repeating his question. 'What is unbelievable?'

'Um, that the British government started the rumours about the angel to make it look like God was on their side,' Daniel said, thinking quickly.

'Actually they did not,' Wetherby said, moving over slightly so that he was blocking Daniel's view. 'The rumour began with a short story by Arthur Machen. He wrote it for a London newspaper, I forget which one. It opened with an account of how the Mons battlefield had been shaken by the sound of British troops calling out the name of St George. The saint duly appeared, along with thousands of archers.'

'Handy,' Bruce said, taking a sip of champagne.

'Very. The air darkened with arrows and ten thousand Germans lay dead, though none bore a wound.'

'I get that with my patients all the time. The old ones anyway. I find an injection of diamorphine into the ball of the foot works best. They can't prove a thing.'

Wetherby nodded thoughtfully, running with Bruce's conceit. 'I imagine the admin is a terrible bore though. All those death certificates. And having to forge medical records to show your patients had been in poor health.'

Bruce grinned.

'What death certificates?' Daniel asked, losing his thread again.

'I was telling Bruce about this short story. Within a few days of publication, Machen received a letter from the editor of the *Occult Review* asking whether the fiction had any foundation in fact. Though he explained that it was entirely made up, the magazine ran an account of it anyway, as if it were based on truth. In the following months, various parish magazines did the same. Even the *Tablet* ran it, complete with a supposedly eyewitness account from an unnamed Catholic army officer. The myth of the Angel of Mons was spreading like . . .'

Daniel was paying attention now. 'A virus?'

'Exactly, exactly, I thought you would like that. The rumour became so widespread that by Christmas nineteen fifteen the *Illustrated London News* had dignified it with an illustration. You could buy sheet music for something called "The Angel of Mons Waltz". Have a copy of it somewhere. Is everything all right, Danny?'

Nancy was drinking from the statue's wine glass. 'Sorry,' Daniel said. 'Carry on. I *am* listening. They cashed in on the hoax?'

Wetherby was gaining an audience among the other guests. He drew himself up, enjoying the role of lecturer. Hai-iki was standing close to his side looking up at him in rapt fascination, her head barely reaching his chest. 'The myth of the Angel of Mons was by this stage evolving and mutating rapidly. According to some versions, the medieval longbow men were strange luminous clouds in human form.'

Bruce shook his head. 'And what did this Machen bloke make of it all?'

'Well, he was getting desperate. He appealed for the nonsense to stop but this merely provoked another author, Harold Begbie, to weigh in. Begbie felt the story was so inspiring for the troops he wrote a book defending it. It was called, let me think, *On the Side of the Angels*, and in this he suggested that the revelation about the Angel of Mons may have come to Machen by telepathic means direct from the battlefield.'

'Poor guy,' Daniel said. 'Machen, I mean.'

Nancy was flicking her hair back, laughing at whatever it was the statue was saying. She couldn't take her eyes off him. How could she do this to him in front of all his colleagues?

'It got worse. There was only one piece of . . .' Wetherby made two inverted comma signs with his long fingers, '"evidence" that was not anonymous. This was a statement from a young nurse, Phyllis Campbell. She had been working at a dressing station near Mons, at one of the railway halts. There she claimed to have met two of the men who had seen the angel, a Lancashire Fusilier who had seen a tall man in golden armour on a white horse, holding up his sword, and a major in the Rifle Brigade who had "seen something", though he was not sure quite what. Machen figured that if he could prove to the world that this evidence was no evidence at all, the myth would die and the record could be set straight once and for all. So he publicly challenged Nurse Campbell to produce sworn affidavits from the two soldiers. She partly wriggled out of it by saying that the fusilier refused to go on the record because he feared this would get him into trouble. All she would offer was a quotation from a letter that she said the major had sent her, though she would not show it to Machen. The passage described how the major had had hallucinations while marching at night. He said everyone in his company had been reeling about the road and seeing things too.'

Bruce grinned again. 'Such as?'

'Flashing lights. Strange shapes. And an ethereal figure who calmly walked through a hail of bullets towards them and then led them to safety.'

Bruce drained his glass. 'So the only evidence offered for the Angel of Mons was a letter describing hallucinations suffered by soldiers drunk from fatigue?'

Camilla was clinking a glass with a spoon. 'It's ready! If everyone would like to come through . . .'

Daniel was relieved when he saw the statue was seated at one end of the table next to Hai-iki, while Nancy was in the middle, opposite him, in between Bruce and Wetherby.

Nancy made no attempt to disguise her dislike of Bruce, turning her back on him as soon as they sat down. He already had his broad back to her. 'So,' she said, addressing Wetherby. 'What have you got to say for yourself?'

Wetherby looked shocked. Said nothing.

'Neither witty nor spontaneous,' Nancy continued. 'I like that in a man.'

Wetherby nodded and smiled. Nancy was his kind of woman. 'Thank you,' he said.

'I can't keep calling you Wetherby,' Nancy continued. 'What do your friends call you?'

'Wetherby.'

Nancy grinned and patted his leg. 'How's the brace?'

He smiled again, unconvincingly. 'Good, I think.'

'No trapped food?'

'No.'

'And how's work? You keeping busy?'

'One struggles on.'

'I appreciate what you've been doing for Daniel, with the professorship thing. Means a lot to him.'

'And he means a lot to us.'

'How about you? You're happy at Trinity? You've been there for ever, haven't you? When are you going to take over from the provost, what's his name . . .' She clicked her fingers impatiently.

Wetherby leaned in to her, close enough for Nancy to detect the sour smell of champagne on his breath. 'It allows me to indulge my true passion,' he murmured.

'Which is?'

'Detective work. I have been trying to track down an alternative opening to Mahler's Ninth.'

Two plates of asparagus were placed in front of them.

'A new recording?'

'No, no, an alternative version written by Mahler himself but lost, or destroyed. I am sure you are familiar with the Ninth.'

Nancy thought for a moment. Shook her head. 'I'd probably recognize it.'

'It was his last completed symphony. His meditation on dying. A premonition of his own death and the imminent carnage of the First World War. The long passages for strings at the end are as close as music has come to expressing silence itself. But it is the opening movement that has always intrigued scholars. It is long and sinuous, a loose sonata in major and minor keys that combines tenderness with savagery. Not to everyone's taste and I must confess I have always found it jarring and unsatisfactory. Mahler may have been having a mental breakdown when he wrote it. Not only had his young wife's infidelity recently been revealed to him, but he had also been diagnosed with a heart condition. It is thought that the hesitant, syncopated motif of the opening reflects Mahler's irregular heartbeat. Can you keep a secret?'

'No.'

Wetherby smiled thinly. 'A letter has come into my possession which proves that he wrote drafts and sketches for an alternative opening, one which makes more sense in terms of its musical and philosophical development. He published a limited edition of it, but subsequently changed his mind and had all but one copy of the sheet music destroyed. No one knows where it is but the Mahler community has known about the rumours for years. Hai-iki there is helping me trace it.' He gave a little wave down the table and Hai-iki raised her glass of water to acknowledge him. 'She has recently returned from a research trip to Berlin.'

Nancy nodded. 'And the letter says?'

'He mentions to whom he gave the missing copy. Not by name, but . . . Let us say the field has been narrowed considerably.'

'Hum it,' Nancy said, picking up an asparagus spear and taking a bite.

'The original version? I could not do it justice. But it is

beautiful . . .' He leaned over so that Nancy could feel his hot breath in her ear as he added in a whisper, 'Like you.'

Nancy stopped chewing.

'It's on at the Barbican,' Wetherby continued nonchalantly. 'I'm going to it next week. Perhaps you would consider accompanying me.'

'That's a kind offer.'

'And *that* is a non-committal answer.' Wetherby stared at the untouched asparagus on his plate. 'I have embarrassed you.'

'Not at all.'

Wetherby leaned in closer again. 'You are used to being told you are beautiful, I think.'

Nancy smiled.

'Used to it,' Wetherby continued in a whisper, 'but not tired of it.'

'Do you ever tire of being called an intellectual?'

'Never.' Wetherby smiled and brushed the back of his hand against Nancy's leg. 'The truth, of course, is that I am in love with you.'

Nancy's eyes widened.

'You probably do not remember when we first met,' Wetherby continued in his barely audible voice. 'But I do, and I have been unable to stop thinking of you since.'

'Now *that's* embarrassing,' Nancy said under her breath, dipping her fingers in a small bowl of water provided for that purpose. 'You have spun me off my axis.'

'Steady on, Wethers old boy.'

'I love you.'

'Don't squander those words.'

'*Amor tussisque non celantur.*'

'You'll have to translate.'

' "Love, and a cough, are not concealed." Ovid.'

'What are you two whispering about?' Daniel said from across the table.

'I was trying to seduce your wife,' Wetherby said, 'with the offer of free tickets to a Mahler concert.'

'We're not married,' Nancy corrected.

'They'd be wasted on her,' Daniel said, scratching his stomach. 'She only listens to hip-hop.'

Nancy stared at Daniel, her face flushed.

'Well, I suspect it will be hideous anyway,' Wetherby said. 'They are for a Friday night, when the Classic FM crowd are usually in. They come by the coachload from the shires and applaud between movements.'

'Is that bad?' Daniel said, removing a thread of asparagus from his teeth. He appeared to be unaware of the cold look Nancy was directing at him across the table.

'The Ninth represents Mahler at his most intense, introspective and profound. It can only be appreciated as a whole. Broken up by applause between movements it becomes meaningless.'

'Daniel always applauds between movements,' Nancy said.

'That's right, darling, I have a low brow and you have a high brow. We complete each other.'

A heavy silence filled the room, broken only by a scrape of silver on china and the babble of a glass of wine being too quickly poured.

The couple did not speak as, two hours later, they climbed into the back seat of a minicab. Daniel clicked his seat belt; Nancy left hers unfastened. They had been driving for twenty minutes before Nancy wound her window down to release a chemical smell of air freshener. 'We're not going to talk about this, are we?' she said.

'Oh, do you think?'

A further minute of silence. Daniel broke it this time. 'Do you want to talk?'

Nancy shook her head.

'Why not?'

'Because,' she shook her head again, 'there's too much to say.'

Silence again.

'Do you have to do that false laugh?' Nancy said. 'You were making everyone cringe.'

'Do you have to be so obvious when you flirt with people?'

Nancy flicked back her hair, mentally squaring up for a fight, not looking at Daniel. 'Are you talking about Wetherby?'

'What? No. Course not. That stockbroker.'

'Paul?'

'That was his name, was it?'

'He's a hedge fund manager.'

'That's all right then. For a moment there I thought he might be some kind of cynical opportunist out to bring down the global economy in order to turn a quick profit for himself.'

'Did I ever tell you how attractive you look when you're jealous?'

'Did you have to be so obvious? You were all over him.'

'*Paul* is happily married.'

The comment shocked them both into silence. It settled between them like a cloud of toxic gas, heavier than air, lowering the temperature. *Paul is happily married.* Nancy had curled her lip as she said it, a rhetorical whipcrack. She tilted her head to look at Daniel's profile, challenging him to stare back. His features were alternating between indistinct and clear, the gloom in the back of the cab dispelled every other second by the orange of streetlights as the cab circled the common. Daniel was staring straight ahead of him. Nancy wanted to punch him, bruise his face with her fist, shake him from his complacency. She wanted to bite him as Sylvia Plath was said to have bitten Ted Hughes – take a chunk out of his stupid, complacent cheek. She could feel anger rising in her chest, making her breathe more quickly through her nose. It was colourless, this anger. Odourless. She knew she couldn't stop herself. Even without sinking her teeth into his cheek, she had tasted blood. Her aim now was to damage him. This wasn't about Paul, but she didn't know how to tell Daniel what it was about. 'Paul loves his wife.'

Daniel caught the eye of the cab driver in the rear-view mirror. 'Don't, Nancy.'

'Paul is a man.'

'Don't.'

'Don't what?'

Daniel appeared unsure, as if he had no stomach for where this was going. 'I'm too tired.'

'Tired or afraid?'

'Don't say anything you can't take back.'

How has he the nerve, Nancy thought. How has he the nerve to try to negotiate his way out of this by making *me* feel guilty? Talking about a man loving his wife had broken a self-imposed taboo for Nancy. She knew now what she wanted. She wanted Daniel to be strong. She wanted him to protect her. She wanted him to be a man. It wasn't so much to ask. She didn't want to have to be the strong one. She wanted the man she loved, the father of her child, to love her so passionately he would sacrifice his life for her. There could be no conditions. There had been a time when she could have unequivocally said of Daniel that she loved him so much she could give her life to save his. Sitting in this cab, in the flitting London shadows, she could no longer say it – and it irritated her the way he stared directly in front of himself, unmanned and unmanly. She realized too, with frightening clarity, that the subject could no longer be avoided. It would continue to grow, expanding to fill the space between them, pushing them apart. There could be no retreat. Her heart was pounding. She could hardly breathe. The weight of the subject was crushing her. 'What *are* we talking about here exactly, Dan? Huh? You tell me.'

'Stop it,' Daniel said with an unexpected firmness and confidence. 'Not here.'

This was good, Nancy thought. She had found the tender spot, enamel at which she could scrape. This would make things easier. *He* was angry now. Become infected by her anger. It gave her a licence to go further, to stop manoeuvring and start fighting. The way her hair had loosened up proclaimed her readiness. She leaned forward to talk in the cab driver's ear. 'Sorry, is our conversation bothering you?'

The driver talked without moving his head. 'Forget I'm here, love.'

'He says we should forget he is there,' Nancy said to Daniel.

'I'm trying to save you from yourself,' Daniel said, his voice taut.

'*You* save *me*? This is a first.'

Daniel looked at her. 'It's you, not me,' he said, gambling that the best form of defence was attack. 'I've tried talking about it. But I can't. You're like this stranger to me, some mad stranger always angry, always stomping around slamming things, feeling sorry for herself. Hey, guess what, you survived. Get over it. Move on. Get your fucking watch mended.'

It was as if a prison door had yawned open for Nancy. Her long-accumulating anger liberated her. She felt ecstatic, exhilarated, dangerous. In her mind, Daniel had no rights left; his words denied him rights. 'You're a coward,' she said and waited a moment for the word to settle. 'That's right. You're a pathetic little coward. And wipe that stupid grin off your face.' She tapped the cab driver's shoulder. 'Stop the car.'

The driver stopped and Nancy opened her door only to be caught in the headlights of an oncoming car that had to swerve to avoid her.

'What are you doing?' Daniel shouted as he leaned over to the open door. Nancy slammed it shut, marched over to the pavement and stood with her back to the car, staring at the solid black outline of the trees on the common.

'Get back in the car,' Daniel said in a neutral voice as he himself climbed out of it.

Nancy spoke without turning round. 'I'm going to walk home.'

'Don't be ridiculous.'

She could hear Daniel walking up behind her, sense him reaching for her shoulder but stopping short of touching her. 'I want to walk,' she said.

'You'll be mugged.'

'I can look after myself.'

'I'm not leaving you on your own.'

'Wouldn't be the first time.'

The comment lingered in the night air like another cloud

of poisonous gas. The sound of a distant police siren perforated the silence. Nancy shut her eyes and said: 'Daniel.'

He didn't respond. Was he hoping that if he didn't acknowledge his name there might still be a way out?

Nancy heard herself speak more calmly than she felt: 'We need a break.'

The cab driver honked his horn. 'You getting back in?' he shouted.

Daniel jogged over and handed him two twenty-pound notes. He didn't wait for the change before jogging back. It was as if the implication of Nancy's words could find no grip in his mind. 'What are you talking about? Break from what?'

'From each other.'

Nancy would later torment herself for escalating things more than she had to. At this stage she still had room to back down. Instead she went further, clarifying her meaning. 'Breathing space.' She wheeled round to face him. 'I can't breathe.'

The cab drove off. Their eyes lingered on its disappearing tail-lights. There was a movement over by the trees. A fox. Its robot eyes were shining in the glare of another oncoming car. It tested the air for a moment and, when the car had passed, trotted across the road within feet of where Daniel and Nancy were standing. Without looking around it disappeared behind the cricket nets, back into the night.

'That was one cool fox,' Daniel said.

'The Steve McQueen of foxes.'

'Steve McFox.' There was a new quality to Daniel's voice, neither anger nor fear but defeat and sadness. Something that had been building invisibly between them was now a physical presence. 'We can discuss this . . . whatever it is . . . when I get back from Boston.'

They set off in the direction of their house, two roads away. The clacking of Nancy's heels on the pavement was impossibly loud. Daniel's plimsolls were making no noise. It was their habit to link arms as they walked, but a force was keeping them apart tonight, polar equals repelling one another. Nancy felt that they were acting out assigned roles, that it would be undignified to step out of character. 'Didn't know you were going to Boston,' she said.

'Only just found out. The *Selfish Planet* team are going out there to film a newly born lemur for the next series. They want me to do a piece to camera from there.'

'Are work OK with you taking time off like this?'

'They should be fine. If I can take academic ownership of this story, I think . . . it would reflect well on the department. I could get a paper out of it. Might help with my tenure. I need . . .' He stopped walking. 'Come on, Nance. We don't need to do this.'

She knew now she had hurt him. 'Will you be OK on the flight?' The kindness warmed them both momentarily, sending a weak pulse between them.

'Bruce has given me something, but thanks for asking. Didn't know you cared.'

'Course I care.'

CHAPTER THIRTY-ONE

Le Bizet, Belgium. Second Monday of September, 1918

THE PERCUSSIVE STAMP OF STUDS ON SPRINGY WOODEN FLOOR-
boards grows louder as Andrew is quick-marched into the
improvised courtroom, an echoey village hall in Le Bizet, five miles
east of Nieppe. The escort, a hollow-chested corporal, clatters to a
halt a second after the prisoner, slopes arms and slaps the butt of his
rifle in salute. Three officers are seated behind a long oak table and,
in the stillness that follows, dust motes swirl upwards, caught in a
shaft of autumn sunlight. Andrew recognizes one of his judges: the
scar-faced major who dragged Adilah through the market square.
He looks lopsided – the left half of his tunic is crowded with
medals, eleven of them, including a VC and a 1914 Mons Star. His
eyelids are swollen and there is a pinkness to his eyes: at close
quarters, in the light, they look cloudy and haunted. One of his
leather-gloved hands, Andrew notices, is shaking. The major
notices, too, and steadies it with his other hand.

To his left – the middle officer of the three – is a man who
doesn't look much older than Andrew. He has a Roman profile and
is wearing a tailored buff-coloured tunic made of barathea and
decorated with seven campaign medals. The cross-straps on his Sam
Browne belt have a glassy sheen and support a polished leather
holster on the right hip and a sword on the left. On his red tabs he
has a crossed sword and baton: a brigadier-general. The dirt under

his fingernails indicates that he is a brigadier-general who has recently seen action. His red nose and watery eyes reveal him to have a cold. The officer to his left also wears medals. He is a slightly built man, mid-fifties. His pallor is the same steel-grey as the hair showing below his cap. His eyes are opaque.

Andrew takes in the rest of the room with rapid sideways glances. Everywhere he looks there is the glint of bronze and silver. Seated at either end of the table are two more officers, both wearing medals, and in the shadows, behind the table, is a chaplain with bored eyes. He is wearing a dog collar under his uniform and a cross, enamelled white and edged in gold on his chest, a DSO. His interlocked fingers are resting on a copy of *The Manual of Military Law*. A clerk – a warrant officer with a notepad and pen – is sitting by the door. Andrew takes off his cap and checks his side parting with a brush of his fingers.

The officer at the centre of the table unscrews the lid of his silver fountain pen, taps some papers and clears his throat. When he speaks it is with a nasal voice: 'This Field General Court Martial is now . . .' he searches for the right word, 'convened, on this day, the fourteenth of September, nineteen eighteen. Let the records show that the three officers presiding are Lieutenant-Colonel James of the Royal Field Artillery . . .' he holds his left hand out, palm flat; 'Major Morris of the Second Rifle Brigade . . .' his right hand is raised; 'and myself, Brigadier-General Blakemore of the Seventh Royal Welch Fusiliers.' He turns to the clerk and adds, 'And could you make a note that my ADC, Second Lieutenant Cooper . . .' he nods towards a handsome young man with wavy yellow hair, dimpled cheeks and glasses, 'will be acting as prisoner's friend and Captain Peterson here will be acting as . . .' Unable to think of the correct term, he taps his papers again. '. . . will be acting on behalf of this military tribunal.' He blows his nose and, as he leans forward to stuff his handkerchief back into his pocket, he notices the chaplain. 'And the Reverend Horncastle over there will be acting as the court's legal adviser.' He looks up at Andrew. 'Will the prisoner please identify himself?'

Andrew remains silent, blinking rapidly and eyeing the room.

Lieutenant Cooper coughs to get his attention, raises his eyebrows and prompts: 'Say your name, rank and number.'

'Private Kennedy, A., number nine eight six two, Eleventh Shropshire Fusiliers. Sir.'

'Private Kennedy,' Brigadier-General Blakemore continues, 'you stand accused of dereliction of duty, specifically of shameful desertion in the face of the enemy. How do you plead?'

'Guilty, sir.'

The room falls silent. The brigadier-general's eyes widen in disbelief. 'Are you sure, man?'

Lieutenant Cooper stands. He gives the impression of being a man trying to appear more languid than he feels. 'May I have a word with the prisoner please, sir?'

Blakemore nods. The lieutenant, who is two years younger than the prisoner and looks it, leads Andrew to the rear of the hall, stands with his back to the bench and talks to him in a muted tone. Andrew shakes his head. Nods. When they return he blinks and says: 'I'd like to change my plea to not guilty, sir.'

'Very well,' Blakemore says, blowing his nose again. He turns to Captain Peterson. 'The case for the prosecution please.'

Peterson, a bald man with an Edwardian moustache and small, piercing eyes, scrapes back his chair. The chaplain knocks on the table. 'I believe the prisoner is supposed to be sworn in first . . .'

'Yes of course,' Blakemore says. 'We need a Bible. Has anyone brought a Bible? Padre?'

The chaplain looks awkward. 'I don't have mine with me . . .'

'What about the *King's Regulations*?' Lieutenant Cooper says. 'I've got a copy of them in my bag.'

'I've got a *Book of Common Prayer*,' the chaplain says.

'That'll have to do.' The brigadier-general signals for the book to be handed to the prisoner.

As Peterson sets out the argument for the prosecution, Andrew's mouth opens slightly, awed by the nuances and pedantry of legal procedure. 'On the thirty-first of July nineteen seventeen, the first day of what has become known as the battle of Passchendaele, Private Kennedy was marked as absent at roll call. His colour sergeant major duly declared him missing in action. His family were informed. His possessions were sent home. *In fact,*' Captain Peterson turns to Andrew, 'you were not missing in action at all. In an act of shameful cowardice you had run away from the enemy. You had deserted your company. You had made your way to the town of Nieppe, where you found lodgings in a house on,' he consults his notes, 'on the Rue des Chardonnerets. Your landlady there was,' he checks his notes again, 'Madame Adilah Camier, a widow. I understand that you were having relations with Madame Camier and living in comfort with her at the time of your arrest . . . at a time when your comrades were still fighting for their king and country at the Front. You had assumed a new identity, passing yourself off as a plumber, and had remained undetected for thirteen months. Is that correct?'

'I never lied about who I was, sir.'

Lieutenant Cooper stands up. 'May I remind the FGCM that Private Kennedy used his own name and address to have his birth certificate sent to France?'

'We'll come to that, lieutenant,' Brigadier-General Blakemore says with an air of patience.

The lieutenant sits down and immediately stands up again. 'In my respectful submission, sir, I would also like it to go on record that Private Kennedy was a volunteer.'

Blakemore nods at the clerk. 'Very well.' His tone is hardening.

'Also that he gave himself up.'

Brigadier-General Blakemore no longer disguises his irritation. 'After he gave the redcaps the slip at Nieppe, you mean?'

Lieutenant Cooper looks deflated. His nervousness is showing. 'Correct.'

Captain Peterson takes advantage. 'As this seems to be the moment to put things on the record, may I remind the court of General Routine Order No. 585 issued to the British Expeditionary Force on the thirteenth of January nineteen fifteen?' He turns to a marked page in his sheaf of notes. 'In cases of desertion the presumption of innocence is effectively removed and the burden of proof reversed. Unless an accused soldier can prove his innocence, the courts are entitled to presume his guilt.' He looks up. 'Private Kennedy, it is clear to me that you had no intention of returning to your battalion. You thought you'd got away with it. Started a new life. Sat out the war away from danger. Your prisoner's friend is no doubt going to plead that you were suffering from shell shock, or that you lost your memory. He will, in other words, suggest that you cannot be held responsible for your actions. But let us examine those actions. Tell us, Private Kennedy, why did you run away?'

An expectant hush falls on the court. 'I don't rightly know, sir. I'd lost the rest of my platoon. I was in a shell hole. Everyone around me was dead.'

'So why didn't you try to make it back to your own line?'

'Couldn't move, sir.'

'You were injured?'

'Can't rightly say, sir. I'd been hit by something, on my helmet. I think I was knocked out for a while. I weren't sure where I was. It were dark. I'd lost me rifle.'

'You'd thrown your rifle away?'

'No, sir, I must have dropped it when I dived for cover. Like I says, I'd lost it.'

'How would you describe your mental state when you were hiding in the shell hole?'

'Don't know what you mean, sir.'

'Were you frightened?'

'No, sir. Well, yes, sir. It was frightening. But I'm not a coward, sir.'

'Yet you thought you would save yourself by running away from the enemy?'

'I walked towards them, sir.'

'*What?*'

'I walked towards the German line.'

'Without your gun?'

'Yes, sir.'

'You wanted to be taken prisoner?'

'No, sir.'

'Are you saying you decided to walk towards the German line, on your own, without a gun?'

'I weren't on me own, sir.'

'Who was with you?'

The prisoner purses his lips and shakes his head.

The question is repeated.

'I weren't alone, sir. I were with someone.'

'Someone from your company?'

'Don't know, sir.'

'What do you mean you don't know?'

'He were one of ours.' Andrew touches his temple. 'It was confusing. He led me to safety. Along the German line. To the river.'

The chaplain stands up. Everyone turns to him. 'He was definitely wearing a British uniform?'

'Yes, sir.'

The chaplain is fidgeting. 'You are sure of this?'

'I think so. I can't remember right well. There were a lot of lights. I couldn't see him proper because of the lights.'

'Flares?'

'Yes, sir. Must have been.'

The chaplain taps his chin. 'But he asked you to follow him?'

'He didn't speak.'

'So why did you follow him?'

'He were signalling at me to come towards him. He turned and started walking towards the German line so I stands up as well and walks after him.'

'And how long did you follow him for?'

'Couple of hours.'

Colonel James throws his pencil on to the table in front of him and speaks for the first time. 'Do you expect us to believe that you and this other fellow managed to take a Sunday stroll for two hours in no-man's-land in the middle of an offensive?'

Andrew looks at him placidly. 'It's what happened, sir.'

Colonel James turns to the defence counsel. 'I'm a little confused. Have you briefed your client to enter a plea of insanity?'

Lieutenant Cooper shakes his head. He looks baffled.

Colonel James returns to Andrew. 'Are you trying to persuade the court that you took leave of your senses?'

'No, sir.'

'So the two of you carried on walking to Nieppe?'

'No, sir. When we reached the river the man pointed to the remains of a barrel in the mud. I lay on it and pushed myself out into the water. I didn't see him again after that.'

'You then threw away your uniform?'

'No, sir. I'm wearing it now.'

'But it doesn't fit you.'

'I know, sir. It were all they had when I enlisted.'

Brigadier-General Blakemore has to suppress a smile at this.

'Did you throw away your tags?' Colonel James continues.

Andrew reaches in his collar, lifts up his identity discs and jiggles them with his fingers.

'Sir, is there any point to this?' Colonel James says, turning to face the brigadier-general. 'He's admitted he's a deserter.'

'I agree. I think we've heard enough. Defence, do you have anything to add?'

Lieutenant Cooper looks at his notes. 'I have a character witness, sir.'

The brigadier-general turns to the chaplain. 'Are we agreed that this is permissible, padre?'

'I can find no objection in military law, sir.'

'Very well. Call the witness.'

Adilah is escorted in. In her nurse's uniform, with her Légion d'honneur on a ribbon around her neck, she looks dignified and elegant. Her starched white wimple bears a red cross on it. She is resting her hand on her stomach, her pregnancy obvious. The members of the court martial exchange glances.

'Madame Camier,' Lieutenant Cooper says, 'would you tell the court who the father of your child is?'

Adilah looks up, her face blank.

The chaplain translates.

'Monsieur Kennedy,' she says, pointing at the prisoner.

'Did you know Private Kennedy was a soldier?'

She waits for the translation. Nods.

'Please answer.'

'Yes, I knew. I guessed.'

'Was it your impression that he intended to return to the army?'

'Yes. I assumed he would one day. But he wanted to help me. He looked after me.' She glances at the cuff of her left sleeve, pinned to her shoulder. 'He protected me.'

'What's she saying?' Brigadier-General Blakemore asks impatiently.

'She says she thought the prisoner would return to the army,' the chaplain translates.

Colonel James interrupts again: 'Is there any point to this?'

Cooper's gamble, that Madame Camier will make the court feel sympathy for the accused, has not paid off. It is the prosecution's turn. Captain Peterson stands up. 'Madame Camier, did Private Kennedy tell you he was a deserter?'

As the padre translates, Adilah looks across at the prisoner. '*Non. Mais ce n'est pas un lâche. Il est revenu pour moi.*'

The chaplain translates again. 'She said: "No, but he is not a coward. He came back for me."'

Captain Peterson continues. 'You planned to marry him? Is that correct?'

'That is correct.'

'Did Private Kennedy tell you he was already married? That, in other words, he was intending to commit the crime of bigamy?'

The colour drains from Madame Camier's face as this is translated. She shakes her head.

'Please answer.'

'*Non.*'

'Thank you, madame,' Blakemore says. 'You may step down . . . Are there any more witnesses?'

'The ADMS, sir,' Cooper says.

Surgeon-Major John Hayes, the assistant director of medical services, is a retired GP. His practice was in Norfolk. He has thick jowls and turned-down lips.

Blakemore is direct. 'In your opinion, is this man suffering from shell shock?'

'I am satisfied that he has been having nightmares and hallucinations,' the surgeon-major says in a voice like fine sandpaper. 'Shell shock is more complicated. He may well have been suffering from it at the time. He may well have neurasthenia now.'

'Yes or no?'

Andrew's mind keeps wandering, as if it is not he being talked about. Out of the window he can see open pastureland. He can hear the clip-clop of iron-shod hooves and the rattle of a passing limber. The medical officer, he notices, has writing on his hand. What does it say? Andrew is not close enough to read it. He shifts his attention to the MO's lips. They are moving but it takes a moment of concentration before his words come into focus. 'He hasn't seen action for more than a year,' Hayes is saying, 'so at the moment he is probably not suffering from shell shock. At the time he almost certainly was, I would say. But I believe he may have been in what is known as a fugue state – memory loss following a traumatic incident.'

'Private Kennedy used his own name and address to have his birth certificate sent from England in order to commit bigamy,' Blakemore points out. 'Does that sound like the action of a man who has lost his memory?'

Hayes looks from side to side, up at the ceiling, down at the floor. He draws a deep breath. 'Memories are unpredictable. Perhaps he forgot he was married.'

'He may be a fool but that doesn't mean he lost his memory. Having remained undetected for so many months he had become complacent.' Blakemore waves a hand at the witness. 'You may step down.'

The ADMS turns from the bench and begins walking away. Stops. Turns back again. 'This is madness,' he says in a barely audible voice, as if softly swallowing the words. 'You know that, don't you? I've seen too many good men pointlessly killed in this war. Private Kennedy volunteered, for God's sake. He did his duty as best he could. He didn't know his nerves would fail him. None of us knows until we are tested in battle. Show leniency. Have some humanity.' He walks up the long table, rests his hands on it and stares at each of the three judging officers in turn. 'The Germans are back to the Hindenburg Line, for Christ's sake. The war is all but won. We'll be home in a few weeks.'

Major Morris bangs his fist against the table and speaks for the first time. He has a resonant voice. 'The man's a coward. Cowards don't deserve pity.'

'You know as well as I do that the woods around Étaples were full of deserters,' Hayes counters. 'There were thousands of them. There probably still are. Do you plan to shoot all of them?'

'Those we catch, yes. Make an example of them. I'll shoot the bastards myself.'

'Major!' There is cold fury in the reproach. The ADMS draws himself up. 'Show some self-control. A man's life hangs in the balance.'

The major straightens his back and turns his heavy-lidded gaze from the ADMS to the prisoner. 'Our business here is finished.'

'We are not savages, sir,' Hayes says, his cheeks colouring.

The major's eyes are burning and wet. 'Our business here is finished,' he repeats.

The brigadier-general blows his nose. 'Yes, well. Are there any more points to be made? Prisoner's friend?'

'No, sir.'

'Prosecution?'

'No, sir.'

'Is the court martial officer satisfied with procedure?'

The chaplain tilts his head. He has a degree in jurisprudence from Cambridge but little of what he learned there applies to the vacillations of this court. 'I should point out that, in order to convict, the court must be certain that the defendant was not only absent without leave but had formed the intention of never return-ing to his unit.'

'Very well,' Blakemore says with a nod. 'We know the answer to that. Thank you, padre. We shall adjourn to consider our verdict. Take the prisoner away.'

Andrew has been waiting for four minutes when a hoarse yell summons him back inside. A crackle of excitement passes through the court. With an excess of tight-lipped military smartness the clerk stands to attention and reads from a piece of paper. 'Private Andrew Kennedy, you have been found guilty of shameful desertion in the face of the enemy and it is the sentence of this Field General Court Martial upon you that you suffer death by shooting at dawn on the fifteenth of September. May the Lord have mercy on your soul.'

The chaplain says: 'Amen.'

Andrew salutes and remains standing to attention.

Blakemore isn't sure what to do next. He looks at the prisoner expectantly. 'Have you anything to say?'

'The fifteenth, sir. When is that?'

'Tomorrow.'

The prisoner makes as if to speak again but instead clicks his heels together. From start to finish his trial has lasted twenty-three minutes.

CHAPTER THIRTY-TWO

London. Present day. Five months after the crash

WITH HER HAIR STILL WET FROM THE SHOWER, NANCY WENT through an underwear drawer, holding up several items before choosing black silk hipster briefs with a lace trim. As she stepped into them, she had to hop twice and steady herself on the ottoman. Half standing, half sitting against this, she opened a new packet of black hold-up stockings and rolled them on. She chose a bra next, a black demi-cup that flattened her breasts slightly so that the Theo Fennell cross she intended putting on would hang better. Next she sprayed a mist of scent from a bottle, walked through it and stood in front of her full-length mirror to look over her shoulder at the curve of her hips and the taut roundness of her buttocks. She patted her left cheek to test the elasticity of her skin; rubbed her forehead. Why had she said yes when Tom had asked her and Martha over for Sunday lunch? She had bumped into him near her house. She rubbed again. What had he been doing near her house? And why had she mentioned that Daniel was away in Boston? 'Why are you making an effort?' she said out loud to her reflection. She knew why and it brought a flutter of nerves to her belly. Infidelity begins in the imagination and it had begun for Nancy that afternoon when Tom had walked her to her car. She had, in moments of reverie, been imagining herself having sex with him ever since, vengeful sex, dirty sex, and this mental adultery had been making her furtive and jumpy. The deed itself was a mere technicality.

She took her BlackBerry from her handbag and sent Daniel an email to appease her guilt. 'Why not look Susie up while you're in Boston?' it began. 'She and I have been emailing each other and I'm sure she would appreciate the chance to talk to a fellow survivor, someone other than me, I mean. You might get something out of it, too. I know she's still struggling to come to terms with what happened to Greg. Poor thing. It broke her heart. In the last email I got from her she said she had gone back to college. I think she has also found religion, but don't hold that against her. She said she starts each day with a visit to the cathedral x.'

A few seconds after sending the message, she sent another: 'We miss you . . . The bins need emptying x.'

Long after the message had been sent, she continued staring at the screen. As if of its own accord, her hand returned to the bag and felt for a packet of anti-depressants. The flat metallic wrapping held eight pills, each separated by an expanse of empty foil. They were like prisoners in solitary confinement. Lonely and enclosed, hermetically sealed and claustrophobic. Their solitude cruelly reflected hers. *They must feel as I feel. Why aren't they all in the same bottle?* She popped each one of them out and pushed them together like gamblers' chips. The staring again. Taking one without water, she clicked her handbag shut. The sound was reassuring, decisive, thrilling.

Tom lived in a Victorian redbrick in Dulwich. It was semi-detached and three storeys tall. 'I inherited it from an uncle,' he explained apologetically as Nancy looked down at the black and white marble tiles on the floor and up at the high ceiling in the hall. He led the way through an airy kitchen and, holding open a fridge door covered in brightly coloured magnets, offered Martha a can of Coke.

'Diet?' Martha questioned.

'Diet,' Tom confirmed.

'Sorry. She has to be careful about her sugar intake,' Nancy explained.

There was a hiss as Tom pulled the ring on the can and put it to his lips to stop it foaming over. 'I'll get you another one,' he said.

'That one's fine,' Martha said sharply.

Tom shrugged and led the way out to the garden where there was a bottle of champagne cold-sweating in an ice bucket. Next to it, on a mahogany table, were two long-stemmed crystal flutes. As he expertly unwrapped the wire, he asked Nancy if she would join him in a glass. Nancy's affirmative answer was lost behind the sound of the cork being popped.

'You seem happier,' Tom said as he tilted both the bottle and the glass.

'Feel happier. Thanks to you.'

'I don't think I've done anything. You needed someone to listen, that was all.'

'You ever seen a counsellor?'

'Why do you think I became one? My counsellor saved my life.'

'Really?'

Tom rolled up his sleeves and showed the thin white scars on his wrists.

Nancy put her hand to her mouth. 'Why?'

'It was after my wife died. The only way I could think to make the blackness go away.'

'I didn't know . . . You never mentioned a wife.'

'Bit of a conversation killer . . . "Hello, my name's Tom. By the way, I'm a widower."'

'How long ago?'

'Eight years, nearly nine. But she had been dying for a year before that. A horribly slow journey.'

'You poor man.' Nancy touched his arm. 'I'm so sorry.'

'Let's change the subject . . . To happier days.'

They clinked glasses.

'Happier days.'

They ate outside under a large canvas umbrella. Tom had cooked lamb with new potatoes and fresh mint, and when they finished the champagne they opened a bottle of red. Feeling light-headed, Nancy had to support herself when she rose from the table. She was still smiling at her own clumsiness when, a minute later, in the bathroom, she looked in Tom's medicine cupboard and found several bottles of anti-depressants. She recognized them. The same ones she used.

Afterwards, while Tom filled the dishwasher, she leaned over a kitchen counter with her chin resting on her fists and watched Martha playing with Kevin the Dog in the garden. She was feeling drunk, as if she needed to sit down. When she felt Tom's fingers kneading her shoulders, she rolled her neck slightly, giving him permission to continue. He bunched her golden brown hair and savoured its weight, smell and texture before laying it gently over her shoulder and kissing the nape of her neck. She closed her eyes as his hands reached around and cupped her breasts, a shockingly intimate gesture. How rude. How deliciously rude. The unfamiliar hands were a thousand times more erotic than if they had been Daniel's familiar ones. When she still did not protest, he hitched her skirt up to her hips; it was tight and she had to help him by wriggling slightly. She felt him press his lips against the exposed curve of skin at the top of her briefs. Feathery kisses now. Goose bumps. Oh my God. He was kissing the backs of her knees. She closed her eyes, breathed through her nose, stopped herself. She then stopped Tom. This was wrong. She wriggled again as she tugged at the hem of the ruched skirt, smoothing it down.

'What are you doing, Mum?'

Nancy opened her eyes. Martha was standing in the doorway directly in front of her. If she moved her head a fraction to either side she would see Tom. 'I was just thinking, darling.' As Nancy said this she lifted a distracted hand to her loosening hair. 'And call me Mummy.'

'What were you thinking?'

'I was thinking that we should be getting going. Can you go and call Kevin in.'

★

The following morning, a raw-boned Monday, Wetherby closed the provost's door behind him, hovered across the corridor to his own office, sat down, tilted back his chair and smiled sparingly to himself. The meeting had gone well. Exceptionally well. It could not have gone any better. The provost was normally like a water spider skitting across the surface of conversation. It was to do with his wandering focus: the way he nodded and smiled constantly, but rarely concentrated on what Wetherby was saying, still less on what he himself was saying. But this time . . . Wetherby's brain reversed current as he retraced his steps back across the hall and replayed the conversation, savouring its nuances, enjoying its dramatic structure. The water spider had also played his part well, given the performance of a lifetime. Sensing Wetherby's reluctance to share what was clearly preying on his mind, he had stopped writing and laid down his pen, affecting his usual air of irritation at being a busy man interrupted.

'So, Larry, what is this matter to which you feel my attention should be drawn?'

When Wetherby told him, with a plastic sigh, that a senior member of staff had been in contact with a terrorist suspect – had, indeed, brought on to campus a man MI5 suspected of being a jihadist trying to recruit Muslim students – the provost, self-important dolt that he was, had looked stunned. Literally stunned, as if zapped by a Taser. There had been utter confusion in his eyes. Wetherby had enjoyed that.

'I do not think it right to say who the member of staff is, at this stage,' Wetherby said, magnanimity personified. 'I would not wish to accuse a man, and potentially ruin his career, without *ablativus absolutus.*'

The provost insisted. Because the provost always insisted. Because the provost was an insistent creep. 'A name. I must have a name. I insist.'

When Wetherby divested himself of the name, the provost shook his head in disbelief. 'Daniel Kennedy? That can't be right.'

Wetherby unfolded the copy of the Trinity College newspaper he was holding and pushed it across the table. The provost stared at the photograph of Daniel in the refectory with a young Muslim man who had a few weeks' beard growth and a chequered scarf wrapped around his neck. After this, the questions came in a torrent. How did Wetherby know? What should they do? Did he think it an isolated incident?

Wetherby mentioned his phone conversation with Geoff Turner, the MI5 officer specializing in counter-terrorism. (He neglected to add that he had been the one to ring Turner, rather than the other way round. There was no need for that information. It would have distracted the provost, a man of limited concentration.) 'Turner does not think we are dealing with a typical cellular formation here. There is no stable command hierarchy. No army council. That is not how AQ – Turner refers to Al-Qaeda only by its initials – operates. They are more organic. More spontaneous. A loose-knit unit. In all probability the jihadist cell on campus—'

'*There's a jihadist cell on campus? Jesus!*'

Wetherby ignored the provost's lazy-minded blasphemy. 'The jihadist cell on campus,' he repeated, 'will have started as an informal conversation between a small group of like-minded young male students. They are always male, though not necessarily fundamentalist. Not to begin with anyway. This will mutate as the conversational stakes get raised at the next meeting. Then one member will broach the subject of a terror attack. They will discover that they have particular talents or resources, access to materials, skills in chemistry and so on. Their behaviour then resembles that of a playground gang and their bond becomes something close to the psychology of a group dare. None wants to be the first to abandon the project – and thus it develops its own momentum. They tend to be ill-disciplined. They fantasize. GCHQ has picked up chatter from a group thought to be connected to the campus group – chatter about kidnapping British and American children and filming them being tortured. The problem for MI5 is when to send in the police. Too soon and there will be no evidence to prosecute. Too late and . . .' Wetherby made an exploding gesture with his hands.

The blood had drained from the provost's face. 'Unbelievable,' he said. 'This is unbelievable. How many Muslim students do we have?'

'About thirty, I believe.'

'It makes no sense. We go out of our way to address their needs.'

'Turner thinks that might be the problem. The better educated, the more privileged, the greater the likelihood they will become radicalized.'

'But why Daniel? The man's an atheist.'

'Good cover.'

'You mean he's not an atheist?'

'No, I mean, that is why they are using him. They know he is a liberal, a political soft touch. That he is a high-profile atheist as well is a bonus. Puts him above suspicion.'

'Is he aware he is being used?'

'Who knows?'

Wetherby closed his eyes as he respooled the next part of their conversation, allowing it to linger in his memory like the smell of incense after Solemn Mass. Predictably, the provost had been concerned that 'all this' should be kept out of the press – that his, the provost's, name should be kept out of the papers. Wetherby agreed there was a risk the story would leak out. If that happened, the press would want to know why the provost had not acted as soon as he had known – why he had not suspended Dr Kennedy, pending an inquiry.

The provost shook his head gravely. 'Yes, suspension is the only option. But it must be done with tact. And there is the issue of Daniel's pastoral care to consider – the university has a responsibility to him.'

'Of course, of course.' Wetherby assured the provost that he would see to it personally; that he would handle matters discreetly. He was, after all, sure it was all a misunderstanding; that it was merely a symptom of Daniel's having been under a lot of strain lately.

'Strain? What strain?'

This was the point at which Wetherby mentioned the trial separation. It slipped out. 'Oh, you know, the trial separation.'

The news about Daniel's delusional behaviour slipped out, too.

'He's seeing things? What things?' The provost stood up and began pacing the room as he said this. 'Has Daniel told you he's seeing things?'

Even better, Wetherby thought but did not say. 'No, no, Daniel's doctor told me.'

'But surely doctors aren't allowed to discuss their patients?'

'True, but he told me in confidence, as a friend. As a mutual friend.'

Wetherby had explained that the doctor feared Daniel was having a nervous breakdown. The doctor, moreover, had wanted to know how he had been behaving at work. It was only sensible to tell the doctor, the friend, the mutual friend, about the nine lectures and seminars in two weeks that Daniel had missed or cancelled. Also about the one he had managed to give which ended abruptly with him collapsing in a fit of uncontrolled giggling, the one broadcast on the web – apparently it was getting thousands of hits on YouTube. Wetherby thought it sensible, as well, to mention the concern of his colleagues: even Sang-mi, the new professor of theoretical physics, had commented on Daniel's odd and, frankly, anti-social behaviour.

The provost protested that he had no idea things had become this bad. 'I had no idea. No idea . . .' He wondered whether he should call Daniel in for a talk. This was the cue for Wetherby's *pièce de résistance*. The provost could not see Daniel because Daniel . . . he paused to savour the moment . . . Daniel was on one of his trips abroad, filming his television series in Boston. Had the provost not been informed?

Wetherby left the provost massaging his temples with little circles of pressure from his fingertips. Yes, the meeting had gone well. His performance, his timing, the way he had been so in touch with his inner bastard, all of it had gone well. He checked his watch. Almost lunchtime. Holding a decanter by the neck, he poured himself a glass of port. Earnest, narcissistic, blasphemous Daniel Kennedy, he thought as the rim of the glass touched his thin lips, was getting what he deserved.

This called for a celebration. A private tutorial with Hai-iki. Where would she be? He checked the music department timetable then rang her mobile. What a relief he had decided against the deportation option with her. He drummed his fingers. Come on, Hai-iki, answer. Wetherby is in the mood for love.

Daniel awoke from a shallow sleep in which he had been following Nancy and Martha down a busy street, unable to catch up with them, unable to make them hear his calls. Where was he? Boston. His hotel in Boston. With sweat on his brow he skittered around the channels on a sizeable television screen. Nothing would arrest his attention. Every other channel appeared to feature a tele-evangelist in a shiny suit on a stage with a microphone, the congregation answering him with 'That's right!'s and 'Amen's. There were also workout channels with muscular women in leotards, weather channels warning about hurricanes on the eastern seaboard, and numerous identical news channels, with ticking information panels detailing falls on the Dow Jones. He stopped channel-hopping when he found BBC World. There had been another security alert in London. A Church of England school evacuated. Another false alarm. In other news, the Department of Homeland Security had uncovered an Al-Qaeda plot to kidnap American children, film them being beheaded and post the footage on Islamic websites. 'We will butcher them like pigs,' one message had read. It was thought that they would use children to do the beheading, following a case in which the Taliban had filmed an eleven-year-old boy beheading a 'traitor' with a kitchen knife in Afghanistan. A commentator came on to interpret the Al-Qaeda 'message' – that this would prove they were more committed than their decadent Western enemies; that jihad would go on being fought into the next generation; that the jihadists would never draw a line. 'We're not going to go away. That's their message.'

Feeling sick, Daniel switched to CNN. A Creationist was talking about the ring-tailed lemur with the feathers. He watched as a preacher worked himself up into a frenzy. Perhaps the unreconstructed Marxists on campus were right. Even with a liberal president, America was still a fundamentalist state, one that was overheating the planet. He turned the television off, put on his sleeping mask from the plane and took it off again as he looked for the ear plugs that had come with it. He couldn't find them and had to listen to the clanking of a bell in the harbour; that and the melancholy two-tone horn of a freight train. When a pneumatic drill started up and a distorted, metallic voice announced departures – he was near the station – he checked his watch with a double tap: 7.30. He had been awake for four hours. At the window he took in the semicircle of old warehouses on the wharf. With their slate roofs and copper flashing they looked like they were forming the spokes of a giant fan. Beyond them was Antony's restaurant on Pier 4 where he had listened to some rough-edged jazz and eaten clam chowder the night before. There were moored yachts bobbing in the marina. Sleeping. Being lulled asleep by the water lapping against their bows. Ropes were clapping and clanking contentedly against their vertical spars. A metallic lullaby. It would be the middle of the night in London; he checked his iPhone anyway. A message from Nancy. 'We miss you . . . The bins need emptying x.' He smiled. 'Miss you, too,' he messaged back. 'Can't sleep. Took two hours to get through security at Logan. There's a lot of water between us x.'

There was another message from Nancy below it, about Susie. After reading this, he looked in the phone's photo library and tapped the one he had taken of Nancy at the moment he had told her about the surprise holiday. He scrolled back and came to one Nancy had taken of him swinging Martha around by her arms. It enlarged to fill the screen. The next photograph showed Martha laughing as she tried to remain standing after the spin. He sent her a text now. 'Didn't get chance say goodbye before Boston. So. Goodbye. Daddy. x.'

Half a minute later a text came back: '*Auf Wiedersehen.*'

Daniel grinned and tapped in: '*Au revoir.*'

Twenty seconds later came: '*Arrivederci*.'

'*Sayonara*.'

'*Do svidaniya*.'

'*Chao* darling. See you at weekend. Look after Mummy. Love you xxx.'

'Luv u 2 xxx. Bring me back a present.'

'OK.'

'And not some cheap tat from the airport.'

'OKaaaay.'

'Something book.'

Daniel smiled. Martha had taught him that 'book' was a textonym for 'cool' – the predictive text facility on mobiles, she explained, always gave 'book' when the word 'cool' was typed. 'OK, something book.'

'But not a book.'

'xxx.'

'Mum liked the roses.'

'Roses?'

'The ones you sent.'

An item on the news distracted him. A microscope. Images of sperm wriggling. The reporter was saying: 'Scientists have identified the hundreds of proteins that constitute the head and tail of the smallest cell in a man's body – so small that five hundred million of them can fit into a teaspoon. They believe the proteins could lead to new insights into how the sperm manages the equivalent of a transatlantic swim as well as sabotaging the efforts of rival sperm in the race to be first to reach the egg.' Daniel looked at the swimming trunks hanging over the back of a chair. He had brought them in case he felt strong enough to try a swim. Fifteen minutes later, as he stood in these trunks at the deep end of the hotel's pool, he felt his limbs grow numb. His arms were poised in front of him, but he could not dive. A middle-aged man with hairy shoulders stood alongside him and dived in without hesitation. His body appeared to shrink as the water distorted and bent the path of ordinary light. Daniel recalled his long swim. It had helped him then to imagine he was merely swimming a length of the pool. One more length.

Half a length. Quarter of a length. This memory made him feel sick again. He rose up on his toes and took a deep breath, but still he could not dive. After ten minutes he gave up and went to sit in the steam room.

As he emerged from the hotel forty minutes later, he half read the front page of a complimentary copy of the *New York Times* – RATE CUT BY FED PROMPTS RALLY ON WALL STREET – but could not take in its meaning. A liveried doorman gave him a lazy salute of acknowledgement. At the same moment, two cab drivers shouted at him. He couldn't make out what they were saying. Realizing they were asking if he wanted a lift, he shook his head, turned up his collar and walked in the direction of the Boston Tea Party Ship. There was a salty mist and the streets were empty and wet from a recent shower.

Daniel was enjoying the solitude, the feeling of having the early morning to himself. When he came to a junction, he headed inland away from the harbour, towards Chinatown along a block of brownstones before reaching a more genteel road of clapboard houses. He left this at the next turning and wandered for a quarter of a mile, savouring the energy of the city as it throbbed into life. There was a plane overhead. It was arcing skyward, leaving a thin trail of smoke in its wake. He was lost. How far had he walked? Why didn't he recognize these streets? He knew Boston as well as he knew London. Better. Ahead he could make out the Gothic cruciform of the Catholic cathedral and wondered if Susie would be in there. Wasn't that what Nancy's email had said?

As he approached it, he saw two women blocking the pavement outside the entrance as they talked. They stood apart to let him through and, once inside, he found the interior cool and, apart from arrangements of small guttering candles, gloomy. He wandered along an aisle, his footsteps echoing, and sat down in an empty pew. The entire interior was a clear space, broken only by two rows of columns extending along the nave and supporting the central roof. On the mildewed walls were the Stations of the Cross depicted in a tapestry and, above them, tattered militia battle flags from the War of Independence. He looked up at the barrelled ceiling, nodded to himself and drowsily inhaled the moist smell of mildew and incense. The noise of the traffic and the chatter in his head subsided. The silence was pure. Is this, he wondered, what people mean by silent waiting on the truth, sitting in the presence of the question mark? His mind emptied. He closed his eyes.

Who the hell has been sending Nancy roses?

He opened his eyes and noticed a schoolgirl kneeling in front of him, head bowed, a plait of blonde hair following the bend in her spine. He cocked his head and studied her, almost envying her simple faith and certainty, but also pitying her. His iPhone pinged in his pocket, disturbing the silence and causing the girl to look round. The message was from the genetics department at Trinity.

'Hi, Dan. Afraid we couldn't get any trace from that Q-tip you gave us. Tried both ends! Was it important?'

Daniel was still staring at the screen when, two minutes later, the girl stood up, dipped her knee as she crossed herself and turned to walk out. She must have noticed Daniel looking at her because, with echoing footsteps, she walked towards him. He looked away, staring down at his footstool.

'Professor Kennedy?'

The young woman was looking at him over the top of her glasses.

'It's me, Susie.' A big smile. Expensive American teeth. 'Galápagos Islands?'

'Oh my god. Susie.' Daniel stood up and held both her hands, a gesture which turned into a kiss on both her scarred cheeks. 'Nancy said you came here. How have you been?'

'Not great. Getting better . . . I've gone back to college.'

'So Nancy said. What are you reading?'

'Art history.'

'Good subject.'

'How are you? How's the biology thing going?' Her voice was chewier than Daniel remembered it.

'Good. Though I'm not Professor Kennedy yet, technically speaking. Anyway, call me Daniel.'

'How is Nancy?'

'Fine.'

'She emailed me to say you were in town.'

'Yeah, she said you came here.' He smiled. 'I've already said that.'

'I know you don't approve. Don't worry, I'm not Born Again or anything. I just . . .' She looked up at the ceiling and spread her arms. 'I found it helped after the crash.'

'I don't really disapprove, it's more . . .'

'You hate the argument that science answers the how questions, but only theology can answer the why questions?' She grinned. 'You wrote that on your blog . . . Now you think I'm a stalker.'

Daniel laughed. 'I do find that a bit embarrassing, as an argument.'

'"A pointless cliché".'

Daniel laughed again. 'Exactly. A pointless cliché. Not worthy of an educated mind.'

'Anyway, knowing that Greg is with the Lord now . . . I come here every morning on my way in. I find I can talk to him here.'

'Greg?'

'The Lord. Both of them, I suppose.'

'It's certainly very peaceful. I'd never been in before.'

'Have you . . .?' She didn't finish the sentence but waved her arms.

'No. No, I'm still with the other lot . . .'

Susie quoted him. '"I'm an atheist fundamentalist. I don't believe in anything, very, very strongly."'

'You really *have* been reading my blog . . . I guess I came in here because I couldn't sleep. Jetlag. I'm staying nearby, at the George Washington overlooking the harbour. Do you know it?'

'Yeah.'

'Do you fancy a coffee? There's a Starbucks across the road.'

'Sure.'

Seeing the polystyrene cups being thrown away prompted Daniel to start his speech on global warming and recycling but when Susie was able to recite it with him, almost word for word from his blog, he grinned and gave up. He noticed a tautness to Susie that hadn't been there before the crash. A fragility too. It was to do with the scars on her pallid face, the ones caused by the flying glass. Those and her mobile, questioning eyebrows. Her voice was unexpectedly light too, floating like thistledown. 'What are you doing in Boston? You were at school here, weren't you?'

'You remembered. MIT . . . I'm here because of the lemur. Have you been reading about it?'

'The one with the feathers?'

'We don't know that's what they are yet. I'm with a film crew. We're going to include it in the next series of *The Selfish Planet*. I remember you said you watched it . . . I was thinking more about how the lemur was a perfect example of random mutation as an explanation of evolution. I'm supposed to be meeting the crew there in an hour so I'd better . . .' He stood up. 'Do you fancy coming along?'

'I can't. I've got a tutorial at ten . . . Do you have a card?'

Daniel opened his wallet and handed over his card.

In a fine, rolling hand, Susie wrote her number down on a napkin. 'Here. Any time . . . You know I found out I was pregnant after the crash?'

'No, I . . .'

'It didn't go to term.' Daniel sat down again and placed his hand on top of Susie's across the table. She held it firmly. 'It was a boy.' She looked awkward. The mention of the baby had paralysed her. Daniel, feeling the contagion of her awkwardness, removed his hand and sipped his coffee.

The Wildlife Foundation, a zoo in all but name, was in Dorchester, a forty-minute drive away. The director, a craggy-faced man in his fifties, was waiting to greet him: he wanted to lower Daniel's expectations before he saw the baby lemur. 'The tabloids have gotten a little carried away,' he said as he walked alongside Daniel and passed him the mask and smock he would have to wear.

The baby lemur was in an incubator. Daniel peered in. It was no more than ten inches long and if it had feathers it was not obvious where they were. Though only a few weeks old, the baby resembled the adult it would grow into. The palms on its forelimbs were padded with soft, leathery skin and its narrow face was pale with black lozenge-shaped patches around its eyes and a vulpine muzzle. It had yet to grow its bushy, black-and-white-ringed tail but its underbelly was grey and white. Its slender fingers had flat, human-like nails and its eyes were bright orange. The director rolled the lemur on to its front and pointed at two small, feathery clumps of hair on its back. Daniel cocked his head to one side and said, 'I see what you mean.'

'We're calling him Red Sox. The papers got that right.'

As the baby was in intensive care, the cameras were not allowed to film him directly. They had to do it from the next room, through a window. Daniel did the piece to camera he had prepared from there, too. The producer was happy after three takes and said there was no need for him to hang around if he didn't want to – they were going to interview one of the keepers who had witnessed the birth and then do some general shots of the zoo. Daniel decided to stick around for half an hour in case he was needed again; half an hour in which he could take in the rest of the site. He watched a tiger pacing up and down neurotically in its cage before making his way to the aquarium.

The vivid electric yellows, blues and oranges of the tropical fish he found beautiful but haunting. As he stood contemplating them, time went into reverse and he was back in the Pacific Ocean once more. A memory ripped through his thoughts like tearing metal. It was of the plane bucking: its death throws. He could smell electrical burn, acrid like battery acid, and could see a film of smoke filling the cabin. The seaplane, he remembered, accelerated as it spiralled towards the water, the horizon appearing at an angle of forty-five degrees. Nancy had extracted her hand from his, lowered her head down to her knees and cupped the back of her head with both hands.

Who had sent Nancy those flowers?

As he stared into the tank, Daniel replayed another fragmented memory: at one point the plane had gone into a nosedive and he had known then that he was about to die, yet part of him had clung to the hope that he wouldn't, that Nancy and he would escape. Part of him, the small, non-scientific part, still believed he was immune to death. The flight attendant's pidgin English filled his head: '. . . You also remove high-heel shoe, take off you glasses and pour drink into the seatback pocket. Place you life jacket over head but not to inflate until ready to leave aircraft. When you hear the command "Brace! Brace!" we want you assume brace position, with head on you knees, feet tuck underneath and hands over you heads.'

We get through this together.

Daniel pressed his forehead against the cold glass and closed his eyes. He could see the flight attendant demonstrating the brace position as he moved unsteadily through the cabin, his hands shaking. He had made all the passengers demonstrate it in turn. He pushed Nancy's head down lower. 'Good,' he said. 'Now check you seat belts are tight and you seats are in upright position. Thank you.' He repeated the emergency procedure in Spanish. Daniel remembered thinking: *He must be as scared as we are, but he is showing courage. He is being a man. He is toughing it out.*

Feeling short of breath, Daniel staggered, unbuttoned his jacket and removed his scarf.

'You OK, honey?'

A doughy, silver-haired woman in a motorized wheelchair was staring up at him. Attached to the arms of the chair were carrier bags bulging with groceries.

'Just a bit hot.'

'You're English?'

'Yes.'

'You sure you're OK, honey? You look like you could do with a glass of water.'

'I need some fresh air.'

The woman smiled, pressed a lever on the arm of her wheelchair and, with an electric sigh, drove off around the next corner. Daniel walked in the opposite direction and came to an abrupt halt as he found himself looking into the bulging, heavy-lidded eyes of a giant leatherback turtle. It was as long as a man and was floating directly in front of him, as if suspended in air. Daniel thought it might be dead, until it opened and closed its beak. Hello. Transfixed by the long digits fused through its flippers, he brought his hand slowly up and pressed it against the glass. The turtle did not move. It was reading his mind, an impression prompted by a cold sensation at the back of his skull. Daniel waved the out-held hand slowly from side to side. With a powerful wing-like beat of its flippers the turtle swam off, giving a brief view of the thick, oily skin on its heart-shaped shell before becoming an indistinct shadow in the murky water at the back of the tank.

Daniel groaned. He was feeling feverish and achy. This place, this turtle, these memories – he needed to get away from them. With no recollection of how he got there, he found himself sitting in the back seat of a taxi. A numbness had sluiced over him. He double-tapped his watch face and asked the driver to take him back to his hotel. As they drove along the Massachusetts Turnpike he gazed up at a vast reproduction of a Stanley Spencer painting on Huntingdon Avenue. It was on a hoarding advertising an exhibition of First World War artists at the Museum of Fine Art. He asked the driver to drop him there instead.

With its air-conditioned coolness and its tasteful gloom – small, evenly spaced pools of illumination – the gallery had an atmosphere similar to the cathedral. Another place of worship. The altar of art. Admission seventeen dollars. He jogged up the marble stairs that led to the rotunda, saw a sign for the First World War exhibition and cut across a room dedicated to German Expressionism. When he reached the room where the temporary collections were exhibited, he felt dizzy and so lethargic he could barely pull open the heavy double doors with their rubber sound-proofing seals.

The oil paintings here struck him as being improbably bright and colourful, in contrast to the black and white images normally associated with the trenches. Green swirling gas in thick impasto paint. Golden starbursts in night skies, defying the patina of age. Barbed wire gleaming under Verey lights as humpbacked howitzers emitted lemon flashes from their great barrels. Some of the paintings were quite abstract and naive, influenced, so Daniel read on the introductory panel, by the Vorticist movement – patterns of duckboards and helmets with cigarette smoke rising from beneath them; ghostly chiaroscuro figures in gas masks walking across ploughed fields carpeted with the dead; huddled groups of greatcoats reduced to solid blocks of colour in dark, cratered landscapes. As Daniel strolled between them he clasped his hands behind his back and nodded to himself. One sketch showed a dog-toothed trench lip disgorging men along its length. Some were being hurled up like foamy waves breaking backwards on to a black ocean. There was a cartoonish quality to the sketches. Something almost childlike. Explosives reduced to fireworks. Under one of the Paul Nash paintings – a black landscape of splintered tree stumps – Daniel read a letter the artist had written to his wife in November 1917. His eyes flitted over it and fixed on one word. It was a word that Hamdi had used only days earlier.

No glimmer of God's hand is seen. Sunset and sunrise are blasphemous, they are mockeries to man; only the black rain out of the bruised and swollen clouds or through the bitter black of night is fit atmosphere in such a land. The rain drives on, the stinking mud becomes more evilly yellow, the shell holes fill up with green white water, the road and tracks are covered in inches of slime, the black dying trees ooze and sweat and the shells never cease.

He looked at the painting again. It was a good description. Nash was as good with words as with paint. Perhaps only words could do the hellishness justice, Daniel thought. He remembered the Siegfried Sassoon poem his father had quoted: 'I died in hell – (They called it Passchendaele).' These words now felt sodden and black with meaning. Daniel could feel their weight. Hell. Passchendaele. Blasphemy. It was as if the trenches were entering his own memory; his own consciousness. They were squatting over him, giving him a terrible sense of foreboding, evoking words that had not held meaning for him since he had abandoned them as a child. There was evil here. This was a godless landscape. A blasphemous place. His great-grandfather had been here, in this mud. He looked again at the paintings and realized these were visions of hell far more nightmarish than any drawn by Hieronymus Bosch. This was not some imagined hell. This was man-made. A hell on earth. A hell with dark fires. He could see his own features reflected in the glass and it was as if the painting was coming to life. It was also producing a sense memory, as the aquarium had done; a feeling of being back in the plane as it was falling to earth. He had been certain then that he was about to die and the imminent prospect of his death, of the nothingness it represented, the hell of not being, terrified him.

Swaying in the cool shadows of the gallery, Daniel found himself in mortal terror once more. The walls of the gallery were closing in. A ball of panic ripped upwards through his diaphragm and into his chest. All around him there was mud, a roiling sea of glutinous, gas-poisoned black. Feeling nauseous and claustrophobic, he backed away from the paintings, attracting the attention of a man with collar-length white hair and a spotted bowtie. A schoolgirl with a brace stared at him, too, smiling at first, then looking alarmed. He wanted to create distance between himself and them. He ran down the steps and out of the main doors, across the grass and left on to Huntingdon. He was sprinting now, keeping pace with a tram trundling along in parallel to the road. At the Symphony Hall, he turned left again in the direction of the Charles River and the comforting embrace of the MIT buildings on the far bank. Ignoring the red hand sign on the pedestrian crossing, he found himself on the Harvard Bridge. He was sweating and when he reached the middle he stopped, bent double and gulped mouthfuls of air. Though a pewter ceiling of cloud was pressing down on him, he could still make out his shadow in the water. As he looked down with vertiginous disgust at the inky, churning liquid below, he felt off balance and cursed his own weakness in the gallery, his childishness, his cowardice.

The river was a broad scar across the city and, judging by the thick, melting folds on its glassy surface, its current was strong. There were black-feathered coots with red eyes and white bills bobbing on the surface. They were causing ripples. The water was absorbing the light, swallowing it up in its black dimples and whirlpools. He saw what looked like a sheet of dark metal, a shell perhaps, a leatherback. It was gone. Stupid, stupid, stupid. You don't get leatherbacks in rivers.

He understood this river. He understood why it was here and how it worked. Though it began inland, it was near to the point at which it joined the sea and was almost tidal, the point at which the water began to turn, lost in indecision, running back on itself. As a student he had watched the rowing teams train here, keeping track of the mileage between the bridges. He looked down now and saw a metal plaque commemorating an escape Houdini performed off the bridge in 1908. Perhaps Daniel could escape death, too. He'd done it once, on the plane. It wasn't so far down, twenty or thirty feet. He held his hand out in front of him and contemplated it.

A low fog was hugging the river. The wrought iron felt cold against his legs and hands as he climbed over the side of the bridge. He remained staring directly in front of him, gently buffeted by the breeze, postponing the moment when he would look down. When he did, he no longer felt afraid. On the contrary, he had an urge to swim that he had not felt since the crash. He began to strip.

For the fifth time that afternoon, Nancy's mobile rang. When she saw Tom's name flashing up on the caller ID, for the fifth time she let it go to voicemail. He had left six messages on her home answerphone the night before, and she had not opened the four new emails from him in her inbox. This had been going on for three days, since she told him she couldn't see him again, that it had been a mistake. Now she was feeling unnerved. Another text came through. 'You there? Why won't you answer my calls? Tom xx.'

She replied to this one: 'PLEASE STOP THIS TOM. YOU ARE MAKING ME UNCOMFORTABLE.'

The text came back almost instantly. 'Sorry, sorry. Can't we at least talk?'

Nancy replied: 'I DON'T NEED THIS RIGHT NOW.'

She didn't need it. She had much on her mind. Daniel was due back from the States the morning after next and was planning to stay the night, possibly several nights, with Bruce. This would take some explaining to Martha, who was in a strange mood anyway. She had been sulking since their lunch at Tom's, that and giving Nancy knowing looks, as if she had worked out what Tom had been up to.

When Nancy pulled up outside her house she saw Tom's car across the road. He was sitting in the driver's seat. A smile. A wave. She marched over to him and rapped on his window. When it came down she said: 'This has to stop. Enough.' Tom's wounded expression softened her. 'Look. I led you on. I shouldn't have. But you shouldn't have . . . You knew how vulnerable I was . . . I know you're a decent guy. Let's not spoil this. I'll ring you in a couple of weeks. I'll ring you, please don't try and ring me.' She strode away in the direction of her house before the driver of the car had a chance to say anything.

The engine started. The car drove off. Ten minutes later, it re-appeared on the other side of the square and parked in a space that had a restricted view of the house.

That evening, as Daniel was lying on his bed in a T-shirt and boxer shorts reading the *New Yorker*, he heard a swishing noise: paper being pushed under the door. An envelope. He loped off the bed and opened the door in time to see a young woman walking away.

'Susie?'

'Hi. Sorry. I didn't want to disturb you.'

'You didn't.' He opened the letter. It was a photograph of him and Nancy on the flight to the Galápagos Islands, the one Susie had taken.

'I managed to keep hold of my camera during the crash. I thought you might like it.'

'That's sweet of you. Won't you come in?'

Susie followed him into the room and, after closing the door behind her, ran her hand along the top of the flatscreen TV, languidly circled the bed, and played with the dimmer switch before opting for muted lighting that cast her scarred features into partial shadow. When she settled it was on the bed, with the side of her head resting on an upturned hand, as if offering it on a plate.

'Just opened a bottle of Pinot Grigio, but I think it's corked,' Daniel said as he slipped his jeans on and buckled the belt. 'Have something from the minibar. I'm on expenses.'

Susie smiled shyly. 'I don't drink actually,' she said. 'But I do smoke.' She held up a small bag of grass. 'Are you allowed to smoke in the rooms?'

Daniel shrugged.

'Do you mind?'

Daniel shook his head. 'Smoke it myself from time to time.'

Susie sat down on the bed and began rolling.

Daniel put some music on, a jazz compilation provided by the hotel. He tidied up some magazines and clothes and sat down at his desk. His bare feet felt cold and achy. He stared at the photograph. 'Nancy and I are having – what was the expression she used? – "breathing space".'

'Oh.' Susie licked the cigarette paper, rolled and twisted one end. Next she tore off a strip of card, curled it into a roach and inserted it in the other end. This she put into her mouth as she struck a match. A blue spiral of smoke circled her as she stood up and walked towards the window. 'Nice view,' she said as she exhaled. 'All those pretty boats in the marina. And there's the water shuttle. You ever used it?'

'No. Well, once. Long time ago.'

A pungent, aromatic smell filled the room.

'Don't you hate hotels that have windows that don't open?' Susie said. 'I feel like I'm trapped in a box.' The mournful bellow of a fire engine could be heard far below. Susie pressed her cheek against the glass as she looked down. When she stood back, there was a cloud on the glass left by her breath. She squeakily drew a peace sign on it.

'Doesn't make much difference to me. I'm no good with heights anyway so I tend to avoid the windows.' Daniel stared at his guest. 'It's my fault.'

'What is?'

'That Nancy and I have separated. I climbed over her to save myself.'

'I know.'

'You know?'

Susie took another drag. 'Nancy told me when we were waiting to be rescued.'

Daniel looked at his toes. 'We still haven't discussed it. Not properly. Don't suppose we ever will. I don't think we can. As soon as it is out there, between us . . . I don't know, I guess we couldn't take it back.'

'You know, you were a hero that day. You saved me. Don't you remember? I was trying to open my lap belt like a car seat belt and you unclipped it for me. You saved Greg, too. He told me . . . I wish I could have saved him.'

'You were next to him when . . . ?'

As she walked back across the room, Susie handed the joint to Daniel. He nipped it between his thumb and finger and took a deep drag, holding it down for a few seconds before exhaling, looking at the spliff and nodding. He felt instantly light-headed.

Susie sat back down on the bed. 'I don't know how long he'd been face down in the water. Someone shouted, "Hey, look!" and I looked and he was floating face down. The thing I find strange is that he was so . . . loud. He was always . . . It seems odd that he would have gone so quietly. The coroner said he died of hyponatraemia, brought on by the cold. It's a type of kidney failure. It was an existing condition . . . He was so strong. I kept holding him until the helicopter came . . . I was pregnant.'

'You said.'

'I told you I miscarried. That was a lie. I had an abortion . . . I couldn't face . . . It was a legal one. The doctors said it was,' she tapped her head, ' "psychologically justified".' A tear trickled down one of the lines on her cheek and settled in the dimple at the corner of her mouth. She sniffed. 'Look at me. I was determined not to cry.'

'Crying is good for you.'

Susie sniffed again and wiped her face with the heel of her hand. 'Is it true the salinity of tears is the same as the salinity of the seawater?'

'Think so. If it isn't it ought to be.'

'We both survived, you and me.'

Daniel noticed that Susie wasn't wearing a bra, as she hadn't been wearing one on the seaplane. 'Sort of,' he said distractedly. 'I still don't feel like I did before the crash. I feel off-centre. Sometimes I wake myself up with my own shouting. Sometimes I'm afraid to sleep. I'll get all shivery like I have a fever but at the same time I'll be feeling clear-headed. It's hard to describe. It's like everything is more vivid. Wet seems wetter. Blue seems bluer. I feel more energized and restless. People tell me I keep smiling. I sometimes feel that, since the crash, I have found my true self – that a glass wall that separated me from the rest of the world has come down. It was like, before it happened, I was underwater and everything was muffled. I was hearing sounds coming from a distance. Now I hear everything clearly. Does that make sense?'

'I guess.'

'At the Wildlife Foundation this morning, I got freaked by some-thing I saw. It was a leatherback turtle. Something about his face. I had to get away. Ended up at the Museum of Fine Art, and I was looking at some paintings there and it was as if I was really seeing them. Like they were real. Like I could step into them. Like I had never seen a painting before. It was fascinating and horrible at the same time. I found myself wanting to run away from there, too. Running, running, running. Found myself standing on the Harvard Bridge looking down into the river. I'd taken my clothes off. I don't think I was going to jump. The truth is, I don't know what I was thinking. I found myself there, the wrong side of the railing, hanging on, staring at the water, naked. A cyclist stopped and asked me what I was doing. I said I didn't know. I was like this surprised spectator.'

'So you climbed back over?'

'Yeah. Put my clothes back on. The cyclist asked me if I was sure I was OK, then he went on his way. I hailed a cab and came back here.'

Susie placed the ashtray on the bed, took off her glasses. Thought. 'I was a virgin when we married,' she said. 'All my girl-friends teased me about it but it was one of those pledge things. Greg had been with lots of girls . . . I haven't been with anyone since. It hasn't seemed right. Too soon.'

'When it's the right time, you'll know.'

Susie patted a space on the bed next to her. Daniel hesitated then sat, bringing with him a mug he was using as an ashtray. He handed the joint back to her and she grinned and said: 'Wanna blowback?'

Daniel let out a loose and unexpected peel of laughter. He hadn't heard the expression 'blowback' for years, since he was a student, and it struck him as comic. 'Your generation still calls it that?'

'I thought we invented it.' With the joint burned almost all the way through, Susie placed the lit end in her mouth, with her lips clenched tightly on the unburning end, and formed a tube with her hands. This she pressed to Daniel's open mouth and exhaled, forcing the smoke through. Daniel felt the room slide. The smoke alarm went off. Susie mashed up the joint in the ashtray and wafted her hand over it. They both erupted into giggles. When the alarm stopped, the jazz seemed louder. Oscar Peterson. Daniel began miming to it, playing a piano with fingers alternately stiff and loose, wrists broken, shoulders hunched, nodding.

Susie copied him.

'You haven't heard music until you've heard it stoned,' Daniel said. 'You hear every note so clearly, almost three-dimensionally. You can shift your focus from instrument to instrument as if you are actually inside the music looking around.'

Susie placed the ashtray on the floor and laid her head in the crook of his elbow. Soon the sound of her sleeping could be heard. Daniel turned the bedside light off and fell asleep, too. When he woke up it was still dark and he was alone. He turned the light back on and checked his watch. There was a note on the bedside table. 'Nancy is a lucky woman. Call me when you're next in town. Susie xx.' Alongside this was the photograph of him and Nancy. He lay back on the bed and kissed it.

His flight was leaving in three and a half hours. No point trying to get back to sleep. Time to have a shower and pack. He could get breakfast at the airport.

For the first half of the flight he rehearsed what he wanted to say to Nancy. That he knew how she was feeling. That he felt it too. That he was deeply sorry about what happened on that flight to the Galápagos Islands, but that he was only human. Another time he might have acted differently, might have put her life first, but in those confusing, adrenalin-charged seconds the fight or flight mechanism had proved too strong. That wasn't him. He hadn't been the one to desert her. Biology was to blame. Two million years of evolution. He would tell her that the crash had left them both traumatized, but that they could overcome whatever problems they were having by talking, by listening. He would tell her how, in Boston, he had lost his equilibrium. He would tell her about the cathedral, the turtle, and the paintings in the museum that came to life. He might even tell her about what happened on the bridge. She would understand. Nancy always understood.

He decided not to take any diazepam for the flight – he would need a clear head when he landed – but he regretted it the moment the seat belt signs came on and the plane was buffeted by mild turbulence. He drained his glass of red wine so that it wouldn't spill, and watched the first twenty minutes of a film, a disappointing thriller starring Robert De Niro. He managed to doze, only to wake in panic – the wide-awake, teeth-gritting panic of realizing that you are twelve miles above the earth in a hundred tons of metal – a hundred tons of metal that is carrying a further hundred tons of cargo. He clung on to his armrests for the remainder of the flight. At Heathrow, as soon as he had collected his luggage, he sent

Nancy a text. 'Just landed. Can I come round? Some things I need to collect. Martha there?'

'Martha at school. Don't be long. Am going to gym.'

As the black cab pulled into the Clapham Old Town square, Daniel's heart began palpitating. He breathed deeply, marched up the steps and knocked on the door.

CHAPTER THIRTY-THREE

IN A DOUBLE-FRONTED GEORGIAN TOWNHOUSE IN KEW, AN OLD man was looking out over the rank of framed photographs on his desk: his son in a Scout uniform; his muddy-faced grandfather in a trench with another soldier who has his arm around him. There was his second wife on the beach, but no photograph of his first. It seemed tactless.

Philip picked up a photograph of himself as a ten-year-old posing with his mother and his sister Hillary, the three of them standing by his father's grave at the Bayeux War Cemetery, the twin spires of the cathedral in the background. He was wearing his Sunday best that day: shorts, snake belt, kneesocks, checked shirt, clip-on bowtie. His chin was tilted up. Arms pressed flat against his sides. Standing to attention.

A noise. The clink of silver against china. Amanda was placing a cup of tea on the table beside him. She must think him asleep. He half opened his eyes to see her leaving the room and looked again at the framed photograph in his parchment-dry hands. It was taken on 6 June 1954, the tenth anniversary of D-Day. His first visit to the cemetery.

As Philip looked into his own eyes – the eyes of the ten-year-old boy – time slowed, stopped and, like the propellers on an ocean liner changing course, spun in reverse. Spin. A shift of tense from past to present . . .

Philip can hear the screech of seagulls as they cross on the ferry;

taste again the salty air; feel the warmth of his mother's hand as he steadies himself against the sways and dips.

The streets of Bayeux are criss-crossed with bunting: Stars and Stripes, Union Jacks and Maple Leaves. There are no Australian or New Zealand flags that he can see. Must have been too far for them to come. His mother has said that the Queen may be coming over to Normandy for the anniversary. He hadn't seen her coronation the previous year. They had no television. But he had seen her picture in *The Times*. She looked nice. She looked a little like his mother.

When the coach stops, Philip is the first off it and, when he runs to the entrance of the cemetery, he gasps at the sight. More than 4,000 white headstones, row upon row, gleaming in the sunshine and aligned perfectly in every direction, horizontally and diagonally. Not a single blade of grass is out of place. He can hear his mother's voice calling after him to wait.

Other coaches arrive and the pathways become busy. Widows, uncles, parents, sisters, grandmothers. The headstones all look the same, apart from the occasional one in the shape of a Star of David, or carved with a half-moon and facing a different way. Philip likes that the glorious dead are buried as they paraded, in ranks. Yet they must all have been different, he thinks: some short, some tall, some fat, some thin, some brave, some cowardly. The most common age on the white headstones, he soon realizes, is nineteen. This means they would still have been in their twenties if they had survived D-Day. As he stands among them he feels as if he is in the middle of an army.

His father's grave proves difficult to find and his mother has to go back with them to the entrance to consult the book in which all the names of the dead are listed. It shows where they are on a map. When they do find the one they are looking for, they are surprised to see fresh flowers have been laid on it. They look around. A number of the other graves have flowers, too. The flowers must be for those with medals. Philip looks up at his mother. She has tears running down her powdered cheeks. Her lips are moving, shaping the words on the headstone.

Capt W Kennedy, VC, MC
48/Royal Marines
Killed in action 27 June 1944
He died that others might live

Philip had once overheard his mother talking on the phone to someone about the wording. The army wanted to include his father's age but there was some confusion about what that was. According to their records, he was twenty-five. But he had always maintained to her that he was a year older. As they hadn't been able to trace his birth certificate, the age was left off the headstone.

His mother tugs a handkerchief from her sleeve and dabs her eyes. Philip steps forward and looks up at her again, this time for permission to touch the stone. She nods. It is cold. Portland stone. He takes out his pocket watch, the one that his father left him in his will, opens it and shows it to the gravestone. He can hear his mother sniff behind him. His sister steps forward and she touches the stone as well, tentatively, as if worried it might give off an electrical charge. She holds out a drawing she has done of a soldier and places it on the grave.

Philip steps back and feels for his mother's hand. His sister does the same and the three stand contemplating the gravestone in silence, heads bowed. A gardener working two rows away distracts Philip. He watches him straighten his back and massage its base with both hands before bending once more to untie his knee supports – which look like cut-up sections of an old car tyre. He places them in his wheel-barrow, on top of the clods of turf he has sliced from the edges of lawn. On these he places his shears and spade and a strange-looking cutting tool which is semicircular in shape. He takes off his jacket and rolls up his sleeves, exposing white hairs. It is getting hot. The gardener takes off his cap too, wipes his bald head, and puts it back on. With his knees bent, he grips the arms of the wheelbarrow, lifts with a sigh and pushes. The creaking of the wheel seems to provide a sympathetic echo to his steps. He is coming towards them. Philip follows his progress out of the corner of his eye. When he senses the gardener is standing behind them, he turns round.

'This is my daddy,' Philip says.

The gardener looks at the headstone: 'You must be proud of him.'

'He won his VC postu, postum—'

'Posthumously,' his mother finishes.

'How did he win it?'

'He attacked a German machine-gun nest,' Philip says. 'He was very brave.'

'Can you take a photograph of me next to Daddy?' Hillary says, tugging at her mother's sleeve.

Her mother reaches in her handbag for the Brownie 127 camera she paid one pound, four shillings and sixpence for on the ferry. Philip and Hillary take up their positions either side of the headstone.

'Would you like me to take one of you all together?' the gardener asks.

Their mother considers this for a moment before winding the camera on and handing it over: 'Would you mind?' She takes up her place behind the headstone and adjusts her hat. All three wear expressions of appropriate solemnity.

Click. Pause. *Clack.*

Philip opened his eyes. The sound memory had roused him from his reverie. He took a sip from the tea. It was cold. Leaning on his walking stick in order to rise out of his armchair, he walked stiffly across to the section of his library containing memoirs from the Second World War. His fingers closed around the spine of a book written by Brigadier Frank Waterhouse, a former commando who died in 1998. It fell open on a passage he knew by heart. Daniel must know it by heart, too – as a child he had often requested it as a bedtime story. Philip hoped that he might have left enough time since his last reading of it to have forgotten some of the phrases and thereby enjoy them afresh. It was written in the dry, self-deprecating style favoured by retired soldiers of that generation – none of the boastfulness of contemporary memoirs. Extraordinary deeds rendered ordinary – and more powerful for being understated.

Philip read:

In war, men are judged only on their bravery. Nothing else matters. One of the bravest men I had the privilege of serving with was Captain William Kennedy, 'Silky Kennedy' as he was known. I liked Silky. Handsome and strong-jawed, he had what the poet Keith Douglas called that 'famous unconcern' – and a habit of carelessly rubbing the back of his neck while assessing the battle ahead. He was one of those officers who affected a certain homosexual nonchalance and flamboyance. On entertainment nights he would sometimes wear women's clothing and dance with fellow officers. His nickname came from his preference for silk underwear, which he always bought from a shop in Jermyn Street. I do not think he was actually homosexual – I discovered after the war that he was married with two young children – I suspect it was more that he was 'acting up' as a counterweight to the savage business of killing. Homosexuals were seen as paragons of wit and whimsy, after all, and such qualities were considered life-enhancing in wartime. When I met him, I was a lowly subaltern and he was a captain and already had an MC. He also had a bit of a reputation. There was a saying that you should never stand too close to an MC in battle. It was partly because they would take unnecessary risks in order to win the next medal to complete their collection, partly because there was a superstition that their luck might run out.

Silky Kennedy's luck did run out on the road to Tilly-sur-Seulles on D-Day plus 21. Our column was being held up by a Waffen-SS unit in a ruined farmhouse on a spur about 400 yards up the valley. They were not being terribly friendly. There were three or four machine guns, we reckoned, plus mortars, and they had our range. A Spit had strafed them but they had kept their heads down and resumed firing as soon as the raid was over. Normally we would have waited for the artillery to arrive and blast them out, but the big guns were being held up behind us, along with a convoy of American and Canadian trucks. There were no other roads in the area and the surrounding fields had been mined. The order came through on the radio from the battalion commander that the obstacle had to be cleared 'at all costs'.

Two attacks had already been attempted – one going round the

317

open right flank, the other the left. They had been forced to take cover and the Germans still had them pinned down. The only option left was to wait for nightfall and attack head on, crawling straight up the slope under the brow of the spur. We would have to hope they did not have flares. Either way, it would be a 'VC job', army jargon for a suicide mission. Volunteers only. We took it for granted that Kennedy would want to do it, as indeed he did. In fact, he seemed exhilarated by the prospect – his eyes, I remember, were wide and shining. The question was, who would go with him? My fear was not of dying but of giving in to my fear, freezing up when I should be providing covering fire. But there was something about Kennedy's insouciance that made me put my hand up that day. Half a dozen other men did the same. We put cam-cream on our faces and checked our Thompson sub machine guns, all of us except Lance Corporal Carter who was carrying a Bren. I remember someone suggested a flamethrower but it would have been too bulky – the Germans would have seen us coming a mile away. Each man carried six grenades instead.

It took us about an hour to crawl the first 300 yards, spreading out and inching forward on our elbows. At a signal from Kennedy, Carter took up a position behind some rocks to the left. The rest of us crawled on. When we were about twenty yards from the farmhouse a flare went up – it must have been on a tripwire – and the night sky was ablaze with bullets. I could feel the wind from them on my face. Kennedy was up and charging. I tried to cover him with my Thompson but it jammed. There was an explosion. He had taken out one of the machine-gun nests with a grenade and was running along the wall in a crouching position towards the rubble of the next window. It was getting pretty hairy by this stage. Bullets were chipping bits off the wall. Three of our men had been hit. I took a Thompson off one of the dead men and gave Kennedy covering fire. There was another explosion and another machine gun was out of action. We now realized that there was a second outer building behind the main farmhouse and there was another machine gun firing from it. There were more flares and more grenades exploding, then I saw Kennedy dragging one of our wounded men out of the line of fire, ignoring the bullets. Then he was up and charging again. He lobbed a grenade through the window, but not before the machine gun had hit him with a burst. The remaining Germans surrendered after that, about a dozen of them, some wounded. Another flare went up and Carter went over to where Kennedy was lying on his back. Because they had been fired at point-blank range, the bullets had gone right through his stomach in a tight circle. According to Carter, Kennedy looked down at the bloody holes in his tunic and said: 'You have to admire the grouping!' I didn't hear him myself, but it would be nice to think that those were his last words. He was awarded a posthumous Victoria Cross. Collection completed.

Philip clapped the book shut and slipped it back into its space on the shelf. He could no longer put off the visit he needed to make to the National Archives. No more excuses.

When Nancy opened the door and saw Daniel standing on the step, she could tell he had a speech prepared. He couldn't meet her eye. His breathing was uneven. He looked smartly dressed, by his standards. Pressed blue shirt and chinos. Clean-shaven. The smell of Listerine and aftershave.

He said nothing.

Nancy was barefoot and wearing a loose-fitting grey sweatshirt with matching bottoms. In her hand were her trainers and a balled-up pair of sports ankle socks. After showering and cleaning her teeth she had rubbed Ambre Solaire on her skin. That hint of holiday. She wondered if he would notice.

The moment when they should have kissed each other's cheeks in formal greeting had passed. Daniel put his bag down and took a step towards her. She had her back to the wall. He took another step and kissed her on the mouth, tentatively at first, parting her lips with his tongue. It took Nancy by surprise. The softness of his lips, the warmth and mintiness of his breath, stirred something long buried in her, an ache, an unfolding. After a few seconds she pushed him away, closed the front door with her foot and held up her arms. He tugged her sweatshirt off. Slid his fingers behind the material of her sports bra. Kissed her throat.

She pushed him back again, pulled off his shirt and grazed his chest with her teeth. It was as if they were engaged in a duel, parrying and testing one another – as if, too, she was trying to lose herself, play a role, become unrecognizable. She tugged off her tracksuit bottoms and briefs and looped her arms around his neck. He was a stranger now, and this she found intoxicating. Sex with a stranger. He raised his head to hers and they snaked and rolled their necks as if in a mating ritual, as if waiting for the moment to attack. Her shoulders were against the wall and the stranger's hands were supporting her weight, holding her legs up and resting them on his hips. She used her hand to guide him, then, for the first time in five months, felt him inside her. As ripples passed up her body she was jolted momentarily to her senses, then was lost again, locking her heels behind his back, trying to press as much of her body against his as possible. She clenched him, impaled herself, read with her fingertips the relief of vertebrae down his back. Had he been working out? His muscle tone was different. She tightened her grip, shivered the length of her body and closed her eyes. In her belly she felt an expansive, vertiginous sensation. It moved to her lower back, the base of her spine, through her pelvic saddle – a thousand tiny electrical shocks. Her consciousness of being in her body had disappeared. She was moving bonelessly, scoring him with her nails. 'Fuck me,' she said, her voice thick, rising from her gut, an incantation from the back of her throat. 'Fuck me.' The words felt strange and wet on her tongue, as if she was possessed, as if she was a stranger, too, as if a stranger had taken over her body, her mouth, her mind. 'Fuck me, you bastard.' Time went slack. She became aware of the stranger breathing hotly in her ear.

'What are we doing here, Nance?' he was saying. 'This feels more like a fight than a fuck. Is this what you want? Is it? You want a fight?'

Her hips bucked in answer – an uncontrolled, shuddering fury of movement. She felt as yielding as liquid: heavy, heat-filled, viscous liquid. She was drowning in herself, her own suffocating sexuality, gasping for breath, for meaning. What was happening? What was the stranger doing? She looked down over the breasts bulging up out of the cups of her sports bra, down over the span of her belly, down to where he was appearing and disappearing.

'I love you,' he said.

He said he loved me. The stranger said he loved me.

He kissed her again and she saw her eyes reflected in his. They were deranged. The eyes of a stranger. A smile was appearing at the corners of his mouth. His brow was glistening with sweat. Strands of hair were clinging to it.

She felt her hand on his face, fingers splayed, flattening his nose, pushing him away. Then both her hands were slapping and gouging his skin before balling into fists and pummelling his chest. His hands now slipped down over hers, knitting their fingers together. Momentarily muddled by the sensation, not knowing where she ended and he began, she said: 'You broke my heart.'

Both were breathing raggedly, as if coming up for air. She rolled her hips. He answered her movements with pelvic rotations. There were more deep kisses, more rising and falling, then came the final throes and the stranger's head flopped into the crook of her shoulder, as though he were dead.

Nancy lowered her legs but did not move away. They remained standing like this in the hallway for a minute, recovering their breath, their distance. 'You can't stay,' she said. 'I don't think you should stay.'

CHAPTER THIRTY-FOUR

SITTING RIGIDLY AT AN OCTAGONAL TABLE BEARING EIGHT GREEN-shaded lamps, Philip waited for the documents he had ordered. He checked his table number, clicked open his pocket watch and saw his features reflected on the same silver surface that had once reflected his father's face, and his grandfather's. The archivist had said it would take half an hour for the requested files to be retrieved and delivered. He had been waiting forty-five minutes. The files, he had been told, were from the 'burnt collection'. This referred to the British army records for the First World War, 60 per cent of which were burnt during a German raid on the War Office in 1940. Philip had been warned to expect gaps in the records he had requested.

He had been meaning to visit the National Archives for several weeks – it was a short walk from his house – but a nagging unease had prevented him. When, ten minutes later, a manuscript box tied with string was placed in front of him, he hesitated before opening it, slowly running his fingers over its waxy surface: acid-free cardboard that protected the documents inside. The expectant stillness of the room prohibited abrupt movements. With rheumy eyes, he read and reread the name on the lid: 'Private Andrew Kennedy, 11/ Shropshire Fusiliers'.

Mechanically he began unwinding the string.

The box contained a birth certificate with an accompanying letter from Somerset House, an army paybook stained with what looked like coffee, or mud, and a solitary file with hints of reddish sealing wax clinging to its edges. Written in a spiky copperplate on the cover was a list of its contents. Underneath this was a stamp stating that the file was incomplete as certain sections of it were still classified. Philip's hands were shaking as he opened it.

The flat in Chelsea was spread over the ground floor and basement of a five-storey Victorian house. It had a distinctive front door, painted pastel blue. When Bruce answered it and took in the sight of his friend standing grinning on the step, he groaned.

Daniel waved the bottle of vodka he was holding by the neck. 'Got it for you in Duty Free.'

Bruce shook his head emphatically and said: 'No way.'

'One game.'

'Fuck off.'

'It'll do us both good.'

'It'll do you good because you always win. I'll end up cunted again. I had to have my stomach pumped last time.'

'No you didn't.'

'That's not the point.'

'I'll let you be white.'

'No. I'm not well. I think I have the early stages of pneumonia. My lungs feel . . .'

Daniel crossed the threshold into a room decorated with ornate filigree lamps, swags of plush velvet, and a mural of semi-naked young Athenian men languishing on the steps of a temple. He dropped his canvas weekend bag on the floor and went over to a baby grand piano where a chessboard with vodka shot glasses for pieces was set up. He placed the board on a glass coffee table, next to a vase of tulips, unscrewed the top of the vodka bottle and carefully filled each glass to the rim. 'Do you know what I like about chess?' he said.

'You always win?'

'It has a beginning, a middle and an end. And you never know when you are in the middle game, because that depends on how abruptly the end game is going to come. You could be two moves away from checkmate and not know.'

'Sounds like another reason to hate chess.'

'I was playing with Martha the other night and instead of knocking her own king over when I checkmated her, she lifted him slowly from the table, as if he were ascending to heaven.'

'You wouldn't even pretend to lose to your own nine-year-old daughter? You are one sick fuck.'

'Thanks for letting me stay.'

'Just don't blow my chances with my tenant, that's all.'

'Peter?'

'He's due home any minute.'

'You time when he gets home?'

Bruce raised his eyebrow at Daniel, a world-weary expression. 'When you meet him you will understand.' Bruce sighed again as he sat opposite Daniel and moved the white queen's pawn. 'The muscled contours of his upper body have clearly been hardened by hours in the gym. And he moves in beauty like the night. I think he is searching for love, too. Such a tragic, epicene figure with no one to protect him. Alone in my study at night I think of his angelic face and shed a tear.'

'Among other bodily fluids.'

'How are things between you and Morticia?'

'Confusing . . . Why don't you like her, Bear?'

'I do like her. No, that's not true. *But it's her.* She can't stand me. I can sense her impatience when I'm around.'

'Everyone gets impatient with you.' Daniel shook his head as he developed a knight. Bruce moved his king's pawn. Daniel took it with his knight and handed Bruce the pawn glass to drink.

★

Ten minutes after he returned from his visit to the National Archives, Philip stood to attention in front of a full-length bedroom mirror. He was wearing his dress uniform; his back bowed slightly under the weight of the medals. On his stable belt – equal horizontal bands of dull cherry, royal blue and gold – was a silver buckle. In his collar were regimental pins, miniatures of his cap badge, the heads of the snakes facing away from each other. Tutting to himself, he swapped them over, so that they were looking towards each other – a nuance that signified he was retired. By his side was the silver sword he had received upon retirement. He held his scabbard with his left hand – RAMC officers do not draw their swords – and saluted his reflection with his right.

The doorbell rang. Momentarily forgetting what he was wearing, Philip answered it. It was Nancy, her hand raised to touch the doorbell a second time. She looked him up and down, said, 'We aren't at war again are we, Phil?' and offered him her cheek for a kiss. 'No one ever tells me anything.'

Nancy was the only person who called Philip Kennedy 'Phil'. It amused her. He was very much a Philip.

The old man looked puzzled for a moment, then smiled. 'I was checking it still fitted. Got a regimental dinner coming up.' It wasn't a lie, though it wasn't the whole truth either.

'I brought your grandfather's letters back. I've translated them. They're rather moving.'

'Thank you, dear,' Philip said, taking them. 'That was kind of you. Come in.'

Nancy talked over her shoulder as she walked past the old man into the hallway, leaving a trail of gardenia in her wake. 'We'd left them in a hotel safe in Quito before the flight. The manager sent them on.'

'So Daniel said. I'm looking forward to reading them. Amanda has gone shopping. Cup of tea?'

'Thanks.'

Nancy led the way into the kitchen, filled the kettle up herself and, with impatient hands, flicked its switch on. She took off her duffle coat, folded it in two and laid it on the counter. She was wearing a short dogstooth skirt over black woollen tights. Her boots were knee-length, with pointed toes and kitten heels.

'How have you been?' Philip asked, placing two cups and saucers on the kitchen table.

'Been better,' Nancy said, warming a china teapot before dropping two teabags into it. 'I've been seeing a trauma counsellor. You heard from Daniel?'

'You'll have to speak up. That noisy old kettle.'

'Did you know Daniel had moved out?'

Tell me the rest of it, Philip's eyes said.

'He's staying with the Bear.'

'The Bear?'

'Bruce. Bruce Golding.'

'No. I didn't know that.' Pause. 'Always liked Bruce. I remember he came to me for advice when he was considering becoming a doctor.'

Nancy emptied the kettle into the pot and stretched her arms as she waited for the tea to brew. 'Of course it's Dan who should be seeing the counsellor. He's suffering from guilt.'

'About what?'

Nancy pouted, weighing up how much she was prepared to hurt Daniel; how cruel she could be to Philip. 'He climbed over me when the plane crashed.' She said it too quickly, as if fearing she would not be able to get the words out other than in a rush. 'To save himself.' She placed her hand, fingers splayed, gently on Philip's face. 'He did this. Left me to die.' Her hand dropped to her side and she began pouring the tea. 'Remind me, do you still take sugar?'

Philip looked as if he had been punched. He fell silent for a moment. When he did speak his voice was hoarse. 'But I thought Dan rescued everyone.'

'He did. Afterwards. And he did come back and save me, but . . . Listen, I don't blame him. People do these things. I'd have probably done the same. It's instinct.'

'But that's . . . that's . . . *terrible.*' Philip was looking into the middle distance as if hearing voices.

It was Nancy's turn to feel guilty. The old man looked ashen. She softened her tone. 'He's not sure I know.'

'You poor, poor thing.' His sword clanking against his belt, Philip moved towards her and placed a bony, loose-skinned hand on her shoulder.

Feeling hot tears welling, Nancy buried her face in Philip's chest. 'I don't know what to do, Phil,' she said, her words muffled by the ribbons on his uniform. 'I feel lost.'

Philip put an arm around her and rubbed the small of her back. 'I never taught him how to be a man,' he whispered.

'Were you disappointed when he didn't want to join the army?'

'It wasn't that.'

Nancy stepped back so that she could face the old man. 'What about the Medical Corps?'

'It's not for everyone. Medical officers are party to dreadful secrets. Men on the point of death often cry out in terror. I tried to give them privacy, but that's not always possible on a battlefield.'

'Why did you join?'

Philip considered this. 'It was a poem. A famous one. "In Flanders Fields". Written by a medical officer.'

'The one about the poppies?'

'I must have bored on about it before.'

Nancy smiled indulgently. 'Bore me with it again.'

Philip closed his eyes, as if reading the words off his eyelids. ' "In Flanders fields the poppies blow / Between the crosses row on row . . ." '

'Beautiful.'

'Sad.'

'Does your grandfather have a grave?'

'No. He's listed among the missing on the Menin Gate Memorial . . .' His throat constricted at these words. He changed the subject too quickly. 'Did I ever show you this?' He led Nancy slowly by the hand into his study where, against a dim backdrop of chipped cornicing and age-darkened oil paintings, he stood on a cracked leather armchair and reached on to a high shelf. 'It's from

Normandy.' He handed down a small glass tank full of turf. 'I've been meaning to collect some turf from Flanders, too.'

Nancy didn't want to patronize the old man by lying. 'You *have* shown it to me before, Phil. But thanks for showing me it again. It's quite something.' She took the tank from him and held it up to the light. 'You visit your dad's grave every year, don't you?'

'This is the first year I haven't. I must go soon. For a few years, back in the seventies, I used to find flowers and letters on his grave.'

'Left by men who served with him?'

'I presumed so. Never opened them. It would have been an invasion of his privacy. I brought them home with me, before they turned to pulp in the rain. I still have them here somewhere, in a box.' He took the tank back and placed it carefully on the shelf.

They sat down and sipped tea in a comfortable silence.

Philip was the first to break it. 'I find sentimentality intolerable,' he said. 'Such a false feeling.'

'Lips tight, face hard. That's the way to deal with emotions, eh, Phil?'

'Actually it is. I don't feel sentimental about Daniel's mother because . . . How can I put this? . . . I believe in a sort of life after death. We live on in the memories of the people who loved us, our wives and husbands, our friends, our children and, if we are lucky, our grandchildren. In that way we live on, for a generation or two at least, then we fade, become those old sepia photographs which no one knows what to do with because no one can identify the faces.'

'Don't think I've ever heard you talk so much, Phil.'

The old man shrugged.

'So your father lives on through you?'

'No,' Philip said. 'I have no memories of him. All I have is remembrance, which is not quite the same.'

Nancy stirred her cup of tea. 'I heard a nice thing the other day. You know the expression "gone for a Burton"?'

Philip nodded.

'It's a euphemism. From the Second World War. Instead of pronouncing a comrade dead, RAF pilots would say he had merely "gone for a Burton", as in a pint of Burton Ale. That's rather touching, don't you think? Intended to soften the pain of the news.'

'English at its most eloquently unspoken.' Philip looked on the point of tears.

Nancy had never seen him like this before. Daniel had told her once that his father had never cried in his life. She tenderly brushed his cheek with her hand.

Philip's face cleared immediately, his voice became firm. 'My eyes are old,' he said. 'They get watery in the cold.'

'Sorry. Didn't mean anything by it.' Nancy felt annoyed with herself. 'I have to go. School run.' She shook her head. 'I shouldn't have told you about Daniel.'

'Glad you did.'

'All he ever wanted was to live up to you, you know.'

After he had seen her to the door, Philip sat in a chair by the fire and read the translations of his grandfather's letters, resting his hands in his lap to keep them steady, nodding to himself. When he had finished them he held them to his nose. He could smell Nancy's perfume on them. He changed out of his uniform. Answered the phone.

'Hello, Philip. It's Geoff. Look, there's something you need to know. One of the professors at Trinity, a Laurence Wetherby, has approached us about Daniel . . . Hello, Philip?'

'Yes, I'm here.'

'I think he might be in trouble.'

Philip said nothing.

'He's become friendly with someone we're keeping an eye on.'

'Does this someone know you're keeping an eye on him?'

'Yes. We want him to know.'

'Is there anything I can do?'

'You could persuade Daniel to disappear for the next few days. Get out of London.'

'What about his work?'

'They're going to suspend him. He doesn't know yet.'

'Wetherby told you this?'

'The suspension is his idea.'

Philip packed his suitcase, then went online to book two tickets for the Eurotunnel and two hotel rooms in Ypres. After this he rang Daniel's mobile.

CHAPTER THIRTY-FIVE

Le Bizet, Belgium. Second Monday of September, 1918

IN HIS CELL, ANDREW LISTENS TO THE SOUND OF A COFFIN BEING hammered together: as the guard has reminded him, coffins are a luxury not afforded to those killed at the Front. He is being held in the town police station. There is a stained mattress on the floor, two chairs and a bucket. His cell smells of paraffin. When he holds on to the bars of the high window and lifts himself up, he can see two soldiers digging a hole in the yard. He feels curious as he watches them, but not afraid. A sense of calm detachment has settled upon him, anchoring him. With the help of a French dictionary lent to him by the Scottish provost marshal, he begins writing a letter to Adilah and is halfway through it when she is brought in to see him. The APM follows her in and stands by the door. 'Yous got five minutes, laddie.' He looks straight ahead of him at the wall. It is the closest they will get to privacy.

'I am sorry, Andrew,' Adilah says, unable to meet his eye. 'I am not any help at the trial, I think.'

'Having you in there did help.'

'What is she like, your England wife?'

Andrew reaches for Adilah's hand. The APM glowers at him, then his expression softens and he shakes his head. 'I never loved her the way I love you . . .' Andrew says this quietly, withdrawing his hand. 'I do love you. I love you more than I can say.'

'I love you, also, Andrew.' A catch in her voice. 'I am glad we had our together time.' She dabs at her eyes.

He finds his hands reaching to her belly. 'If it's a boy, I'd like him to be called William.'

Adilah nods and sniffs. She holds his hands to the bump before taking his fingers in hers and pressing them to the swell of her breast. He has learned every detail of these breasts, the softness of the skin, the faint blue veins buried just below the surface, the pinkness of the buds.

'No touching,' the APM says. But there is kindness in his voice.

'When William is older will you give him this?' Andrew backs away and holds up his pocket watch. After a nod from the APM, he presses it into Adilah's hand, taking the opportunity to brush her skin with his finger as he does so.

Adilah sniffs again.

'Please don't. I can't be strong if you cry.'

'You have to go now, madame,' the APM says.

Adilah composes herself and levels her gaze at Andrew. 'Goodnight,' she says.

He smiles tensely. '*Bonne nuit.*'

CHAPTER THIRTY-SIX

Northern France. Present day. Five and a half months after the crash

THE SHADOWS WERE LENGTHENING AS THE TYRES OF PHILIP'S twelve-year-old Daimler rolled with a metallic clatter down the ramp on to salt-stained French tarmac. There had been a two-hour hold-up on the Eurotunnel – a security alert on the English side – and now there was a further delay as the car was ushered to a siding and security staff asked father and son to step out of it so that they could run a nitroaromatic explosives detector rod over its interior. As Daniel was driving, he was the one asked to open the boot. There was a bucket crammed with rubber gloves, two scrubbing brushes and detergent. Behind their bags were two spades, a pick, an axe, a large red torch and several rolls of bin liners. Nothing to arouse the suspicion of the police then. Thanks, Dad.

As he stood, Philip felt in his waistcoat pocket for his fob watch, pulled it out by its chain and flicked it open with his thumb. He began shifting his weight from one foot to the other. For reasons he would not elaborate upon, he had wanted to cross into Belgium and reach Ypres by 8pm.

'Don't forget to put your watch forward an hour,' Daniel said, winding on his own watch. 'It's six thirty, not five thirty.' He immediately regretted saying this, as his father had clearly not allowed for the time difference. He tried to make light of it:

'Anyway we're going back in time, Dad. Isn't that what this is all about?' His father made no comment but, when they set off again, he tapped the windscreen and pointed to a sign reminding English drivers to drive on the right. Daniel had forgotten. Touché, he thought.

Out of habit, Daniel extended a hand towards where the satellite navigation display would have been on his hybrid – what Nancy and he called the Navigatrix, because of the bossiness of its recorded female voice – but after hovering for a moment the hand returned to the steering wheel. He asked his father about the best route instead, hoping it would distract him. Philip would enjoy unfolding his map and spreading it out over his lap and on the fascia containing the airbag. Some of the road numbers were out of date. Nevertheless, a route was soon worked out that meant they would follow the coastline for half an hour past Dunkirk before turning inland. As they passed fields of oilseed rape and unripened wheat, Daniel helped himself to one of his father's Mint Imperials and tuned the radio to a French jazz station. John Coltrane was playing 'A Love Supreme'. He would have liked to listen to it but he retuned to a classical station, knowing this was what his father preferred.

When a sign for Ypres came up, they forked off the motorway and made a south-easterly approach to the town, past a sign to the British and Australian war cemetery at Polygon Wood, and along the Menin Road. When they reached a roundabout, Philip said: 'This is Hellfire Corner.'

'I've heard of it,' Daniel said.

'You should have. Everyone should have. This place is a byword for unrelenting death.'

'Funny, it doesn't seem so bad. I mean, obviously the Belgians drive like nutters but . . .' Daniel caught his father's expression and dropped the gag. He always found his father's seriousness brought out the joker in him, an attempt to dispel dark clouds with breeziness of manner.

They had reached the outskirts of the town.

'Here,' Philip said. 'Pull over.'

Daniel checked his rear-view mirror, indicated and found a parking space on the side of the road. It was a fairly mild evening, but crisp enough for Daniel to reach for his suede jacket to put over his hoody. He grabbed Philip's wax jacket from the back of the car too and held it up. Philip shook his head and said: 'No need . . . but could you pass my stick.' Father and son slammed the doors of the car behind them in unison and began stretching and rolling their necks. Daniel checked the parking meter. Free after 6pm.

'This way,' Philip said, setting off with his walking stick. Ahead of them was the barrel-vaulted archway of the Menin Gate Memorial. When they reached it they were greeted by a powerful smell of flowers wrapped in cellophane and left among the wreaths of artificial poppies. 'They built it here,' Philip said, 'because it was the route every British soldier would have taken on his way to the Front.'

'Through the gate?'

'There was no gate. Not even an arch. It was a gap in the ramparts which encircled the town, a bridge across a moat.' He checked his pocket watch again. 'Good. We have time.' They walked up to the memorial and took in its sombre stone-and-brick arch. A crowd of secondary-school children, aged fourteen and fifteen, was gathering underneath it: teenage boys in football shirts and sunglasses; girls wearing tops that didn't cover their midriffs.

'They come here by the coachload,' Philip whispered. 'Fifty coaches every day. The First World War is on the National Curriculum, you see. The locals get upset because the children don't know how to behave. They jump over the gravestones, drop litter, swear.'

As Daniel stared up at the single span of stone above him he whistled under his breath. It had a coffered, half-elliptical arch and, at both ends, two flatter arches. Each was flanked in turn by an enormous Doric column and surmounted by an entablature. To the sides of the staircases and inside the loggias on the north and south sides of the memorial were tens of thousands of names engraved on vast panels. Every surface had been carved with chiselled capitals over leagues of white stone. The names on the outer sections up the steps had weathered, he noticed, having been exposed to the rain.

'So this is everyone killed along the Ypres Salient during the war?' Daniel said. 'Lot of names.'

'No, these are the ones who have no known grave. More than fifty thousand. And it doesn't include the thirty-odd thousand who went missing here in the last year of the . . .' He trailed off, distracted as he searched the names. Cars were still driving under the arch, over the cobbled stone, and one had to swerve slightly to miss Philip. He had forgotten which direction the traffic would be coming from.

'Careful, Dad,' Daniel said, leading him to the side by his arm. 'You nearly became one of the missing yourself then.'

A broad staircase led from the hall up to the ramparts and the loggias. Daniel read the inscription over its entrance out loud: ' "*In maiorem dei gloriam*. Here are recorded names of officers and men who fell in Ypres Salient but to whom the fortune of war denied the known and honoured burial given to their comrades in death." So where is he?'

Philip pointed an arthritically crooked finger. 'There.' Above them was the panel dedicated to the missing of the Shropshire Fusiliers. Halfway down it were dozens of Kennedys and at the top of them was KENNEDY A. The sun was almost below the horizon. Philip took out his pocket watch again and clicked it open. 'It is time.'

The noise of the traffic ceased abruptly and a muffling stillness descended, as though an invisible eiderdown had been spread over the town. The crowd of people choking the road bowed their heads. Three buglers in starched and colourful uniforms marched under the archway and, after the cathedral bells chimed the hour, played Last Post. A teenage girl near Daniel began rubbing her mother's back. As the last note faded, a two-minute silence began. Partial silence. The bleeping of cameras could be heard, as well as a baby crying. After twenty seconds a mobile phone began ringing and a young and female English voice could be heard answering it – informing the caller in a loud whisper that she was at the memorial in Ypres and that she had come with her school. 'Nah, bit boring really.' The partial silence over, cars and lorries started up again and the crowd parted to allow them under the arch.

Philip looked disappointed that Daniel wasn't more moved. 'Glad we got here in time for that,' he said.

'Yeah, it was nice.'

With a stiff-legged walk, Philip led the way up the steps to an area of lawn where a group of schoolchildren were assembling. They were being told to form up in pairs for a head count. A roll call was taken. 'Is this a re-enactment of the roll calls in the trenches?' Daniel asked his father. 'The head count after a big push?'

'Let's check into our hotel and then get something to eat,' Philip said, ignoring his son's question. 'There is something I need to tell you, but let's do it over a drink.' Philip led the way down the monument steps and back to the car where they collected their overnight bags. He retraced his steps back under the memorial and along a cobbled alley lined with shops selling British Army books and souvenirs. The window of one of them, Tommys Gift Shop – without an apostrophe – was festooned with Union Jacks and poppies. It sold poppy-pattern umbrellas, replica Vickers guns and helmets, mugs and spoons emblazoned with images of British Tommies. The alley led out on to a vast open square, the Grote Markt. Though the sun had not yet set, the floodlighting had come on.

Daniel's eyes widened as he took in the gothic spire of the Cloth Hall. 'Beautiful.'

'A beautiful fake. All this was rubble,' Philip said with a sweep of his arms. 'In nineteen eighteen, a man on a horse could see from one end of the town to the other.'

Daniel tried to imagine the ranks of British soldiers marching through the square on their way to the Front. 'So the Belgians rebuilt it.'

'The British rebuilt it according to the original medieval plans. The Germans paid for it.'

'They should have got the Germans to rebuild it.'

Philip shook his head. 'The British *wanted* to rebuild it, because it meant work for British servicemen who had been demobbed. Better than selling matchboxes on street corners. They came back here where they could be with their old comrades and be paid to use their skills as bricklayers, plumbers and engineers. They found they no longer fitted in at home anyway. They couldn't talk about what they had been through here, other than to fellow soldiers.'

Daniel nodded. He liked it when his father talked about the army. It was the only subject about which he ever talked at any length.

They found their hotel in the area of the square overlooking the Cloth Hall. It had three flags flying outside it: Canadian, British and Australian. 'Guess there's only one reason foreigners visit this town,' Daniel said.

The hotel was like a museum: paintings of the original Cloth Hall in flames hung from the walls in the gloomy foyer alongside grainy photographs of bedraggled soldiers trailing through the market square with ammunition limbers and horses. Their rooms were next to one another. Daniel dropped his canvas bag on a nylon quilt covering the bed. The walls were papered with wood-chip. There was a cupboard made of plywood with the door hanging off its hinges. And the room was dominated by a bulky television hanging on an angle off its wall bracket. The bathroom sink, meanwhile, had two cold taps with blue tops. When Daniel tested them he discovered one ran hot water. When he saw that damp was coming through the polystyrene tiles on the ceiling, he grinned. It was always the same when he left the booking of hotels to his father. He went for the cheapest available.

'Thought you said this whole town was rebuilt,' Daniel said after knocking on his father's door and walking in. 'I think this hotel might have been one of the few things that survived.'

Philip had his back to the door with one arm in his shirt. As he slipped the other arm on, Daniel noticed the skin-coloured patches on his shoulders. They looked like nicotine patches, but couldn't be. His father hadn't smoked for years. Without turning round,

Philip removed something from his mouth. Daniel could see it was a handkerchief.

'It's cheap,' Philip said, regaining his composure. 'And at least it has a view over the square.'

When Daniel went to lock his door he found the lock broken and so asked if he could leave his bag in Philip's room while they went out for dinner. This time he noticed how thin his father's legs looked, and how his chest had barrelled. He also noticed the paraphernalia of old age: the bottles of pills in the bathroom, the rubber ferrule at the bottom of the walking stick propped against the door, the surgical stocking on the bed. He also noticed the whiskers his father had missed shaving, and the smoky smell of urine on his trousers.

On their way out, Daniel was surprised to see the old man turn and walk slowly and cautiously backwards down the stairs. Neither of them commented on it.

Having found a restaurant in the corner of the square that was surrounded by hanging baskets, they sat at a table outside it. Though they asked for a menu and wine list in French they were handed menus in English. Daniel ordered an expensive bottle of burgundy and tested it by swirling it around the glass and inhaling rather than sipping it. He nodded at the waiter and smiled to himself as he realized he was still trying to impress his father, still trying to win his approval. The wine connoisseur at dinner. How pathetic.

As usual it was Daniel who felt he had to lead the conversation. He began talking about college, about how there had been much more administration and red tape lately; about how the provost was always trying to modernize and introduce new computing systems. He was talking too quickly, building up to what he wanted to say. It came out abruptly: 'By the way, Dad. I've been suspended.'

Philip took a sip of wine and nodded. Daniel couldn't decide whether he was nodding in approval of the wine, in acknowledgement of what Daniel had said, or because he already knew. 'It's a misunderstanding,' he continued. 'Office politics, really. My friend Wetherby is fighting my corner. He thinks it will all blow over.' Pause. 'It's to do with Islamist radicalization on campus. I invited a Muslim on to campus who they say is a radical preacher or something. He's nothing of the sort, of course. He's a teacher at Martha's school. I thought I . . .' Another pause. A sigh this time. Daniel still hadn't found a convincing way to articulate what had happened. 'After the crash, when I was swimming for help . . .' Another sigh, heavier. 'I was hallucinating.' Daniel realized he was gabbling and that, as usual, his father was listening in silence. 'Well, it's always good to talk, Dad.' He drained his glass. 'We should do this more often.'

'Wetherby is a friend of yours?'

'Yes. You know him?'

'He's the music professor, isn't he?'

'Yeah. He's working on something to do with Mahler. I over-heard him telling Nancy about it. He reckons Mahler wrote an alternative opening to one of his symphonies . . . You OK, Dad?'

Philip had closed his eyes. He was choosing his words. 'There is something I have to tell you, too.'

Daniel blinked and swallowed. His hands moved to the edge of the table and took hold. 'Go on.'

'There is a name on the memorial that shouldn't be there.'

The waiter returned. 'Are you ready to order?'

Philip put his glasses on and tightened the strap at the back that compensated for his missing ear. He scanned the menu. 'I'll have the moules,' he said.

'A cheese omelette and salad for me.'

'Still a vegetarian?'

'Still a carnivore?' Daniel watched the waiter walk away before prompting his father: 'You were saying?'

'The name Andrew Kennedy, it shouldn't be on there.'

'His body's been found?'

Silence. 'It was never missing. There's no easy way to say this, Daniel . . . Andrew Kennedy was shot at dawn. He was a deserter. Court-martialled and shot.'

Daniel tilted his head back and frowned. He couldn't take it in. 'I don't understand . . . Have you always known this?'

'Had no idea until earlier this week. It was in his file at the

National Archives. The court record of his trial. It's only recently been declassified.'

'But wasn't your grandmother told he'd been killed in action?'

'Families of deserters were rarely told the truth. The letter home usually said "died of wounds".'

'Is that what ours said?'

'No, not quite. I have it here.' Philip handed over a pre-printed letter with spaces that had been filled in by hand.

Sir, it is my painful duty to inform you that no further news having been recorded relative to (No) . . . 9862. (Rank) . . . Private. (Name) . . . Andrew Kennedy. (Regiment) . . . Shropshire Fusiliers who has been missing since . . . 31 – 7 – 17 the Army Council has been regretfully constrained to conclude that he is dead, and that his death took place on . . . 31 – 7 – 17. I am to express to you the sympathy of the Army Council with your loss.

The Regimental Adjutant

'They *thought* he was missing in action,' Philip explained. 'Then they realized he'd run away.'

Daniel let out a low whistle. 'Poor bugger. How did they catch him?'

'He was gone for more than a year. Went to live in Nieppe, a town about fifteen miles from here. Met a French woman.'

'A year!'

'He met a French woman.'

'Those letters . . .'

Philip nodded. 'They were going to get married. He needed his birth certificate sent over from England to make it official. It came back addressed to him care of his regiment. He was easy to track down after that.'

'But he was already married . . .'

Philip sighed. Took a white plastic bottle from his jacket pocket and sipped from it.

'What's that? A hip flask?'

Philip ignored the question. 'The French woman's name was

Adilah Camier. She was called as a witness at his court martial. According to the records, she was pregnant.'

Two plates of food arrived. Daniel broke off a chunk of bread and buttered it. 'Andrew was the father?'

'So it seems. He refers to the baby in his letters to her.'

'And do we know what became of this baby?'

'That is what I'm hoping to find out. I thought we could drive over to Nieppe tomorrow afternoon, have a look around, see if we can find the house where he lived. What do you reckon?'

'Course. I'm still trying to take this in.' Daniel drained his glass and refilled it, leaning over to top Philip's up, too. 'So you might have had an uncle or aunt you didn't know about?'

'It's possible but . . . There was always something that never quite added up about when my father was born. There was no birth certificate, for one thing. Everyone in our family was always cagey on the subject. My mother, I remember, would never talk about it. And I always suspected that my sister knew something I didn't, that she was somehow protecting me.'

'You think that baby might have been your father, my grandfather?'

'I don't know.'

'We could drive over to Nieppe first thing.'

'I've arranged to meet an archaeologist tomorrow morning. A friend of mine. I work with him on the British War Graves Commission. He is on a dig over on the Passchendaele Ridge. We can go after that.'

'Sounds good.'

The scrape of cutlery on plates.

Daniel could feel the wine warming his belly, taking the edges off their conversation. He spoke first. 'It's not, I mean, there's no stigma attached to it these days, is there? Being shot at dawn. Everyone knows the poor sods were all suffering from shell shock. Didn't they pardon them all a few years ago?'

'I think they called it "a retrospective recommendation for mercy", but yes. All three hundred and six recorded cases posthumously pardoned.'

'Presumably that number didn't include Andrew?'

'Think it was meant to cover everyone.'

'I wonder if it's genetic.'

'What?'

'Cowardice.'

The sound of shells being cracked open, sauce being sipped. Then Philip said: 'What do you mean?'

'Well, I wonder if there is a gene for cowardice. Obviously it skipped two generations in the case of our family – my great-grandfather, then me.'

Philip avoided his son's eye. 'Why do you say that?'

'You know: you and your father. The medals. The hero gene.' Daniel searched his father's face; ran a piece of bread around the rim of his plate. 'My great-grandfather and me, the yellow streak . . .'

'I don't know what you're talking about, Daniel.'

'Nancy told you what happened on the plane, didn't she?'

Philip hesitated. Nodded. He was still avoiding his son's eyes. 'She hinted at something. Didn't go into detail.'

'Well, let me fill you in. I saved myself and left her to drown.'

'I'm sure . . .' Philip didn't know how to finish the sentence. 'I've always had the highest regard for Nancy.'

'You're changing the subject.'

'You have to fight for her. Fight to keep her.'

'I am, Dad, but lately . . . She called me a coward. I'm surprised she didn't present me with a white feather. She has every right to.'

'She is a beautiful woman . . . Beautiful . . . Like your mother.'

Daniel blinked. He was astonished to hear his father talk in this way. He couldn't remember the last time he had heard him talk about his mother. It was a taboo between them. 'I know. Don't think I don't know how lucky I am.' Realizing he had drunk most of the bottle of wine on his own, he added: 'Sorry, Dad, you hardly had any. Let me order another.'

'Might have a brandy.'

Daniel caught the waiter's eye and held up two fingers. '*Deux cognacs, s'il vous plaît.*'

When they arrived, Daniel said, '*Merci, et l'addition, s'il vous plaît.*'

'Certainly, sir,' the waiter said in English.

'I blame myself,' Philip said. 'Too protective of you . . . after your mother died.'

'Were you? That's not how I remember it.'

'Never let you hurt yourself. Get stung by nettles. Fall out of trees.'

Daniel sensed his father's embarrassment but continued anyway. He was feeling drunk, reckless and affectionate. 'Why have we never talked about my mother?'

Philip exhaled and played with the glasses hanging from a cord around his neck. 'Don't know. You were very angry about her death. Angry with God.'

'Was I?' Daniel sounded distant. 'Why does it take something like this to get us talking? We never really have talked, have we?'

'That's not true, Daniel.'

Both men felt awkward about the exchange. It hung in the air and neither could think how to dispel it.

CHAPTER THIRTY-SEVEN

Le Bizet, Belgium. Second Monday of September, 1918

MAJOR MORRIS FINDS THE CHAPLAIN IN THE VESTRY OF THE church. He taps on the open door. Removes his cap. 'I've come to apologize,' he says in a thin voice.

The chaplain has not heard him enter and jumps slightly. 'For what?'

'For my behaviour at the court martial.'

The chaplain looks puzzled.

'I've come to ask for your forgiveness.'

'My forgiveness?'

'God's.'

'I see. Well.' He gestures towards a chair.

'Will you pray with me?'

'By all means.' The two men kneel together and say the Lord's Prayer.

Sensing more is needed, the chaplain places his hand on the officer's head and blesses him.

'Thank you,' Morris says, still kneeling. 'What did you make of Private Kennedy's testimony in court? That business about him following the soldier across no-man's-land?'

'I don't know. Why?'

'Have you heard of the Angel of Mons?'

The chaplain removes his hand. 'Everyone has.'

Morris raises his head and looks the chaplain in the eye. 'Well, I saw it. I was there.'

'The Angel of Mons is a myth, surely.' The chaplain studies his face. 'You expect me to believe you saw St George wearing a suit of armour and riding a white horse?'

'No, it was a soldier. He just stood there, oblivious to the bullets. They went through him as if he was made of air.'

'Why didn't you mention this at the trial?'

'Because it would have made me sound mad. Because I couldn't believe my own eyes. We were exhausted. When you haven't slept for days you see things.' Morris reaches for the chaplain's hand. 'I'm not mad, you know. I never told anyone, apart from a nurse who I had heard was investigating the claim. I wrote to her.'

'I see. And do you think Kennedy saw the same figure?'

Morris looks away. 'I don't know. It doesn't matter now anyway. Doesn't change the fact that he deserted his post.' A long sigh. 'Thank you for listening, padre. It is a weight off my mind.' He gets to his feet. 'Now, if you will excuse me, there is something to which I must attend.'

Once outside, Morris dismisses his waiting driver and gets behind the wheel himself. Five minutes later, when he parks in front of the armoury, a converted schoolroom, sentries challenge him. With a scrawling signature, he signs for a dozen short-magazine Lee Enfield rifles. These he carries out to the car two at a time and lays against the running board. Next he retrieves a box of .303 ammunition which he has in the boot of his car, loads a cartridge into the chamber of each gun and sets the safety catch before laying the weapon carefully down on the slatted wooden seats in the back. He sets off for the police station now, narrowly missing a dispatch rider on a motorbike as he swings out into the road.

★

Because the ground floor of his house had recently been decorated with an expensive silk wallpaper from Paris, the mayor of Le Bizet had not allowed it to be commandeered without protest. But he was relieved to learn it was officers who would be using it as a mess, not men. Two of them are standing in the drawing room now, reflecting on the court martial.

'What do you make of Major Morris?' Brigadier-General Blakemore says, staring out of the window.

Lieutenant Cooper purses his dry lips. 'Don't know, sir. Don't know him.'

'Know how he got his VC?'

'No, sir.'

'Neither do I.'

'I can find out if you like, sir.'

'No need. It's just he's asked to take personal charge of the firing squad. What kind of man does that?' The brigadier-general turns to face the lieutenant. 'What was he, do you know?'

'What do you mean?'

'Before the war.'

'Morris, sir? I'd heard he was a conductor.' As if further explanation is needed, he adds: 'Symphonies and so on. But that's only a rumour.'

'Good God.' Blakemore walks heavily up to a cabinet and pours himself a whisky from a decanter. 'Did you see the way his hands shook?'

'Yes, sir. He's been in it from the start. Fought at Mons.'

The chug-chug of a motorcycle on the road outside signals a dispatch from general headquarters. Both the officers know this means Field Marshal Haig has signed the death warrant. They would have had a phone call otherwise.

'Well, that's it,' Blakemore says, looking up after reading it. 'I thought he might show leniency this near the end.' He studies the amber liquid in his glass, swirling it around.

'Sir?' Cooper says. 'I've been thinking. Private Kennedy's wife in England thinks he was killed at Passchendaele. Do we need to disabuse her?'

Blakemore takes a swig as he considers this. 'No, I suppose not ... Strange, that business with the French nurse. Attractive woman. Has she been sent back to Nieppe?'

Cooper's smile is embarrassed. 'I said she could visit the prisoner, sir. For five minutes.'

'You still have compassion, Cooper ... How old are you?'

'Nineteen, sir.'

Blakemore sets down his empty glass. 'Do you know how old I am?'

'No, sir.'

'Twenty-eight. Does that surprise you?'

'Don't know, sir.'

'Kennedy is twenty-two. It was on his birth certificate.' He picks up the decanter of whisky and hands it to Cooper. 'Would you do me a favour and take this to his cell. Best not to mention where it came from.'

CHAPTER THIRTY-EIGHT

Ypres. Present day. Five and a half months after the crash

DANIEL STUDIED HIS REFLECTION IN THE HOTEL SHAVING MIRROR
as he applied his moisturizer. He could not see his father's features
staring back at him, as men approaching middle age are said to do.
But there was a shadow of ancestral recognition. The double helix
was performing its trick. He had been genetically encoded with his
great-grandfather's cast of eye and delicate features. They were
haunting his face.

He read for barely a minute before turning out his bedside light
and slipping into a peripheral sleep that soon deepened into a
dream about Nancy and Martha walking ahead of him down
Clapham High Street. He couldn't catch up with them.
People kept getting in his way. When he saw them walking
through the gates of a vast cemetery he followed them in, but he
could not see them among the rows of headstones. He began
running and calling their names. Now he saw them over in the
farthest corner, kneeling under a tree. They stood up and were
walking away again. He was shouting but they did not hear
him. He wanted to see the gravestone they had been visiting but
the closer he got to it, the farther away it became. Nancy and
Martha were miles away now, back at the entrance gate. He was
shouting after them. Trying to shout. Someone was telling him not
to worry.

Feeling the touch of cold lips on his brow, he opened his eyes. There was no one in the room. He remembered where he was. Ypres. In a hotel. His father was next door. Everything was all right because that human rock, that anchor, was next door. He checked his watch with a double tap and heard a commotion downstairs. A drunken guest was trying to get back into the hotel. Perhaps that was what had woken him. The night porter had clearly gone off duty and the guest didn't realize that his room key was also the key that opened the door to the hotel. He was shaking the handle of the front door so violently it was vibrating the thin walls of the building. Daniel, feeling dehydrated and hungover, muttered to himself: '*Use your key. Use your key.*' When he put a pillow over his head and turned over, he found it was cold and damp from his own sweat.

The guest, an Australian judging by his accent, was becoming more and more frustrated and was ramming the door with his shoulder, as well as kicking it. He was also shouting: 'Fucking country! Open the fucking door!' He walked away, returned five minutes later and started shouting and rattling the door again. Daniel got out of bed and looked out of the window. The man was urinating in front of the Cloth Hall now. He looked to be in his mid-forties. Presumably he had come to visit his great-grandfather's grave, too. Daniel tried ringing reception but there was no answer. He considered walking down and letting the Australian in, but worried the man might attack him, thinking he was the porter. Cowardice again. Be a man. He was about to phone the police when the drunk went away. Daniel couldn't get back to sleep, gave up trying and stared at the stained square of polystyrene above him. It was orange in the street lighting.

At 5.30am, when lorries began trundling past outside, the sound of their tyres amplified on the cobbles, he turned on his light. At 7am, when the sky became slate grey, low and heavy with the promise of rain, Daniel went down to breakfast. His father was already seated, immaculate in a tattersall check shirt, a regimental tie and neatly pressed cavalry twills.

'There was shouting in the night,' Philip said.

Daniel helped himself to a glass of orange, a baguette and four slices of cheese. 'I heard it, too.'

'No, before that. It was coming from your room.'

'I was shouting?' Daniel shook his head. 'Nancy says I do that sometimes, since the crash. Night terrors. I wake up sweating and delirious.'

'Have you seen a doctor?'

'Bruce gives me beta blockers. I take them when I'm feeling panicky.'

'I used to prescribe them for men suffering from post-traumatic stress.'

'Did *you* ever need them?'

Philip shook his head. 'Some men don't. It's not about bravery, it's about luck.'

'I imagine your father was the same . . . Funny, I always think of him as your father rather than my grandfather. Because I never met him, I suppose.'

'I never met him either.'

'Must have been weird not knowing him. I mean, you know about his VC and all that, and there's that passage about him in that war memoir, but you don't know whether he preferred tea or coffee, whether he was left- or right-handed, what he sounded like.'

'Weird is one way of putting it.'

'Did you ever talk to men who served with him?'

'Met a couple, but their generation never talked much about the war.'

'Thought that was all they ever talked about.'

'They talked about it, but not to people who weren't there. A lot of soldiers are like that.' Philip buttered some bread. 'Clearly he was brave, my father, but I don't think he ever felt fear. To be truly brave you have to know fear. It's much worse for men who are afraid. "The coward dies a thousand times, the brave man only once."'

'How about you, Dad? Did you feel afraid?'

Philip tilted his head to one side. Made as if to speak. Checked himself. He began tapping his fingers on the table. 'In the Gulf? I was going to say that of course I was afraid but that isn't true.

351

I don't think I did feel fear. Not in the way some men do. I have seen men crying before going into battle. But some men felt immune from death, as if they had an antenna on their heads that was warning them of impending danger, keeping them safe.'

'That's what I felt when . . . That's what I was trying to explain last night about . . .' He searched for the name but could not recall it. 'Martha's teacher. The Muslim guy. After the plane went down I was swimming for help and he appeared out of nowhere in the water and I felt like . . . like he was keeping me safe. Like he was leading me to safety, pointing me in the right direction, towards the islands. I was hallucinating, of course. Had sunstroke and hypothermia. And I was dehydrated. All the symptoms. But . . . Am I making sense?' Daniel felt in his jacket for the news cutting from the Trinity College student newspaper, the one with the photograph of himself and Hamdi sitting together in the refectory. 'Thought I had a picture of him. Must have left it upstairs.'

'You felt he was your guardian angel?'

Daniel wafted his hand and gave a dismissive laugh. 'For the . . . *No!* Course not. I told you, *I was hallucinating.* I've been through it all with Bruce. I'd had a knock on the head during the crash and that might have caused temporal lobe epilepsy. There's this small shadow on my brain.'

Philip looked concerned. 'Why didn't you tell me?'

'Bruce has it in hand. Didn't want to worry you about it.'

'I've had some experience of temporal lobe epilepsy. Did you have convulsions?'

'Not really. It was more like migraine. A blinding light.'

'And you haven't had that since?'

'I've had headaches. That's all.'

'You should have told me. I know some excellent neuro-surgeons. It's associated with out-of-body experiences and quasi-religious visions, you know.'

'I know.'

Philip hesitated. 'Have you considered that it might have been a genuine vision?'

'No such thing.'

352

'How do you know?'

'I'm a scientist, Dad. I know.'

'Yes but *how* do you know?'

Daniel took a sip of coffee. 'Never been any proof of them.'

'Science cannot disprove them either.'

'Well, it can actually. If they are not testable according to the known laws of physics and biology then—'

'Perhaps that is why God chose you.'

'Chose me!' Daniel laughed again, more edgily than before.

'Someone who knew the meaning of scientific proof. A Darwinist. A Darwinist in the Galápagos Islands.'

'You saying the Big Fella likes a challenge? Hadn't thought of it like that. I suppose life must get quite boring if you're a supreme being who can do anything he wants whenever he wants. Short of challenges. I suppose that's why he became so jealous and insecure. Demanding people worship him and no other. Smiting those who take his name in vain.'

Philip smiled with his eyes, a rare event. 'Careful, Daniel, you're talking about Him as if He exists.'

Daniel looked up at the sky. 'OK, Allah, Yahweh, whatever you like to be called, if you exist, give me a sign. Just one. Doesn't have to be an angel . . . I promise, if you give me a sign right now I'll sacrifice my first born on the altar, as that seems to be what you get off on . . .' He cocked his head. 'Nothing. No bolt of lighting. Not even a shooting star.'

' "Now faith is the substance of things hoped for, the evidence of things not seen." '

'That's from Hebrews, isn't it . . . Surprised I know that? I read the Bible cover to cover when I was a student. Have to know your enemy. You taught me that.'

'Perhaps the evidence you seek has been with you all along and you can't see it, or you won't allow yourself to see it. Sometimes believing is seeing.'

'That's called superstition.'

'It's called faith.'

'Sorry, Dad, but faith isn't enough. I *know* this table exists.' Daniel lowered his head to the table and mimed banging it repeatedly. 'I don't have to *believe* it exists as an act of faith.'

'You always say religion is for closed minds, but I think the opposite. I think it's for open minds. Minds that are open to the possibility of there being something more, something we can't explain.'

'Sorry, Dad, but it's just not true. We know how a child is conceived, to take an obvious example, and that knowledge allows us to dismiss the idea of a virgin birth.'

'What about IVF?'

Daniel gave a forced grin. 'OK. You got me there. The Resurrection then. We know that didn't happen because we know how life and death work. If Jesus was alive three days after coming down off the cross it was because he was *still* alive. He never died. He slipped into a coma. I don't suppose there were too many trained medics on hand with thermometers, sphygmomanometers and watches to check for vital signs. Look, we know he didn't come back to life because coming back to life is a biological impossibility.'

'Perhaps that was the point. Perhaps it had to be something impossible, something that mankind would take notice of and still be talking about two thousand years after it happened.'

There was a loud clink as Daniel slammed his coffee cup down in its saucer. 'Dad! You're a doctor! How can you say that?'

'I can say it because I believe in God.'

Daniel sighed. 'Scientists are open to belief, but only if it's supported by hard evidence. That's what people don't get about us. We *are* open. We *are* prepared to change our views, but only when some proof is offered. Proof you can hold in your hand.' He shook his head. 'How long have men been believing in gods? Since the beginning of recorded history. What's that? Five, six thousand years? And probably for thousands of years before that. In all that time there has not been one trace of evidence. Not one shred. Nothing you could hold in your hand and say, "Look! Here it is! *Proof!*" '

Philip caught his breath and swivelled around in his chair, as if an electrical current had passed down his back. He was clenching and unclenching his fists.

The dig was a ten-minute drive from Ypres and, for the duration of the journey, the windscreen wipers thrashed against a downpour. Daniel dipped his head whenever the screen came clear to look for signs to Passchendaele – there weren't any, the village that gave the battle its name having been wiped off the map by British artillery during the First World War. In its place were pastureland and fields of maize, as well as warehouses and a sewage treatment plant. There were also poppies in bloom, but only in the ditches where the weedkiller hadn't reached them. As they came to a fork that took them on to a lane that followed the Passchendaele Ridge – not so much a ridge as an undulation in the otherwise flat landscape – they saw the verge was littered with piles of rusting ordnance, some of the several hundred tons of shells ploughed up by farmers each year. Those that were clearly unexploded had been left in the gaps of the concrete telegraph poles for Belgian bomb disposal experts to take away on their weekly collections.

As they drove, Daniel noticed that the rushing air was dragging the beads of rain on the driver's side window, making them look like spermatozoa swimming across a Petri dish under a microscope. He was so distracted by this he did not see the orange backhoe loader on an articulated arm that was biting into the ground ahead of him.

Philip tapped him on the shoulder and pointed in its direction. It was trailing mud as it excavated the earth, and next to it was a small bulldozer with caterpillar tracks. Beyond that was a large white tent around which stood a team of half a dozen men and women in luminous jackets, hard hats and wellington boots. One was wearing headphones and sweeping a metal detector back and forth across the ground.

Father and son parked and found two umbrellas in the boot of the car. A short and jowly man was jogging towards them, grinning broadly and pushing his spectacles further up the bridge of his nose.

He was wearing a lumberjack hat with earflaps hanging down loosely and a cagoule over a pink shirt that was flecked with mud. 'This is Clive,' Philip whispered. 'Bit of a chatterbox but don't let that put you off him. He's a good man.'

'Philip, Philip, how are you?' Clive said breathlessly as he shook hands. His glasses had steamed up. His mottled cheeks were pouched at the bottom. He turned to Daniel. 'Good to see you again, Professor Kennedy . . .'

Daniel blinked twice. 'Actually I'm not a . . .' He held out his hand, a look of bemusement playing across his face. 'Hello . . . again . . . I'm trying to think . . .'

'Trinity College. I was the porter there until . . . well, we don't need to go into that. It was a job to pay the bills. This is my real passion. I do battlefield tours. I'm also an amateur archaeologist.'

'One of the most professional I've come across,' Philip corrected.

Clive beamed. 'Very exciting. This morning. Two more bodies. Germans, we think. Thank goodness we got to them first. Local farmers tend not to report Germans. I've heard of them spitting on the bones. We have to inform the local police in case the bodies are murder victims. Do you have wellies?'

Daniel and Philip shook their heads.

'Never mind. You might be OK without them. You will have to wear hard hats though. There's a couple in the tent over there. Careful how you go. It's slippy.' The archaeologist led the way to the tent, where he swapped his own lumberjack hat for a hard hat and handed out one each for Daniel and Philip. All three made their way to a muddy hole in the ground, their footwear sucking in the orange mud. Rain was splashing in the pools at the bottom of the hole. The remains of duckboards and rotting A-frames could be seen in the sodden ground. 'When we uncover bodies we have to be certain of the identification before we can give them a formal burial,' Clive shouted above the sluicing of the rain, scarcely pausing for breath. 'Only then can we take them off the missing list. Things like watches and cigarette cases engraved with initials are not enough on their own because bones often got melded together. You know, if one man was carrying another when a shell hit them.

Couldn't tell which was which. Identification is usually impossible because dog tags were made from cardboard and leather and so have rotted away. We found this yesterday.' Clive held up a rusting entrenching tool. 'We usually find human remains nearby. That's why this place is known as "the boneyard of Belgium". And come and have a look over here.' He pointed to a cross-section of earth ten feet deep where layers of rusting metal could be seen at intervals below the turf and the clay. 'There was so much lead falling from the skies here, over such a long period of time, it has settled into its very own geological formation. Look! A solid mass of rusty matter. Isn't that amazing?'

Daniel nodded under his umbrella.

'This whole area was a maze of tunnels and bunkers. Cows sometimes disappear down the shafts when a shelf of soil gives way. Even tractors disappear sometimes. The ground opens up and swallows them.'

'The present collapsing into the past,' Daniel said.

'Or the past rising up into the present. We've got one over here.' Clive led the way to a fenced-off hole. 'Look down there.'

Daniel peered over the edge and immediately staggered back. 'Sorry. Not good with heights.'

Clive was shining a torch down the hole. 'You can't see the bottom. Must be fifty feet straight down. The entrance to a tunnel. Unexploded mines go off sometimes, especially when there's lightning. They throw up soil that hasn't been in contact with air since the First World War. Look at this.' He held up a dirty bottle. 'HP sauce. That has to be British. Would you like to keep it as a souvenir?'

Daniel glanced at his father as if asking for permission.

'Now,' Clive said, handing over the bottle. 'Am I right in thinking your great-grandfather fought at Passchendaele?'

Feeling delirious from lack of sleep and not in the mood for such enthusiasm, Daniel said: 'Went over on the first day.' He glanced at his father again. It wasn't a lie.

'And he was with the Shropshire Fusiliers, wasn't he? Well, where we are standing now was the front line on the eve of the attack.' He pointed to the remains of a concrete bunker a few yards away. 'The Germans were only that far away on the higher ground. They could hear them talking. They could smell the bacon they cooked for breakfast. I'd have to check, but I'm pretty sure the Shropshire Fusiliers were in this sector. They went over in the third wave. According to our maps we are above a trench they named Clapham Common.'

Daniel made as if to say something but rubbed his arms instead. His jacket was saturated, the fibres gorged with rain.

'They liked to give the trenches familiar names, to make the men feel at home. They *were* quite homely. By the summer of nineteen seventeen, they had had two years to work on these trench systems. The engineering was very sophisticated.' The rain had turned to a fine drizzle. Clive held out his hand. 'Think it's more or less stopped. Come with me. I want to show you something in the Land Rover. Are you coming, Philip?'

'Eh?'

'You coming over to the car?'

'Actually I need to go back to our car for something. You go.'

'Can you take this with you, Dad?' Daniel handed over the HP bottle.

Clive kept up the chatter as he bustled along. 'I should think he's sick of hearing me bore on about Passchendaele. We work together on the War Graves Commission, you know.'

'I know.'

'Expect he's told you all about it?'

'The commission?'

'Passchendaele.'

'Not really. You know what he's like.'

'He is quite . . .' Clive looked over his shoulder. 'What's the word?'

'Taciturn?'

'Well, empty vessels like me make most noise.'

'Some find him rude. I think it's because he's a bit deaf. Finds it hard to join in. He can go days, even weeks, without talking.'

'So what would you like to know?'

Daniel looked at his father's straight back as he was walking away. 'Did he ask you to give me a history lesson?'

Clive grinned as he unlocked a Land Rover, raised his blotchy hands and described an arc. 'On the occasions when the rain lifted, foaming black smoke hung over the landscape, blotting out the sun. More than half a million British and German troops were killed during the fighting here – and often the dead would be buried under a deluge of soil, only to be disinterred by the next shell and reburied by the next. In the summer months, those bodies left on the surface would either be eaten by rats or stripped down to the skeleton by maggots, a process which took eight days. And it stank like the cauldron of hell: cordite, mustard, putrefying horseflesh.'

'What was the first day like?'

Clive pointed with his umbrella to a distant spinney. 'The British took the Pilckem Ridge over there, one of their objectives. But we had twenty-seven thousand killed, wounded and missing that day. The Germans a similar number. In his diary entry for the first of August, Field Marshal Haig recorded the thirty-first of July as "a fine day's work". He described the losses as "small".'

Daniel puckered his lips as he took this in. He looked at the grassland around him and nodded as he saw it was still dimpled and cratered by shells. He looked back towards Ypres but could not see its spires through the rain. When he turned back to his guide he was fifteen yards away standing on a block of concrete, holding a large scroll and signalling for Daniel to join him.

'This,' Clive said, tapping the block with the scroll, 'is a German pillbox. Ferrous concrete. When your great-grandfather went over the top on the first day here he would have seen whole battalions reduced to husks by the Devil's Paintbrush. That's what the Tommies called the Maxim gun. They placed them on the top of these.' He stamped his foot. 'This whole salient,' another sweep of his arms, 'was a quagmire. Liquid mud. Soldiers who slipped from the duckboards drowned. Marching men were ordered to ignore the cries for help. To stop with a battalion behind you on a slippery duckboard eighteen inches wide was impossible.'

With the spires of Ypres becoming visible through the mist

behind him, Clive unscrolled the black and white panoramic photograph he had collected from his Land Rover. He asked Daniel to take one end. It was fifteen feet long and showed a charred and jagged landscape that was almost featureless apart from barbed wire and a few splintered tree stumps over on the Passchendaele Ridge. 'This is the view your great-grandfather would have had on the morning of the attack,' he said. 'Would you fancy heading out into that?'

Daniel shook his head. 'Can't say I would.'

Back at the car, they found Philip asleep in the passenger seat, his mouth open. His skin looked grey. He was holding the HP bottle in his hand.

Daniel tapped on the window. 'You OK, Dad?'

'Mm? Oh . . . Had a bad night.'

Daniel found himself driving slowly along the road to Nieppe. It seemed the respectful thing to do.

An elderly woman with hair like cauliflower was leaning out of a window halfway up a grey block of flats in the centre of Nieppe. Unsupported by teeth, her mouth had folded in on itself. She was staring at the big car with the English number plates that had parked below her – and, as she watched with clouded eyes, a lithe and delicate-faced man got out of the driver's side and walked over to a board showing a map of the town. The man studied the board for a moment, tapped it twice, looked up and smiled at the old woman. When she did not return the smile, he looked down the street he had come from and, with his hands on his hips, nodded to himself. A warm breeze was picking up, blowing grit down the street in flurries.

Though blighted by satellite dishes, Nieppe was more whole-some than other towns that marked the line of what had once been the Western Front. It had a country market feel to it, with dusty hens scratching around and several loose-skinned cats resting their bones on garden walls. There were fuchsia-filled baskets swaying from porches and streets lined with poplars. Most of the houses were of red brick and some of them – the main difference between this and the other towns through which they had passed – appeared to be original, having survived the Great War. The canal looked clean – clean enough for fish to live in, judging by the anglers on its banks. The Château de Nieppe looked sooty and neglected, but its slender turret was solidly intact. Daniel walked back to the car and opened the passenger door. 'We're on the Rue d'Armentières, Dad,' he said. 'The main road through the town. The road we want is behind that church over there.' He wagged a finger towards a steeple. 'May as well leave the car here and walk. You feeling up to that?'

With Daniel acting as traffic policeman, Philip tapped his way across the main road, but his progress was slow and a woman holding the hem of her skirt down against the gathering wind easily overtook him. When he reached the other side, Philip waved his stick in gratitude at a waiting car. They cut through a narrow alley and across a cobbled square that brought them out on to the Rue des Chardonnerets. According to the files Philip had seen in the National Archives, the house at which Andrew Kennedy had been arrested was Number 11. It was a modestly sized, gable-ended dwelling with a slate roof and boarded-up windows. Graffiti about Le Pen had been sprayed on the boards. Father and son looked at one another and shrugged despondently before walking back the way they had come. They continued past the car, around a fountain that spouted no water, and up towards the town hall: an old stucco-fronted building from the Napoleonic era. It had a Tricolour draped down one side of its stone frontage and an EU flag down the other. Engraved across its façade were the words MAIRIE DE NIEPPE and below this: LIBERTÉ. EGALITÉ. FRATERNITÉ. Daniel spoke in pidgin French to the receptionist and was directed to the land registry department. There he approached a young clerk who was reading a text on her phone and handed her a piece of paper with '11 Rue des Chardonnerets, Nieppe' written on it. He explained he was after any information on the building, anything at all. The clerk returned ten minutes later with a thin file.

'That house has been empty for the past four years, monsieur. The Lemarre family last owned it. They bought it in nineteen seventy-three. Before that it had been in the same family for forty years.'

'Do you know the name of that family?'

She handed over the file. It was warm from her hands. 'Their name was Boudain. They had bought it in nineteen thirty-three. It's in there.'

'Does it say who lived there before that?' Daniel asked as he flicked through the pages.

The clerk sighed testily as she took the documents back. 'Camier.' She snapped the file shut and drummed her fingers on it.

'You wouldn't happen to know where they moved to, would you?'

'No.' She resumed her texting, stopped and raked her hair to one side. 'I think there is a Camier family living on the Rue d'Armentières, opposite the Hyundai garage. One of them did some decorating for my father.'

The wind determined the slow pace, with Philip, his stick tapping the pavement, bowed like a spinnaker before it. But when they found the garage, they slowed down even more, as if they were both prolonging the journey, to postpone any disappointment they might have at their destination. They looked at one another before knocking on the door. After half a minute it opened on a chain.

'*Oui?*' A woman's voice.

'Madame Camier?' Daniel said.

A finger appeared and pointed next door.

When Daniel knocked, an unshaven man in his fifties answered. He was wearing a vest. His fingers were nicotine yellow.

'*Oui?*' More a grunt than a word.

'*Parlez-vous anglais?*'

'Small.'

'We are trying to trace a relative of ours. He lived in Nieppe during the Great War.'

'Here?'

'No. He lived on the Rue des Chardonnerets. His landlady was called Adilah Camier. We were told a family by the name of Camier live here.'

The man scratched his belly and cocked his head to the other side as he studied the two strangers in his doorway.

'She was married to Henri Camier.' The voice was as dry as wood bark. It belonged to an old woman. The man stepped to one side and a stooping figure waved them in. She had a leathery face framed with the grey tendrils of a carelessly assembled bun. 'He was killed at Verdun. Come in, please.'

Philip and Daniel followed her along a peeling hallway to a small sitting room that smelled of cat food and was dominated by a sun-bleached poster of the Virgin Mary. She ushered them to sit down on a green sofa that had springs uncomfortably close to its surface. A cat jumped on to Daniel's lap. A wind chime sounded in another room. The man in the vest went noisily upstairs and the old lady disappeared and reappeared with two cans of lemon Fanta and a bowl of Twiglets on a tray. 'After Henri died, Adilah met an Englishman, a soldier. She had a child by him. Please . . .' She pulled the ring on one of the cans and handed it to Daniel. 'You are thirsty, I think.'

The can was sweating condensation and so cold it made Daniel's hand tingle. As he drank he watched the old lady rummage in first one drawer of a dresser then another. She was slight and wan, as if painted in watercolour rather than oil. A trick of the eye, he concluded – no electric lamps were on and, as the afternoon was overcast, the light that was floating in through the sash windows was soft and grainy. She pulled out a shoebox of small sepia photographs and began to sift through them. After a long minute, she held one up and looked at what was written on the back. It showed a handsome woman with hauntingly pale eyes. She was wearing her hair down around her shoulders and the empty sleeve of one arm pinned up. In the other arm she carried an infant wrapped in a cot blanket. 'This is her.'

The front door opened, a growl of wind carried through the

house. It swung shut again. Philip looked up briefly; returned his gaze to the photograph. 'So she was your . . . ?'

'Adilah Camier was my aunt. No, my great-aunt. I get confused. My memory.' The old woman was studying the scarred rump of Philip's missing ear. 'It is many years since I have been to England. I used to go there for school trips. I taught English for . . .' She trailed off. 'You are from London?'

'Yes,' Philip said. 'Kew. Daniel here lives in Clapham. I'm sorry, we haven't introduced ourselves properly. My name is Philip Kennedy. This is my son, Daniel.'

'My name is Marie Camier.' The old woman held out a small and liver-spotted hand. Philip took it in his. 'I have visited Kew. They have a wonderful garden there.'

'We're very close to it.'

'You said you were tracing a relative?'

Philip hesitated. 'The English soldier you mentioned, he was my grandfather. Andrew Kennedy. He died in the Great War . . .' He hesitated again. Handed the photograph of Adilah to Daniel. 'I think Adilah's child might have been my father. I never knew him. He was killed, too, fighting the Germans in the Second World War.' He took a sip of Fanta.

'What was your father's name?'

'William.'

The old lady nodded. She was staring at Philip's muddy shoes now. 'Yes, I believe the child was given an English name.'

'As far as I've been able to work out, what happened was this . . .' Philip tapped the palm of his left hand with two fingers of his right. 'Andrew Kennedy, my grandfather, already had a wife in England. Her name was Dorothy. I always assumed that Dorothy was my grandmother because she was the one who raised my father.'

'On her own?'

'No, she lived with a man called Will Macintyre. He had been a friend of my grandfather's. They had both been plumbers in Market Drayton before the First World War and had joined up together and come to France. My father was named after him . . . What I don't

364

understand is how Adilah's baby, my father, came to be living in England.'

The old woman smiled, exposing discoloured teeth. 'You know that Adilah died in La Grippe, the great flu epidemic?'

'No, I didn't know that. In nineteen nineteen?'

'*Oui*. This plumber . . .'

'Will Macintyre.'

'I heard about him. He must have been the one who returned to France after the war to help rebuild Ypres. He came here to Nieppe to see Adilah. Then, when she died, he took the baby back with him to England. I always knew . . .' The sentence was left unfinished. 'He came back, you know.'

'Who did?'

'The plumber.'

'Will?'

'I get confused. It must have been in the nineteen fifties. I met him.'

'You met Will?'

The old woman touched her head. 'I mean your grandfather, don't I? Who was Will? My mind is not what it was.'

Ten minutes later, back at the car, they found a note left under the wiper. It was a complaint that they were blocking someone's drive. Philip spread his map out on the bonnet. 'There is a village called Le Bizet five miles away,' he said, prodding the map. 'That was where Andrew was taken to be court-martialled after his arrest. He was held in the police station there and executed in the grounds. It's on the way back so we may as well take a look. I'll drive if you like.'

Daniel tossed the keys over the roof. Philip missed them. As they were putting on their seat belts, a cloying smell of urine became noticeable. Daniel surreptitiously wound the car window down. He slid his finger along the screen of his iPhone, waited a second and tapped the internet icon. He tapped again and studied a webpage for a minute. 'There's a page here on the psychology of firing squads. Says that because no single member of the squad could save the condemned man's life by not firing, the moral incentive to disobey the order to shoot was reduced. The phenomenon is known as "diffusion of responsibility".'

Philip was gritting his teeth.

Daniel stared at him, then back at his screen. 'In some cases,' he continued, 'one member of the squad was issued with a gun containing a blank. The idea was that each member of the squad could hope beforehand that he was the one with the blank. It reduced flinching. It also allowed everyone to believe afterwards that he had not personally fired a fatal shot. Normally they could tell the difference between a blank and a live cartridge because of the recoil, but there was a psychological incentive not to pay attention to the recoil and, over time, to remember it as soft.'

'I've heard that.'

'Would Andrew have died instantly?'

Philip slowed down as he approached a traffic light. When he stopped he looked across at his son. 'Bullets fired at the chest boil volatile fats and rupture the heart, large blood vessels and lungs so that the victim dies of haemorrhage and shock. Death is nearly always instantaneous. But . . .'

'What?'

'I can't quite put my finger on why . . .'

'Why what?'

'Why I think he somehow managed to survive the firing squad. Marie Camier said Will Macintyre had come back here in the fifties, but he died in the thirties. In nineteen thirty-four, as I recall. I have this feeling that . . . I think it might have been Andrew she met.'

On the floor of his South West London bedsit, Hamdi was on his knees. A few feet away were the flip-flops he had taken off, neatly aligned, up against the wall. He touched his head to the small prayer rug that ensured the cleanliness of his place of prayer. The sajada, as the rug was known, was as much a compass as a threadbare oblong of embroidered colour, one that orientated him towards the centre of the world, towards the sacred black stone Ka'ba in Mecca. He rocked back on his heels, mumbled an ancient incantation to himself and made a gesture as if using his hands to splash his face with water – the elaborate 'dry ablution' ritual of the desert. Next he kissed his copy of the Koran, rolled the rug up and placed it on a chair before walking barefoot to his small bathroom.

He looked in the mirror, picked up a pair of scissors and cut off the beard he had been growing for several weeks – he found it too itchy and distracting. The black hairs lay in the sink like a dead dog, an unclean animal, and he was able to gather them in two clumps and drop them in the pan. He removed his shirt next and squirted shaving foam on to the palm of his hand before dabbing it on to his face and chest. He started with the chest first, shaving upwards with his razor towards his neck, removing the few impure wisps that had grown back there. Next he shaved his cheeks and chin, carefully, turning his jaw on an angle to catch the light and ensure he had not missed any stubble. He splashed cold water on his face, an echo of the earlier gesture, and began again. When he had shaved a second time he squirted foam under his arms and, after removing his trousers and briefs, around his groin. This was a more delicate operation. He was smooth now, no longer corrupted by body hair. He ran a hand down his chest, enjoying the absence of friction.

Afterwards he showered with equal care, working his cracked bar of soap into a lather as the nozzle sipped back the water several times before finding its full pressure. He covered his body with circular motions, across the back of his neck, over his flanks and buttocks, behind his knees, under his testicles. With the plastic shower curtain clinging to his shoulders like an extra layer of skin, he shampooed his hair, dipping his head under the spout and spitting out the soapy water that entered his mouth.

Once he had dried himself on a crusty towel he changed into a suit and tie, opened his front door, hesitated, closed the door again and walked over to a phone on the kitchen table. After a few rings an answering machine cut in. Daniel's voice. 'If you would like to leave a message for either Daniel or Nancy, please do so after the beep.' The beep was more an electronic whine. 'Professor Kennedy, it is Hamdi. I have been thinking about our conversation. You asked about angels and I did not give you a very satisfactory explanation. Muslims believe that Allah has created an unseen world, including angels and jinn. I can explain it to you better next time we meet. That is all.'

In another part of London, behind a bank of digital recording and editing equipment, an MI5 operative wearing a headset made a note of this conversation, her fingers a blur of movement across her keyboard. She took a sip from a small plastic bottle of water and spellchecked what she had written.

Before closing the door to his flat, Hamdi felt his jacket pocket for the rattle of car keys. He then stepped out on to his balcony and negotiated the metal stairs of the fire escape, carrying his cello case in front of him. His Mini Cooper, parked in front of the block of flats, did not start first time. On the second attempt it revved raucously. Hamdi indicated, pulled out and drove off. Twenty yards behind him, a green Volvo did the same.

'Target now leaving,' the driver of the Volvo said into a microphone.

Le Bizet was not so much a separate village on the border of Belgium and France as a sprawling and anonymous suburb of Armentières. The police station, Philip discovered after asking a postman, was off the main road and was now a private house. It had been renovated quite recently, judging by how freshly painted the outside walls were. Its shutters were a vivid yellow. He knocked on the door. No answer. He looked in the window. Dustsheets on the furniture. 'I think whoever lives here is away for the summer,' he said as he walked around the back to an enclosed garden with an immaculate lawn over which time-activated sprinklers were hissing.

'Should we be doing this, Dad?' Daniel said. 'Aren't we trespassing?'

'That must have been the wall.' Philip was looking at a high, moss-covered wall behind a shrubbery. Trees obscured sections of it, but it clearly ran for thirty yards. 'The post they tied him to would have been in front of it.'

Sunshine was emerging from the clouds and was slanting through the leaves, dappling the garden. 'I wonder if you can still see bullet holes,' Daniel said, taking off his sunglasses.

Philip scrambled around the back of a greenhouse and on to a flowerbed. There he let out a cry of pain.

Daniel hurried to his side. 'You all right, Dad? Did you slip?'

'I'm fine. I'm fine.' Philip appeared distracted, talking almost to himself. 'He's buried here somewhere; I know it. Unmarked and unknown.' Using his walking stick, the old man pushed back the branches and found the wall overgrown with ivy and bindweed. Daniel came over and held the weed back while his father felt along the wall with his fingers, as if he were a fireman testing for heat. They progressed in this way for five yards before Philip came to an object that was set in from the wall. Under a dark and tangled knot of roots, its shape was hard to determine. Daniel pulled back the ivy with renewed effort.

It was flat and upright with a curved top covered in slimy green lichen.

'Portland stone,' Philip said with a nod. 'Absorbs everything. Can you fetch that torch from the car? Can you also bring that bucket with the scrubbing brush and the detergent? And try and find some water.'

'Was wondering what you had brought them for.'

When Daniel returned, Philip was feeling the engraving with his fingers. 'Letters are worn down,' he said.

'Is it Andrew's?'

'Don't think so. Shine the torch.' Philip was on his knees. 'Good God! It's a VC!'

When they finished scrubbing the top half of the stone they

stood back and read the inscription in full: MAJOR PETER MORRIS VC, MC & BAR, DSO & BAR, DFC, MONS STAR, BWM, VM. 2/RIFLE BRIGADE. 1880–1918.

Daniel pulled weed from the lower half and continued scrubbing. The stone was still green but more words were becoming readable.

' "Greater love hath no man than this," ' Philip said, reading the epitaph out loud, ' "that he lay down his life for his friends." How extraordinary. I've never heard of him. He should be buried in a British military cemetery.'

'There's a reason presumably. Perhaps he was shot at dawn, too.'

Philip clenched both his fists and tensed his jaw.

'You all right, Dad?'

'This is precisely why we set up the commission . . . I'm going to see to it that he is disinterred and reburied with full honours.' He stared at the headstone for a few moments, lost in his thoughts. 'They usually buried executed men near to where they were shot, so I'm guessing Andrew is buried here somewhere too.'

'I suppose they weren't allowed to bury him in consecrated ground.'

Philip ran his arthritically bowed hand over the curve of the headstone. 'You still an atheist, Daniel?'

'Course. You still a Christian?'

'I struggle with the question of why God allows . . . When you think of the carnage of Passchendaele.'

'It isn't God that allows it, Dad. It's man.'

'It's God.'

'Then God is an arsehole.'

'Don't blaspheme.'

Daniel was on his knees clearing away more weeds and feeling the wall as he went along. 'It's funny, someone else said that to me.' He tried to recall Hamdi's name. 'The Muslim guy I mentioned.' He stopped pulling and straightened his back. 'But you can't blaspheme against something that isn't there. A blasphemy against man and nature, on the other hand . . . Passchendaele was a blasphemy. What I did to Nancy was a blasphemy . . .' Noticing a small movement a few yards away, he put a finger to his lips and whispered: 'Over there. Look.'

Philip looked to where a rat with a long naked tail was perched, watching them.

CHAPTER THIRTY-NINE

Le Bizet, Belgium. Second Monday of September, 1918

HAVING DRIVEN HIS CAR UP TO THE STEPS OF THE POLICE STATION, Major Morris laboriously carries the rifles inside, two at a time again, and places them against a bed in an empty cell. As he is carrying in the last two, he passes Adilah emerging from Andrew's cell. Each affects not to see the other – Morris looks at the floor, Adilah straight ahead at the studded wooden double doors that lead out to the garden. The APM is the next to emerge from the condemned cell and he carefully closes the door behind him before jangling a ring of large keys until he finds the right one. Morris taps him on the shoulder and, nodding towards the cell with the rifles, says: 'That door is to be kept locked until five thirty tomorrow morning. You will then lay the rifles out in the garden exactly one yard apart in two rows of six, the first row fifteen feet from the post, the second twenty feet. Is that clear?'

The APM salutes. 'Sir.'

Morris walks out into the garden to inspect the wooden post that has been driven into the ground near the wall. He lights a cigarette with shaking hands and draws on it as he walks to where the hole is being dug. Its yawning mouth demands a body, its soil longs to absorb human blood. Morris stares into it as he smokes quickly, barely holding the smoke down in his lungs before exhaling and jabbing the cigarette back to his lips. When he finishes it, he tosses its stub in the hole. Only now does he turn to the police station and see Andrew's pale face at a barred window. The two men regard one another impassively for a moment, each holding up a ghostly mirror to the other. Morris blinks slowly, as if in a trance, strolls up to the window and tosses in the rest of his packet of cigarettes. As he is walking away he hears the prisoner acknowledge this unexpected act of kindness.

'Thanks.'

Morris does not turn round.

An hour passes before Andrew's next visitor arrives. The condemned man does not recognize his old friend. Macintyre has aged twenty years since their arrival together at Ypres the previous year. He is hollow-eyed and chap-lipped. There is a suppurating sore on his neck. His once-round face is gaunt and ashen; his hairline receded, his centre parting prematurely grey. There are corporal's stripes on the arm of his grimy and tattered uniform and he is wearing a waistcoat made from rabbit fur. He smells rank, as if his flesh is rotting. 'It's me,' he says. 'Will.'

'You look different.'

'Lost weight.' Macintyre has a cigarette tucked behind his ear. He pulls it out, snaps it in half, puts both ends in his mouth, lights them and hands one to Andrew. 'Look what I got at Wipers,' he says, pulling out an Iron Cross from his trouser pocket. 'Here, have a hold of it.'

As Andrew stares at the medal in his hand, Macintyre stares at Andrew. Both men are acting, as if in the company of strangers. Macintyre begins scratching and says bluntly: 'Can I have your boots?'

'Help yourself. They never fit me properly anyhow. Hardly worn.' Andrew gives a weary, off-centre smile. 'Suppose that was the problem.'

Macintyre does not laugh. He stares up at the bars of the

window and rolls his shoulders as if trying to shake weariness from them. The difference in him is more than physical. Something is missing. He is distracted. Somewhere outside a car backfires. 'What was that?' Macintyre says, jumping.

'Must be practising,' Andrew says, trying to put his old friend at ease. He realizes what the difference is now. Macintyre has lost his sense of humour.

'Asked the quartermaster to send up some scran for you. Stewed beef and sixty pounders. It being your last . . .' Macintyre's voice trails off.

'Thanks, 'preciate it . . . One of the officers brought me that.' Andrew nods at a decanter of whisky. 'Want some?'

Macintyre takes a deep swig and then starts coughing. 'Bloody hell,' he says, handing the decanter over.

Andrew takes a smaller sip. 'Heard from anyone in Market Drayton?'

'Wrote to Dorothy when . . . We thought you'd copped it on the first day.'

'Think I did die that day.'

'You was well out of it. Pissed down for the whole of August. Place turned to liquid shit. Brown for as far as the eye could see. Lot of lads drowned in it. It were November before . . . I tell you, mate, if I thought I had to go through that again I'd . . .' He points two closed fingers at his foot and mimes shooting himself.

Andrew tries to recall faces from his platoon. 'How's the CSM?'

'Sniper. Three weeks in. I were next to him. There were this crack and then he stares at me with this curious look. As he's staring, a hole appears right here.' Macintyre taps the centre of his forehead. 'When he slides down I can see the back of his head is open.'

Andrew is shocked. The CSM had seemed invincible, a force of nature, too strong to be felled by a single bullet. He touches his own forehead with his finger and says: 'What do you think it feels like?'

'Being shot? You don't feel owt. Blokes I know who've been wounded say it feels like being punched – a dull pain. Sharp pain only comes later if you survive long enough to feel it . . . Sorry, Andy, this ain't tactful, is it.'

No one has called him that name in more than a year. It sounds odd to him now. A stranger's name. He scratches his neck. 'I'm not afraid. I don't know why, but I'm not. Not any more.'

'What's this about you and some French bint then?'

'Her name is Adilah . . . She's expecting my child. I've asked her to call it William if it's a boy.'

The dignity of the answer shocks Macintyre. 'Sorry,' he says. 'Didn't realize it were serious like. The lads said . . . You want to name the baby after me?'

'You're my oldest friend.' Andrew takes another sip from the decanter. 'Can you keep an eye on them for me, Adilah and the kid?'

'Sure.' As Macintyre says this he begins scratching his belly. One of the buttons on his tunic slips open and he unselfconsciously begins picking lint from his navel.

'Do you swear it?'

'Swear . . .' Macintyre buttons himself up again and takes a drag on his Woodbine, nipping the end between thumb and finger. 'What happened to you then?'

'When we went over the top?' Andrew doesn't know how to explain. 'I thought I'd died and gone to hell. Then I followed some-one. After that I carried on walking. I met Adilah and I knew then there was no going back. I didn't mean to let you down . . . Do you hate me for what I done?'

'No one blames you. We've all thought of doing it.' Macintyre stubs out his cigarette. 'There's something you should know. I'm the last of the platoon, or I will be when . . . That means I have to be in the firing squad. Them's the rules.'

Andrew blinks and falls into a thoughtful silence. 'Well, aim straight. You won't be doing me no favours otherwise.' He puts an arm on Macintyre's shoulder. Withdraws it. 'I'm glad it'll be you doing it, Will.'

'Better go.' Macintyre stands and, as they move to shake hands, they fall into an awkward embrace instead. 'I missed you, mate,' he says.

The words hang in the air. Andrew wants to make a joke of them – 'So long as you don't miss me tomorrow!', something like that – but his throat has contracted. He pats his friend on the back and steers him to the door.

Lieutenant Cooper and Surgeon-Major John Hayes stare at the body on the floor. It is pale, as pale as the pool of liquid around it is dark. Cooper shakes his head. 'Who would have thought there was so much blood in a man.'

'The rate he was bleeding it must only have taken a few minutes,' Hayes says, closing Morris's eyes and checking his watch. 'Knew exactly what he was doing. Look . . .' He points. 'Cut right through the femoral artery.' He dabs a finger in the blood. It is cold.

Brigadier-General Blakemore appears in the doorway with the chaplain. They both grimace when they see Morris's body is bloody and naked, apart from the trousers around his ankles.

'Jesus!' Blakemore says. 'Cover him up, would you.'

'Is there a note?' the chaplain asks.

'No, sir.'

'Morris came to see me before he did it, you know. Asked me to bless him. He was agitated but it never occurred to me that he was planning to do this. Makes no sense.'

All four men are standing in a semicircle around the body, their boots in the pool of blood. Hayes stares at a punch dagger a few feet away that is stuck in the floorboard at a perpendicular angle. 'Perhaps he wanted to take back some control over his life,' he says. 'Was he married?'

'I'll find out, sir,' Cooper says.

'Jesus!' Blakemore repeats with a shake of his head. 'What a waste.'

'Why do you suppose he did it?' Cooper asks, directing his

question to no one in particular. 'Now, I mean, with the Germans about to surrender?'

'I imagine that was the problem,' Hayes says. 'He must have known he couldn't go back to his old life. None of us is fit to go back. You can't turn a man into a killer and then expect . . .'

'We must find out how old he was . . .' Blakemore interrupts. 'Can you organize a headstone, Cooper? Make it a decent one. Mention his VC.'

'Sir.'

'Where should we bury him?'

The chaplain frowns. 'Hadn't thought of that. Suicides are not supposed to be buried in consecrated ground.'

'I'll leave that to you, padre.' Blakemore turns to Cooper. 'That reminds me, with Morris gone, we're going to need someone in charge of proceedings tomorrow morning. Would you mind?'

'Course not, sir.'

'See if you can find a drummer. We should do the thing properly. And Cooper . . .'

'Sir?'

'Discipline will need to be tight. The men won't want to do it. Pick a good RSM.' Blakemore leaves, followed by Cooper.

The chaplain and the MO look at the body, then at each other.

As the daylight wanes, the chaplain visits the condemned man in his cell. He looks like a ghost. His skin is transparent, his eyes blank and unfocused. He is fingering in his hand a lock of hair tied with ribbon, worrying it like a rosary. As the chaplain sits down and folds his hands in his lap, Andrew tucks his shirt into his high-waisted serge trousers.

'I've written this,' he says, handing over a letter. 'Could you get it to Madame Camier? The address is there.'

'Consider it done.'

'I said Will Macintyre could have my boots.'

The chaplain lights a lantern and squints up at him from its flame. 'Is there anything you want to talk about? That is what I'm here for.'

Though he is not tired, Andrew begins yawning uncontrollably. 'I've always been afraid of rats, but there was one in the hut where they locked me up and when I looked at it I realized it was just a rat.'

'It was probably more frightened of you,' the chaplain says, trying to stifle a yawn of his own. 'I'll keep you company all night, if you like.'

'That's all right, father. You should get some rest.'

'I have to say, Kennedy, you are showing great courage. I've seen some men . . .' He pats his knees. 'But I do think it best to put a brave face on things. Much easier. Are you an Anglican?'

'That's Church of England, ain't it?'

The chaplain nods.

'Then yes.'

'Would you like me to give you communion and assurance of pardon for sins?'

It is Andrew's turn to nod. He watches intrigued as the chaplain lays out a small chalice and tips some ruby liquid into it from a hip flask. He produces a wafer from a hanky and blesses it. Afterwards they both get to their knees to pray.

'Never been a church-goer,' Andrew says when they return to their chairs. He takes a swig from the whisky decanter. 'Can't get drunk,' he says, yawning again. 'Would you like some?'

'No thank you.'

Andrew is finding it difficult to concentrate on the chaplain's words. The alcohol is at last numbing him and the heavier his body becomes the more his mind floats away. 'Will my grave be marked?'

'Don't know.'

'Don't matter if it's not. I've already been buried once. My grave is in no-man's-land. I died and went to hell and then I came back. I was saved, you see. An angel saved me.'

The chaplain holds the soldier by the wrists. Looks him in the eyes. 'Why didn't you say that at your trial?'

'They'd have laughed at me.'

'You've heard of the Angel of Mons?'

'Weren't like that.'

The chaplain nods. 'Will you put it down in writing, what happened to you? A testament. You can dictate it to me if you like, then you can read it through and sign it.'

CHAPTER FORTY

London. Present day. Five and a half months after the crash

'CAN I COME AND LIVE WITH YOU?'

Hamdi looked up from the textbook he was marking to see Martha standing by the door studying her shoes.

'What are you still doing here, Martha? Your mummy running late?'

'Can I come and live with you?' Martha repeated.

Hamdi laughed. 'No you can't. Why do you say that?'

'Because . . .'

Because her heart felt like a big bumblebee trying to escape her chest whenever she looked at him. Because she had given it a lot of thought and it was time the world knew that she loved him, always had and always would. Because when she was old enough they were going to get married. It would be a spring wedding, when the lambs were being born and the leaves were on the trees. She could picture the house they would live in, a thatched cottage in the country, by a wood, with a stream running alongside it full of fat trout. She also knew what car they would drive, a hybrid utility vehicle, because Mr and Mrs Said-Ibrahim were going to be an environmentally aware couple. She had named the three children they would raise. Peter, Sally and little George. She would be a primary school teacher herself by then. Marriage was a big commitment to make at her age but she had no doubts, she knew that. None at all. She knew in her heart that she and Hamdi were destined to be together for ever. Because with love comes certainty.

'Because what?' prompted Hamdi.

'Just because.'

'Is everything OK at home?'

'No.'

'Want to talk about it?'

Martha was still examining her shoes. 'No.'

Hamdi checked the parents' book. 'You were supposed to be going home for tea with Clare and her mummy.'

'I know.'

'Is Clare's mummy late?'

'Told her there had been a change of plan.'

Hamdi frowned. He didn't need this complication. It would make him even further behind with his marking. 'I'd better ring your mummy,' he said in a tone that was calculated to sound unfriendly. He looked in his desk for the sheet with all the parents' numbers on it.

'I've got it programmed into my mobile,' Martha said, placing her iPhone on the teacher's desk. 'You can use it if you like.'

'You have an iPhone?'

'Daddy bought me it. It's ringing.'

'Lucky girl.' As it rang he looked at Martha and smiled tightly. 'Answering machine. Hello. This is Hamdi Said-Ibrahim, Martha's teacher. There's been a mix-up. She was supposed to be going home with Clare's mother. It's . . .' He checked his watch. 'Three forty-five now. I'm going to be driving past your house so I can drop her off . . . I have my mobile with me if you need me. And Martha has hers.'

'You and Daddy are friends, aren't you?'

'Yes,' Hamdi said. 'I suppose we are.'

In the Mini, Martha continued staring at her shoes. Hamdi studied her out of the corner of his eye. He clicked the radio on to Classic FM.

Martha said, 'Have you ever been in love?'

'Why?'

'It's a yes or no answer.'

'I'm sorry, Martha, but I don't feel comfortable talking about such things with you. These are inappropriate conversations for a teacher to have with his pupil.'

She was in a passage of the conversation that she had rehearsed. 'Do you love me?'

Hamdi swerved slightly. 'Enough, Martha. We cannot have this conversation.'

'I need to know if you love me or not.'

As Daniel and Philip came out on the English side of the Channel Tunnel, sitting in their car inside the train carriage, their mobiles bleeped in unison – a re-entry into the modern world after a brief, subterranean silence. Daniel looked at his screen and frowned. '*Twelve* missed calls?'

'I've got six,' Philip said. He looked puzzled.

They both pressed their phones to their ears. As they waited to be connected to their messages, the air in the car seemed to loosen. The colour drained from Daniel's lips as he listened. 'It's Martha,' he said in a distant voice. 'She's gone missing.'

The three MI5 officers standing in front of the screen moved to one side to allow Bloom to join them. He was carrying a tray with four steaming cardboard mugs on it. These he handed round. 'Who was having skinny?' he said in a gristly New York accent.

'Mine,' Turner said, reaching for it.

All four men stood taking careful sips of coffee as they rewound a film and watched a young man in a jacket and tie leave his house with a cello case and get into a Mini Cooper. 'We got enough to pull him in yet?' Bloom said.

'Depends,' Turner said, pausing the image on the screen.

'It's not so much what he's done as what the chatter says his lot are planning to do.'

'We're sure they *are* his lot?'

'Fits the profile. They've been looking for a teacher.'

'They're after a child, that's not the same thing.'

'Do we know which website they are planning to show their little snuff movie on?'

'Not yet.'

'On Tuesday we saw this one using a mobile and immediately afterwards he walked into a phone box to make another call.' Turner sat down and put his feet on the desk in front of him, revealing red socks that were an apology for the greyness of his suit.

Bloom took another sip. 'Perhaps his phone needed recharging.'

'Perhaps he didn't want his number traced.'

Bloom was opening a sandwich. He carefully removed the lettuce from it and left it on the side of his plate. 'He knows his phone is being tapped. That guy Kennedy told him. Wouldn't you use a pay phone?'

'He shreds his paper,' Turner said. 'Why would a teacher bother to shred his paper?'

The square in Clapham Old Town was being cordoned off with police tape as Daniel and Philip pulled up outside the house. 'Missing girl' posters were going up. Because three police cars were blocking the road, Daniel left his engine running and the driver's side door open. He shouted instructions over his shoulder as he ran up the steps to his front door. 'Can you find a parking space, Dad?'

Nancy was wearing paint-flecked jeans and a baggy grey sweatshirt with the sleeves rolled up. Her hair was wound up on top of her head and held by a white headscarf. She was in the kitchen staring blankly at the mobile in her shaking hand. Mascara had run in dark lines from the corners of her eyes. Her nose was pink and her face looked puffy. When she saw Daniel she ran to him, spread her arms and began crying again.

'Anything?' Daniel said, his own eyes welling.

Nancy sniffed, wiped her nose and shook her head.

'She was supposed to be going back for tea with Clare, right?'

'She told Clare's mother . . .' Nancy's breathing snagged. Her voice sounded hollow. 'She told Clare's mother that there had been a change of plan and that she was coming home with me.' It was as if Nancy were rehearsing the details, reassuring herself her own version of events was consistent.

'What time was that?'

'Three thirty. Pick-up time.' They both looked at the clock on the kitchen wall. It was ten to seven. Still light, just.

'Did anyone see her leave the school?' Daniel asked. 'She couldn't have got her days mixed up and thought she was doing an after-school club? What night is her chess club?'

Nancy shook her head again, dark fronds tumbling across her face.

'Cello was last night, right? Have you tried . . .' He struggled to remember Hamdi's name. 'Her form teacher, the guy who takes her for cello?'

A small-boned man in a charcoal-grey suit approached them. 'Nothing reported yet from the school. We're questioning all the teaching staff, as well as her schoolfriends.' He held out his hand. 'Detective Chief Inspector Alan Mayhew . . . I want you to know we're doing everything that can be done at this stage. There are photographs going out to every station.'

Daniel held on to his hand. It was as cool as wax. 'You've checked the common?'

'Several times. Battersea Park, too.'

'What about the Bowling Green Café? She loves it there.'

The detective extracted his hand gently. 'We have an officer there now, in case she turns up.'

384

'We've tried the toy shop on Northcote Road and the Latchmere swimming pool,' Nancy said. 'And Mum and Dad haven't heard from her. Nor has Amanda.'

Daniel stood in the centre of the kitchen, rubbing his face with his hands. 'Clapham Picture House?'

'Checked.'

Daniel's shoulders sagged. 'What about the Natural History Museum? She could have taken a taxi.'

'Unlikely. Black cab drivers aren't allowed to pick up un-accompanied minors,' DCI Mayhew said. 'Can she use the Tube on her own?'

Nancy shook her head.

'We've got an officer at Clapham Common, Clapham North and Clapham South. And there's an alert out to all Underground staff. And we'll ask the museum to keep a lookout. Anywhere else she goes?'

'She might have tried going to my college. Trinity . . . I'll call Wetherby.'

Philip had entered the kitchen and was clearing his throat. 'Kew Gardens?' he offered.

'We'll notify both places.'

Daniel said, 'What about that counsellor you've been seeing?'

Nancy recoiled. 'No, I . . . I've tried him.'

'You definitely checked her phone?'

Nancy looked at the kitchen counter. Daniel followed her sight line. Martha's iPhone was next to her school satchel.

'She came home?'

'Someone deleted a message on the answering machine. It had been left at three forty-five. Her *Finding Nemo* rucksack is missing and her toothbrush and . . .' Nancy ran to the sink and heaved. Nothing came out.

Daniel crossed the kitchen and stroked her back.

'Crush. She's taken Crush with her.' Nancy wiped her mouth. 'They think she might have tried to run away from home. Look.' She pointed to four crusts that had been cut off on the counter. 'She's made herself sandwiches.'

385

'If that's what's happened,' DCI Mayhew interrupted, 'her prospects are good. We get called out to situations like this more often than you'd think and the missing child usually turns up within a few hours. In all probability she is sitting in a café somewhere wondering how best to get home.'

Nancy was rubbing her temples. 'Kevin isn't here. I think she might have taken him too.'

Mayhew: 'Kevin?'

'Our dog . . . When a child is abducted . . .'

'We don't know she's been abducted,' Daniel interrupted. 'If she's taken Crush and Kevin it is far more likely that she ran away.'

'Once a child sees her abductor's face . . .' Nancy continued.

'Stop it, Nance. It won't help to think . . .' Daniel frowned. 'Did she have any money?'

Nancy shook her head and chewed on her lower lip. 'And she doesn't have her insulin pouch with her.'

Daniel picked up Martha's iPhone. 'You've checked this for texts and photographs?'

'Nothing,' Nancy said.

'Anything we should be doing?' Daniel said helplessly.

DCI Mayhew said, 'Have you phoned everyone you can think of?'

'I could call Bruce,' Daniel said. 'He's her godfather.'

An hour and a half passed as phone calls were made and remade from police lines, so that the home landline would be left free. Mayhew kept checking his watch. At 8.40pm he nodded at his sergeant and squared his shoulders. He didn't want to alarm the parents more than was necessary. 'Are you familiar with the Amber Alert System?'

Nancy put her hand to her mouth. 'That's for abducted children.'

'Missing children,' Mayhew corrected gently, resting a hand on Nancy's arm. 'We've scanned a photograph of Martha and it's been sent to every police force in the country. All the airports and seaports are covered.' He blew out his cheeks. 'We now need to start thinking about a media appeal.' He checked his watch. 'It's been five hours since she was last seen. The child rescue alert system is a procedure designed to achieve rapid cross-border publicity. We send out texts and emails and Martha's picture will be broadcast with a police contact number every hour on ITV and Sky. We should also be thinking about getting you in front of a news crew as soon as possible.'

The sergeant stepped forward. 'We have a crew waiting outside, sir,' she said.

'Good.' He looked at Nancy. 'Do you think you can manage this? It's best coming from the mother. Keep it simple. It will be pre-recorded. We should be able to get it on the nine o'clock bulletins.'

Nancy and Daniel were holding hands as they stood on the steps of their house, blinking in the lights. Nancy didn't look at the camera as she spoke softly and haltingly, on the threshold of tears. 'If anyone has seen. Our beautiful little. Girl. Can they please contact the police.' She looked at Daniel. Put her hand to her mouth. The tears came. 'If someone has. Taken her . . . please . . . please do not hurt. Her.'

Daniel squeezed her hand and spoke in a stronger voice: 'Please let us know where to find Martha, or put her in a place of safety and tell somebody where that is. She is nine years old with long blonde hair in a ponytail. She has green eyes and a discoloration of skin on her neck. She was wearing a dark green school uniform and a pink jacket. She is short for her age. She may have a mongrel dog with her called Kevin.'

'She's diabetic,' Nancy added, her voice clotting again. 'If she doesn't get her insulin she will . . .'

For twenty-five minutes after the appeal was broadcast, Nancy sat on the sofa in the drawing room, sometimes crying, sometimes staring blankly ahead, sometimes drawing her knees up and wrapping her arms around them. Daniel sat next to her. He held her hand. Put his arm around her. But he couldn't sit still for long. Instead, he kept standing up to check his own iPhone and the message alerts on his MacBook. He made fresh cups of tea. Tapped his watch face. Stood by the window staring out across the garden.

Every ten minutes or so he wandered next door to the kitchen where the three policemen assigned to their house were waiting with Philip. Had they heard anything yet? Every time the phone rang, both parents jumped. It was always a friend or relative who had seen the appeal. After a while they let the calls go straight to the answering machine, screening them as the messages came over the speaker.

Daniel poured two large brandies and handed one to Nancy. She gulped it down and said, 'I'm going to check her room again.' She could hear Daniel following her up the two flights of stairs. In the bedroom, with the door closed, the cacophony of phones, police radios, televisions, doorbells and distant sirens downstairs was shut out. Nancy sat on the bed and tugged at her hair, holding it off her head through open fingers then letting it drop. Daniel pinched the bridge of his nose. 'If I'd been here, this . . .' He didn't finish the sentence. 'You've checked the drawers?'

'Won't harm to check again.' There were tears below Nancy's surface again. They could be heard rather than seen – a catch in her voice.

With each drawer that was pulled open, Nancy felt a stab of pain. The sight of small, neatly folded T-shirts, pants and socks were a judgement on her. Underneath them was a secret hoard of sweets: Haribos, Refreshers, Creme Eggs. 'I should have let her have sweets.'

'You're a dentist. You know what sweets do.'

'Should have let her have sweets,' Nancy repeated, straightening her spine. She had her back to Daniel but could see his face in a triptych of dressing table mirrors. She could also see the sun-bleached poster of Girls Aloud on the wall behind him and, next to that, the photograph of the school play and the certificates for gymnastics and skating. She turned and stared at the pencil lines measuring heights alongside the door frame, each with a date. They were close together, these marks. Martha was not growing fast. Her gaze ran along the shelf stacked with Harry Potter books and came back across to the dressing table and the Barbie dolls, three of them, in a sitting position on its glass surface. On the mirror were tiny sparkling stickers of butterflies. Next to them was a SpongeBob SquarePants mug that had left a hot chocolate ring alongside it. She picked up Martha's hairbrush, teased a ball of hair from it and held it to her nose. Her gaze shifted to the floor and to the roller blades she had bought, the hockey stick, the cello case, the PlayStation incongruously close to the Snow White costume out of which Martha had grown. One colour predominated in the room: the pink plastic CD player, the pink ring-bound school jotter and the pink spangled purse.

Nancy exhaled slowly, sat down next to Daniel and felt the bend of his arm move around her waist. She shrugged him off and turned her back to him.

Daniel got on his knees and, putting a hand on both her shoulders, turned her to face him. 'Look at me, Nancy,' he said. 'Hey! Look at me.'

Nancy shook her head. 'I had an argument with her this morning.'

'What about?'

'Nothing. She wanted a nose stud . . . The other morning she asked why we never kiss any more.'

'She'll be all right.'

'What if she isn't?'

They sat in silence for a full minute as they weighed this. Daniel spoke first. 'I think there's something wrong with Dad.'

'What do you mean?'

'I think he's ill. He was drinking from these bottles of morphine and he has these patches on his shoulders. I caught him stuffing a handkerchief in his mouth.'

'Why?'

'So I wouldn't hear him crying out in pain, I guess.'

'Has he said anything?'

'You know Dad.'

'Poor Phil. Maybe it isn't too serious.'

'Maybe.'

The atmospheric pressure in the bedroom changed. The air thickened. Nancy put her hand to her chest, over her heart. The cold pain she had been feeling there all evening melted and lost some of its weight. 'Poor, poor Phil. I went round to see him only the other day. I'd translated those letters.'

'Thanks. He was desperate to see them.'

'Don't think he's had a happy life.'

'No.'

'Typical of him not to mention he was ill.'

'Yeah.'

'Does Amanda know?'

'No idea.'

'You want to talk about it?'

'Not really.'

Nancy placed a hand on Daniel's leg. 'I know.'

Daniel lifted Nancy's face, framing it in his hands and wiping her tear stains away with his thumbs. She opened her arms. They held on to each other tightly and lay down, her back to his front, with their heads at the feet end of the child-sized bed. Daniel felt for Martha's pillow and lifted it down so that Nancy could rest her head on it. They stayed like this for five minutes before Nancy sat up and saw the diary with the leopard-print cover that had been hidden under Martha's pillow. She reached across for it and flicked to the last entry. It was about Hamdi; Martha's love for Hamdi; Martha's plans to run away with Hamdi and get married and buy a thatched cottage by a stream. There were dozens of love hearts on the page: large, small, coloured in red.

They hurried down the stairs and met the inspector on his way up. 'We've had a strong lead,' Mayhew said. 'A neighbour of yours. Martha was spotted in a car at four o'clock.'

'What car?' Nancy said. 'Who was driving?'

'A man.'

Daniel and Nancy exchanged a look of panic. 'Who?' Nancy said.

'Your neighbour described him as being young-looking, smartly dressed, jacket and tie. "Of Middle Eastern appearance".'

Daniel blinked. 'Middle Eastern?'

'Do you know anyone fitting that description?' the inspector asked him.

He numbly placed the diary on the table.

Philip put a hand on his shoulder and repeated the inspector's question. 'Do you know anyone fitting that description?'

By the time Nancy, Philip and Daniel pulled up outside Hamdi's flat a mile away in Balham, a TV news crew had laid out cable and was training its arc lights on a balcony that had a metal fire escape leading down from it. Seven police cars, their lights flashing, had formed a corral. Within this was a cordon of blue and white tape. A policeman was giving instructions into a loudhailer.

Mayhew knocked on the window: 'He's her form teacher, correct?'

Nancy nodded, trying not to cry. 'Martha had a bit of a thing about him. She . . . thought the world of him.'

They overheard a voice crackling over the police radio: 'The suspect's name is Hamdi Said-Ibrahim. Repeat, Hamdi Said-Ibrahim. He is known to the Counter-Terrorist Branch. Do not approach him. An Armed Response Unit is on its way.'

'God knows how surveillance missed him giving Martha a lift,' Mayhew said. 'What were they playing at?'

'Are you the parents?' a reporter asked as Daniel stepped out of the car. He ignored the question.

An armed response unit arrived in a Range Rover with blackened windows. They were wearing black body armour and baseball caps and carrying Heckler & Koch assault rifles. They immediately trained them on the balcony. Daniel recognized the two plain-clothed men who pulled up in a black BMW at the same time: the shaven-headed American and the older, leaner man with the heavily lined face. He seemed to recognize Daniel in turn and came over, only to walk past him and shake hands with Philip.

'Geoff,' Philip said. 'I feel reassured to see you here. It's my granddaughter, Martha.'

'I know. It's going to be OK. We've had our eye on this one for a while.'

After ten minutes, Hamdi appeared with his arms raised over his head, wearing only his underwear. As he was being restrained, a white forensic suit was pulled over him and he was handcuffed. A policeman behind him held a hand to the back of his head, keeping it bowed slightly as he led the way down the echoing metal stairs that served as a fire escape. Another policeman emerged from the flat talking into his radio mic. His crackly voice could be heard in a nearby police car saying: 'No sign of the kid.'

'Hey!' Daniel shouted. 'Where's Martha?'

Hamdi looked up. 'Professor! What's going on?'

'What have you done with Martha?'

'Don't know where she is. On my honour. I dropped her off at your house. That was the last I saw of her.'

'Please, my friend, you must tell us . . .'

The hyperthyroid bulge of Hamdi's eyes was more pronounced than ever. He was twisting his neck to keep Daniel in his sight, as if he were a lifeline. 'She talked about someone called Tom. Said she had lunch with him and that he lived in a big house. Do you know a Tom?'

Sirens sounded as the suspect was driven away for interrogation. DCI Mayhew addressed Nancy, Daniel and Philip together. 'He's being taken to Paddington Green high security station. We should get some information about Martha soon. You can come with me if you like, but if I were you I'd head back home and wait there. We've left a couple of officers at the house. I'll keep you up to date with any developments.'

When the three got back into their car, Daniel started the engine only to stop it again. He was looking at Nancy. She was covering her mouth with her hand.

'What is it, Nance?'

'He said "Tom". He said Martha was talking about Tom.'

'Tom the counsellor? Thought you said you'd tried him.'

Nancy did not answer. She was tapping a number into her mobile. 'I did. He said he would call if he heard anything . . . He's not answering. I think we should go round there.' She tried again. 'Tom! It's Nancy.' Pause. 'No, she's still missing . . . Has she tried to call you? . . . Well, if she does can you call me straight away on this number?' There was fear in her eyes. She ended the call and pressed the mobile to her chest. 'She's there. I know she's there.'

'Where does he live?'

'Dulwich . . . twenty-two or twenty-one Alice Grove. Twenty-two. Definitely twenty-two. It's opposite the college. I went for lunch. We went there, Martha and me. She could easily have remembered the address. You know what she's like.'

Philip sounded dazed. 'Who is Tom?'

'My counsellor. Tom Cochrane.'

'Why would . . .' Daniel's voice trailed off as he noticed Philip looking confused. 'You OK, Dad?'

'It's Hamdi – I think I recognize him. I can't think where I've seen him before but I recognize him.'

A fire engine – blue and red lights flashing, siren off – turned into Alice Grove ahead of them and parked outside number twenty-two. A firefighter jumped out and began sealing off the road with 'Do Not Cross' tape. It shimmered across the street, rolling in on itself, stirring and twisting. There was a smell of gas in the night air. The firefighter began knocking on doors. The street was being evacuated.

'That's the house.' Nancy pointed. 'I recognize it.'

'Everyone back, please,' a firefighter said. 'There's a gas leak.'

'I think my daughter might be in that house,' Nancy said, still pointing.

'We've knocked on that one. There's no one in. Now please, stand back. There's a risk of an explosion.'

'Please. She's nine.'

'OK, we'll check it again, but you must get back.'

A second fire engine arrived and parked across the end of the street, blocking it to further traffic. As Nancy and Philip walked around it, Daniel saw an open compartment full of maroon and gold-coloured coats. He grabbed one, along with a helmet, and slipped it on as he followed the firefighters walking down the street towards the house. As he got near it, he broke away and followed two more firefighters carrying a metal ladder around the side of the house. They laid it on the ground and returned to the fire engine. Daniel, his face now hidden by the helmet, marched over. The ladder was lighter than it looked – longer too, reaching as high as the guttering. Once at the top of it, he half crawled along a gully at the join of two slate roofs and, lying flat on his belly, looked down on to the glass of the conservatory, twelve feet below. No lights were on but he could make out a shape – the crown of a man's head. The man was swaying in the semi-darkness, staring at what looked like a lighter in his hand, as if unsure what it was. Daniel felt off-balance. A swoop of vertigo. He removed his helmet. A linking door to the kitchen, he could now see, was wedged open. Towels and blankets were sealing the bottoms of the other doors. What was going on? Another shape. A child. It was Martha, wearing her pink coat, cuddling her velveteen turtle, sitting on a sofa looking drowsy.

Kevin walked into the room and looked up. If the dog starts barking, Daniel thought, Tom will surely follow his gaze. He now knew he had to jump, but he also knew his nerves were failing him. As he crawled backwards, concealing himself, a firefighter appeared on the roof behind them. Daniel put his hand to his lips and pointed at the conservatory roof. He peered down again and could see that the man was a foreshortened and isolated figure with a small bald patch. How dare he take his daughter? How dare he lock her in a room and turn on the gas? He looked across at Martha. Her eyes were closed, her freckled face cushioned on the palm of her hand. As she slept, her small, rubbery fingers clenched. She stretched her arms and legs, her muscles rolling softly. The gas smelled stronger than before. Daniel realized it would be rising to meet him. It was harmless to breathe these days, he knew that, but an acid taste of bile nevertheless bubbled up in the sump of his throat. The point of no return. The realization of the unthinkable. He tried to compose himself.

He looked back to see a second fireman arriving, using urgent hand signals, demanding that he come back down. Unsteadily, he got to his feet and held his arms out for balance. He could now see Nancy in the drive below. She was rubbing Philip's back. What were they talking about? Nancy looked up, saw him and covered her mouth. Philip followed her gaze. They were both looking at him now, silhouetted against the moonlight. Philip appeared to be nodding.

There was a flash of light, a white ray of stabbing pain on Daniel's retina. Assuming it was the gas igniting, he ran instinctively towards it and, his stomach lurching, jumped in the direction of Martha. His arms described small circles as he fell for an impossibly long moment. The sensation he felt was of falling through time, of finding its inward flow. When his boots met the glass, it was as if he had broken through the surface of an ice-covered lake and was being slowed down by the drag of water. It was the drag of time. Outward, linear time had expanded and slowed almost to a halt. Below him, the earth was losing its gravitational pull. There was a pungent smell of gas in his nostrils; gas escaping past him through the shattered ceiling of the conservatory, into the night. As his arms flailed they disturbed particles of silver dust: shattered glass suspended in air, floating as if in a vacuum. He had been here before, living out these final moments, these fractions of seconds – falling to earth, through the earth, into a deep place where the sun is silent.

He landed heavily, his knees buckling, and as he pitched

sideways, he felt his skull crack against something solid. The fragments of glass darkened and thickened. They were everywhere, showering him, suffocating him, burying him alive. And then he felt nothing.

CHAPTER FORTY-ONE

Le Bizet, Belgium. Second Tuesday of September, 1918

SLEEP DROPS AWAY AS ABRUPTLY AS A TRAP DOOR AND ANDREW SITS up in bed. He has a sense of a noise dimming, a shadow sound, a dog barking somewhere. He is baffled momentarily by a hollow sensation in his stomach then, as he remembers what is to happen this day, he finds his voice. 'What time is it?' The words are shouted.

No one answers. He stands up. Light is edging under the door – a dirty white dawn. He contemplates the clothes draped over the chair and knows that he does not want to die in a uniform that does not fit him. When the assistant provost marshal unlocks the door, Andrew is standing naked, squaring his shoulders defiantly.

'I want a uniform that fits me,' he says.

The APM turns his head and, without taking his eyes off the prisoner, speaks to his own shoulder. 'Medic.'

Surgeon-Major Hayes steps out from behind him, unrolls a cloth pouch and lifts up a syringe. 'We need to give you this, Kennedy.'

'What is it?'

'A tranquillizer. You won't know anything.'

'Don't need it, sir. Not afraid. No fear left.'

The chaplain is the next to appear in the doorway. He is wearing purple insignia and a white clerical stole. He holds the prisoner's arm tight to reassure him. Distracted by this, Andrew does not notice Hayes step behind him until it is too late. As he

397

turns, the surgeon-major jabs the needle into his left buttock. He slumps forward into the chaplain's arms. The APM wraps the now limp body in a blanket and carries him out as if he were carrying a sleeping child, down the steps of the police station and into the yard.

When the firing squad arrives half an hour later they are surprised to see the prisoner already tethered to the post. A rope is tied tightly around his chest to stop him slipping down. He is wearing a hood. His head is lolling forward. The APM pins an off-white aiming mark to the prisoner's tunic, over his heart. The mark is a four-by-two flannelette used for rifle cleaning.

Several members of the firing squad are swaying, anaesthetized with drink. The twelve rifles are laid out ready – Major Morris's final order has been followed. The soldiers line up, one behind each gun in two rows of six. All raise their rifles to their shoulders and take aim, with the back rank remaining standing while the front rank, on an order from the RSM, get down on one knee. Lieutenant Cooper nods at a drummer boy and a roll begins. The RSM raises a handkerchief at a ninety-degree angle in front of him and, as he lets it go, a ragged volley is fired. The prisoner's body sags on the wooden post. Surgeon-Major Hayes marches over to it, feels for a pulse and holds a stethoscope to the chest before nodding at Lieutenant Cooper. The subaltern puts away his revolver, relieved that he will not have to deliver the *coup de grâce*.

Hayes unties the ropes and supports the dead weight as he lays it out on the ground. 'You there,' he barks at Macintyre, 'give me a hand.' With Macintyre taking the feet and Hayes lifting under the arms, the two men carry the body over to a waiting coffin and tip it in. The coffin is too small: the body looks big inside it. Macintyre looks at the prisoner's bare feet, unable to hide his disappointment. 'He said I could have his boots,' he mutters.

They each take one end of the coffin lid and lay it on top.

'Sir?' Macintyre says.

'Yes?'

'How come there's no blood?'

The surgeon-major does not answer. As he marches back inside the police station to fill out a death certificate, the members of the firing squad stand around. The only sound is the clattering of bolts being drawn back and spent cases tumbling down into the dust.

'Any recoil?' one says.

'Not much.'

'Me neither.'

'Thought I felt a kick, but I'm not sure.'

CHAPTER FORTY-TWO

Le Bizet, Belgium. Present day. Seven months after the crash

A SMALL CROWD OF VILLAGERS HAD GATHERED IN THE GROUNDS OF the old police station. The owners of the house were among them, back from their holiday. They had not been aware of the headstone in their garden, still less that an English war hero was buried underneath it. Not only had they given their permission for his exhumation, they had turned it into an event – inviting neighbours, handing around drinks on trays. A gendarme and a priest were here in a semi-official capacity, as was the mayor of Le Bizet who was to accompany the remains to their new burial place, the Tyne Cot Commonwealth War Graves Cemetery on the Passchendaele Ridge. This was why Clive and Philip were here, too. For Philip, making the journey through the Eurotunnel without Daniel had been distressing, but he felt he had no choice. There was unfinished business here. He knew Daniel would have wanted him to come back.

The remains were to be joined at Tyne Cot by the headstone, once it had been cleaned. A photographer from the local paper was recording the occasion. Whenever he used his flash, he gave depth to an otherwise flat and grey afternoon.

'You know Morris was a conductor before the war?' Clive said to Philip as the two men stood slightly apart from the others.

'Yes.'

'Quite a distinguished one. There's a reference to him in a diary that a friend of mine bought at auction a couple of years ago, part of a job lot. He's sending it to me . . .'

The headstone was worked free and carried with awkward solemnity by two officials from the Nord *département* towards a waiting van. When they returned, they marked with their spades the outline of where the grave should be. The first nestled his boot on the lug and his hand drew leverage against the inside of his knee. The spade bit into the soil easily and a square of turf was cut out, then another. As the hole widened, the second official joined in with his spade. After a few minutes they stopped to pull from the ground what looked like a rat's nest made from threads of soil-matted fibre. A rotting plank of wood was attached to the end of it. They dug a hole four feet deep before they found something similar. A sandbag. It took both of them to pull it out.

'How does that poem go?' Clive said taking a step closer. ' "There shall be / In that rich earth . . ." '

Philip finished the line: ' "A richer dust concealed." '

The first official pulled out another rotten plank of wood, longer this time. The shape of the other piece of wood was consistent with it. A third plank was visible. It was nailed to another one, a lid of some sort. The coffin proper. They lifted it out, trailing soil with it, and scraped back a layer with their spades. They could see more rotting sandbags. A row of them. Five in all. They opened one. It was heavy and solid, the sand hard and imprinted with the hessian's weft. They laid all the bags on the ground side by side and stood panting as they looked in the hole. There were no bones.

Philip walked back to the house, supporting himself on his cane. Clive watched him disappear from view before following. When he turned the corner he found his friend with a handkerchief stuffed in his mouth. He was clenching his fists.

'You OK?'

Philip removed the handkerchief and recoiled as a spasm of pain carried through his age-silted body. His mind emptied. The air left his lungs. The past was rushing in on him.

'Philip?'

'Can you fetch the underground monitor,' Philip said, once he caught his breath. 'A radius of twenty feet from the grave.'

A yellow and white device resembling a lawn mower was brought over from the van. As Clive pushed it at walking pace back and forth within the radius Philip had specified, a transmitter mounted on its right side emitted a ground-penetrating radar pulse that was picked up by a receiver mounted on its left. The results were displayed on a liquid-crystal screen. 'I think we've found something,' Clive said a few minutes later. He was on an area of lawn twelve yards from the grave. 'According to this, whatever it is should be about three feet below the surface.' He looked across to the owners of the house and, when they shrugged and nodded, he signalled for the officials with the spades.

Once they were three feet down, they stopped digging. One of them slipped on a pair of latex gloves and pulled from the ground an object the size of a shoe. He laid it on a sheet of plastic. It was alive with worms. While Clive shone a torch on it, the official brushed away the soil to reveal that it was a bone fragment, its surface greasy with dark yellow-brownish discoloration. The bone was human. A femur.

A fleeting coolness roused Philip from sleep. He was in his high-winged armchair in front of the inglenook fireplace in his study and there was a package beside him on a small table. Amanda must have put it there and her walking in front of the fire must have caused the coolness, like a passing ghost. His arthritic fingers struggled to pull apart the layers of Sellotape in which the package was bound. His fumbling was compounded by his eagerness. It was the parcel he had been expecting: a diary. There was an accompanying letter, handwritten.

Dear Philip,

This is the diary I mentioned, written by an army chaplain called the

Rev. Horncastle. He died in 1927 and has no surviving relatives as far as we can determine. It came with a job lot of medals and memorabilia my friend picked up at a First World War auction at Sotheby's a couple of years ago. Not worth much, fifty quid at most. He says it's yours if you want it. He was going to donate it to the Imperial War Museum, so if you don't want it, perhaps you could donate it for him. The entry I thought you should read is for 15 September 1918. I think you will find it interesting. It concerns the death of Major Morris.

Yours ever,
Clive

The diary was written in pencil on yellowing paper. A Post-it note marked 15 September 1918.

Major Peter Morris VC killed himself yesterday. He was one of the judges at the court martial. Let God be his judge. Apparently he was a conductor. Friend of Gustav Mahler's. We have no record of a next of kin and we weren't sure what to do with his body, as we could not bury a suicide in consecrated ground. Came to an arrangement with the MO and the APM. Buried him in the grounds of the police station and marked his grave. A proper headstone is being organised. The same will not apply to the soldier shot at dawn yesterday.

Philip turned to the previous day's entry, 14 September 1918. There was a heaviness to the page, even though it was tissue-thin.

Soldier court-martialled for desertion today. He had gone missing for more than a year. Settled down in a French town. Met a French widow. I acted as the court's legal advisor. The fellow didn't say much during his trial, but afterwards I went to visit him in his cell and asked him to tell me exactly what had happened. Got the impression he said what he said for my benefit. Must have heard the Angel of Mons rumours. Nevertheless I wrote it down and got the poor blighter to sign it.

Philip's jaw went into spasm for a second. He took a sip of morphine. The reverend hadn't even bothered to mention the private's name. He examined the diary; it had a leather skin, the back cover of which had been badly stitched. A thread was hanging and he tugged at it. A leather flap hung loose from the lining, like a disembowelled stomach. There was a piece of paper inside, folded into four. It was a statement signed 'Private Andrew Kennedy, Shropshire Fusiliers' and dated 14 September 1918. Philip closed it again. He would read it with Daniel, once he recovered. Whatever it said, they should find out together.

He read the entry for 15 September once more, tapped the page twice with his finger, opened his drawer and took out the rusting shortbread tin. The lid came off easily and he reached inside for the copy of *Punch*. This opened, he removed the sheet of music, held it up to the light under a magnifying glass and examined its dark stains, looking for the name 'Gustav'. He stared at it for a moment, lost in thought, before struggling across the room to his desk and turning on his computer. After googling 'Mahler signature', he held the score up to the screen to compare the writing, nodded to himself and reached for the phone.

'Professor Wetherby please, department of music . . .'

'Wetherby speaking.'

'Hello, professor, we haven't met. I'm Daniel Kennedy's father.'

Wetherby was silent.

'I have something,' Philip continued, 'which I believe you have been looking for.'

'What?'

'Rather not discuss it over the phone. When might be a convenient time for me to come and see you?'

'My secretary keeps my diary.'

'How about now?'

'I have a college formal tonight, but that is not until eight.'

Philip's next call was to Geoff Turner. 'It's me, Philip. I have another favour to ask.'

★

'What do you reckon?'

'Fifty-fifty. Better than when he was first brought in. The REMs are promising.'

'Think he can hear us?'

'No.'

'Probably as well.'

'Yeah.'

There were two people. A man and a woman. They were speaking in a whisper.

Daniel tried to open his eyes. They were glued. He felt a sleeve brush across his face. Hands were plumping up his pillow. His position was being shifted but he could not feel his body, only a heaviness where his limbs should be. What he did feel was a spiralling drift into sleep.

When he next awoke he tried to open his eyes and managed a slit, but they stung under the harsh strip lighting. He thought he could make out the blurred fronds of a spider plant in the corner of the room. There was a cage around him, a chrome contraption with pulleys. He could see a face reflected in it but not one he recognized. The eyes were puffy and bruised, the lips blistered. The nostrils had splints in them and the bridge of the nose was taped. There was gauze on the chin that was black with congealed blood and across the cheek there was a line of stitching. His tongue felt heavy. An involuntary heave of his stomach. A taste of bile in his throat. He closed his eyes again and retreated back into unconsciousness.

As he moved unsteadily with his stick across the flagstones leading to the portico, Philip could see college servants, dressed formally in black waistcoats, lighting the candles in the dining hall. Antique college silver had been brought out and was gleaming gratefully in their light, like nursing home residents allowed out in the sunshine after a winter indoors. To his right, at a bow window with armorial bearings carved in the mullions, he could see a tall, lean, balding man adjusting his bowtie in the reflection. Wetherby, he presumed. He would need all his strength for this. Could not allow pain to distract him. A gulp of morphine from the small, white bottle in his pocket helped. When he knocked on the door marked VICE PROVOST, he heard a voice say, 'Enter.'

Wetherby was lying out at full length on a Regency chaise longue. He was wearing a black velvet jacket that added to, rather than subtracted from, the impression he gave of suppressed violence. In one hand he held an antique magnifying glass, in the other a slim volume of poetry, its mildewed pages open in the middle. His face was half in shadow, an effect created by a floriate lampshade, the only lamp that was on in the room. He snapped the volume shut and placed it on the side table next to him, on top of an arrangement of dainty silver spoons. Only now, with graceful movements, did he rise, cross the room and hold out his hand.

As they shook with a testing firmness, the two men eyed one another. Physically, Wetherby was the taller man, but they were not dissimilar.

'Come in, come in. Take a seat,' Wetherby said, his voice a croaky thread. 'My dinner is in half an hour. Going to say grace in Latin, I think. Give the college benefactors their money's worth.'

'Thank you, but I prefer to stand.' Philip became distracted by a small watercolour on the wall, a preparatory study by William Blake. It showed a naked and bound young man on his knees, his muscular torso exposed as he leaned back in agony. Two bearded men in robes were stoning him.

'They knew how to deal with blasphemers in those days,' Wetherby said. 'It was left to the college and I suppose it should be locked away somewhere, but I cannot quite bring myself to do it.' He clapped. 'So . . . Can I offer you a port or a brandy? I think I have some gin and tonic somewhere if you prefer. A sherry. I have some dry sherry left.'

'Not for me, thank you. I'll come to the point. When Daniel recovers, I want you to reinstate him and give him the zoology chair that should have been his.'

'Yes, I was sorry to hear about his accident. I trust he is on the mend.'

'It wasn't an accident. He jumped to save my granddaughter's life.'

'Of course, of course. I will see what I can do, but, as you must know, it is the provost's decision.'

'You have the provost's ear.'

'Your son was encouraging Islamist radicalization on campus.'

'You know that's not true.'

'I would help him if I could. I regard him as a friend.'

'You know that's not true either.'

Wetherby stiffened. 'Meaning?'

'I mean you have been no friend to him. You reported him to the counter-terrorism squad. You pushed for his suspension. You blocked his promotion.'

'He told you this?'

'I have my sources. I don't know how he wronged you or why you have been waging this vendetta against him but I want you to know he is a good man. You don't know him as I do.'

'I see, I see. So why would I want to stick my neck out to help him?'

'In return for this.' Philip reached in his pocket and produced the music score.

Wetherby took it and immediately saw what it was. He tried to disguise his excitement as he read it, his eyes flicking greedily over the notes, his finger following them and twitching as it conducted in his head. Perhaps realizing he was breathing too quickly, he affected nonchalance. 'Sheet music. Early-twentieth-century German. Part of a larger orchestral score. Bad condition. May be of marginal interest to a collector but . . . I suppose you want to know if it is worth anything?' His eyes studied the old man's face for a reaction.

'No. I know what it's worth . . . to you.'

Wetherby looked up and gave a sickly smile. 'You know what it is?'

'Mahler's alternative opening to the Ninth.'

'Ah.'

'I believe you've been looking for it.'

Wetherby held his arms up in mock surrender. 'I have. I have. It is an incredible find, if authentic.' He laid it out carefully on the table before reaching for a clear folder. 'May I?'

'Go ahead.'

Wetherby used a pair of tweezers to pick the score up by its corner and slot it into the folder. 'I have been looking for this all my life. I almost stopped believing it existed. How did you come across it?'

'It was tucked inside a copy of *Punch* from nineteen eighteen.'

'You bought it at auction?'

'It was among some personal effects left by my grandfather.'

'Did you photocopy it?'

'No.'

'Have you mentioned it to anyone?'

'No.'

'Extraordinary. Extraordinary. Do you know how it came to be in your grandfather's possession?'

'The copy of *Punch* had belonged to a Major Morris. It had his name on it. He was a conductor. Killed himself.'

'Peter Morris? My God . . . I never thought . . . Ralph Vaughan Williams refers to him once or twice in his letters from the Front. They served together and he mentions that they discussed Mahler, but I had no idea the connection between Mahler and Morris was anything more than—'

'It *is* genuine, isn't it?'

Wetherby looked away. 'I could not say.'

'It would be easy enough for me to get it authenticated, carbon dating, signature analysis.'

Wetherby sighed. 'There is no need. It is genuine. May I play it?'

'If you like.'

Wetherby stood up, silently crossed the room and laid his elongated fingers on yellowing piano keys warped by the sun. By the time he had finished playing, his cheeks were damp with tears. 'Beautiful. Just beautiful. So contemplative. It has none of the darkness of the authorized version. Pure light and delicacy . . . Are you prepared to sell it?'

'You can have it, in return for reinstating Daniel and giving him the zoology chair.'

Wetherby thought about this for a moment. 'And no one else knows about it?'

'No.'

'You have proof of ownership?'

'I'm sorry, you speak very quietly. I'm a little deaf.'

'I asked if you have proof of ownership?'

'Why?'

'Because I am not going to have your son reinstated.'

Philip held out his hand. 'In that case I will have the music back please.'

'I think not.'

'What do you mean?'

'I mean, I shall be keeping this and there is nothing you can do about it. As it is out of copyright, even Mahler's estate does not have a claim on it.'

Philip walked around the side of the desk to reach for the music. 'Give it back.'

'No.'

'I shall report you to the provost.'

'He is hardly likely to accept your word against mine. He does everything I tell him and, anyway, I have a feeling his days as provost here are numbered. As for Daniel, dear Daniel, yes, you are right, I knew he had nothing to do with the Islamists, but I could not allow that to get in the way of his suspension.'

Philip moved his lips. They looked wrinkled and purple. No sound emerged.

'Was there anything else?'

Philip found his voice. 'It's supposed to be cursed, you know. The Ninth.'

'I will take my chances.'

Philip hesitated in the doorway, in case Wetherby wanted to call him back. He didn't. Instead he felt the professor's eyes on his back as he crossed the quadrangle and made his way slowly past the Porter's Lodge to where a car was waiting for him. Once seated, he took a small digital recording device from his pocket and handed it to the driver, a lean man with a heavily lined face.

'As expected?' Turner asked.

'As expected.'

'Didn't notice the mic?'

Philip shook his head.

Turner opened a thin laptop, leaned it against the steering wheel and plugged in the digital recorder. He connected to the internet and, with supple fingers moving over the keyboard, sent the sound file as an attachment in an email to the provost. 'This should be interesting then,' he said.

CHAPTER FORTY-THREE

DANIEL'S NEXT CONTACT WITH THE WORLD WAS MORE A SENSED presence. It was Nancy, he knew that much. Nancy was his dentist, the mother of his child, the woman he loved. She was edging her chair closer to his bed with fluid shunts of its legs. And now she was using a cold and damp compress to dab his forehead. He could hear a familiar voice talking in a whisper, too. Not Nancy. Someone he knew well though.

'He's not responding. Watch what happens when I do this to his foot . . . Nothing.'

'But when he comes out of the coma?'

'You never know. Don't get your hopes up. The skin should react to a pinprick.'

Daniel was outside his body now, in a room with a bed. There was someone lying on it. A man. He had a large white brace around his neck, a tube taped to his mouth and a yellow contusion across his brow. There were wires, monitors and drips. This was clearly a hospital but there was something not right about it. The walls were too soft, as if they were melting. He tried to concentrate on the two seated figures by the bed. Though he could not see their faces he knew it was Nancy and the Bear. They were small, as if at the wrong end of a long telescope.

'Can you hear me, darling? It's me, Nancy.' Her voice was cloudy, rising up through layers of consciousness. 'Martha's safe. You saved her. A paramedic resuscitated her.'

411

Daniel was confused. He could not concentrate. His mind was shying away from something. Who was Nancy talking to? Who was the man on the bed wearing the green hospital-issue gown? He felt a numbness, a sensation of hugeness, as if he was filling the room, as if he was part of the fabric of the room. He wanted to tell Nancy he loved her, but his teeth were loose and chalky and his tongue was too heavy to shape the words. There was a weight on his chest and an intolerable sensitivity to his skin, as if he were becoming transparent. Even his thoughts ached – an electrochemical jelly that would not cool and harden.

Days floated by without Daniel noticing them. Then he could hear a song. He recognized the voice singing along to it tonelessly and getting the lyrics slightly wrong. 'It's Hall and Oates, Dan. Can you hear it? You hate Hall and Oates. Wake up, Dan. Listen. "Because my kiss, my kiss is on your lips." Can you hear it, Dan? Tell me to turn it off.'

The room fell silent. Hours passed. Days. Weeks. Then he found himself lying on his back. Eyes open. Miles below the ceiling. Was that Martha he could hear? She was nearby. Crying. A thin blackness descended, slowing his mind.

Now he was on a rubber-wheeled gurney being pushed down a corridor and he could hear Nancy's voice again. She sounded upset, her voice crackling with anger. 'Daniel! Daniel! You have to fight this! Daniel! Danny. Please, Dan. Can you hear me? You must fight.' Her breath smelled of chocolate.

Later, there were strangers' voices. 'What happened?' 'Jumped through a conservatory roof to save his daughter. Landed on his head. Lacerations all over. Lost a lot of blood.' 'The guy in the paper?' 'Yeah, him.'

The genes. The survival of the genes. The survival of my daughter. I saved my daughter.

He was outside his body again and the room was tilting. Circulating in his head were fragments of conversation.

Do you think he can hear us? . . . The scan results were inconclusive . . . Paul is happily married . . . We get through this together . . . I'm assuming it's a fissure in his brain . . . You have to fight this!

412

In moments of lucidity Daniel realized that he was delusional, that he was hovering above himself, that this was the madness of paralysis. It was almost liberating, this awareness. It was allowing him to cast adrift from the world of phenomena, become pure thought, a cold brain trapped in an unfeeling body, wandering the universe. But his thoughts would turn to liquid again. Questions, doubts and randomly recalled lines would tangle his senses once more, writhing like worms through his cerebral cortex.

There was an explosion of colour. Kaleidoscopic shapes and patterns. In a rush of images, one merging into the other, he could see the head of a match igniting, a double helix, a spermatozoon, a mushroom cloud, a sun spot . . . then the images blurred, a runny stream-of-consciousness, now hot, now cold. He was high above the room again, riding the thermals, defying gravity.

You cannot defy gravity. This is impossible.

Daniel was trying hard not to think. His old certainties were weightless. It was his doubts that were anchoring him. He sighed heavily, as if his lungs were being entirely emptied of breath by some outside pressure. His intestines felt at once bloated and shrunken, his lips swollen, his head engorged with chatter.

He was next aware of someone repeating his name, but his eyes felt too heavy to open properly. There was a man's image on his retina though, a giant, friendly bear towering over him, his chin creasing into chins. He was chewing sympathetically on the inside of his cheek.

'You know about his vision?' Bruce asked. The question wasn't directed at Daniel. Someone else was in the room.

'Vision?' It was Nancy's voice.

'After the crash. He thought he saw a man in the water when he was swimming for help after the crash. He was about to give up and take off his—'

'*Dan* said he had a vision?'

The corners of Bruce's mouth flickered upwards. 'Well, you know, hallucination. We worked out it was brought on by frontal lobe epilepsy. Did he tell you about the small shadow we found on his brain?'

'No.'

'Well, no reason why he should have, really. We don't think it's significant. Certainly not malign.'

'But did *he* think it might have been a vision?'

'You're a Catholic, right?'

'There was a time I could have said yes unequivocally.'

'But you're Catholic enough. He would have told you rather than me if he really did think he'd had a vision.' Bruce lowered his eyes as if what he had to say would be easier were he not looking at Nancy. 'I loved him too, you know.'

Who is the Bear talking about? Is he talking about me?

'I know. Dan knew, too.'

Why are they talking about me as if I'm not here?

As Father Donne paced across the square towards the steps of Westminster Cathedral, his torch picked out dozens of small white patches on the pavement: discarded chewing gum that had become flattened under the feet of the faithful. He turned the torch off as he reached the steps and listened to the sound of London at night. The distant house alarm, the barking dog, the brushes of a motorized street cleaner scraping the kerb along Victoria Street. There was a full moon and the cathedral was floodlit. Neither was needed. Father Donne generated his own light. He had chalky skin and a silver fringe that emphasized the blackness of his cassock. As he searched through the numerous keys he carried on a bulky chain, he made a mental note to arrange for the square to be scrubbed of chewing gum. He concentrated on the matter in hand, the reason he had been called from his flat so late at night.

Only when he had found the key to the side door did he think to try the latch. It was unlocked. A check of his watch showed that it was ten to eleven; fifty minutes after the doors were normally locked to the public. Once inside, he stood between the two red granite columns in the entrance and looked down the dark nave to a small pool of fragile light, a rack of votive candles flickering in the transept. A tall, bony man was sitting in the pew next to them, staring up at the organ. He was unshaven, wearing jeans and a fleece. As he got nearer, the priest saw the man had a domed forehead that glistened in the light and that by his side was a cardboard box containing framed photographs, files and ornaments. A Chinese girl was sitting the other side of him, partially obscured from view. She was pregnant. Father Donne cleared his throat loudly. The man looked startled, coming out of a trance.

'I'm claiming sanctuary,' the man said.

He smelled of alcohol.

The priest tapped his watch. 'It is a bit late, you know.'

The man stared up at the gallery again. 'The crowning glory of Henry Willis and Sons.'

'She is a nice organ.'

'When they revoiced the stops and added a two-hundred-and-fifty-six-level capture system it made the registration changes so much easier . . . Father?'

'Yes?'

'I've been fired.' The man tapped the box with lank fingers the colour of ivory. 'Had to clear my desk after a quarter of a century teaching at the same university. Pension. Health plan. All gone. They even took away my computer as part of their . . .' he pulled a mock-serious face, ' "internal inquiry".'

'Have you been drinking?'

'Of course. Will you hear my confession?'

The priest looked at his watch again.

'I do not suppose the Lord sticks to Greenwich Mean Time.'

The priest smiled. 'No, I don't suppose He does.'

'There is no need for the box. We can do it here.'

'I'd rather do it in the confessional, if you don't mind.'

The Chinese girl remained seated as the priest turned on his torch and led the way towards the confessional. He pulled the cord on a small strip light on his side of the box. In the adjoining compartment, the tall man sat in the semi-darkness gathering his thoughts.

'So what is it?' the priest prompted through the grille.

'I'm a wicked man.'

'Why's that now?'

'I've behaved abominably to a man who considered me a friend. I could easily have . . . Perhaps I thought, I don't know, *accipere quam facere praestat injuriam*. I've tried to ruin his career and all because I'm . . .' The sound of a hip flask being opened and liquid being swallowed. 'I sent his wife flowers, you know. Well, common-law wife. I wanted her to . . . I don't know what I wanted. Most of all, I'm jealous that he had a vision. He did not deserve it. He is an atheist, you see . . . I thought, why should he be blessed? Why him?' The man took another swig before adding as an afterthought: 'I also got one of my students pregnant.'

There was silence in the next compartment.

'Don't worry, I didn't let her have a termination.'

The priest remained silent.

'Though she wanted one.'

Silence.

'I'm going to live in sin with her, I think. Go abroad. A godless country such as China. I've had it with faith, you see, and the strange thing is, I feel happier. That was why I came here. To say goodbye. To you. To the Church.'

There was a pause before the priest spoke into the darkness. 'A vision, you say?'

Philip looked through the peephole into a cell five paces by three. The white light angling in through the bars was illuminating a figure sitting cross-legged on the floor. His feet were bare, he was wearing what looked like a skullcap and he was rocking. There was a copy of the Koran on a rug in front of him. 'Why is he wearing that orange uniform?' Philip whispered.

'Category A,' Turner said. 'Solitary confinement. You want to go in?'

Philip nodded and stood back. A prison guard stepped forward with a set of keys and the mechanism in the lock turned with a heavy clunk. He held open the door and moved to one side. The prisoner raised his head and smiled. 'Welcome to Belmarsh.'

'Thank you,' Philip said. 'I'm Daniel's father.'

'How is he?'

'Still in a coma.'

'Sorry to hear that. And Martha?'

'Fine, fine. She was asking after you. Thank you for alerting us to Tom. We know you had nothing to do with it . . . How are they treating you?'

'Like a suspect detained without charge or trial under the Anti-terrorism, Crime and Security Act, since you ask.'

Philip studied the prisoner's face. There was something about his bulging, wide-set eyes and guileless smile that was familiar . . . 'If there is anything I can do to help, Hamdi, I promise I will. I know a good QC at Matrix Chambers. Specializes in human rights.'

'Is that what you came to tell me?'

'I wanted to know . . .' Philip began. 'I have to know. Where have I seen you before?'

'You were there the night I was arrested.'

'Before that.'

The prisoner stared at his visitor for a moment. 'I'm afraid I don't think we have ever met before.'

'From here it looks like his eyes are open,' Nancy said.

A blur of daylight was slanting in through the hospital window.

'That's just the muscles in his eyelids going,' Bruce said. 'Look . . .' Fingers were being waved in front of Daniel's face. 'Nothing.'

'There was a message from the provost. Said Dan could take off as long as he needs and whenever he feels ready to come back to work the zoology chair will be his. Don't think they realize how bad he is. The papers don't help. Did you see this?' A crackle of a magazine being passed from one hand to another. 'It's about

Martha's abduction. An account of the rescue. Pretty good. Accurate, I mean. Daniel would have been amused by the headline.'

Bruce read it out loud. 'LEAP OF FAITH.' He tossed the magazine on the bed. 'I heard about your friend Tom.'

'What did you hear?'

'He reckoned you and he had been, you know . . .'

'Well, we hadn't. Did you also hear that he told me his wife was dead when in fact she'd taken out a restraining order on him? That was before he was sectioned. Apparently he did three years in therapy after he was released. Volunteered to become a therapist himself. Ended up working as a part-time trauma counsellor. No one checked his references.' Nancy's shadow looked down, her hair flopping at the sides to blinker her eyes. 'If I hadn't led him on, Martha would have been . . .You know she went there on her own? She'd remembered his address.'

Bruce cupped her chin and raised her face. 'You mustn't blame yourself.' A dry laugh. 'On the other hand, Dan did warn you that this guy was a charlatan.'

Nancy echoed the laugh. 'He talked about that?'

'We talked about everything . . . Haven't heard you laugh in ages.'

'Haven't had much to laugh about . . . Dan told you about what happened when the plane went down?'

Bruce nodded. 'Everything.'

Nancy held out her wrist to show Bruce her watch. 'I've had it fixed. It broke during the crash but I never got round to . . .' She stared at it. 'I overreacted. I misjudged him. I wanted to tell Dan that his dad was proud of him. He went with him in the ambulance, you know. Holding his hand.' Nancy looked down again. 'I was proud of him, too.'

There was a long silence before Bruce said: 'How many weeks?'

Nancy hesitated, then she said: 'Oooh. You're good.'

'It's a doctor thing . . . Also you keep touching your tummy.'

'Coming up to three months . . . Got an appointment for a scan.'

'It's Dan's, right?'

'Course.'

'Did you know he was going to propose to you on your trip to the Galápagos Islands?'

Nancy took Daniel's hand in hers and began stroking it. She leaned forward and kissed each knuckle in turn, so softly her lips barely touched his skin. From this position she first knelt on the floor then sat, with the side of her head resting on the bed. She placed Daniel's hand on her hair and closed her eyes. 'There's something I have to tell you, Bear,' she said. 'And I don't know how to . . . so I'm just . . . If things take a turn for the worse, and it may never come to this, but if they, you know, if they do, the hospital will need my permission to turn off his life-support machine. I'm not saying . . . They're not saying . . . I mean, he could go on for years like this, but they . . . They want me to allow for that possibility.'

A few hundred yards from Kew Gardens, in the musty embrace of his study, Philip picked up the army chaplain's diary and carried on reading. When he came to 23 September 1918, he held the diary closer to himself, then farther away, before finding his distance.

And on the third day he rose again . . . Had a long chat with the MO. He wonders whether the APM can be trusted. I pointed out that he has more to lose than we have. I told him my conscience was clear and that his should be also. In war men have to do what they think is right, regardless of the consequences. Does it even matter any more? Thank the Lord; with the Hun now in full retreat, this war appears to be drawing to a close. They have a body. The headcount tallies. The quartermaster is missing some sandbags.

Philip stared dry-eyed at the page for a full minute before rising stiffly from his armchair. He walked slowly upstairs to his attic, pulled a small tea chest out from behind a water tank and carried it unsteadily back downstairs to his study. After sifting through the papers it contained, he found the bundle of letters he was looking for: eight of them, the ones left on his father's grave at Bayeux in the seventies. He had always assumed they had been left by one of his father's comrades; partly because the handwriting had been the same on all of them; partly because, in the early eighties, the letters had stopped appearing, presumably when the comrade had died.

He took the top one out. The ink had run on the envelope. Rainwater must have diluted it; words fading into the past. The letter was thin, like a seam of sedimentary rock compacted by the pressure of the years. He removed a sheet of paper folded in two and his eye fell upon the words at the bottom: 'Regards, Your Pa'. The handwriting was shaky but it matched the handwritten signature on the statement his grandfather had signed after his court martial.

Dear William,

I have a new bike. The old one fell appart. It has a pump and two stripes on its crossbar, a red one and a blue one. I have retired from looking after the graves here now. I spend my afternoons playing dominos with my friends, Jean and Henri. They know me as Jacques. They like to look at pictures of an actress called Brigitte Bardot.

The world is changing. The Americans have put a man on the moon. In England they have a 'pop group' called the Bay City Rollers who are even bigger than the Beatles. In the summer, I hear English voices when the tourists come. I sometimes wonder if I will meet your son again. He looked like a fine young boy. Yelow hair. Straight back. He was wearing a bowe tie. You would have been prowd of him. He told me what you done to get your VC. I am glad you was brave. I wish the angel had come to save you as well though. I still think of your mother every day. She was very beautifull.

Regards, Your Pa

Philip understood now.

It had been Andrew who had taken the photograph of him that day at the Bayeux War Cemetery.

He shook his head. Why had it never occurred to him that it was odd that a gardener in France had spoken English to him? He was nodding now. Ten-year-old boys assume everyone is English.

Philip wondered what thoughts had haunted Andrew as he had stood over his son's grave in Normandy and stared at the letters 'VC'. He had never known what his son looked like, even from a photograph. Philip could have shown him one, but the old man had been too ashamed to introduce himself. He had simply taken the photograph of the widow and her two children – his own grandchildren – and walked away without saying a word.

Philip stared at the glass case containing his medal collection. 'Bloody medals,' he said. 'Bloody, stupid medals.'

Breathing heavily, he picked up the case and dashed it against a shelf of books, the glass shattering into a hundred shards. He then tipped the box of documents over and swept his arm along his desk, knocking over his photographs and his lamp. He stared at the mess with confusion in his eyes, knelt down and crawled over the broken pieces on all fours, crunching them under hands mottled with liver spots, oblivious to the perforations that were being made in his papery skin.

He had seen a photograph frame lying face down underneath his desk. He reached for it with a bleeding hand and turned it over. It was the photograph of his grandfather and another muddy-faced soldier in a trench. There was a crack in the glass, running almost straight down the middle, dividing the two figures.

On the fringe of sleep, Daniel thinks he hears his father say: 'Sometimes you have to believe before you can see.' Aware of dry lips lightly touching his forehead, he half opens his eyes to see his father's back shadowing through the doorway. He tries to call after him but can find no voice. The empty doorway holds his attention for a couple of minutes until he becomes aware of something new in the room, sensing its presence before it enters his peripheral vision, as if it is giving off a static charge. Lowering his gaze he can see a flat object held between his finger and thumb. It has been placed in his frozen grip. He forces his eyes to focus. It is the photograph of his great-grandfather in the trench, the one he has seen on his father's desk, the one as fragile as the glass plate on which it was recorded four generations ago. It is no longer in its frame. He realizes Philip must have placed it in his hand while he was asleep. As he studies it, he feels a tingling in his brow, as though he has antennae there that are twitching. The monkey chatter that has filled his head in recent weeks falls away. A string has been plucked and, on the threshold of audibility, a single harmonic note is being sustained. It is more a mood than a sound, a feeling of luminous certainty. Though he has glanced at the photograph a number of times before, he has never seen it. Not properly. Not in its entirety. He has paid no attention to the soldier who has his arm around Andrew Kennedy's shoulder. With his protuberant, wide-set eyes and his broad smile, this unseen soldier seems familiar to Daniel. A name, the shape of a name, forms on the edge of his tongue and pushes against his teeth. He hasn't been able to say it before, nor summon it to mind. Now it comes, a force of air down the palate, breathed as much as said. 'Hamdi.'

EPILOGUE

Northern France. Second Monday of September, 1918

THOUGH HIS BILLET IS ONLY A TWO-MINUTE DRIVE AWAY FROM THE police station where the condemned prisoner is being held, the journey takes Major Morris eight minutes – he keeps stopping to look at the steering wheel in his hands, as if unsure what it is. On two occasions, as revealed by tyre tracks on the grassy verge, the car weaves off the road and back on again. Upon reaching the billet, he climbs out unsteadily, leaving the engine running and the door open. A platoon of Welsh guardsmen stare openly at him as they march past, some giving a muffled cheer at what they assume is the sight of an officer the worse for drink. Their sergeant has to bark: 'Eyes front!'

In the sanctuary of his billet, Morris mentally unfolds his score of Mahler's Ninth, the one he has lost. As the memorized notes swim before his red-rimmed eyes, he removes his punch dagger from its scabbard and runs his thumb along its blade. With a heavy sigh, he raises it in the air as if it is a baton, closes his eyes and sees an orchestra before him – the perpendiculars of the strings, the balancing arches and curves of the cellos. He stands still for a moment before clenching his fist and giving a tiny, almost imperceptible flick of his wrist. An upbeat.

The first sounds are from the cellos to his left, below his podium. They are soft; the uneven throb of a heartbeat. Morris leaves a minute-long pause between the first two notes, indicating a sharper second beat, as if he is at a church door silencing a latecomer. From the back of the orchestra, the answering sound: a French horn playing the same note — long, then short. With his mind's eye, Morris looks across at the fourth horn — giving him assurance, bidding him to keep it pianissimo — before giving a taut, third beat to the right. He is into bar three now — the restrained entrance of the harp being plucked behind the first violins. It is joined by a loud horn phrase, rasping and harsh, the notes stopped with the horn player's hand pressed into the bell. As the cello and the fourth horn continue their long-short heartbeat, Morris adds the delicate sound of the double basses from behind the cellos. They play a long-held harmonic, one octave higher. Now, at bar four, he encourages the second horn to play strongly but also to keep his hand pressed into the bell, making the sound suppressed and cruel. There is a stretching of time as he allows his second violins to begin their hypnotic melody. The bell-like tolling of the harp is replaced by a more gentle and yielding sound. With bar five comes a delicate, almost spectral shuddering from the violas: six notes with an accent on the first, agonizingly soft then falling away. He is conducting by heart rather than memory now. Though he has never yet managed to conduct this far, he knows what is coming. The stillness and lulling beauty of the opening herald a crashing dissonance, one as inevitable as death. His death. Mahler's death. Private Kennedy's death. Like two chief mourners, the second horn and bassoon enter at bar fourteen. With six beats, Morris introduces the first violins, asking them with his eyes to play so softly they will become shadows. The conductor's arms are out-stretched. His breath is held. The shape of his body is flowing upwards, reflecting the shape of the music, an elastic stretching of time. As he turns back to the cellos for a rising figure that will introduce the movement's first loud sound, his brow furrows in pain. He wishes he didn't have to hear what is coming, but come it must. The horn enters with a minor half-tone, a death knell, and, within two bars, Morris is in the middle of a dark, swirling fortissimo.

The crashing of guns.

He is intoxicated now, filmy with sweat, his shoulders expansive and his arms sweeping violently. With each fling comes a thrill of intensity. Before him, a thousand musicians are galvanized beyond control, a phantom army on the march. They are responding to every signal from his body, reading his eyes, his posture. They can sense, as he can sense, the power contained in the tip of his baton. Power enough to drive a man insane. His eyes are closed tightly. The music in his head is tumultuous. His baton flails and thrashes. He demands urgency from the violins, from the sweeping machine guns, and he shakes his fist at the trombone and tuba, a signal to draw from them the most jarring, almost atonal sound they can manage as they lurch towards the hate-filled climax. When Morris hears the snarling trumpets there is cold horror in his eyes. Out of breath and shivering with exhaustion, he comes to the resolution, the consoling sound of the horn – the hate melody turned into love, the dying away into dusky silence. He stands still. Arms limp by his side. Spent.

As the baton slips from his fingers and bites, point first, into the floorboard, Morris opens his eyes. What was that noise? There are drips of red paint around his feet. The foreshortened handle of a punch dagger is vibrating. A slow blink. Another question forms in his head. Have I stabbed myself? He now sees his breeches are slashed, the cuts forming diagonal lines. They are also wet with blood. He slips his braces. Allows the serge material to fall around his ankles. Bends at the waist. There are plump lips on his thigh, parted to reveal layers of fat and rising bone. He looks at them with curiosity, as if this mortal wound is not his own.

ACKNOWLEDGEMENTS

I am grateful to John Preston, Emma Howard, Chris Lang, my agent David Miller and my editor Marianne Velmans for their close reading and astute comments. Above all, I am grateful to my wife Mary, not only for her wise suggestions about the book but also for her patience and good humour.

Nigel Farndale is the author of *Haw-Haw: The Tragedy of William and Margaret Joyce*, which was shortlisted for the Whitbread Prize and the James Tait Black Memorial Prize. He lives on the Hampshire–Sussex border with his wife and their three children.